THE
LAST
BROTHER

ANDREW
GROSS

PAN BOOKS

First published 2018 by Minotaur Books

First published in the UK 2018 by Macmillan

This paperback edition first published 2019 by Pan Books
an imprint of Pan Macmillan
20 New Wharf Road, London N1 9RR
Associated companies throughout the world
www.panmacmillan.com

ISBN 978-1-5098-7839-0

1 3 5 7 9 8 6 4 2

A CIP catalogue record for this book is available from the British Library.

Printed and bound by CPI Group (UK) Ltd, Croydon, CR0 4YY

Visit **www.panmacmillan.com** to read more about all our books
and to buy them. You will also find features, author interviews and
news of any author events, and you can sign up for e-newsletters
so that you're always first to hear about our new releases.

To
Fred P. Pomerantz, Pop.
Only wish you were around to read this . . .

Lies is lies . . . Howsoever they come, and they come from the father of lies. . . . Don't you tell no more of them, Pip. *That* ain't the way to get out of being common. If you can't get to be uncommon through going straight, you'll never get to do it by going crooked.

—CHARLES DICKENS,
Great Expectations

If I am not for myself, who will be for me. But if I am only for myself, what am I?

—RABBI HILLEL,
quoted in the Pirkei Avot

THE
LAST
BROTHER

Prologue

1905

For the rest of her life, Bella Rabishevsky would remember the day the K'hal Jeshurun temple burned as the day she lost her son.

She stood over the coal stove that day in the cramped third-floor apartment on Essex Street on Manhattan's Lower East Side that she, her husband, and her six children shared. The heat from the steaming pot, wafting with the sweltering August temperature outside, was almost too much to bear. She stirred the *krupnik,* the soup of boiled meat, potatoes, and cabbage that would be the family's meal that night. The twins, Shemuel and Harold, who were six, and even on a calm day a handful, were in the midst of a game they called *zuzim,* a version of tag from back in Minsk, where the family had emigrated from three years ago.

Except, as always, the game's playing field stretched far beyond the three sparse rooms that the eight of them shared, onto the roof, up and down the rickety staircase of their building's five stories, eventually spilling onto the street, amid the endless throng of horse-drawn wagons, pushcarts, and shouting peddlers there.

1

"Two zuzim!" Harold declared, digging his fist into his brother's back, almost knocking his mother into the steaming pot.

Shemuel, who always played the part of the victim, cried out in Yiddish, "*Ow!* He hurt me, Momma. Make him stop."

"*Genug iz genug,* Harold!" his mother barked back. Enough is enough. "You'll spill the soup and then none of us will have a thing to eat tonight. And I'll have to tell your father who was to blame."

"Yes, Momma," Harold said, softly enough to appear contrite, but with an impish smile creeping through as he continued to taunt his twin.

"*Three* zuzim!" Shemuel called out from his hiding place, upping the ante. Their eyes met in a kind of wordless dare, then suddenly Shemuel bolted past him and out the front door, bounding up the stairs, with Harold whining, "See, Momma, he's just a little cheat! That's all he is." Then he took off after him.

"Boys, you must stop it now!" Bella shouted after them, wiping her arm across her brow. "This silly game has gone too far."

But by that time they were already out the door and all she heard was the heavy pounding of their footsteps as they ran up to the fourth and fifth floor.

Harold, the older by four minutes, always played the instigator in these affairs. Anything to keep him from doing his chores or schoolwork. But when sufficiently riled, it was Shemuel who, in the end, would lose his temper and up their rivalry to a whole new level.

"Anna, please, the soup is about to boil. Go and find the boys," Bella called to her daughter. Nine-year-old Anna was practicing ballet steps near the window while keeping an eye on Morris, the youngest, who was almost two. Her older sister, Bess, was eleven but always lost in a book, so she wasn't much help around the house.

Dance had been Anna's dream since she first put her face to the window of the Mishnoff School on Norfolk Street and watched the students practicing inside. But of course, all she could do was watch, as they could hardly afford such a luxury as to send her to classes there. When they moved here, Jacob, who had studied to be a rabbi back in Russia, could only find work as the shammash of their temple: opening and closing the doors, sweeping up after services, and adjusting the Torah scroll each morning to the reading of that day.

"Tell them they must behave," Bella instructed Anna, "or you know Mr. Yanklovitch," the cranky neighbor upstairs, "will complain for certain."

And they were already a week behind in the rent.

"Samuel, Harry, come down now!" Anna went to the door and shouted up the staircase in English. "Momma insists that you stop."

As she stepped away from him, Morris moved closer to the window, which she had opened in search of a breeze.

Though each season came with its challenges, for Bella it was always summer that was the most difficult to bear. In summer, it felt like a furnace in their cramped, suffocating rooms. There was little ventilation, and opening the windows only seemed to sweep in more heat from the outside. On top of that, they had to deal with the sweltering hiss from the countless steam irons and the incessant whir of sewing machines of women trying to earn a dollar or two from doing piecework that emanated from almost every apartment.

Of course, in the winter they all huddled in blankets, as there was rarely heat and often no water from the spigots to boil.

But in summer, when school was closed, there was never a moment's peace. The children were always around, the apartment feeling like a cattle car with nowhere for any of them to go. Her husband was always at the temple—if not straightening up the teaching rooms or checking the boiler, then with the men, studying the Talmud. Bella did what little she could to help out with money, sewing garments herself after the dinner plates were cleaned and the rest of the family had gone to bed. Every dollar helped. Outside, there was the constant clop of horse wagons on the cobblestone streets, their drivers selling ice or making deliveries, the clatter of hundreds of peddlers with their overstuffed pushcarts until well after dark, the ever-present haggling back and forth in a dozen accents over prices or bickering if someone felt wronged.

Bella had given birth to four boys, and loved each as if he was her only one, but if she was truthful, there was one who occupied the space closest to her heart. Yes, Shemuel always hid in her skirt when his brother reached his boiling point. But he was also the sweetest thing she knew, a wounded bird compared to his far more devilish twin. Each of her boys had their own distinct qualities. Sol, the oldest son, was the smart one, his head swimming with numbers and logic. He would surely stay in school and become an accountant or a teacher one day. Harold was as temperamental as he was lazy, always doing his best to slough his responsibilities onto his twin. But he was also the most handsome, with a charm no one could deny. And Morris . . . Little Morris was the feistiest. He was never still for a moment, even in the womb. He would go far in life, Bella was sure; she just didn't know where. Just far. But Shemuel, with his apple-red cheeks and doe-like eyes, *he* was her favorite. She always said a smile from him could make the birds laugh in the trees.

The twins ran back in, Shemuel in tears. Either from pain or anger. "Harry hurt me, Momma."

"What a baby." His brother mocked him, tauntingly wiping his eyes. *"Wah, wah, wah!"*

"I'm not a baby. But you're a cheater," Shemuel shot back.

"All right, all right . . ." Bella exhaled in frustration. "Harold, help me peel the potatoes for the soup. Quit trying to avoid your chores."

"Let Samuel do it," Harold protested. Then he rubbed his eyes some more with a glance at his brother. "Wah, wah, wah."

"I said, *stop,* Harold! And now! Or you won't have even a spoonful of soup for supper," Bella scolded him in English, smacking the top of his head with her open hand. Maybe she did baby Shemuel just a bit. But Harold just would not quit.

"Okay, okay . . ." Harold finally surrendered. The boys knew when she spoke English, she meant business. But after a moment, the impish smile returned to his face and he grinned at his brother. "Last one . . . ?"

Shemuel glared at him accusingly. "Momma said stop."

"I heard her. But five zuzim . . . ," he said. He winked at his brother mischievously. "For all the marbles."

It took a second, the kind of silent dare that ran like an electrical current between them. In answer, Shemuel thrust out his fist and found the center of Harold's back. Harold cried, "See!" as Shemuel dashed out of the apartment, this time bolting down the stairs, Harold only yards behind.

"Boys! Boys!" Bella yelled after them, at her limit.

In a second they were out of earshot. Bella went to the window to angrily call them both back up. "Where is Morris?" she said to Anna, who was now back to her practicing, suddenly noticing he wasn't anywhere in sight.

"I thought he was with you, Momma."

"He's not with me. I told you to watch him—" Her nerves lit up. That boy could wander off in an instant. She never liked to let him out of her sight.

Up the street, she heard the loud clang of a bell and leaned out the window. A fire wagon drawn by four horses headed down the block at a steady clop. She caught a whiff of smoke in the air—it seemed to be coming from over on Chrystie, two blocks away. People were running that way. "The temple is burning! The temple is burning!" she heard them shouting.

The temple. Her mind flashed to her husband.

Jacob.

Worry rising in her, Bella searched the street for her twins. She'd have to go, she knew. The temple was their lifeblood. They'd need every hand. But in the meantime, this foolery between her boys must end. They would go straight to bed now, she promised herself, with no dinner. Both of them.

"There he is," Anna said. "By the stove."

The fire wagon rumbled toward her, people darting out of the way. "Watch out! Let the fire wagon through!" If it was the temple she must go there herself. There were important documents that would need to be saved. The hand-woven prayer shawls in the cupboards, many of which she'd made herself. And the prayer books. They must be saved too.

That was when she saw Shemuel darting out of the building into the street. Harold stopped on the sidewalk.

"*Harold! Shemuel!* Come back up! Now!" she shouted down at them.

Laughing, Shemuel turned to look up at her. Then he spun back to his brother. "Five zuzim!" he yelled with a giddy smile, his eyes wide in triumph.

Someone screamed, "Watch out!"

Above the sudden neigh of horses being reined in, the fire wagon swept upon him. There was another shout, not a stranger's, but one far more recognizable, not filled with mischief this time, or even anger, but terror.

6

Harold's voice. *"Samuel, look out!"*

The wooden spoon fell from Bella's hand.

A pall of dread swept over her, the dread only a mother might know, as forces terrible and yet completely unstoppable came together.

"Shemuel! Anna, watch Morris," Bella said, her heart churning out of control. "Something has happened."

"What, Momma?"

"Just watch him. Now!"

She ran out of the apartment and hurled herself down the stairs, a voice inside her pleading with her brain that what she had seen could not be true. But yet she knew it was true. No matter how she tried to banish it from her mind.

Outside, she ran straight into Mr. Mandlebaum, the butcher next door, who grabbed her and held her as she tried to pull past him. "Mrs. Rabishevsky, please . . ."

"Let me go. Let me go. *Shemuel!"*

Amid the tangle of horses' legs, she saw his feet. His body twisted at an angle she had never seen before. His neck, more sideways than straight.

"He just ran right out in front of me." One of the firemen, who had climbed down from the wagon, shook his head in dismay. "I didn't see him."

"Let me go, please!" Bella wrenched herself out of Mr. Mandlebaum's grip. She ran over and kneeled above her son, put out her hand and gently touched his shoes, his bare leg, his face, softly stained with blood. His smooth, red cheek. "Shemuel," she said again, stroking his face.

She knew there was no life in him.

And Harold, burying his face in her skirt, tears streaming down his cheeks. "I'm sorry, Momma," he said, his arms wrapped tightly around her. "I'm sorry," he kept saying. "I'm sorry."

A dim voice whispered faintly inside her: *My little boy,* it said, as she stroked Shemuel's face, knowing his soul had already left him. *My little boy.*

My favorite.

PART ONE

ALL OF THEM

1934

Chapter One

There was a chill in the air, for April, as Morris Raab headed back down Seventh Avenue. And a chill was always good for the coat business, anyone on the street would say.

He and his brother Sol had had their own firm for seven years now. They had sixty machines in operation, a steady production in two other factories on Allen and Rivington Streets downtown, and a growing business even in the teeth of the Depression, when dozens of their competitors had been forced to close their doors. There were six years between them—six years which could have been twenty. Sol had always planned to pursue a reliable trade, like accounting or the law. But as the oldest son, when their father died it had fallen on him to take care of the family, so he dropped out of accounting school and found work preparing the books for the bridal shop on Orchard Street and for an engraver on Grand.

It was Morris, his younger brother, who had asked him to come on board.

"What would I possibly do for you?" Sol asked skeptically. "I don't know garments. I know numbers."

"I know all you'll need to know," his younger brother said. "And what I can't teach you, you'll learn. It's not exactly rocket science."

"If it was, I doubt you'd be much of a success," Sol said.

From the start it was a *schlecht shidech,* their mother always said. A bad marriage. A circle made of two squares.

And yet the "marriage" had worked.

To Sol, who labored over every dime, Morris never seemed to spend a minute thinking much on anything. He only saw things as he wanted them to be, as he felt he could make them happen. Morris was tall, over six feet, with full shoulders and muscular arms that made him appear even larger. And he never backed down from anything. Sol was shorter and thin, with already receding hair and fists that had never been clenched in anger. The two were as different as two people could be who had come out of the same womb.

"Ich zol azoy vissen fun tsoris," Sol would mutter in Yiddish with a shake of his head. I should only have half the trouble you cause for me. "You know that, right?"

"Du machst nich veynen," Morris would reply with a dismissive wave. You're making me cry.

They had grown up rough-and-tumble on the Lower East Side. While Sol was always in the books, Morris saw no point in staying in school when, at twelve, he was already set to make his way in the world. He was handsome in a rugged sort of way. He had a firm jaw and a wide, flattened nose, as if reshaped by a heavyweight's jab. His hands were solid and rough, his knuckles scarred from a hundred scraps, not the hands of a man used to solving things by sitting across the table. And he had learned how to use them early on, and capably.

When he was only fifteen he had forged his mother's consent and enlisted to go fight in Europe in the Great War. By then, he had already dropped out of PS 48 on East Fourth and joined in the trade. They sent him to basic training at a camp near Aqueduct Raceway in Queens. He was the only Jew in his unit; his fellow recruits, all street-hardened Irish and Italian boys, acted like they'd never even met one before. A week into their training, Morris's corporal and four of his tent mates wrestled him from behind and shoved him into the latrine, basically a ditch dug outside half-filled with piss and excrement, while the rest looked on, laughing, peppering him with taunts of "Christ killer" and "Rumpleforeskin." Two or three even opened their flies and let go. When Morris crawled back out in shame, soiled with piss and shit, the corporal said he smelled so vile he'd have to go sleep with the horses in the stables. When Morris finally told him to go fuck himself and charged, the rest of the unit tackled him and held him down while the corporal ran a sharp-bristled horse brush down his back until his skin was bloody and raw. Morris spent two days in the hospital, bandaged and covered in salve. When the sergeant found out, he tried to get Morris to divulge what had happened, but Morris refused to give up a name.

A second sergeant got involved, this one a Jew. A drill sergeant, with arms like cannons and a demeanor as tough as any soldier in camp. "I figure you'd like to get back at these bastards," he said to Morris, sizing up what had taken place. Morris said, yeah, he damn well would like to get back at them. "Well, not here," the sergeant said. They had a boxing team on base, so he said they would take it out in the ring.

Morris, who was ready wherever, said, "Fine. Pick any one of them," leering at the corporal.

"Not any *one*." The sergeant looked at him and handed him his gloves. "All." *All* ... Morris looked back at him, sure he hadn't heard correctly. These were tough Irish and Italian kids, all with three years on him. Why would another Jew set him up for the biggest licking of his life?

13

"And if you take a quick fall," the sergeant said, with an earnestness that made Morris sure he meant it, "be sure I'll step in the ring myself and you'll have to deal with me. *Fershtayst . . . ?*"

"Farshteyst." Morris looked at him and nodded. I understand.

So one by one he took them on. All. And each who came up cockily went down just as quickly, staggering sideways back to their corner, rubbing their jaws. The last to go was the corporal who had pushed him into the latrine and run the wire brush across his back, who turned out not to be so tough without his unit to back him up. At the end, his nose broken, his eyes puffed out twice their size, Morris himself could barely stand. He staggered back to his corner and collapsed onto the mat. He looked at the sergeant, blood streaming down his face. "You said *all,* right?"

"Yeah." The sergeant finally smiled and nodded. "All."

Soon after, the army found out Morris's true age and sent him home. Which turned out to be a good thing in the end, since his unit ended up wiped out to a man at Belleau Wood.

But from then on, Morris was a man who others knew had the will to stand up for himself, and the means to back it up. And he operated his firm with the same conviction. There were pressures in the business, things that could sink a company every day. And not just the teetering economy, which had put enough of his competitors on their backs. The unions, which were no longer unions in any traditional sense, but rackets, taken over by the gangsters, who squeezed companies for payments—worker benefit funds, they were called, ostensibly for the slow periods, but everyone knew exactly what they were. Protection money. Protection from the unions themselves. And they had taken over the suppliers as well, forcing firms into agreements to buy only from them, adding a nickel here or a dime there to their costs, which went straight into the union's pockets. And anyone who refused to pay up or play by the rules didn't stay in business very long.

So far Morris and Sol had been left alone, but they both knew it was only a matter of time.

As he turned onto Thirty-sixth Street, where many of the garment firms had moved now, the block buzzed with activity. Pushcarts piled high with bolts of fabric manned by beige-smocked warehouse workers, wheels clattering on the pavement; trolleys of dresses and coats being rushed from factory to warehouse that could knock a careless person on his face. On the corner, O'Malley's, the Irish bar where the owner booked bets in the back room, was doing its usual lunchtime trade, salesmen at the bar trading stories, swigging a last rye before their next call.

That was where Morris first caught sight that something was wrong.

A crowd had formed halfway down the block toward Broadway, people staring upward. Three police cars were pulled up in front of a gray stone building. *His* building, he could now see. Blocked, trucks and cars were honking to get by. Edging his way through the crowd, Morris looked around to see what had brought them there.

On the street he kneeled next to Buck, the vagrant in the ragged wool coat who camped out near their entrance. Morris often stuffed a dollar in his hand when he left at night. "What's going on, Buck?"

"It's Mr. Gutman, Mr. Raab, sir," the down-on-his-luck black man said. "Some men went up there for him. And they didn't look like any men you want to mess with."

A knot of worry tightened in Morris's gut. Manny Gutman had been a friend of his for years—as much a mentor as a friend. And Morris didn't have to ask which men, or from where.

He knew damn well what had happened.

The Isidor Gutman Fur Company was started in 1883 by Manny's father, who peddled furs out West and to New England in towns so small they had no retail stores, then, in the '20s, rode the wave of raccoon coats and ankle-length beavers to become one of

15

the largest makers on the block. An Isidor Gutman signature woven in the lining of a coat was a mark that it was only the very best quality. Manny had taken over from his father and been running the firm for thirty years.

The past two years, they'd been forced to buckle under to pressure from the International Fur Dressers Protective. Since the days of the Triangle Shirtwaist fire in 1911, Isidor Gutman was always a union shop—"I'm a garment maker, not a union crusader," Manny would declare. But since then the gangsters had seized control, first demanding protection money, then forcing them into buying cooperatives which pushed lesser-quality pelts and trims and drove their prices up, even in the teeth of the Depression. To stay afloat, Manny came up with a plan to buy some furs from the union suppliers forced on him and some from his own resources, firms they had been doing business with since his father's time and who sold only the finest quality. Those of lesser quality they shipped to accounts who might not appreciate the difference, the finer stock to their longtime accounts who would know. But the union seemed to have ears everywhere, and what had begun as mere threats—intimidating phone calls, strong-armed people coming around—soon escalated into hijacking their delivery trucks, defacing finished inventory with red dye, and warning them to get in line or else. Still, Manny tried to keep on a few of his old suppliers in secret—off the books, so to speak, without purchase orders—dressing the furs himself at his own expense. "I mean, how would they ever know?" he said to Morris, "if there's no documentation."

But apparently they did know. An ambulance drove up, siren blaring.

And this was their response.

"How many were there?" Morris asked Buck, watching a medical team with a stretcher rushing in.

"I dunno, six or eight, Mr. Raab. They all ran out and climbed into two cars. Maybe twenty minutes ago."

"Thanks." Morris pressed a five into his hand. "I'd get off the street if I were you. Things are going to get hectic."

He headed inside. He didn't even stop at his own floors, three and four, but, adrenaline pushing him, bounded up the stairs to Manny's offices on seven, hearing the slow freight elevator clattering on every floor. When he got up there, there were cops milling around in the hall and the wooden door to the Isidor Gutman Fur Company was open.

A young cop manning the entrance put an arm out and stopped him. "Whoa, what's your business, fella?"

Morris knew the police were the last people you needed in these situations. The precinct captains were squarely in the mob's pocket. They had usually been paid off in advance not to find a thing by the very people who had done it.

"I'm a friend," Morris said, pushing past him.

The cop grabbed him by the shoulder. "You wait right there, buddy."

One of Manny's employees, his bookkeeper, Mr. Leavitt, white as a ghost, his tie undone, came up to the cop, seeing Morris's position. "It's okay. Mr. Raab is Mr. Gutman's friend. You can let him through."

There was a receiving area in the front, where raw materials were diverted to the warehouse area; those who had business with the firm came in through a separate wood-and-glass door. Morris went in. When he looked around, at the proud business that had prospered for two generations now in shambles; at Manny's workers, many who had been with the company since his father's time, glassy-eyed, huddled together, Morris's heart sank.

Where piles of expensive and neatly laid-out furs were normally stacked on tables in line to be cut, there were now mounds of torn and mangled skins that had been sheared into worthless strips and scattered akimbo. And not just inexpensive squirrels like Morris used for collars and sleeves, but once-luxurious beavers and minks that would have been in the windows of Altman's and Saks. Now worthless. Many of the pelts had bald spots on them and were singed as if they had been lit by a flame or doused with something corrosive.

A sharp, acrid odor filled the room.

Many of Manny's staff huddled around. Some of the seamstresses were still whimpering as if they'd just witnessed something horrible. The old cutters and sewers seemed dazed, and when they saw Morris, just shook their heads in a blank way, as if to say, *Can you believe what you see here?*

In the stock room, racks of finished garments and excess pelts were similarly defaced. Expensive furs and fur-trimmed coats torn, shredded into jagged strips from neck to hem, linings slit, many giving off that same bitter smell. A few cops stood around, perfunctorily interrogating the employees with their pads open. But Morris knew no arrests would be made.

One of the staff, an old cutter named Oscar, came up to Morris. "Mr. Raab . . ." was all he could mutter, somberly shaking his head.

"Where's Mr. Gutman?" Morris said. He didn't see Manny anywhere.

"It was terrible, Mr. Raab," was all the cutter said. "They came in like back in Russia, handkerchiefs over their faces, knocking people to the floor." He wiped a hand across his face despairingly, as if he was gazing at bloodied bodies, not ruined garments. Morris knew Oscar had fled the pogroms back in Russia and likely survived the most terrifying attacks and slaughter. Still, he was always an upbeat man. Morris had never seen him look like this before.

"Where's Manny, Oscar?" Morris asked him again.

The old cutter pointed toward the rear. On the floor, behind one of the two large cutting tables, Morris saw the doctor from outside kneeling, two cops nearby.

He went over. Manny was sitting upright on the floor. At least he was alive. He was dressed in an open vest, his tie undone, sleeves rolled, his face covered. Morris kneeled next to him.

"Manny..."

His friend looked up and dropped the towel. Blood trickled from his right ear, where he'd clearly been struck, and there was a deep purple bruise on his cheek, his white hair all disheveled. But what Morris then saw on the left side of his face made him wince and hold his breath.

A bright red blotch, like a spreading rose, stretching from cheek to eye. The doctor dabbed a wet rag to the eye, which Manny closed. "Morris, is that you?" He held up a hand. "I'm sorry, I can't see a thing out of this eye."

"Manny, what the hell did they do to you?" Morris took in a breath, his chest tightening with rage. But he knew just by looking at him what had been done to him.

A large oil tin was on its side at Manny's feet and Morris picked it up and smelled inside.

"I wouldn't touch that if I were you," the doctor warned.

Sulfuric acid.

"Who did this to you?" Morris said, gazing around in anger. He set the tin back down.

"What does it matter who did this?" Manny opined. "Look around. Fifty years we've been in business. Fifty years. Now... It's over for me, Morris. I'm done. I'm glad my father's in his grave not to see this."

"Who was it, Manny?" Morris said again, his gut as stinging and raw as if he had taken a swig from that can of acid himself.

But he knew precisely who had done it. And who was behind it as well. The same people who had walked over all of them with the same brutality and indifference to the law. One by one, every business on the street was being forced to knuckle under to the mob's rule or face the same consequences.

"Fifty years, Morris...," Manny kept muttering. "My father used to carry these coats in a sack from town to town. Now..." He looked around numbly and shook his head in dismay.

"Try not to talk," the doctor said.

Morris put his hand on his friend's shoulder. He got up, took a last look around, letting the scene of destruction sink in.

He picked up the can of acid again.

"You stay out of it, Morris," Manny looked up and warned him. "You'll only get yourself killed."

"You've been telling me that for a while," Morris said, "and look around."

"It's not your fight. Be smart. And what are you going to do anyway by getting involved except get your own business ruined, and I'll end up at your funeral."

"It's too late for that, Manny." Morris placed the tin of acid back on the floor. "It *is* our fight now."

"Don't be a fool, son. You can't win this. Just let it be," Manny called after him. "Morris, do you hear me? Do you hear what I'm saying?"

Morris had heard him. He'd heard a dozen fellow garment men make the same plea. All desperate and futile, and nothing changed.

But by that time he was already out the door.

Chapter Two

An hour later he was under the elevated IRT line at the corner of Livonia and Saratoga Avenues in Brownsville, Brooklyn.

Rosie's Tobacco Shop was known as the headquarters of Louis Buchalter. From the back room, he and his partner in crime, Jacob Shapiro, ran their illicit operations, which everyone knew included gambling, murder for the mob, and control of the corrupt garment unions. Murder, Incorporated, they had named it. No matter how many front-page headlines and photos of bloodied bodies crumpled in the street or ruined businessmen like Manny pleading to the cops for protection, they paid off whomever they needed to and operated with free rein in the city.

One of their goons in a check suit and fancy black-and-white wingtips stood watch outside.

Morris had no idea just what he was here to accomplish, only that it was time someone did something. There had been too many bodies and too many businesses ruined, and the ones that remained had been bled dry by thugs who didn't care who they drove out of business and who they didn't.

Don't be a fool, Manny had called after him.

Morris got out of the car.

He knew, this was as foolish as it got.

But it had to end.

It had to end because it was destroying the business. These men didn't care who stayed afloat and who didn't; they were just milking their millions till the end.

It had to end because innocent people were being killed and maimed.

And it had to end with him today, because there was no one else able to stop it.

Not the police. Not the DA. Not the Feds and the fancy commissions they had set up to put an end to organized crime.

The truth was he had known Louis Buchalter a long time.

As he crossed the street, Morris's thoughts went back to the streets he'd grown up on. To an alley off of Delancey, twenty years ago, where in some ways, he'd become a man. He had tried to stay out of it as long as he could, but he could no longer remain on the side.

But once he went through those doors, he didn't know if he'd come back out alive.

He crossed the street and went up to the tobacco shop door. The goon in the check suit came over to block his way.

"What do you want here?" the man said, sizing Morris up as someone who hadn't come for a box of White Owls.

I got a rule for you, Morris Raab, Louis Buchalter had always told him with a wag of his finger. *You just remember, there are some lines you just don't cross. Even you.*

But he was crossing one now. Crossing it, in a way he might never turn back from. In a way he might live to regret.

"I'm here to see Mr. Buchalter," Morris said.

PART TWO

CHERRY STREET

Chapter Three

1915

The boy stood in front of the large oak desk piled high with bulging folders of fabric and boxes of buttons and trim, his tweed cap clasped in his hands.

"You're tall for your age." The man behind the desk looked at Morris and removed his wire glasses.

Menushem Kaufman, owner of the Majestic Garment Company on Chrystie Street, was short and balding, with bushy gray eyebrows. He wore a tie and suspenders, with his sleeves rolled up. His wife, a gray-haired woman in a heavy sweater who made her husband look tiny next to her and who oversaw the company's books, sat at a desk to the side.

"So what's your name?" Mr. Kaufman peered at him. He closed the leather-bound accounting book he'd been paging through, filled with columns of numbers.

"Morris Rabishevsky," the boy answered, dressed in knickers and a brown hand-me-down sweater.

"Rabishevsky. That's a mouthful. And you're twelve? By the looks of it, you haven't even begun to shave."

"Still, he's no child," Morris's mother said in Yiddish, her hands on his shoulders. Then, in broken English, she added, "He doesn't want the school no more. He wants a trade."

"A trade? Very noble," the man behind the desk agreed. "Still, a boy your age ought to be in school, not on a factory floor."

"I'm almost thirteen," Morris said, correcting him.

"Ah, thirteen.... Oh, well, that makes all the difference in the world then," Mr. Kaufman exclaimed. "Still, I suppose if you're old enough to be considered a man in shul, why shouldn't you be one in the world, right?" He looked up at Morris's mother. "I'm told you're recently widowed, ma'am . . . ?"

"Last February." She'd barely removed the black mourning shawl from her husband's yahrzeit. "He was shammash of our temple on Chrystie Street. He helped to rebuild it after the fire in 1905 you may remember."

"Meyn simpatye," Mr. Kaufman said in Yiddish. "I know well the strains such a thing puts upon a family. Well, you've come to the right place, then, young Mr. Rabishevsky, if it's a trade you want." He switched back to English. "Yesterday, every woman in America wore a fitted jacket and skirt. Today, it's a cotton lawn shirtwaist blouse with pleats and fancy collars. *Tomorrow . . . ?* Your guess would be as good as mine, boy." He looked at Morris, studying his face the way a dentist might inspect a questionable set of teeth. "Can you read?"

"I can read," Morris answered bluntly.

"Good. The truth is, we can use a hand to sweep the trimmings off the cutting room floor and run things back and forth from the fabric houses over on Grand Street. You seem strong enough—at the end of the day you can lend a hand with loading the truck. The job calls for five dollars a week. I hope that will be sufficient."

"Five dollars . . . ?" Morris turned back to his mother. He said

26

in Yiddish, "I can make six on the street selling *The Jewish Daily Forward*. Chaim Fineman does, and he doesn't even have to work Saturdays."

"*Zey shtil,* Morris!" His mother nudged him from behind. Hush now.

"Be my guest, then. Go work for the newspapers." Mr. Kaufman reopened his ledger book, as if the interview had come to an end. "You'll freeze your *tuchis* off all winter long, and I see you're not even wearing a proper coat as it is. Anyway, I thought I heard your mother say you were looking to learn a trade."

"He ist. He ist." His mother pinched Morris on the shoulder, more of a command than an answer to Mr. Kaufman's question. "Morris . . . ?"

"*Owww!* All right, Momma. So if I do these things . . . sweep the floor and load the truck, how do I get ahead?"

"*Get ahead?* You hear this, Rose?" Kaufman looked over at his wife. "I haven't even hired the lad and he's already angling for a promotion. Trust me, son, I can shout out that window and come back with five boys older than you who'd be happy with this job. I only called you in as a favor to Mrs. Davidowitz, who is one of my most valuable workers and who seemed to think you had *this* . . ." He snapped his fingers three times. "Zip. Drive. A quality that I'm sad to say in front of your mother that I cannot see." He turned the page of his big leather accounting book and put his spectacles back on. "You decide."

"He is happy with it." Morris's mother nudged him again, this time with impatience. "I assure you, he will do the job."

"He will, will he? Let me ask you, son." Mr. Kaufman leaned forward, knitting his brow. "Have you ever heard the word 'impertinence'?"

Impertinence. Morris couldn't even pronounce it. He shook his head.

"Well, look it up, lad, because you seem to have it. In spades! Still, it bears repeating that somehow Mrs. Davidowitz has vouched for you, so she must see something I can't. At least, she's convinced my wife—and she's the real boss here." He looked over to Mrs. Kaufman and smiled. "Isn't that right, Rose? So that's all that matters. She says you're a smart lad with zip in your step. Good qualities for certain, but all that matters to me is, not can you run the Standard Oil Company, but can you do what's asked of you here?"

"Five dollars a week will go a long ways, Mr. Kaufman," Morris's mother said. "He'll take what you offer. Thank you."

"All the same, Mrs. Rabishevsky . . ." Mr. Kaufman leaned forward. "I'd prefer to hear it from him, if that's okay. So do you have it, boy . . . ?" He snapped his fingers again. One, two, three. "Tell me."

"I have it," Morris said. Though inside he'd hoped to come away with a least a dollar a day.

"One more time, if that's okay . . . ?" Mr. Kaufman put a finger to his ear. "And with some conviction, if you don't mind. My hearing isn't what it used to be."

"I said I have it," Morris said again. *"A sheynem danken,* sir." He turned to Mrs. Kaufman. "And thank you to you too, ma'am."

"So if that's settled . . ." Mr. Kaufman leaned back in his chair, "we work six days a week here. Seven thirty A.M. to seven P.M. We do give the Sabbath off, of course, though if you come in you'll usually find the two of us here. Mrs. Kaufman and I are not religious. You get two sick days a year. Three, I dock your pay. Five, you might as well take that job selling papers, 'cause you'll no longer be working here."

"Feshtayn." Morris nodded dutifully. I understand.

"Good. The truth is," Mr. Kaufman looked at his wife, "I started at twelve myself. Isn't that, right, Rose? As a tailor's assistant. Back in Vilnius. No more of a sense where life was taking me than you

28

now. So what do you say, Rose? Shall we give young Mr. Rabishevsky the chance to acquire his trade?"

"Manny . . ." Mrs. Kaufman turned her chair around and gave her husband a disgruntled narrowing of her brows.

"All right, all right . . ." Mr. Kaufman looked back at Morris with a blanch of guilt. "My wife thinks I've taken advantage of you in your wages. So how 'bout we say, three months from now, if you're doing well enough, we'll see about that dollar a day you're so eager for. Until then, we'll see if you're cut out for this kind of work."

"How about I come in every day at seven and you pay me the dollar a day now?" Morris pressed.

At first there was silence. Morris's mother twisted his ear, causing Morris to yelp loudly, "What's that for?" and he spun around in pain. When he turned back at Mr. Kaufman, Morris didn't know if he was about to be fired before he even began.

"Impertinence, Rose. You hear it, don't you? He's already pushing for a raise and he hasn't even shown up his first day. If this is how he is now I hope we're not making a big mistake on him."

"Three months," Mrs. Kaufman said to Morris, no negotiation in her voice. "Do you hear? And only *if* you're doing well. Understood?"

Morris nodded. "Yes, ma'am."

"But since you've offered, being here at seven and getting a jump on things will not go unnoticed. Is that fair?"

"Morris?" His mother nudged him. *"Zogen di dame."* Tell the lady.

"Yes. I'll be here at seven. Thank you, ma'am. Mr. Kaufman, you as well." Morris put out his hand. His new boss leaned across the desk and took it, with an impressed glance to Morris's mother, at the firmness of his grip.

"He's got a shake for a middleweight. That much I can say. And for the record, son, from now on it's English only here. Leave the Yiddish for the home."

"That's fine with me."

"Good. So we'll be seeing you tomorrow then. Seven A.M. Leave your address. Mrs. Kaufman will put you on the payroll."

"Thank you, sir." Morris put on his cap. He and his mother took a step toward the door.

"And, son . . . ?"

"Sir . . . ?"

"You want to get ahead so badly, keep your eyes open here. Only way to learn this business. You can't learn it in a school. Watch Mr. Seligman in the cutting room. He can do blind what others only wish they could do with their eyes wide open. Or Mr. Beck, when he lays out a marker . . ." His eyes twinkled with pride. "So take things in, and learn. Maybe one day, you'll find that trade. *Farshteyst* . . . ?"

"I thought you said to leave the Yiddish at home, Mr. Kaufman," Morris said, his eyes in a bright smile.

"So I did, didn't I?" For the first time he gave Morris a smile back. "Oh, and one more thing . . . Rabishevsky is a fine Russian name, lad, but it's a mouthful for some people here. Many of the workmen here are Italian. It would be helpful if we could shorten it just a bit. What if we just call you Raab? No disrespect to your late husband, ma'am. Morris Raab. Is that all right, Momma?"

Morris's mother thought about it a moment and then slowly nodded. "Yes, it's all right with me. His father won't know."

"And with you, boy?" He narrowed his bushy eyebrows at Morris.

Morris said it over in his mind. He actually liked the sound of it. It sounded . . . more American. "Morris Raab is good," he replied.

"So then keep those eyes open, Mr. Raab." Mr. Kaufman put his glasses back on and turned the page of his ledger book. "Who knows—do your job well, how this crazy world works, one day you might even end up running the place."

Chapter Four

Of the five dollars Morris brought in each week, four went toward the family's food and rent.

One dollar he was free to keep for himself.

Now that his father had died, and money was even scarcer, the family had been forced to move to smaller and even more modest lodgings on Cherry Street, a mile from the temple. In fact, once he began working full time, Morris started going less and less, until he hardly went at all.

In a part of the city where squalor and overcrowding were a part of life on every block, Cherry Street was among the poorest. Buildings there were barely more than ramshackle tenements owned by indifferent landlords who had no urge to improve them, since most of their tenants were either just off the boat or would be gone soon. Apartments had creaky staircases, scant lighting, furnaces that rarely worked, especially in winter; water that was brown and intermittent, and rarely hot. On each floor the incessant chatter of sewing machines and the hiss of steam pressers could be heard deep into the nights.

The family squeezed into a tiny three-room apartment on the fourth floor. Morris and his brothers: Sol, six years older, had to assume the role of the man in the family now that their father had died. He took courses in accounting at City College, but could not afford to go there full time as he had to bring money in. Harry, four years older: likeable, handsome as a movie star, but lazy and unreliable when it came to a career. Since the tragedy on Essex Street, and the feeling that in her heart his mother always held him responsible, Harry shied away from anything you might call dependable and had begun to hang out with a questionable crowd. His mother always called him *Moisheh Kapoyer*, Mr. Upside Down, because whatever he touched never seemed to come out right. Inwardly, however, her feelings toward him were anything but lighthearted. The hardscrabble life they lived now had taken much of the fight out of her, and Harry always felt a lack of forgiveness in her voice toward him, so that he began to spend less and less of his time at home.

Morris was the only one of them born in the States, and before he could even read, he would pick up *The Jewish Daily Forward* or magazines left on the street and see how other people lived, some even Jews, who resided in fancier neighborhoods uptown, which might as well have been different countries. Once, he and his friend Irv Weschler took the tram up Broadway and walked around Central Park, which to Morris seemed to go on forever—*in his life he had never seen so much green!*—staring at the tall apartment buildings that lined both sides, with white-gloved doormen opening carriages and rich tenants who stepped out. He and Irv looked at each other with awe—such grandeur was a sight they'd only heard tales of—imagining the servants, the high-curtained rooms with glass chandeliers hanging within, until a policeman, noticing their disheveled clothes and unwashed state, shooed them away like they were fleas carrying pestilence. "Go back to your own neighborhood, boys. You don't belong up here."

"One day, I'm gonna live up there," he said to Irv on the long tram ride back home.

"You better save up your pennies then," Irv said, "because it'll take a lot of them."

"It won't always be pennies," Morris said. "You'll see."

Most boys left school in their early teens, needing to bring in money for their families. Oftentimes women continued with their education, as their money-earning options were slim. Anna held a part-time job as a bookkeeper; after school, Bess helped out in a bridal shop. Harry never brought in much of anything, always losing jobs, whether it was as a newspaper hawker or a stock boy, and he started to hang out with a group of older ne'er-do-wells, drawn to pickpocketing and gambling. Still, he did bring in a few bucks playing lookout for some of the back-alley gambling scams, and every dollar was needed. He wasn't a bad kid—he just seemed drawn to the promise of easy cash instead of working for it.

In summers, the neighborhood kids would escape the heat by jumping off the docks into the East River for a swim. It was like a country club to them. Morris was the best swimmer among their friends. He could hold his breath for what seemed like forever. He was able to swim from pier to pier without even coming up for air.

But even their fun contained a measure of danger. Rival gangs of Irish and Italians all used the same overcrowded docks, and they had no urge to share them with newly arrived immigrants who spoke a language no one could figure out, grew their sidelocks long, and looked at a dunk in the river as their weekly bath. There were always fights and people being taunted. Teenagers of all origins went around in packs. One of their neighbors' kids on the fourth floor on Cherry

Street was even drowned one day; one minute he was frolicking next to a barge, the next minute he was gone, and a group of freckle-faced Irish boys were grinning how Jews couldn't swim, weighed down by their big noses. Those who had no urge to fight back required protection just to get around, generally from the Irish or Italian kids, who had turned it into a business. Scrapes and tussles were an everyday event, as were the insults and taunting that went with being a Jew. And as they got older, the bullies began to carry knives. Then lead pipes wrapped in newspapers, and occasionally guns. The jostling and pickpocketing escalated into armed robbery and assault.

Morris's friend Irv was pudgy and curly-haired. He was good in school and talked about one day going to college. His mother was a librarian and his father had an office job for the city, so Irv was reading and speaking English fluently at an early age. At thirteen, he was accepted into the Washington Public School on Irving Place, a half-hour trek through the dangerous neighborhoods north of Houston. Italian ground. And Irv was someone who was far more comfortable with a book than he was using his fists.

"My parents wouldn't let me go unless we found someone to look out for me," he confided to Morris, their feet dangling over the East River pier in the heat of an August Sunday.

"I'll look out for you," Morris said. "I can handle myself."

"I know you can, but you work. Besides, we found someone."

"How much do you have to pay?"

"Two dollars a week."

"Two dollars! Those Italians will rape you if you let them. I'd do it for a buck."

"He's not Italian," Irv said. "He's a *yiddisher* actually."

"A Jew?"

"That's right. He was sent away to a reform school and now he's got his own gang. This guy's even tougher than the Italians. My father says, what a world when such behavior is rewarded."

"Let's take a swim. Last one in has to lug home the towels," Morris said.

Chapter Five

Friday was payday in the factories. By March, Morris had worked four months and earned the raise to a dollar a day that Mrs. Kaufman had promised.

Just making the long walk home from Chrystie Street back to Cherry, his pockets stuffed with a week's wage, temptations and risks arose on every corner. Any card hawker worth his salt knew the look of a ripe young man flush with cash in his pockets, even a twelve-year-old boy, and they would urge Morris to come over, "Just for a look, young fella, you don't have to play. But who knows, you might win big," sometimes even following him halfway down the street.

Once or twice, Morris actually stopped at a three-card monte swindle off Delancey Street and studied how the game was played. One time, sure that he spotted the scheme that was meant to take advantage of an unsuspecting tourist or those just off the boat, Morris plunked his own money down on the table and lost his entire week's pay. When his mother found out, she was furious at him for risking the family's welfare. "You of all people, Morris. You're no one's fool. How could you let yourself be stolen from like that?"

He felt ashamed, and vowed he would never be taken advantage of like that again.

But making his way back through the maze of crowded streets and alleys was fraught with danger too. Especially on Fridays, when anyone keen to take advantage was on the prowl. South of Monroe Street were the Irish; north of Houston, the Italians; to the west, German Catholics, all hostile to a ragtag immigrant who didn't look or talk like them, and who believed that their Savior was not the son of God.

But the toughest of the troublemakers were the Jews themselves. "Don't let the yarmulkes fool you," his mother would say. "These people will cut you blind." Because for every lad looking to make it out through hard work or enterprising spirit, there was one whose ticket to riches was punched by crime. Every corner harbored roving bands of thugs who would shake you down and steal what you had, and rackets—gambling, prostitution, robberies, pickpocketing. And the street-smart Jews preyed on their own kind just as willingly. On any corner, a pushcart filled with clutter could haphazardly knock into you, a pretty girl could sidle up and steal your attention, someone's hand could slip inside your pocket and your hard-earned wages would be gone.

Morris always protected his cash by keeping his hands in his pockets and avoiding signs of suspicious bands of youths—Gentiles or Jews. But one Friday, the wind whipping off the East River, right through Morris's new wool coat—a gift from Mrs. Kaufman, who had gotten it from a friend in the business and who was sympathetic to Morris's long trek to work—Morris was carrying a bag of potatoes and turnips and had six dollar bills in his pocket, when he came face-to-face with a band of cigarette-smoking toughs heading his way.

He thought it wiser to duck through an alley off Broome, which led to Delancey and the safety of crowds. But the alley was narrow and unlit and ahead Morris heard voices—peals of exultation mixed with groans of frustration. He saw a group of men sitting on fruit boxes, with two young toughs overseeing a card game.

The con men were older, one short, in a suit and black coat and homburg, the other in ragtag clothes and a flat wool cap, twice his size. Morris knew how to handle himself, but not against thugs like these; they looked like the real thing. He looked behind and saw the band of street toughs congregating at the alley entrance, so he thought the safer course was to continue on rather than to turn back. He figured if these guys gave him any trouble he could always make a dash for it to the other side.

As he approached the card game, one of the con men caught sight of him and came up with a cocky smirk. He was dressed in an ill-fitting black coat and black homburg, tilted slightly to the side. Though he really wasn't a man at all, but more of a youth trying to look like one, dressed all dapper, chubby-cheeked and with a dimpled chin. Morris pegged him as no older than seventeen. He was shorter than Morris, but not short on boldness, blocking Morris's way. "Want to get through? It'll cost you, kid. A buck. For protection," the tough said.

His crony, the slope-shouldered bruiser in the tweed cap, looked over too.

"I don't need protection," Morris replied.

"Hear that, Jacob," the one in the suit sniffed, "the young man says he doesn't need any protection. Everyone needs protection, kid. It's a rough world to navigate out there."

The tough's large companion sauntered over from the card game. "That's a pretty nice coat you got there, fella."

"It's not the coat, but what's inside it that I'm interested in, Jacob. Friday's payday, isn't it?" the tough in the suit said to Morris in Yiddish. "You got a job, kid? I see you got a nice bag of vegetables there you're taking home to Momma."

"I work." Morris folded the paper bag closed. "And what's in the bag ain't your business," he answered.

Delancey, with its crowds, was only around fifty yards ahead. Getting past these thugs, especially the ox, would be a challenge. But in the end, Morris reasoned there was enough money on the fruit boxes that the two thugs would have to remain with their card game.

Still, the bruiser sauntered out, also blocking Morris's way.

"Why don't you let me see what's in that bag, kid?" The tough in the homburg and coat grinned. He had a flat nose like it had been broken more than once in a fight and a chummy smile, though the invitation was anything but friendly.

First the bag, Morris knew, then his pockets. And after the three-card monte fiasco, he wasn't about to come home empty-handed again, no matter what he had to do.

"Take a hike." Morris tried to walk on past.

"Take a hike! Hear that, Jacob? What does it make you think when a little *pisher* like this tells you to take a hike?"

"It makes me think we hold the brat upside down by the ankles and see what falls out," his large partner said.

"It makes me think we might have been willing to let him pass," the one in the suit said, "but now, things have definitely changed. What do you say you try your luck at the game, kid? You got some money on you, right? Three bucks gets you a seat. Maybe you win big and take a wad home for Momma. Maybe you leave it here. What do you say?"

"I say I don't like the odds," Morris said, again trying to take a step around him.

But the tough scampered ahead of him and blocked his way again. "Our little friend here is quite the handicapper, Jacob. You're right on the odds, kid. But still, better odds than, say, fighting me. I told you, it'll cost you a buck to pass."

The guy wasn't so big, but he still had a wide, cocky smirk on his face and a willing gleam in his eye, and Morris knew this likely wouldn't be the first time he'd used his fists. But he was determined to keep his money. He rolled up the bag of vegetables and looked back at him. "All right, you want to fight so bad, I'll fight you."

"You will, will you?" The tough grinned and glanced at his friend with an amused chortle. "Hear that, Jacob, our friend here says he'll fight me to get by." He met Morris's gaze, a little shorter than he was, but cocky as a peacock. He rolled up his sleeves, as if preparing.

"You, maybe," the larger friend said with a dull shrug. "But I bet not me."

The tough's cohort was larger than any of them, plus four or five years older. He would surely be the biggest person Morris had ever scuffled with. But Morris looked at him, dead on. "If I have to, I'll fight you too."

The one in the suit laughed. "Ha, Jacob, I love this kid. But he clearly doesn't have much between the ears. Still, a whole lot of moxie, I'll hand you that, pal." The tough put his cigarette down on one of the box crates and removed his hat and coat. "So, listen, I make a rule for you. You take me, you get to pass free. I take you, we'll see what's in your pockets. Truth is," he handed his oversized friend his coat, "since I got back from reform school, I haven't had a good row. Isn't that right, Jacob?"

"Let me have a shot at him," his companion said. "We'll find out what he's got on him."

"Take it easy, my large friend," the tough said. "And as you know, Jacob, I prefer to settle my own scores. Won't take but a second. Ready . . . ?" The tough loosened his tie. He stepped in front of Morris, cracking the knuckles on both hands. He was smaller than Morris in frame, but clearly older, and had already been sent upstate, which meant he knew what he was doing. And he seemed to relish the fight. He put up his fists. His nod said he meant business. "But you ought to know, kid, when I do fight, I fight to win."

Morris felt his heart begin to pick up with concern. He didn't like where this was heading, probably a busted nose at the least. Or worse, the loss of a whole week's pay. He began to think that maybe paying the buck was the wiser choice after all. But there didn't seem any way out of it now. He put down his bag and took off his coat as well.

"Come on, kid." The tough winked, bobbing behind his fists. "Let's see what you got."

Morris put his fists up too and said, "I ain't no kid."

"That so? All right then, here's your chance to prove it."

The guy lunged, then jabbed at Morris, probing his defenses. Morris thought that if all else failed he could simply charge the guy and bowl him over. Then keep on running. A bag of onions and turnips wasn't worth losing a week's pay over. But the idea of running didn't sit well with him. He'd heard stories of what went on in these upstate schools. The guy had likely been in scraps more often than Morris had been in temple. But here they were, circling, dodging, the tough with a determined grin on him. No backing down now.

One of the card players spun around. "Listen, you shit heels, I didn't put my money down to watch you duke it out with some twelve-year-old with nothing at stake. Deal the cards. I don't have all day."

The tough circled, dodging behind his fists. "Relax, this won't take but a minute."

He lunged again and Morris sidestepped him and spun him across his lower leg to the ground. The guy jumped back to his feet, chastened and a bit surprised. He gave a glance to his behemoth friend, then back to Morris. "Not your first tussle, huh, pal?"

Morris said, "Look, I just want to get by. That's all."

"Too late for that, I'm afraid." The tough brushed the dust off his pants. "Okay, let's go."

He lunged again, leading with a right this time. Morris took a hard shot to the face. He felt blood ooze out his nose. He wrapped his opponent in a clench and they struggled, the guy grabbing and twisting and trying to elbow Morris below the belt. Morris edged his weight against him and wrestled him back to the ground.

Red-faced, the guy hopped back up onto his feet. This time, any trace of levity had disappeared from his eyes.

"You want me to cut in, say when," his companion chuckled, an edge of mockery in his offer.

"No, I got it, Jacob. I got it just fine." The tough reached inside his pocket and came back out with something gleaming. A knife. "Maybe I didn't get my point across, kid." His smile had changed, ire flashing in it now. "You want to take me on, we play for keeps." He lowered into a crouch, thrusting his blade toward Morris's face. Morris took a step backward, his heart accelerating with real worry now. He'd been in plenty of scraps but never had a knife drawn on him before.

"C'mon," the tough said, beckoning Morris on. "You want a fight so bad, I'm here to give you one." He circled with a malevolent smirk on his face. A smirk that said he was prepared to do anything. "How about I cut that Russian nose of yours down to size, just to show you."

The tough's partner had circled behind Morris, removing any escape. If there had to be blood, then there would be blood, Morris accepted. He was in this far. He wasn't giving up his hard-earned money now.

The tough jabbed the blade. Morris dodged backward and put up his hand. The knife nicked him, slicing a red line of blood on his wrist.

The tough grinned. "Fun's over, huh? C'mon, let's go."

Then the card player turned around and chuffed again, "I said deal, smart guy! Or I'll take my winnings and leave. I didn't come here to get the cops called on us."

"Hey," another of the players grumbled, "you leave now, you leave with my money. You'll have to go through me. I thought this game had rules."

The tough looked at them and stopped. "Gentlemen, gentlemen. It's just a little free entertainment, that's all." He gave Morris a wink and brushed himself off. "On second thought, Jacob, I think the numbers say this time we let the kid go. We'll catch up to him another day." He folded the knife back into his pocket and picked up his hat, with a smile that read, *There's unfinished business between us.* "It's your lucky day, kid. But I give you credit, you're no momma's boy as much as I thought. It occurs to me we can use a tough little *macher* like yourself. What do you say? Plenty of opportunity out here. Want to put a little gelt in your pocket?"

"I already have a job," Morris said.

"He already has a job. Hear that, Jacob, he doesn't want to pal around with the likes of us. Suit yourself then." The tough bent down and picked up what remained of his cigarette off the fruit box. "So what's your name, anyway?"

"Morris Raab." Morris adjusted his sweater. "Yours?"

"Mine . . . ?" The street tough put his hat back on. "Louis Buchalter, that's my name. And you remember it, kid, if you're smart. Not many people get to turn Louis Buchalter down. You're already ahead of the game." He looked at him and adjusted the tilt of his hat to just the right angle. "So, Morris . . ."

Morris bent down and reached for his bag of vegetables. "Yeah?"

The tough reared back and took a swing, catching Morris flush in the jaw. He felt a tooth fly out of his mouth and he stumbled backward a step and went down to one knee, his lip bloody.

"Okay, Morris Raab . . . We'll be seeing you around then," he said in Yiddish. "Enjoy those onions. . . ."

Morris stood up, rubbing his jaw. He spit out a mouthful of blood. "Be seeing you too."

But it was years before Morris did see him again. By then, Morris was grown.

And Louis Buchalter was no longer just running card games in some back alley.

Chapter Six

At Majestic, Morris did keep his eyes open, just as Mr. Kaufman had urged.

He generally got to work every morning at seven, a half hour ahead of the other workers. Often he had the bolts of fabric he knew Mr. Seligman had planned for cutting that day already pulled and on the table by the time the old cutter came in. As he went about his job—sweeping up the remnants on the floor around the cutting table, tacking down the multiple plies of fabric to keep them set, assorting the cut pieces in bins and carrying them over to the sewing stations, Morris carefully watched Mr. Seligman shear around the marker's outline, adhering to every groove and notch with a surgeon's skill, often on fabric piled six to eight ply.

Morris also studied Mr. Beck, the marker maker—a stooped, white-haired Hungarian who always wore a vest and tie, spoke little English, but could size up how to lay out a complex pattern in the most efficient way, fitting the pieces together like an intricate puzzle—sometimes as many as twenty separate pieces per pattern—to achieve the best "yield," the most efficient utilization of fabric.

Every day, Morris would observe as the marker, Mr. Beck, performed what seemed to Morris dizzying calculations in his head or sketched out the proposed layout on the marker's edges to limit the wastage. Morris would lean over and ask him why he had laid out a pattern in a particular way—against the grain or on the bias—when at first it appeared as if that way would in fact consume more goods. The marker would simply wipe his glasses and reach behind his ear for the pencil he perpetually kept there. He would show Morris that the answer lay not in minimizing the yield for a *single* garment, but in the "repeat"—multiple garments interlocked together— and he would sketch it out by drawing three garments, not just the one, to prove his point. "The hre-*peet,* son," Mr. Beck would mutter in his heavy Hungarian accent, rubbing his thumbs and index fingers together. "Dats ver the money is."

Just before Morris turned sixteen (and after Mr. Kaufman had welcomed him back from his three-week enlistment in the army), the old marker maker, who'd worked at Majestic for twenty years, came in and announced it was time for him to step down. He'd been having dizzy spells and could no longer make it to work so easily. His doctors thought it might be a tumor. He'd have to call it quits at the end of the month.

The news threw Mr. and Mrs. Kaufman into a state of dismay. Mr. Beck was as valuable to the firm as anyone in the company, they always insisted. Maybe more.

"These kinds of people just don't come in off the street and introduce themselves," Mr. Kaufman opined. "I'll put an ad in the trade papers. We'll put out feelers and try to lure someone in from another company. In any case, it'll cost us a lot more money."

Mrs. Kaufman said, "I heard J and L Needlework is closing their doors. Maybe they have someone?"

"They do, but he's a hack. Arnold Lochman couldn't engineer a dress that would fit his own mother."

"Maybe Mr. Beck might know someone then," Mrs. Kaufman proposed. "These people often know of others in the same work."

Mr. Kaufman nodded, but without much enthusiasm. "There's always a chance."

That afternoon, Morris knocked on the Kaufmans' office door.

"What do you need, son?" Mr. Kaufman groused impatiently, glasses on, scanning the Help Wanted ads in *Women's Wear Daily*. "This really isn't the time."

Mrs. Kaufman was at her desk. "Yes, Morris, what is it?"

Morris stepped in. He squeezed his cap and cleared his throat. "I can do the job."

"Whose job?" Mr. Kaufman looked up. "As I say, this really isn't the time to—"

"Mr. Beck's job," Morris said. He took another step. "I can do it."

Mr. Kaufman put down his newspaper. "Did I hear you right? You're not even sixteen, boy. We're talking about a man who's learned what he does for over fifty years. Now leave us be, we have important work to do." He shooed Morris away.

"You said to keep my eyes open and I have." Morris squeezed his cap. "I've been watching him steady for three years."

Mr. Kaufman removed his glasses. "Mr. Beck was a master tailor in Budapest. You're still just a boy. And a brash one, at that. Now go on home. You're lucky I don't fire you for a remark like that. For insubordination. Come see me in the morning and we'll see if you still even have a job in this firm."

"Just ask him." Morris shrugged, and went to the door.

"Ask *who* . . . ?" Mr. Kaufman knitted his brow in anger.

"Mr. Beck," Morris said, and left.

"Manny, don't you think you were a little hard on the boy?" Mrs. Kaufman wheeled around at her desk. "He's a smart lad. He picks things up. Maybe we should do like he said."

"He's a boy, Rose!" her husband bellowed, turning red in the face. "This is a job that takes years and years to understand and perfect. It's not a game in the penny arcade."

"Still, maybe we should just ask him. What is there to lose?"

"Ask who, Rose? You're surely not suggesting I go down and ask Mr. Beck?"

"Yes, Manny, that's exactly what I'm suggesting," his wife said.

So they went downstairs and caught the old marker maker as he was buttoning up his vest to leave for the day.

Mr. Kaufman said, "I don't want to insult you, Mr. Beck, but Morris Raab came upstairs and insinuated he can handle your job. I told him it takes a lifetime to learn such skills, that it's impertinent to even suggest he could do it, but somehow he said to ask you. So I'm asking. Respectfully, you understand."

The marker maker set his watch and dropped it into his vest pocket. "I told him to go up and ask."

"*You . . . ?*" Mr. Kaufman stared widely. "He's not even sixteen. You think he can perform a job that requires such an intricate knowledge of construction?"

The marker maker shrugged. "I've taught him a bit. The rest he just picked up. The lad's got quite a smart *kop* on him, you know." Mr. Beck pointed to his head. He closed his bag and took his cane to leave. "If you've come for my opinion, I think you ought to give him a chance to show what he can do."

So in the morning they brought Morris in and watched him lay out the pattern pieces for the style they were about to cut that day. It was a large shirtwaist blouse, made of actual silk, not cotton lawn, with a lot of *blousson* in the waist and sleeves like the French were wearing these days, which consumed a lot of goods. Expensive goods. There were fifteen different pattern pieces.

"Okay." Mr. Kaufman nodded for him to begin. "I'm waiting."

Cautiously, Morris studied the pattern pieces and arranged them carefully on the table. The style had a fancy peplum waist, a collar print that needed to be matched, and blousy sleeves, which, since the goods were narrow, around fifty inches, had to be tucked in tight to the selvage.

"Can I have your pencil?" Morris asked Mr. Beck.

"Of course." The old marker pulled it out from behind his ear.

Morris made a quick sketch of how the pieces fit on the side of the paper.

"C'mon, boy, you're not applying to Rembrandt for the position." Mr. Kaufman tapped the table impatiently.

Morris began to lay out the pieces.

"Wait, why put the peplum there?" Mr. Kaufman interrupted him. "If you tuck it in *here,*" he shifted the pattern piece completely around, "we can save a few inches. See?"

Morris looked at what he'd done. "You're not cutting only one of this style, are you?" he asked.

"*One?* Of course not? Two hundred is more like it," Mr. Kaufman replied.

"And the goods, they're narrow, right, Mrs. K?"

"They are." Mrs. Kaufman took a measuring tape and spread it across the table. "Fifty-two inches."

"And pricey too, I bet?"

"Very pricey." Mrs. Kaufman nodded. "It's silk. Over two dollars fifty per yard."

"Two dollars fifty, huh . . . So you see, if you lay it crosswise, like this . . ." Morris took the peplum piece and returned it to its original position, "I figure you can save about six inches. In the repeat. Six inches, times two hundred pieces . . . ? That's close to forty yards, isn't it, Mrs. K? At two dollars fifty a yard . . . ?" He looked at Mr. Kaufman. "That's over a hundred bucks, by my count. Just on this one cut."

Mr. Beck looked at Mr. Kaufman with a glimmer of pride and satisfaction. "See, I told you."

Mr. Kaufman let out a grunt. He looked at Morris and scratched his chin, then turned to his wife and threw up his hands in exasperation. "All right, have him report here for the time being. No guarantees, mind you," he said to Morris emphatically. "Mr. Beck, if you'd be so kind as to continue to instruct the boy until you are forced to leave."

"Yes, I could do that."

Grunting again, Mr. Kaufman shook his head and turned to go back upstairs.

"Mr. Kaufman . . . ?" Morris said.

"What now, boy? You got your chance."

"The job comes with a raise, don't it?"

"*A raise?* You're lucky I didn't fire you! You're very brash, young man, have I ever told you that? Rose, please talk some sense into the lad. Someone has to."

"I only thought it'll cost you an arm and a leg if you had to go and find someone from outside." Morris shrugged.

"You did, did you?" Mr. Kaufman said, giving him a glare that could melt ice if there was a bucket in front of them. "And are you paid to think such things?" Morris wasn't sure if he was about to tell him to get out on the spot.

"How about forty dollars a week," Mrs. Kaufman said.

"Forty dollars!" Mr. Kaufman's eyebrows rose halfway up his forehead. "Rose, for God's sake, he's making ten now."

"The boy's right," Mrs. Kaufman said to her husband, "about if we had to look outside."

For someone Morris's age, forty dollars was a king's ransom. More than successful people twice his age were paid.

"How does fifty sound?" Morris looked Mrs. Kaufman in the eye. "*If* you keep me in the position full time?"

"*Fifty!*" Mr. Kaufman roared, and shook his head. "Have we all just gone insane?"

Morris said, "Mr. Beck . . . ?"

"I don't like to get involved," the marker maker said, "but fifty seems a reasonable wage to me, for such skills."

Mr. Kaufman looked at his wife, who still seemed to think it was the best deal they had. "All right, give the boy his fifty, Rose. And that's *if* we keep him, you understand? And that's a big *if*, son. Do you hear?"

"Just one more thing," Morris said, as Mr. Kaufman started up the stairs.

He stopped. "What is it now? Do you want me to just hand you over the keys?"

"I'm not a boy. I'm your marker maker now. For as long as I have the job."

Mr. Kaufman narrowed his eyes at him, then, like ice thawing, his hardened face softened into a smile. "Yes, you are, Morris Raab. That you are. See, Rose, I told you this would happen, didn't I? Pretty soon, you'll have the kid running the place."

Chapter Seven

On his twentieth birthday, Harry Rabishevsky saw his reflection in the jewelry shop window.

He was wearing the plaid wool suit his mother had bought for him just the other day to find a job, with a new black bow tie and a Panama straw hat, for which Harry had forked over pretty much every nickel he had in the world. He didn't look at all like the penniless waif who had grown up on Cherry Street, without a dime to his name. But more like a young man with a skip in his step, one going places in life. He felt people taking note of him as he passed on the street. Women smiled. Men in similar suits, maybe on their lunch hours or heading to or from important meetings, gave him respectful nods. Though the truth was he hadn't held a paying job for a while now, having been fired from Garfinkle's Dry Goods for showing up late twice, and as a hawker at the Midnight nightclub for letting people cut the line, gratis.

But, inspecting himself in the window, straightening his tie and feeling a throbbing in his chest, today he was a man on the rise.

Maybe not quite in the way his brothers Sol and Morris might look at it. Someone with a real career, with an office to go to every day and a regular check coming in. Those kinds of ventures hadn't panned out quite so well for Harry just yet.

And maybe his mother would still look at him the way she always did, hiding a frown of scorn or shame she did her best to hide. Mr. Upside-Down. Those words always sent a shameful tremor through him and brought back that day on Essex Street they all had long tried to bury. It certainly wasn't the way she would say, "My youngest, Morris, he's learning the garment trade." With pride. Or, "My Sollie, he's the smartest of all of them. What a whiz with the numbers he is."

Still, it was better than she speak aloud of the blame he knew she had always carried for him in her heart, for taking away from her the thing she loved most in the world. Everyone knew Shemuel had been her favorite. And that no matter how much Harry had coming in, or whatever heights he might rise to, that would always be the way she would look at him. He would never live it down.

It was true, he hadn't done as well in school as Sol, and didn't have the same fire in his belly and determination to succeed as Morris. And that sometimes he forgot to come home when he said he would and pitch in with things, and never had enough money to help out with the rent or food. His latest job at the pool hall had garnered him a new circle of friends. Maybe not the kind of friends Momma or Sol or Morris might have been impressed with. But still, people who wanted to get ahead as much as they did, just in a different way. Mendy Weiss and Maxie Dannenberg had taken a liking to him. Mendy was older, twenty-four, a real prince of a guy if you were on his good side—which Harry apparently was—but clearly not someone you wanted to mess with if you weren't. Harry had seen him beat a man who owed him money to a bloody pulp; the memory of it still made him cringe.

Still, Mendy was good fun to be around and generous with them all, and it made Harry feel good to be part of his crew, even if they mostly just let him run for coffee or deliver an envelope here and there to the big bosses, which he assumed were filled with cash. Mendy and his guys earned their living doing what they had to. Maybe rolling a few unsuspecting rubes flush with their paychecks, or providing protection for a few gambling operations on the streets, or even cracking a head or two if word came down from the bosses that someone needed a lesson taught. But no one really ever got hurt. Harry always promised himself he would draw the line if someone ever did. But he was pretty sure, hanging out with him, that wasn't Mendy's style.

And that's what he would say to Sol and Morris when his brothers sat him down and asked him who he was spending time with in life, or what his plans were. "This is no life for you, Harry. You've got your mother worried sick."

"C'mon, Sol," Harry would say, "they're just pals, that's all. Mendy's just small potatoes. He's not exactly Legs Diamond," speaking of the flamboyant bootlegger, bodyguard for the famous Arnold Rothstein, "or any of those guys."

"Then let them buy you a beer, if they're just pals," Morris would say. And Harry had to admit, his little brother really had a fire in his belly when it came to advancement. Sixteen, and already earning more than a successful person twice his age. Sure, there were times Harry was a little jealous. His little brother seemed to catch all the breaks. And he really didn't like being compared to him. But the way Harry looked at it was that it just hadn't worked out for him yet. Maybe the daily grind simply wasn't his way. But he still would genuinely like to earn some money.

But anyway, that was all changing for him now, in his new suit and new way of looking at things.

At least, as of yesterday.

Mendy's crew hadn't given him any real jobs to do yet. The real jobs went to guys who were a lot tougher, who didn't mind using their fists, and that was fine with him. He didn't quite have the heart for it when it came to that sort of thing. He wasn't a fighter like his brother Morris, and he wouldn't know what to do with a gun if you put one in his hand. Down the line, if he could be relied upon, they might let him run a pool hall or manage one of their speakeasies uptown. That would mean real money coming in. He just had to prove that they could trust him.

"So Harry . . ." Mendy had sat him down next to him at the pool hall yesterday with a slap on the thigh. "I think it's time you put a few bucks in your pocket."

"Sure." Harry looked at him, excited. "That would be great, Mendy. How much we talking about?"

"Oh, I don't know." There was a glint of opportunity in his boss's eyes. "Say, thirty bucks."

"Thirty bucks!"

"All right, fifty, then," Mendy said, grinning.

Harry's chest always expanded with pride whenever Mendy took the time to talk to him, but fifty dollars . . . Fifty bucks was as much as Morris brought in in a week. "I don't have to kill someone, do I, Mendy?" He grinned back.

"Kill someone . . . !" Mendy laughed and nudged Harry in the ribs. "You hear this guy . . ." He turned to Maxie Dannenberg. "In fact, all you have to do for it is something completely legit. Just start up a conversation with a girl. A pretty one. You can do that in your sleep, right, Harry?"

"Sure, Mendy," Harry replied. "Who is she?"

"Just meet us tomorrow across from Sheffler's down on Canal. Just before noon. You know them, right?"

"You mean the jewelers?" Everyone knew it. Right on the corner. Sheffler's was one of the poshest shops on the Lower East Side.

"That's the one."

Fifty bucks. Harry was almost salivating. And just for starting a conversation. He could turn thirty over to his mother. She and his brothers would be over the moon. And he'd still have a wad for himself. "Sure. I'll be there. Noon, huh? Anything else, Mendy?"

"Oh, one thing. Just come in your very best outfit, kid. That is, if you have one."

So there he was, straightening his tie in the jewelry store's window, feeling his stomach churn just a bit, as only the very best people could even afford to shop in such a place. He and Mendy had gone over the plan. As Harry stepped inside, he heard the jingle of the door chimes, and started looking around the displays.

"Can I help you?" A store clerk came up to him. She was pretty as a picture and young, early twenties, possibly Mr. Sheffler's own daughter, the one Mendy had been talking about. She smiled at Harry as if he belonged there.

"I'm looking to buy a ring," he told her, playing out the part by leaning over a display. "For my girl. We're getting married. Nothing too fancy, but . . ."

"Well first, my congratulations." The salesgirl beamed, eyes bright as opals. "I don't know how much you're looking to spend, but these diamond chips over here might be a good option. May I show them to you?"

She led him to a display cabinet on the far side of the store. The rings inside were shimmering and beautiful. The kinds of rings he saw only on the fingers of the fanciest people. Harry caught himself thinking that he would love to buy one for his girl one day. Truth was, he'd love to even have a girl. And this one looked awfully cute.

"Gee, they are nice." Harry leaned down to take a closer look. "Say, what about this one, maybe?"

He pointed to a gold band with a small diamond on top. Harry couldn't even afford the box it came in, much less what was inside. She took out the ring he'd indicated and polished it up with a cloth. "It's two hundred fifty dollars," she said, "but it's one of our nicest, I think," holding it up for him to see. "Don't you?"

Two hundred fifty dollars. The price might have been two thousand. "Yes, you're right." He nodded. "It is a beauty."

"I could put it on for you, if you'd like to see?"

"Could you? That would be swell."

It was ten after twelve now. Canal Street was bustling. The busiest time of day. People on their lunch hours, hundreds of pushcarts, and honking traffic.

The store clerk smiled and slipped it over her ring finger and put it out for Harry to see. "I think she'll love it. What do you think?"

"What do I think? I think it's the most beautiful ring in the world," Harry said.

Almost as pretty as the salesgirl's eyes.

Suddenly he heard the sound of glass shattering. Across the store, two men, their hats angled down, handkerchiefs over their faces, had come in and smashed through the display cabinet in the window and were stuffing their bags.

The salesgirl screamed. *"Papa! Papa!* We're being robbed!"

They reached inside the cabinet with gloves, scooping up bracelets and necklaces—diamonds, emeralds, and rubies. Though their faces were covered, Harry knew exactly who they were.

From the back room, an older man ran out, crying, "Thief! Thief!"

But by that time, Mendy and Maxie had already gotten as much as they could carry and pushed the old man down against the cabinet.

In seconds, they were out of the store.

"Papa, are you all right?" The pretty salesgirl hurried over and kneeled over him.

"Yes," he said, holding his head. "I'm fine."

"You're hurt, Papa!"

Harry ran over to see about him too.

"Police! Call the police!" the owner called out. "Sarah, help me up." He struggled to his feet and ran outside, trying to get a fix on the fleeing thieves, who by now had melded into the sea of noonday traffic on Canal Street.

"Papa, you're bleeding." The salesgirl gasped. A trickle of blood was running down the side of her father's face, where it must have struck the cabinet.

Suddenly whistles were blowing outside.

"Maybe I oughta come back another time," Harry said with an awkward shrug. "I didn't get much of a look at them anyway, so I wouldn't be much help. I'm awfully sorry."

"Come back, I know what you're doing, young man." The girl's father glared. "I know what's going on. Stop!"

Harry ducked out of the store, hunching his shoulders, and turned down the busy street, in the other direction. In seconds he was just another speck in the crowd. At the corner he stopped. His heart was racing. He couldn't make it stop. He caught his breath and looked back. The shop owner was directing two policemen down the block after Maxie and Mendy—the other direction.

But by now, they were long gone.

Sweat wound its way down Harry's neck. He told his heart to calm. But then he realized he'd just made fifty bucks. And who really got hurt? Just a scratch and a little blood. And old man Sheffler likely had dozens more where those bracelets and necklaces had come from. He didn't like the idea that he'd had to lie to that cute salesgirl, though. She was truly a doll, the kind of gal he'd like to find for himself.

But he'd be able to hand his mother more cash than ever before. Even Sol and Morris would have to be impressed. He'd explain it by saying a little luck had come his way at the tables.

On Broome, he stopped and caught his reflection in the window of a bakery. He was pale as a ghost, still drenched in sweat.

To anyone else, though, he had the look of a man on the rise.

Chapter Eight

By the time he had turned twenty, Morris *was* pretty much running the place.

Mr. Kaufman, who was in his midsixties, had developed a hacking cough and was told he had to spend the winters out West. Soon, winter became spring and autumn too.

By that time, no one in the company knew the operation better than Morris. He had become a trusted marker maker and oversaw the entire sewing floor. After that first winter, Mrs. Kaufman went out West along with her husband and put Morris fully in charge. No one had earned the Kaufmans' trust more.

Which meant overseeing the entire manufacturing operation. Over thirty cutters, sewers, sample makers, and pressers. And demanding the same level of quality and construction, always Mr. Kaufman's rule number one, so he had to know the entire operation as well as any of them. It became Morris's rule too. He also learned how to calculate the material requirements of a style and make sure any remaining inventories were fully utilized, and he scrutinized the daily books well past closing time to make sure every sewer was paid for whatever work they had produced. As part of that, he came up with the idea that the manufacturing process would be far more streamlined and efficient if it was organized into separate "sections," each devoted to an individual part of the manufacturing operation, say the setting of a sleeve or a pocket, or the pleating of a skirt, which made all the sewers learn their specific jobs better and earn more money. In fact, Morris's nose was in every part of the business, except for sales. Sales, he just didn't have the confidence for right now. His speech still betrayed that he was right off of the streets, and he often felt embarrassed in the company of people with more education.

By that time Sol had married and had moved up to the Grand Concourse in the Bronx. His sisters Bess and Anna had married too, Bess to an assistant stockbroker and Anna to a shoe salesman. Morris moved his mother out of the Cherry Street tenement to a larger and far more comfortable place with real plumbing and heat. And he moved into his own apartment on West Broadway with Harry, who slept late and was always out at odd hours of the night, so they barely crossed paths.

He was twenty-one years old now and bringing in over four hundred dollars a week, the wage of a successful man twice his age. And, two years later, when Mrs. Kaufman abruptly passed on, and Mr. Kaufman was left with no choice but to sell the business to a competitor, with the understanding the buyer would keep his staff on, Morris said to Sol at a Sunday dinner, "I need someone who knows numbers and who can talk to a customer."

"Need them for what?" his brother inquired, helping himself to another piece of brisket.

"To open our own business."

"Good luck finding him then," Sol said. Then he looked at him and put down his fork. "Your own business, huh? I assume you don't mean me, do you?"

Morris said, "And why not?"

"Let me get this straight," Sol said, staring across the table. "You want *me* to come work for *you*?" Morris was only twenty-three; Sol was six years older and for years had been the man of the family. "And if I even entertained such a suggestion, I'm an accountant. What do I know about garments?"

"You know business. On the factory floor, I know what we need to know. I've got some money saved up. All I need is someone with a little more polish than me to get us a bank line and to sell what we make. Fifty-fifty. Are you in?"

"No, I'm not in." Sol shook his head at his wife and went back to his brisket.

He had a nice, steady career building. He was back taking classes at City College—Harvard for those on the Lower East Side—and doing the books for people in the neighborhood. Twice a week he helped out in his father-in-law's hardware store. In a year or two he could be a real accountant. But he looked back at Morris and saw something twinkling in his younger brother's eyes. Something he could not put his finger on. But he kept looking.

"I may regret this." He pushed back in his chair and threw up his hands.

"You won't. I'll make you rich," Morris said.

"You'll make me crazy is what you'll do. That I do know. But the truth is, someone needs to look out for you."

"It's the right move, Sollie," his mother said in Yiddish. "Morris will make it right."

"All right . . ." Sol stabbed a boiled potato with his fork. "Just for argument's sake, let's say I'll come. What do we call this enterprise? Just for discussion's sake, of course."

"I don't know . . . Why not Raab Brothers?" Morris proposed.

"Raab Brothers, huh." Sol spooned a helping of spinach on his plate. "You know I can't sell for beans, Morris. Besides, my name's still Rabishevsky. And I'm not changing it."

"It'll be easy. We'll knock off what's in big department stores from Paris and make it at a cheaper price. And you don't have to change anything if you don't want. Harry, what do you say? There are three of us. Raab Brothers means there's a place for you, if you're game?"

"I don't know, Morris . . ." Harry shrugged. "I mean, what would I do?"

"You can learn the trade, like I did." Harry was twenty-seven now, working in a pool hall, picking up fives and tens here and there doing errands for Mendy Weiss, who these days was bootlegging and working for some unsavory types, way out of Harry's league.

He looked to their mother, who only turned away from him to their sister. "Anna, you should eat more brisket. One day you'll have to do the cooking yourself."

"Yes, Momma," Anna said.

"Let me think about it," Harry said. "It's a swell offer though."

Morris said, "There is no thinking about it. This is your one chance, Harry. Come in with us. You'll learn a career. I'll teach you. It'll get you away from those types you're with."

"I don't know, Morris." Harry shrugged again and bowed his head. "They're not so bad. It just doesn't sound like me."

"I won't be asking you again."

"I won't expect you to." His brother waited, hearing nothing from his mother like she'd said to Sol. "Thanks, thanks a million, Morris. But I've got some good things happening where I am."

"To Raab Brothers then?" Morris turned to Sol and put across his hand. "Just us."

"Just us, huh?" Sol said, shaking his head and taking his brother's hand. *"Got zol ophiten."* God help us.

Morris looked back at Harry, just for a second. But it would be years before he could look at him again the same way.

Chapter Nine

Twenty-four now, and living in the height of Prohibition, Morris took his friend Irv, in law school now, to the Theatrical Room, a speakeasy up on 120th and Fifth said to be owned by the notorious gambler Arnold Rothstein.

Rothstein had allegedly fixed the 1919 World Series in a big scandal and no one had laid a glove on him, so there was always a table or two of reputed gangsters on the premises, which didn't exactly hurt business.

Morris had grown into a tall, powerfully built man with thick shoulders and pressed dark hair. Women were attracted to him, but he was always at the office and never had the time for a girlfriend, only a few brief flings. He had sprung for a tailored black evening suit with a high-collared shirt and cut a pretty fine impression, though Irv, with his hair askew and twenty extra pounds in the belly, was busting through a suit he had borrowed from a taller and no doubt far slimmer cousin.

The Theatrical Club was packed, bustling with men in fashionable evening jackets, women in glittery, short dresses, the music blaring. Glamorous people came from all over the city to dance and catch a sight of the Babe holding court, or Al Jolson, or maybe Arnold Rothstein himself, or a dozen other notorious gangsters. Smoke filled the room and drinks flowed freely.

Morris had paid for a table and ordered a bottle of champagne for him and Irv. Someone whispered there was Jack Dempsey, the fighter, at a table in the corner, with some writer named Runyon or something Morris had never heard of. People hovering around their table were laughing; the women all seemed to be puffing on cigarettes in long holders, and a cloud of smoke hung over the room. Charlie Whiteman's orchestra was playing "Dardanella" and the dance floor was hopping.

"So what do you think, Irv?" Morris patted his friend on the back as they took the lay of the room.

"It's like a motion picture of how the other half lives." Irv buttoned his bulging jacket, his eyes childishly wide.

Morris took a swig of champagne and looked around for the prettiest unattached girl he could see. "It's like diving in the East River in October," he told Irv. "Don't think. Just jump in."

"You first, Morris. You were always a far better swimmer than me."

"All right." Morris got up and went over to a group he noticed near the bar and asked a pretty brunette who was nursing a drink to dance. She hesitated at first, glancing at her friends, but they all pushed her on. "Oh, go on, Ruthie." She was short and willowy, in a shimmery jade dress above the knees and a matching beret in her hair, which curled around her ears. A tiny nose with long lashes and lively green eyes. Three layers of necklaces jangled beneath her neckline. To Morris she was about the prettiest thing in the club, her small, oval face moon-pale, but she was clearly uptown and obviously moneyed.

"It's just a dance." He smiled, noticing her hesitation.

She finally shrugged and put down her drink. "Sure, why not?"

Morris took her hand and led her out on the crowded floor.

He'd learned to dance as a kid from his sister Anna. As a boy, he would act as her partner as she took him around their cramped apartment trying to learn the new steps. Maybe not the most current dances—the Peabody and the Charleston. But she always complimented his rhythm.

"So where you from?" he asked her. The dance was a Lindy and he twirled her with ease.

"Riverside Drive," she said above the orchestra. "On a hundred and second."

Probably with a view of the river, he thought. The kind of neighborhood Morris could only dream of having a place in one day. "I'm in my senior year at NYU. And you . . . ?"

"West Broadway. Down near Houston," Morris answered.

"Houston . . . ," she said with a kind of knowing nod. He could feel her sizing him up in her mind. He knew the very mention of Houston Street gave him away. Who he was and where he was from.

Still, she gave him a bat of her eyelashes and a smile and seemed to be enjoying herself.

The music picked up into a Jolson song everyone knew and he twirled her around smartly. She was light on her feet herself, with a lithe dancer's body.

"You dance pretty well," she said, melding into his lead. "For a guy from Houston Street."

"I don't know much of the modern stuff," he said with a shrug of apology. He led her deeper onto the floor and held her hand as she twisted in a circle. "In fact, it's just my second time to a place like this. I mostly just work."

"All work, huh? So what do you do, Mr. Houston Street?" She clearly wasn't expecting him to say, *I'm a lawyer.* Or *I work for one of the large banking companies.* Not with his accent.

"I'm in garments," he said. "You know, *schmattas*. It's what we call—"

"I know what *schmattas* are," she said, crisscrossing her hands at the knees.

"Jewish . . . ?" Morris asked, raising his eyes. That was the last thing he expected. To him, she looked like a picture out of *Harper's Bazaar*.

"Guilty." She shrugged. "And you?"

"Guilty too, I guess. I'm—" He caught her concealing a grin. "Oh, you were kidding me, right?"

She smiled mischievously and flashed her lashes as she twirled. "Would never have guessed. Not in a million years."

"Well, what do you know?" He grinned, liking her even more, and led her around the floor.

There was a world apart between the uptown German Jews (which was what Morris took her for), and those from Russia and Eastern Europe encamped in the crowded slums of Brooklyn or the Lower East Side.

Jews from Germany had arrived in the U.S. decades earlier and were already established in fields of power and influence, unapproachable for ragtag Eastern European newcomers: the law, finance, department stores. Morris had heard that the synagogues uptown even held their services in English, not Hebrew, trying to blend in. He liked the way she felt in his arms, light and trusting, like a cloud.

"So this is just your second time out dancing, you say?" she said with surprise.

"Yeah."

"I guess you're just a natural then?" she said and spun, this time with a smile Morris knew wasn't fake.

After a couple more dances he took her back to her friends and Morris invited them all to his table. With a few shrugs and cordial smiles, they all agreed. They were all from fancy colleges and seemed to know people there that night, and he and Irv didn't exactly look the part.

"I'm Ruthie," the one he had danced with introduced herself.

"Morris. And this is my friend, Irv."

He ordered another bottle of champagne, some French brand he couldn't pronounce but would set him back a week's pay; he merely pointed at the most expensive one they had. "Marge, Priscilla, they're at Columbia. Jen's upstate—Skidmore." One look at them—earrings, necklaces, and superior ways—Morris could see they were all way out of his league.

"Irv's in college," Morris announced. In fact, Irv was the only person he knew who was in college.

"That so? So where are you, Irv?" one of the Columbia gals asked.

"I go to Brooklyn," Irv said. He was round and his hair kind of unkempt and curly no matter how he tried to Brilliantine it down.

"Brooklyn? That so?" Priscilla said with a nod laced with amusement to her friends. "And just what are you studying there, Irv, at Brooklyn?"

"Law," he replied, clearly beginning to feel like the butt of a joke he wasn't a part of. "Second year."

"Do you mean how to practice or how to break it?" the Columbia gal asked with a bright laugh. Everyone joined in. Even Irv, though unenthusiastically. "I'm sorry," she said, "but it seems that's what all the people from Brooklyn are doing these days. It was just a joke. Though according to Fitzgerald, there's almost no difference today. Practicing it or breaking it."

Fitzgerald. Some lawyer, Morris reasoned. He had no idea who they were talking about.

"And what about you?" One of them turned to Morris. "Don't tell us you're a budding counselor as well?"

"Morris is a workingman," Ruthie cut in. "He's in garments. He's got his own firm."

"Garments . . . !" Marge, the Columbia girl, declared. Garments meant low wages and sweatshops and a lack of refinement. She rolled her eyes Ruthie's way as if to say, *What a find you've got here.*

When Morris found himself around people like this, worldly, with money and education, he always felt out of place. He read the papers, *The Jewish Daily Forward* mostly, but sometimes he didn't know what they were talking about. And his speech was still peppered with improper grammar that made it clear what part of the city he was from whenever he opened his mouth.

Priscilla looked at him. "You seem awfully young to have your own business, Morris. Your family's firm, I presume?"

"Just my brother and me."

"Only you and your brother?" she replied. She actually did seem genuinely impressed. "A real bunch of go-getters. You must have been just out of grade school when you started out."

"I don't know, just a natural, I suppose." Morris winked Ruthie's way. She smiled back at him.

He didn't care what the rest of them felt.

"Morris." Irv pointed to the far end of the club, just off the dance floor. "Take a look who's here."

At a large, round table, clearly one of the most prestigious in the house, Morris looked and spotted his brother Harry, with Mendy Weiss and Maxie Dannenberg amid several others he didn't know, along with two shapely gals in glittery, low-cut dresses, with necklaces bobbing on their breasts. The sight of Harry so at ease in the company of those kinds of *putzes* was like a punch in Morris's gut. The group was loud and laughing, and the champagne flowing; one of the girls seemed to have spilled her drink on herself and the heavyset man next to her made a big scene about dabbing it up. Morris saw that it was Jacob Orgen—Little Augie, he was known as—a known labor slugger whose bands of strong arms acted as the muscle behind the garment unions.

Morris said, "Excuse me, I'll be back in just a minute," and got up, buttoned his jacket, and made his way through the tightly packed tables as the music played.

"Morris!" Harry looked up in surprise—at the same time uncomfortable to have his brother coming upon him in such company. "What are *you* doing here? This isn't your normal watering hole."

"Hey, Morris!" Mendy Weiss and Maxie Dannenberg waved hellos. They'd all known each other for years, from the same streets. They also knew Morris and Sol were never happy to find their brother in their company.

"Mendy. Maxie . . ." Morris acknowledged them with a nod.

"Well, all of *you* seem to know each other . . . ?" Jacob Orgen exclaimed. Orgen was no more than five foot two in height and barrel-chested, but his reputation for violence far outsized him. He had a fat cigar in the ashtray.

"I'd say we know each other," Harry said. "Morris is my brother. Let me introduce you to some friends, Morris. Say hello to Jack Diamond. . . ."

Jack Diamond, known as Legs, a gangster whose name and reputation for violence were well known, was tall and reed-thin with an easy laugh and amiable face. He stood up and extended his hand to Morris, nodding. "Pleasure." Diamond was a trigger man whose prowess with the gun and with the ladies was legendary, someone who was never more than a few steps away when things got rough and who could count more than a few gangland victims to his name.

Morris shook the gangster's hand. "Mr. Diamond. Nice to meet you."

"Next to him is Jacob Orgen." His was a name everyone knew, whether you were in the garment trade or just read the papers. Little

Augie was one of the toughest thugs on the Lower East Side. He controlled the union muscle, whether it was clothing or the docks. You didn't join up, you got your head cracked or your warehouse torched. Or worse. Word was it was he who had shot down a rival, Nathan Kaplan, right on Essex Street to consolidate his rackets.

Harry had graduated to a dangerous crowd.

"Mr. Orgen." Morris nodded. The diminutive gangster shot him back a brief wave, the other arm around the girl to his right.

"And these are Mandy and Virginia," Harry introduced the girls. "Jack's friends."

"Charmed," one said, diverting her attention from chewing on Orgen's ear for just a second. The other waved an indifferent hello. "How do you do?"

"And last but not least, to your right," Harry motioned, "say hello to Louis Buchalter."

Morris fixed on the small, dark-featured man in the white evening jacket. He hadn't seen him in years, since Delancey Street. But Morris had never forgotten the name. Buchalter nodded back with a wave. By now the gangster went by the name "Lepke," Little Louis, the name his mother supposedly called him. Since Morris had last seen him, Lepke's reputation had grown. With his enforcer, Jacob "Gurrah" Shapiro, the load Morris had dared to egg on that day in the alley, the two had moved up from street-corner gambling scams and burglaries to extortion, prostitution, and acting as strong arms for some of the most notorious gangsters in town. Even the Italian mobsters were said to come to him when they needed a dirty job handled.

"We've actually met," Morris said.

"I know you?" Buchalter stared up at him. He had the chummy, congenial grin and cocker spaniel eyes of a kid on the *bima,* belying his reputation. Morris had already seen how he could turn in the flick of a switch.

"Years ago. In an alley. Off Delancey," Morris said. "You were running a card game there and I happened to come by."

"Well, that *was* my office back in those days," Buchalter said with a grin, "and lots of people used to happen by, so you just might be right."

"And did you win or lose, Mr. Raab?" Jack Diamond asked.

"Neither. I chose not to play."

"Smart. That's the only way I've found to put the odds in your favor."

"*Raab . . . ?* Wait a second. . . ." Buchalter snapped his fingers at Morris, his memory kicking in. "I remember you now. You're that little *pisher* who wanted to fight us that day. Me and Gurrah, right? What has it been, eight, ten years . . . ?"

"That was me. But I think the fighting was more what you wanted," Morris said. "Not me."

"Maybe, but you stood right up. You stood up pretty good, as I recall, for just a young *macher*. . . ."

"Fight Gurrah?" Jacob Orgen nodded at Morris with surprise. "That shows moxie."

"Morris has always had moxie," Harry said. "And plenty of it."

"Well, consider yourself lucky your good sense kicked in, Mr. Raab," Jack Diamond said. "A man would have to have his brains checked if he wanted to take on that ox. So what is it you do now . . . ?"

"Morris is in the garment trade," Harry announced.

"The garment trade . . ." Jacob Orgen looked up. "I've spent some time in it myself."

"He ran the old Majestic Company for Mr. and Mrs. Kaufman until they sold it. Now he's got his own firm with my older brother, Sol. They're going to do real well."

"Majestic?" Little Augie said. "I remember that old fox. So your two brothers, huh . . . ?" He raised a glass to Morris. *"Mazel tov."*

"Thank you," Morris said.

"So, tell me, how the fuck they let *you* escape?" Mendy Weiss elbowed Harry, leaning over to his pal Maxie with a snicker.

"I guess that kind of life just ain't for me." Harry shrugged, not sure if he'd suddenly become the butt of a joke.

"So tell me, Mr. Raab, what do you and your brother call yourselves in this new venture of yours?" Jacob Orgen tapped the ash off his half-smoked cigar.

"Our firm's called Raab Brothers," Morris said. "And there's still room for you anytime you want, Harry. Whenever you guys feel you can let him go, of course. And we won't even have to change the name."

"Harry's his own contractor." Mendy slapped him on the shoulder. "*Right?* He can walk out any day he wants. Clean as a baby's *tuchis*. You don't have to worry, Morris, we got our eyes out after him. Now the rest of us . . . Ain't so easy backing out, once you're in. At least not on your feet."

"So Raab Brothers, you say. . . ." Jacob Orgen flicked a cigar ash on his plate, eyeing Morris like a dog smelling meat. "Tell me, Mr. Raab, are you a union operation?"

"We're just starting out. We're way too small to worry about."

"Maybe now." Orgen shrugged. "But one thing you learn is, even in a small pond, the minnows get fat if they don't get eaten fast enough. Maybe I ought to send around some of my boys. Just to make introductions."

Morris said, "I think we've already made the introductions. Anyway, it's just my brother and me, right now. We job out all our production."

"Well, for when it's time then, perhaps. . . ." The labor slugger looked at Morris; people didn't often decline that invitation. "Tell you what, I'll give you a little room while you fatten yourselves up." He pointed with his cigar. "Just as long as you know, one day we'll be calling. In the meantime, whatever you need, a brother of Harry here, you just call on me and let me know."

Morris nodded. "Thanks, Mr. Orgen."

"So why not sit down and join us for a drink?" Jack Diamond proposed. "The bubbly's flowing, and the night's just getting started. Right, girls . . . ?"

"Yeah, Morris." Harry jumped up, offering his chair. "Jack's right. Have a seat. They've got only the very best here."

"Thanks, but I think I need to head back to my table. I've got some people there."

"Can't say I blame you a bit." Louis Buchalter peered over and got a look at the bevy of pretty girls. "I wouldn't leave them myself. Not for a second. Someone might gobble them up. Feel free to bring them along, if you like?"

"Actually, Harry," Morris said, "I was just thinking why don't you come over and join *us*? Irv's with me."

"Irv, huh . . . ? Yeah, I see him." Harry shrugged, kind of sheepishly. "Thanks, Morris, but I'm good where I am."

"C'mon," Morris pushed. "Like old times."

"It's okay."

"So I'm trying to figure out who's the big brother and who's junior?" Mendy Weiss piped up. "No one's tying your hands, Harry. Your kid brother'd like you to leave."

Harry grinned sheepishly and ran his hand through his thick, dark hair, almost like he did when his mother called him a *moisheh kapover* and he just wanted to slink out of the room. "I think I'll just stay, if it's all the same, Morris. Thanks for the invite though. How about I stop over before we leave?"

"Sure, stop over." Morris looked at him with some disappointment. "Anyway, it was a pleasure to meet the lot of you. Enjoy your evening."

"You as well," Jacob Orgen called after him, and pointed. "And we'll be seeing you."

Morris wove his way back through the tables, annoyed that Harry had made the choice of staying with his table; even more annoyed that he had singled Morris out for the attention of the most notorious labor muscle in town. Right now, dealing with the union was exactly what they *didn't* need.

Back at his table, the college girls seemed distracted and Irv was on the dance floor circling with the one from Skidmore who seemed even more bored.

Morris sat back down next to Ruthie. "Sorry to be so long."

Ruthie leaned close to him on her elbow. "You know those guys?" She widened her eyes with surprise.

"One or two of 'em."

"That was Jacob Orgen you were talking to. And everyone's saying that's Legs Diamond across from him. Those are two of the biggest mobsters in town."

"The other two ain't exactly choirboys themselves," Morris said, referring to Maxie Dannenberg and Mendy Weiss.

"So, hey, how's Harry doing?" Priscilla asked loudly.

"How do you know about Harry?" Morris said.

"Irv told us."

"So your brother's a gangster?" Ruthie said, in a tone that made Morris think his chances with her had now gone from unlikely to nil.

"My brother wouldn't know a gun from a pressing iron," Morris replied. But he could see how even the thought made him look in her eyes. "I don't even know what he's doing with that crew. All he is, is just friends with one of them, that's all. He's a mile out of his league."

Priscilla, the Columbia gal, was whispering to a good-looking young man in a white dinner jacket with gold cuff links, who was leaning over her chair. "A bunch of us are moving the party," she announced to the table. "To the Cotton Club. This guy named Ellington is playing there. Jen, Ruthie, shall we gather up Margie," who was on the dance floor with Irv, "and head out?"

Ruthie shrugged. "I don't know, maybe you all should just . . ."

"C'mon, I bet that guy you're sweet on is there. Anyway, you're not going to be a drip and break up the party."

"C'mon, Ruthie . . . ," her friend Jen pressed, seeing her hesitation. Morris thought maybe she liked him a bit.

Ruthie shrugged. "All right." She halfheartedly picked her purse off the back of her chair and got up. "It is Marge's birthday," she said to Morris with a sigh. "I've got to tag along."

"I get it." Morris stood up too.

"I'd invite you and your friend, but I'm not sure we can all get in. But, listen, thanks for the dance and all the bubbly. I wish you the best in what you do."

"Pleasure's all mine," Morris said, but with a hint of disappointment. "Listen, if it's okay with you, maybe sometime we could—"

"C'mon, Ruthie, we can't sit around here all night," Priscilla cut him off. "Everyone's waiting."

"Maybe I'll see you around here again sometime," Ruthie said. "We show up from time to time."

Morris couldn't decide if that was an invitation or a brush-off. Likely the latter, he figured. "Sure. Maybe I'll see you," he said. "Why not?"

"So who's the company?" the guy in the white dinner jacket inquired. "You gals want to bring them along?"

"Nah, just a couple of rubes from the Lower East Side," the Columbia gal said under her breath, but loud enough for the rest to hear.

Ruthie glared at her, her eyes burning.

"Ruthie, Marge, c'mon, girls. Ben has a cab." She grabbed her bag and turned back to Irv and Morris breezily. "I'm sure we'll see you boys again sometime. Irv, keep up the good work with the law."

Ruthie stayed behind a minute and looked back at Morris with a crestfallen expression. Then Priscilla took hold of her, exclaiming brightly, "Night, everyone," and they disappeared into the crowd.

"You ought to go after her," Irv said. "She liked you."

"Liked me? We might as well have had a sack over our backs for all they cared." Morris sat back down with the half-empty bottle of champagne. He was confident in all other matters, but when it came to women, especially fancy ones, with an education, he couldn't get the right words out of his mouth. Words someone wouldn't laugh at.

But, if that was how they really felt about them—a bunch of rubes from Delancey Street—then, hell with them. Morris filled Irv's champagne flute. "Let's finish this up and leave."

"She's right, you know," Irv said. "That's what we are. Rubes. We don't belong here any more than Harry and his goons do. Look at me—I borrowed this suit just to get in. They were laughing at me the whole night. Next time I come in here, after I pass the bar . . ." He drained the last of his champagne. "No one's gonna be laughing at me. Thanks for the evening, Morris. . . ." He stood up. "But we're gonna spend our whole lives trying to act like we fit in here, and we'll always be exactly what she said. Rubes."

Morris glanced back around at Harry, who was telling a story that had Mendy and Maxie in stitches.

Irv was right. He should have never let her leave. He'd probably never see her again. "Lemme get the check," he said. "I'll go with you."

He caught the waiter's eye and signaled for the bill. It had probably cost him three hundred dollars just to pretend he was a big shot. He looked across at Harry again. He didn't know what his brother saw in that crowd. The bubbly empowering him, he had half a mind to go over and wrestle him away. *Rubes.* Rubes and goons. They were no better, just because they put beer in people's mugs and left a few bodies on the street.

"Any more of that bubbly left?" a woman's voice said above him.

Morris looked up. Ruthie, her eyes sparkling and apologetic, stood over him. "The cab could only hold five." She shrugged. "And anyway, I thought if you were still going to hang around a bit longer, we might catch another dance."

"Another dance would be great," Morris said, expansive. "Whaddya say, Irv, you'll excuse us, right . . . ?" He got up and took Ruthie out to the crowded floor.

They danced for a while without saying much, then she finally stopped and looked at him. "I'm sorry for what Priscilla said. She's drunk, but she's also a bit of an ass. And just for the record, her parents bought her into Columbia. They even named a building after them. Without that, she probably couldn't even get into Brooklyn College."

"That's okay," Morris said. "Anyway, maybe she's right about what she said."

"She's not right." Ruthie looked at him. "At least not about the rube bit anyway. You're okay. And so's your friend. Though his suit's in desperate need of an alteration."

"He borrowed it." Morris grinned and drew her a little closer. "I'm glad you came back." The music picked up and suddenly there was the sound of a glass shattering and everyone whooped with delight, like the evening was just starting to liven up.

"They were jerks to let you go," Morris said with her against him.

"They didn't let me go." Ruthie put her head on his chest. "I left. I ran back two blocks in the rain."

"It was raining, huh?" He twirled her around, feeling like he was the most important person in the room.

Back at the table, he ordered another bottle of bubbly. Irv, who'd stayed, was now turned around, talking to a heavyset girl at the table next to them.

"So when *did* you actually start working?" Ruthie asked, leaning on her elbow, "if you don't mind me asking? You do look pretty young to have started your own business."

"A while," was all Morris said. He didn't want to say how much of a while. He was embarrassed to admit how little education he'd truly had.

"Well, I assume in high school?"

"I never made it to high school." Morris twisted the flute of champagne in circles. "My father died, we were broke. We all had to help out to pay the rent."

"So how old were you then? C'mon, you can tell me."

"Fifteen," Morris lied, hesitating a second. He felt a tremor of shame to do so. But he knew there was no way she would even look at him if she knew the truth. "I never told that to anyone before."

"Fifteen?" Ruthie stared at him. "Wow."

"Well, almost sixteen," Morris said, sinking deeper.

She blinked and gave him an incredulous shake of her head. "Well, we do come from very different worlds, Morris Raab. When they were talking about Fitzgerald, I saw how you averted your eyes."

"Who is he? Some lawyer?"

"Some lawyer?" Ruthie smiled. "He's a famous writer. You probably don't read much, do you?"

"Not that way. Made-up stuff."

"You mean novels?"

"Whatever you call them. I read the papers though. Every day. And the trades."

"The trades?"

"You know, *Women's Wear Daily*. To see what's going on and who's in town." When she merely blinked back at him, Morris grinned. "I guess you're right, we do come from very different worlds."

"Well, I know a book you just might like. One of those 'made-up' things." She smiled. "You've heard of Dickens?"

"I heard of 'scared as the dickens.' But I guess that's not what you mean, is it?" He felt a stab of embarrassment.

Ruthie laughed. "No, *Charles* Dickens, silly. Oh, come on. You're joking, right?"

Morris didn't reply.

"I'm sorry." She saw his chagrin. "He's famous, that's all. British. He died over fifty years ago. You know, *A Christmas Carol*. The Ghost of Christmas Past? Every schoolkid knows it."

"I guess I didn't stay in school that long."

Ruthie nodded, and put her hand on his arm. "I'm sorry. I know that was stupid of me to say. Anyway, the book's called *Great Expectations,* and if you ever come upon it, made-up or not, I think you'd find it worth a read. I think you'd like the main character. His name is Pip. You kind of remind me of him."

"I do, huh? Why?"

"I don't know, that you both came from very humble beginnings. That you have a kind of naïve way about you, and yet you learn the ropes and you're clearly going places. I can see."

"Going places, huh . . . ?" He liked how those words sounded coming from her. He felt like he had the prettiest girl in the place seated next to him, and from his view, maybe the smartest. "Pip, you say . . . ?" Morris had never even looked through a real book in his life, other than the Talmud or the Mishnah, and even those had been a while. He no longer went to shul more than two or three times a year.

"Yes. Pip." She tilted her champagne flute to him. "Do read it. If we ever see each other again, you'll thank me."

They clinked glasses. *"Great Expectations . . ."* He picked up a pencil and started to write the name on a cocktail napkin. He hesitated.

"That's with a 't' and an 'i.'" Ruthie pointed to what he'd written. "Here. . . ." She wrote it out on the napkin. "*Great Expectations*. See? By Charles Dickens."

"Thanks. And by the way, we will. I'm sure of it."

"We will, what . . . ?"

"See each other again. Maybe we'll even read it together sometime."

She cocked her head, smiling in a congenial way, but at the same time, it carried a message. That that wasn't likely to happen. "Look, you're a nice fella, Morris, and intriguing in a way. And I'm very glad I came back in. But we're from very different worlds, and . . . I can't even imagine being with a guy who . . ." She curled her hair around her ear and flicked an ash from her cigarette holder into the ashtray. He knew what she was about to say. "Maybe just don't get your hopes up, that's all. But I admit, there's a certain way about you. And you're clearly nobody's fool. Say, want to take another run at that dance floor?"

"Sure." He was about to get up and help her chair back when Ruthie's gaze suddenly shifted toward the front. "Look, seems we have company."

On the way to his table, Louis Buchalter in his white dinner jacket came up to them. He put a hand on Morris's shoulder.

"Hello again. It's Raab, right . . . ?" The gangster surveyed the table. "I see you've lost your party."

"I don't know, the party seems just fine as it is," Morris said, looking him in the eye. "Meet Louis Buchalter."

Buchalter introduced himself to Ruthie. Then he looked over and gave a nod to Irv. "So why don't you all come over and join us then? The drinks won't stop, and after, we've got some places to go."

"Some other time, maybe," Ruthie spoke up. "I'm perfectly fine where I am, thank you."

"Can't twist your arm, huh? Morris here can tell you from

past experiences, I don't give up so easy when it's something I'm interested in."

"Thanks for the offer, Mr. Buchalter," Morris said. "But you heard her, she said she's fine where she is."

"Suit yourselves. I only ask once." Buchalter had that chummy half-grin and looked over again at Irv, like he had a chew of tobacco in his jaw, but unlike before, Morris could feel no more than a ray of mirth in it. "But you know, that makes twice now, Morris," he said, "if I recall."

"Twice?"

"Twice, I let you get over on me. You think I forgot? Which puts you in a small club, Morris Raab. A very small club. But once again, I make an exception for you. You twice, but once for anyone else. Anyway, enjoy the night, lovebirds." He bowed, casting Ruthie an eye. "I hope the new business goes well, Morris. But just watch out, if you'll take a good piece of advice: these union guys, they're not like me, they never let as much as a piece of lint get by them, the greedy *machers*. You know what I mean?"

"Yeah, I think I know what you mean," Morris said.

Buchalter gave a look to Irv again. "Counselor . . ." He nodded. Then he headed back to his table at the other end of the room.

"Who was that guy?" Ruthie turned back around to Morris.

"No one you need to know."

"But *you* know him."

"I know a lot of people." He looked over at Irv.

"Well, I don't like him. He gives me the chills. Whatever he was referring to, that almost sounded like a threat."

"He gives a lot of people the chills," Morris said. "C'mon, don't pay no attention to him." He pulled back her chair and put out his hand. "Night's still young, whaddya say, you still up for that dance?"

Chapter Ten

Days later, Louis Buchalter sat in the backseat of the Pontiac across from Blinky Cohen's candy store on the corner of Pitkin and Bristol Avenues in Brownsville, Brooklyn. The street was dark and dimly lit, and the store, which sold everything from candy to comics and cigars, was the only thing still lit on the block.

Buchalter watched through the window as the last customers straggled out with bottles of pop, toffee, or baseball cards, and probably a numbers ticket in their pocket. He glanced at his watch. Five of . . . Everyone in the neighborhood knew Blinky shut the doors promptly at eight P.M.

"Look at this guy," Louis chuffed to Jacob Shapiro, who was seated in the front, next to Oscar Hammerschmitt, who was behind the wheel. "He's got more people in there than Macy's on Christmas Eve. It's a wonder he even shuts the door."

"I'd be open till midnight if I had a line like that," Gurrah looked back and said.

"Two things you can count on in life to put a smile on your face." Louis nudged him on the shoulder.

"And what's that?"

"A blow job. And that first bite from a box of Cracker Jacks."

"It's a tough choice," Gurrah said, seemingly thinking on it a second, and this from a man not generally given over to much reflection. "Still, I'll have to go with the blow job."

"You would, huh?" Buchalter gave it a bit more reflection and shrugged. "I don't know. . . ."

At eight, what appeared to be the last customer exited the store. Through the window, Louis saw Blinky, the size of an ox so he was hard to miss, shuffle over and turn the Open sign to Closed. Louis scanned down the darkened block. No one was around. But Blinky had a lot of friends. Sometimes after closing, the police wandered by. That's why he didn't lock the door. They played the numbers too. But tonight, in the cold and drizzle, the street was clear. Louis nudged Gurrah that it was time to go, and opened his door. "That's our sign, my old friend. Shall we go?

"Keep the motor running," he said to Oscar.

He and Gurrah stepped out and, hands in their overcoats, headed across the street.

Things had gone pretty well for Louis Buchalter in the past years. His star was definitely on the rise. He'd carved out his own territory down on the Lower East Side, between Rivington and East Fourth, where his gambling and protection businesses brought in a reliable income. Merchants had to ante up to keep themselves safe, which of course chiefly meant safe from him, since he and Gurrah were not above cracking a knee or two, splitting a skull, or even firebombing a store if a stubborn merchant didn't see it their way.

Still, it was all nickel-and-dime stuff compared to the guys above him. Pocket change. He looked at fat cats like Rothstein and Jacob Orgen and even the guineas like Luciano and Albert Anastasia, who had a temper that could go off at a moment's notice and was known to have once put a steak knife in a suspected informant's chest, seated across the table. And which explained why he and Shapiro were there that night. Blinky Cohen had friends—too many friends. And apparently he was handing out a lot more than just jelly beans to the local cops, which Anastasia said had landed an associate or two of his in jail and was starting to put a dent in his rackets.

Guinea or Jew, Louis had no tolerance for snitches, no matter which language they blabbered in. He took a last look at Gurrah as they turned the handle and stepped into the store. The door chime jingled.

"Sorry, we just closed!" Blinky called out from behind the counter, in the process of filling a cigar humidor. Then he saw who had come in. "Oh . . . Louis, Jacob . . ." His reaction was both surprised and wary. It clearly wasn't a social call. He closed the humidor. "What brings you two all the way out here?"

"Jelly beans, Blinky." Buchalter grinned.

"Jelly beans . . . ?" Blinky went about three hundred pounds, with thinning gray hair and a constant twitch in his left eye, accounting for his nickname. He wore an open white shirt and thick suspenders, his ample belly hanging over his waist. "Whatsamatter, they don't sell 'em no more across the bridge?" he said hesitantly, but with a laugh.

"None like yours." Louis and Gurrah stepped up to the counter.

"Sure, then," Blinky said, his eye wandering to Gurrah, who stood there with his meaty hands stuffed inside his coat pockets. "Cold in here, Jacob . . . ? Whatcha got in there?"

Gurrah just shrugged. "Don't pay it no mind, Blinky."

"Just make sure you gimme enough of those red ones there." Louis pointed to the glass container. "I fucking hate it when you get a handful of jelly beans and only one or two are red. And while you're at it, Blinky, how about you make sure you keep those hands of yours above the counter where I can see them nice and clear, okay?" Everyone knew the candy store owner kept a loaded shotgun underneath the cash register, so no one ever attempted to rob him.

"I know you're not here for fucking jelly beans, Louis," the candy store owner said, a film of sweat starting to break out on his forehead. He scooped a shovelful of beans out from a large glass container and put them in a dish.

"Well, you're right there." Louis looked around. "Y'know, you of all people ought to know how to keep that fat mouth of yours shut, Blinky."

"I don't know what you're talking about, Louis." Blinky shut the glass case. "You know I keep to myself. I don't talk to anyone. I don't know who *you* been talking to. In a million years, I would never give a *yiddisher* up to the cops, if that's what you're saying. You both know me, Louis, Jacob. A long time."

"Well, you might be right on that." Louis nodded, as Blinky turned around with the jelly beans and put them on the counter. "Problem is," he said, looking at him, "in this case, I ain't talking about a *yiddisher*."

The air slowly leaked from the fat man's cheeks, as the reason Louis and Gurrah were there suddenly became clear. "I don't know what you're talking about," the fat man said, "but I think you know, Louis, I got protection. Abe Reles. Not someone you want to fuck with. No matter whose business you're here on. You and I been friends a long time."

"So I thought, Blinky. And you're right again, Abe's a tough *macher*," Louis agreed. "Not a guy you'd want to get on the wrong side of."

Blinky's bad eye started to flutter.

"Here, I think I gave you enough red ones to fucking shit cherries," he said, sliding the dish of jelly beans across, and as Louis reached for one, Blinky thrust his other hand underneath the counter for the shotgun there. In the same motion, Gurrah removed his hand from inside his coat pocket and drove the ice pick he'd been holding in there through Blinky's left hand, impaling it to the counter.

"*Shit!*" Blinky howled in pain. "You fucking wop pussy-licking kike." Blood began to ooze from his hand as he tried to bring it up. But it stayed there, fixed. With his other hand, he reached under the counter for the shotgun.

Louis removed his own gun from his coat pocket and placed it between Blinky's eyes. "I don't care what language you're singing in, Blinky, a canary's a fucking canary, you fat snitch."

He pulled the trigger.

There was a pop, and Blinky's head snapped back, a dark, crimson hole dotting the candy store owner's forehead.

"*Zay gezunt,* Blinky," Louis muttered. He pulled the trigger again. Say good-bye.

The top of Blinky's head blew open in red, and the candy store owner slumped, pulling at the ice pick impaling his left hand, until Gurrah lifted the pick back out and the fat man sank to the floor.

In a rage, Louis ran around the counter. "You fat fucking whale snitch." He kicked Blinky in the head. By that point the candy store owner was already dead, but Louis continued to stomp on him, mashing his face in with his heel.

"Louis," Gurrah called out to him.

"In a minute." Louis took his gun and inserted it into the fat man's gaping mouth and pulled the trigger one more time. And then again, until what a minute ago was Blinky's jowly face was now little more than a red, indecipherable maw. He stomped on him two or three more times until he grew flushed in the cheeks and short of breath.

"Louis," Gurrah said again.

"Okay!" Louis reached and grabbed a fistful of jelly beans off the counter. "You want to use that mouth of yours so bad—*here*. . . ." He stuffed the candy in Blinky's hanging, bloody jaw. "Chew on these!"

"Louis!" Gurrah tried to get his partner's attention. "We gotta get out of here. Oscar's waiting. No telling who's around."

Louis blew out a breath and wiped some of the dead man's blood off his coat sleeve. "You're right. I'm coming." He came back around from the counter. Gurrah was at the door. He opened it a notch, the chime tinkling, and he waved outside. Oscar swung the car around and flung open the passenger's side door.

"C'mon, let's go!"

"All right. Just one more second . . . ," Louis said, to Gurrah's irritation. He hurried back over to the candy counter like he was going to stomp on Blinky's head one last time.

"Louis, what the fuck you doing?" Gurrah said. "The fucker's dead. Don't worry 'bout him. People could've heard the shots. We gotta go."

"Not him. . . ." Buchalter paused at the counter and grabbed a couple of boxes of candy. He came back to the door. "These . . ."

"Fucking Cracker Jack?" Gurrah's eyes grew wide.

"I don't think Blinky's gonna miss 'em too much. Anyway, relax. . . ." Louis stuffed a box in Gurrah's coat. "I took one for you."

Chapter Eleven

Three days later

In a barber's chair in Guiseppe's Barber Shop in Flatbush, Brooklyn, Louis Buchalter sat across from Albert Anastasia, who was getting a shave.

"You know what, you Jews gotta learn the meaning of a true shave," the Italian grinned, reclined, his face covered in shaving cream, a cigar sticking out. Guiseppe, the owner, carefully eased the straight-edged razor over the contours of the crime boss's face. "You have no idea what you're missing."

"I shave just fine, Albert." Louis ran his hand across his own cheeks, which in fact were smooth.

"I'm talkin' a *real* shave, Louis," the Italian gangster said, glancing over to him. "Not walking around with all this fucking hair on the sides of your face and those heavy beards. It's unsanitary. What is it with you guys anyway?"

"It's in the Bible somewhere." Louis shrugged. "Jews are not permitted to use a razor on our faces. It's forbidden."

"The Bible . . . ?"

"Yeah. Leviticus, I'm thinking. You read the fucking Bible, don't you, Albert?" Louis winked at the barber.

"Last time I read the Bible, I probably couldn't even count to ten. Least not in English." He laughed. "C'mon, let my friend Guiseppe here have a crack at you when I'm done. On me. I promise, you'll feel like a million bucks."

"If it's all the same, Albert . . ." Louis sat up and looked at the Italian crime lord. "I'm gonna let someone put a razor to my neck without putting a bullet in his head—it won't be no Guinea. No disrespect, of course, Guiseppe."

"None taken, Mr. Buchalter," the barber said.

The barber finished up, and handed Anastasia a steaming towel. The crime boss wiped off whatever was left on his face, and ran a hand across his cheeks. "You know what they say, Louis: clean face, clean conscience. You'll sleep like a fucking babe."

"You know, I sleep just fine as it is, Albert."

"Perfect, Guiseppe." He took out a twenty and pressed it into the barber's hands. "Now leave us alone a couple of minutes, if you don't mind. Mr. Buchalter and I need to talk some things over a bit."

"Always a pleasure, Mr. Anastasia." The old barber folded the twenty into his vest pocket and stepped into the back room. The gangster waited until the door had completely shut.

Anastasia swiveled the barber's chair Louis's way. Though he was a man linked to many violent deaths, including stories of bludgeoning and garroting by his own hands, the Italian's face did give off the sheen of a baby's. "I want to thank you for coming all the way out here, Louis. And for doing that job the other day. I heard you messed our friend Blinky up pretty good."

"He got what was coming to him. I don't have any use for a snitch, no matter what language they're talking."

"My feelings exactly," the Italian said. "I was happy to be able to count on you. If I had to do it myself, it would've started a war.

Trust me, I won't forget. I can see you have ambition, Louis, though let me tell you, too much of it in this business isn't always the best thing."

"I do what I can," Louis said. He reached to the counter and dabbed a little aftershave on his hands and then onto his cheeks as well. They stung.

"Sure I can't tempt you . . . ?" Anastasia asked one more time. He rubbed his knuckles across his face. "Last chance."

"Next time, maybe. I'll have a shave here and you can have your dick cut by this mohel I know down on Delancey."

"Ha!" the Italian laughed. "That would be quite a deal, wouldn't it? Which is what I thought we might talk about, Louis. There's an opportunity here. You and your boys turn out to be quite good at what you do. I said to Masseria just the other day, who knew fuck-ing Hebes could be so tough? We always thought you were a bunch of sissy bedwetters. So the idea I'm thinking is, a kind of partnership. Your people bring the poppers. . . ."

"You mean we do all the work and take the risk. And you bring exactly what, Albert?" Louis asked.

"We bring the business, Louis." Anastasia sat up and grinned. "You know us Italians, we always seem to have grudges against some-body. There's always someone who needs to be taken care of. I got the idea from Lansky himself. It should be just like a business, he said. And why not? Murder and Company. Or Murder, Incorporated. How's that?" The Mafia man chuckled. "Doesn't have a bad ring to it, Louis. I know a lot of people who'd like to be shareholders. Any-way, you and me, I know we came up the same way. We never minded getting our hands dirty. *Mettendo le mani nella salsiccia,* we say in Italian. Putting our hands in the sausage."

"Something to talk about." Louis nodded. But inside, he couldn't help but marvel: Lansky, Masseria, Anastasia . . . These were the big-gest names. People were noticing. Louis felt his stock rising. "But before we start handing out business cards, I'd like to get something a little steadier going for myself. The rackets are fine, but it would be good to find something, I don't know, a bit more day-to-day. Where I didn't have to put my neck out all the time. You know what I mean?"

"Day-to-day, huh . . . ?" The Italian thought on it a second, chewing on his cigar. "You know what you ought to get into, Louis . . . ?"

"What's that?"

"Garments. If I were you I'd look very closely at the garment business. For your kind, that's where the real money seems to be."

"Garments?" Buchalter let out a laugh. "I'm afraid you got the wrong Jew, Albert. What the fuck do I know about making clothes?"

Anastasia leaned forward, looked over at him and smiled sagely. "Whoever said anything about making clothes, Louis?"

It hit Louis just what the crime boss was telling him. "You're talking the unions. . . ."

Albert nodded. "That's where the real money is, Louis. And you'll never have to buy a fucking yard of fabric. It's all about the dues. We got the dockworkers. It comes right out of their paycheck every month. Just like the IRS. It's a license to steal, my friend. And you oughta have the garment makers."

For the past decade, since the revolution that took place in Russia, the unions had been a growing force. Workers needed to have a voice, all the papers said. You heard it everywhere. Someone had to represent them. Since the Triangle Shirtwaist fire in 1911, the garment trade was no different. The unions had grown stronger and stronger, and with them, the money that was collected each month.

But there was a wrinkle. Louis swiveled around in his chair and looked Anastasia in the eye. "The garment unions are Little Augie's thing, Albert. You know well as I do, he'll never give 'em up."

"You're right. That's something that might have to be given some thought." The Italian shrugged and flicked an ash off his cigar. "That

Augie's a stubborn bastard. He won't give up an inch. But from my thinking," Anastasia looked back at him, "that's a thing you seem to have the means to resolve, Louis. You understand what I'm saying?"

The Italian got up from the chair, folded his face cloth, and laid it neatly on the counter. "Tell me, how many factories you think are making garments in this city these days?"

Louis gave it some thought. "I don't know. Thousands, I figure."

"My people tell me it's the second-largest business in the city these days. That's a lotta fucking dues, Louis. You do your job right, you're talking millions. Week in, week out. Straight outta their pay-checks. And here's the thing, what you do with 'em . . ." Anastasia shrugged. "Well, that's entirely your business, Louis. It's totally up to those in charge. And that would be you, right? You understand?"

Louis ran the numbers around in his head. He had no idea for sure, but Albert had to be right. It was millions they were talking about. Right in front of his eyes. And all Little Augie cared about was cracking a few heads. He wasn't a businessman. He couldn't see the big picture.

But Louis saw it. He saw it come together like a fucking Michel-angelo being painted right in front of his eyes.

"Still, you're right on one thing. . . ." Anastasia lifted his jacket off a hanger and put his arm through. "Little Augie would never stand for it. Not for a minute. That's a problem that would need to be solved." He put his hat on and adjusted his tie. "But you did say you were looking for something, didn't you, how did you put it, a bit more 'day-to-day' . . . ?"

"Yeah." Louis nodded. The idea was already taking shape in his mind.

"Well, this is pretty fucking 'day-to-day,' my friend." The crime boss laughed and nudged his shoulder.

If Louis had learned one thing, it was that in this business you had to take the opportunities when they presented themselves. Otherwise, someone else would gobble you up. Little Augie might be small in height but he was no little fish in stature. Arnold Rothstein was his friend. And he was never very far away from that Jack Diamond, who was no one to fuck with, himself.

Still, Albert Anastasia had just given him the okay.

"So, see, you can tell a lot about a man . . ." Anastasia patted Louis on the shoulder, "from his shave. And besides," he rubbed his cheeks and winked, "it makes the babes go fucking wild."

But Louis was no longer thinking about shaves as he followed Anastasia out.

Or babes.

His mind was a million miles away.

He was thinking of putting his hands in the sausage.

Chapter Twelve

Morris did take Ruthie out again—the following week. To the Crimson Room at Delmonico's for a steak. Where they sat across from movie producer Samuel Goldwyn, who Morris knew from the neighborhood.

Then he took her to Yankee Stadium and sat in field-level boxes and they saw the Babe belt two homers, and to the Zigfeld to see Al Jolson perform along with a comedian named Jack Benny.

Each time Ruthie seemed to laugh and have a good enough time, but she always implied when he took her home that this might be the last time they would see each other.

He would ask, "You have anyone else?"

And she would simply shrug and shake her head that, "No, that's not it." Politely enough not to say what she truly felt. He knew they were from completely different backgrounds. Her fancy Ivy League friends probably laughed and made fun of her that she would even give an unsophisticated rube like him the time of day.

But instead of backing down, he just kept asking her out. He didn't take no for an answer.

And after their fourth date, with a little champagne in her, she even let him kiss her goodnight. "Just don't get your hopes up, Morris Raab," she insisted again. "It's just a little kiss. We're not boyfriend and girlfriend. Let me make that clear."

"I know, I know," he said. "We're from different worlds."

"Markedly so," she said. He dropped her off in a cab at her family's apartment on 102nd and Riverside.

"Maybe we'll go dancing Saturday?" he called after her.

The doorman opened the door as she slipped through, and turned back. "Come if you like. I might be down. But I don't know."

"Eight o'clock," he said.

When he went home he asked Sol what "markedly" meant.

The next day he took off at lunchtime and grabbed a cab to a bookstore called Brentano's on Fifth.

He'd never stepped foot inside a real bookstore before. And this one was huge, bustling with customers browsing through the wooden shelves. There were more titles stacked in tall bookcases, it seemed, than there were shells on Coney Island beach. Morris had no idea where to even begin. He started looking through the racks at random, whatever was in front of him, too embarrassed to give away that this was all so new to him. He'd never seen so many books, on subjects he'd never even known people wrote about. No one named Dickens, however. His heart began to pick up, and he thought maybe he should just give up on this. Who was he kidding anyway? It was a foolish idea. He'd never read a real book in his life.

Finally a salesman saw him foundering and came up to him. "You look lost, sir. May I be of help?"

"Yeah. I'm looking for this book called *Great Expectations*?" He took out the napkin Ruthie had scribbled it down on. "I can't find it anywhere. It's by some guy from England. Named Dickens."

"Charles Dickens. Of course we carry *Great Expectations*." The salesman smiled. "It's quite a well-known title. But that would be in our Fiction department, sir. Over there." He pointed across the store. "I'm afraid this is History."

On their sixth date, they went to the RKO Orpheum to see Valentino in *The Son of the Sheik*. Morris loved the way she latched onto his arm when the hero was captured and held for ransom by the bandits. It made him feel like they were indeed a couple. Afterward, they went across the street to the Horn & Hardart for a cup of coffee. They sat near the window. Ruthie seemed distracted, even a little bored, until she finally confronted him. "What do you intend to do with your life?"

"What do you mean, what do I intend to do? I intend to build up my company," Morris said.

"And then?"

"And then . . . ?" Truth was, he'd never thought about anything else. He'd only had one goal his whole life. "Take care of my family, I suppose. Maybe buy a place out of the city."

"See, I would never let a man take care of me," Ruthie said resolutely. Almost attacking him.

"You wouldn't, huh?"

"Not at all. Julia Richman says independence and education is all that gives a woman strength today. I would never be tied down to that kind of life. It's a new world now. And there lies the difference between us."

"What kind of life?" Morris asked. He only knew one kind of life.

"A life where the woman is merely the child-bearer. A woman is able to work in the same fields as a man, and with the same capacity."

"I didn't say she couldn't. Anyway, who is this Julia Richman you're talking about?"

"She's an educator. And suffragette. She has a school on the Lower East Side. You must know of her."

"I guess I don't know much of anything." Morris shrugged, starting to get a little peeved.

She looked at him. *"See?"*

He sipped at his coffee in silence and picked at his pastry until he couldn't hold back anymore. "I guess for me, I only see one kind of woman. Women who work on factory floors. Seamstresses. Who don't have nothing to their names. I don't see the kind of women you're talking about, who go to fancy schools. And have choices. Who can decide what kind of path they want their life to go down, the way your kind of women do."

"But maybe they will, if you pay them a fair wage. Or then their children will. That's where I want my life to be. In education. Not just teaching. Lifting the lower classes. I want to open schools. For those who have less possibilities. In the Bronx. Or Harlem. Who knows, maybe even the Lower East Side."

"I do pay a fair wage. I pay them more than a fair wage."

"See, I told you there are unbridgeable differences between us, Morris. And it's not just our backgrounds. It's so many things. This won't work."

"Well, you keep saying that," Morris said, unable to hold back what he'd wanted to say for a long time, "and yet you keep going out with me. And I know you feel safe with me and have fun. I know I'm not the most polished or educated guy in the world. So if you really think there's no chance for us, don't go out with me next time."

Ruthie nursed her coffee for a while, quietly, then shrugged. "I don't know, Morris, maybe I won't, then."

Morris put down his cup. He was steaming even more than the coffee. "You know, it's like that book you told me to read."

"Which book?"

"By that English guy you talked about. Dickens."

"*Great Expectations*?" She stared widely at him with surprise.

"So was there another one you asked me to read . . . ?" He glared.

"Truth is, you got me wrong. I don't think I'm much like that guy Pip at all. I mean, I guess I kind of see what you mean. How he started with nothing and then rose up to become a gentleman. But things happened for him. I mean, it was all made-up, right? So it's not real. Me, I never had any Miss Havershamer, or whatever her name was. Or any of those, what were they called . . . factors of some kind . . . ?"

"Benefactors." Now she smiled as she corrected him.

"Yeah. But all that's for some made-up story, not real life. At least, not for me. Me, I had to go to work. And if I didn't, we would have been out on the street and who knows where I'd be now, delivering papers, or pushing some broom around somewhere. Certainly not here with you."

"You actually read the book?" she said, her surprise now bordering on delight.

"Yeah. But maybe I was wrong." He picked up his fork and pushed through whatever was left on his plate. "While I was reading I had the thought, this is all made-up, but maybe one thing was true. Maybe I did find my Estella. Like Pip in the book. But like I say, I guess I was wrong."

They sat for a while in silence, the feel of a heavy weight hanging over them.

"You read the book," Ruthie finally said, visibly pleased.

"You asked me to," he said.

"All the way through?"

"Yeah. All the way. What is this, a test? I even went back and bought another one by him."

"Another Dickens?" Her eyes stapled wide with astonishment.

"Yeah. About these French guys. And an English guy who falls in love. During a war. And he gets, you know, his head chopped off. What's it called, gillertin, or something?"

"Guillotined. Why, Morris Raab. . . ." Her eyes shone brightly and she smiled. "I honestly do believe there is hope for you yet, Morris Raab."

"Maybe. But I have a story too. You want to hear mine? You can tell me if it belongs in some book."

He'd never shared much about his life growing up. He was always too embarrassed, sure it would only bring up the differences between them she always spoke about and she would never want to see him again. Maybe he was trying to keep up some pretense too.

But this time he told her. About his time in the army, the humiliation he was forced to feel so keenly in that ditch, covered in piss and shit. Then having no choice but to fight his entire unit, one at a time. It felt so real to him, he could still see their faces today.

"Oh, Morris." Ruthie's eyes shimmered with emotion and grew wide.

"And something else," he said. "I lied to you about something that night."

"What night?"

"When we met. At the club. I wasn't fifteen when I left school to go to work. By fifteen I already had someone else's job. I was twelve."

"Twelve?" Ruthie stared back at him.

"Yeah. Twelve. And I'm sorry I lied to you. But let me ask, would you have even taken a second look at me if you knew that?"

Ruthie's eyes dimmed as she saw the shame on his face, and she wrapped her hand over his. "Morris, I'm so sorry."

"And, trust me, I don't need to read some book to know what it feels like to be the brunt of snobs and phonies in this world, like all those uppity friends of yours, in their fancy schools, waiting for their parents to introduce them to some equally rich guy and take them away. We never had those choices. I learned from the time I was six and couldn't walk across my own neighborhood without hearing some mick call me a kike or get into a fight exactly who my bene-factor was. It was me."

"Morris, please. . . ."

"And Estella, in that book, she's what in the end . . . ? Not some fancy socialite. She's just a housemaid's daughter. So all those airs people put on, they mean nothing when it comes to who you really are. It's what's in *here*. . . ." Morris tapped his chest. "That's what *I* read in the book. It's about when people have to show who they are, like when you're fifteen and you have to climb out of some ditch, and do what you have to do next. Just to survive. That's what it's all about. You know what I'm sayin' to you, Ruthie?"

She nodded, wordless and hurting for him.

"So you're right." He pushed away his plate. "We do come from different worlds. And I'm tired of hearing that. But maybe for the first time, I'm thinking, I'm not so embarrassed by that anymore. I'm okay with my world. It gave me the strength to understand what's right, even when it was hard. What's right in here, Ruthie." He tapped his chest again. "Inside.

"So I know I'm not exactly what you always had in mind for yourself, for who you'd end up with in life, but you keep saying I'm going places, and no one's fool, and if that's not enough for you, enough to come along, to trust me, on the journey, well, I don't know then. . . ."

He took out a five and put it under his saucer. "Let's go."

"Morris, I don't know what to say. . . ."

"Just tell me, if I hadn't lied, would you have taken a second look at me?"

She didn't answer.

"Would you?"

They finished up and left, and on the street, Ruthie turned and looked up to him and said, "Look, Morris, I don't know, maybe you're right about us. Maybe I'm just not the one to—"

He pulled her close to him and kissed her right there. On Eighty-sixth Street, the lights from the RKO theater flashing behind them. A real kiss, this time. Filled with promise, the present and future, the road ahead he was offering. Where life might take them together. She was taken by surprise; her arm dangled loosely by his side. But she didn't pull away.

And when it was over she just looked at him, breathless. "I think you should read more books, Morris."

The following week, she asked him to come upstairs when he came to pick her up.

"Bernstein," he announced to the doorman, who replied, "14C," and they whisked him into a wood-paneled elevator.

He met her father, a big-shot lawyer who worked for some important firm and wrote contracts, as best as Morris could figure out. Her mother was nice too; the place went on forever and they had a maid and a view of the Hudson. They both seemed to be walking on eggshells to be nice to Morris and not say what was likely in their minds. That their daughter was still in school and when she finished up she had things to accomplish, and that it wasn't so easy anyway, this German–Eastern Europe thing, even though they were all Jews.

"So we hear you're in garments, Morris," her father said as they sat down in the spacious living room.

"That's right. I am. And I'm going to marry your daughter," Morris replied.

"Morris." Ruthie cut him off, her cheeks blushing. "We're a long ways off from even thinking about anything like that. I'm still in school. We're barely dating. I—"

He looked at her father. "I was just letting you know."

Six months later, he asked her again.

This time she said, "Absolutely."

Chapter Thirteen

On October 17th, morning readers of the *Journal-News* on the streets of New York were greeted by a half-page photo of a crumpled, bloody corpse under the following headline:

STREETS OF FIRE:
Famous Mobster Gunned Down on Lower East Side

Labor Racketeer Jacob Orgen, known in the underworld as "Little Augie" for his stout but diminutive frame, came to a bloody end in a hail of bullets from a passing car on Norfolk Street on the New York's Lower East Side late last night.

Orgen, 36, a protégé of Arnold Rothstein, was a feared bootlegger who exerted a stranglehold over various unions in the garment field.

There were no immediate suspects, though sources indicate the list of people who could have wanted him dead ranged from crime boss Meyer Lansky to up-and-coming crime figures like Albert Anastasia and Louis "Lepke"

Buchalter, all making a play to expand their influence over the unions.

His bodyguard, the flamboyant mob figure Jack Diamond, hit with three bullets himself, managed to survive.

PART THREE

RAAB BROTHERS

Chapter Fourteen

So I'll tell you how I became a success.

Sol and I had been in business three years. We were making a go of it in women's coats—I handled all the production and he did the books and handled the sales, mostly to places like S. Klein and Abraham and Strauss in Brooklyn. Whatever we did, though, we couldn't seem to break into the big national buying offices.

Every season we tried to get our goods in front of important buyers, like at Interstate Department Stores or Certified stores. They had accounts all over the country and the leeway to write orders directly when they found something good.

But every season Sol would come back with his suitcase full of the same samples he went out with that morning and simply shrug. "They keep saying there's nothing special." Frustrated, I'd reply, "Maybe I should go out and sell them then?" And he'd go, "You think you can do a better job, go right ahead. Be my guest." But he knew I would never do it. I didn't have the nerve back then. I always felt like I had marbles in my mouth. We were doing enough business to scratch by. We just weren't growing.

That year, the world was saying that women's fur collars were going to be big. I had a friend in the fur business, and as it turned out, he got stuck with a large shipment of squirrel skins. Squirrel was big because it was cheap, and perfect for collars and cuffs. I bought the entire lot at a big discount.

So we put together our samples, knocking off styles I had seen in all the store windows the previous year. And that March, Sol went out to Ben F. Levis. They had hundreds of stores across the country. The buyer was this woman everyone knew. She had the biggest pencil on the street. Everyone was afraid of her. Muriel Mossman was her name. So Sol goes up and I know this time we have a good line at the right price. This time I was sure it would be different. I knew she liked chocolates, so we brought her this expensive box of Swiss candies from this fancy chocolate store on Broadway. But at five o'clock Sol comes back to the office and throws his hands in the air.

"What happened?" I asked.

"What happened? Nothing happened. There was a big wait. Her assistant said she had to see the lines she already buys."

"You mean you didn't even get to show her the line?" I was angry. I knew we had something right for her. All we had to do was get it in front of her.

"You think it's so easy?" He flung the box of chocolates across the table. "You fucking do it. Be my guest."

"All right, maybe I will," I said back in the same anger. I'd never seen my brother lose his temper before. But I was nervous as hell. In production I was the boss and could do anything I wanted. But sales . . . I didn't even know how to make a sales call. That night, I got drunk and went over and over what I would say.

At eight o'clock the next morning, an hour early, I dragged the sample case up to her office at 1225 Broadway on an open sales call. I *was nervous as a kid playing the violin at Carnegie Hall. This was the first time I'd ever been in front of a customer on my own.*

I figure I'll be the first in line, but to my shock, when I get there, there are already at least thirty salesmen ahead of me waiting to show their lines. And every one seems to have wool coats with fur on them—fur collars, fur sleeves. A few people there knew me from the trade and knew I didn't go on sales calls. They gave me questioning looks like, What the hell are you doing here, Morris? Aren't you in the wrong place? *One by one the ones in front of me go in—there's an assistant at a desk in front of a frosted-glass partition open at the top, Mrs. Mossman behind it. You could hear her voice—stern, no-nonsense. All business. One after one, the salesmen come back out, most of them with the same look Sol had on him the other day, like their own mothers had passed away. Once in a while, one would come out with a bit of a smile, and maybe gives a friend who was still on the line a wink and a thumbs-up. Then the telephone would ring and no one would go in for a while. I waited. An hour passed. Then two. I practiced over and over what I would say.*

I sat there for over four hours. At one thirty, there were still at least ten people ahead of me. I asked the assistant how long she saw sales-men for and she told me, "Mrs. Mossman has to leave today at two. She has an appointment in the market."

Two? I saw clearly I wasn't even going to be able to show her my line. I wasn't even close.

But I wasn't going back without her seeing me.

I opened my case and went up to the partition. The assistant said, "Sir, I told you you'll have to wait your—"

I took my two best fur-collared numbers and flung them over the partition. Then I yelled out so anyone behind it could clearly hear me, "Sixteen seventy-five for either of them. See if you can beat it!"

At first, there was no response. Just silence. I figure I'd dug my own grave, but so what, at least I wasn't going back without her seeing what we did.

Horrified, the assistant ran in the buyer's office, going, "I'm sorry, Mrs. Mossman, I tried to tell him you were—"

But before she even got the words out of her mouth, Muriel Mossman came out with one of my samples. Gray haired, a tweed suit well below her knees; heavy, low-heeled shoes. She looked like that drill sergeant who had thrown me in the ring in the army.

"Who's the wise guy?" she asks dourly and looks around. I'm standing there and her gaze centers on me. I figured I'd just collect my samples and be told to leave and never come back.

Instead, I go, "I'm the wise guy. Sixteen seventy-five for either of them. You won't find a coat like that at a better price."

"Roselle, who is this person?" She glared at me.

I didn't scare easy, but the way she looked at me, fire in her eyes, my insides were rolling over. Behind me, I heard a few of the salesmen snickering.

"I'm Morris Raab," I said.

"Morris Raab . . . I've heard of you," she said. Still, I figured the next words out of her mouth would be, Well, Morris Raab, collect your samples and get the hell out.

Instead she held the fur-trimmed number out. "And you can deliver these? Just like they look here. Same quality? For that price?"

"As many as you need," I said. Though I knew I had to figure out how to back up my word.

"All right, then Morris Raab, come on in," she said, motioning me into her office. "Roselle, hold my calls."

I didn't get back to the office until almost five. I dragged my sample case into the office and threw it on the desk. Sol was going over some figures, no doubt seeing my downcast face and thinking I'd suffered the same fate as him.

"So . . . ? Get anything? It's not as easy as you think out there, is it?"

"I got one." I dug into my case and produced a signed purchase order from a store in Pennsylvania and put it on his desk.

He picked it up. Three styles. Eight of a number. He looked up and his face split into a smile. "Sonovabitch, Morris! I've been trying to crack Muriel Mossman for two years and you finally did it." He got up and slapped me on the back with true excitement.

"I got this one too," I said, and pulled out another. From a store in Kalamazoo, Michigan. Four styles. Twelve of a number.

Sol looked it over and his face lit up. That was two more than he'd been able to get in two years.

"And this one . . ." I reached inside my case and brought out a third order. This one, from Perkins-Watkins, a big department store down South. Three styles. Sixty of a number.

By then he was dumbstruck.

"I forgot, this one too . . ." To his amazement, I kept taking out orders from my case and dropping them on the desk. "Oh, yeah, and this one . . ." Soon, the pile of orders I'd received was eight inches high. From all over the country.

It was a lot. A real lot.

Stunned, Sol sat back down. He started going through them one by one, writing down the quantities in a column, punching them into an adding machine. I kept hearing the ka-ching, ka-ching of the machine, totaling them up, knowing each one was a block on which our future would be built.

"There's sixty," he finally said, and looked at me. "Over three thousand pieces." He turned over the last one. "That's over fifty thousand dollars, Morris."

"Fifty-three thousand, six hundred and three," I said. "And we deliver 'em, just like we showed 'em, next time we'll get ten times that amount."

From then on Muriel Mossman became like a mentor to me. And there wasn't much argument that I was in charge of the firm.

Chapter Fifteen

1933

The Amalgamated Needle Trade Workers Union had been representing workers in the garment trade for fifty years, and for thirty of them, Abraham Langer had been its most successful rep.

In the early years, it was fruitless work, as Abe went company to company with no one wanting to hear his message; even the workers themselves were afraid just listening would cost them their jobs. Then, in 1911, there was the tragic Triangle Shirtwaist Factory fire in the Asch Building near Washington Place and Greene Street: 146 sewers lost their lives, most of them young immigrant women; the outer doors had been blocked against escape so that they wouldn't take unauthorized bathroom breaks. The entire city was appalled. The newspapers took up the labor cause, headlines excoriating the firetrap and the victims' deplorable working conditions. One by one, garment makers were forced to give in. In 1917, the Russian Revolution championed the plight of workers worldwide. Strikes were organized, speakers ranted in the streets against greed and capitalism and the abuse of labor for profit; newspaper headlines took up the cause of women. All Abe ever wanted was to give a voice to the small and the powerless. Suddenly it was as if the whole world had taken up his cause.

He went from shop to shop, factory to factory, listening to the workers' complaints, but Abe's way wasn't to overthrow anyone. Everyone knew him, worker and factory owner alike. His easy way and natural sense of humor made him as liked as anyone on the street. Anyone would be able to find him in his booth at Eddie's, the restaurant on the Lower East Side that was his makeshift office. "Why don't you cut your workers a break," he would tell a stubborn factory owner over coffee. "You want to keep them happy, don't you? Happy workers make happy clothes. The better workmanship alone will pay the difference in wages."

One by one, they all began to come in line.

But in the late 1920s, things began to change. The gangsters got in the game. Suddenly the unions no longer had the interests of the workers in mind. They were taken over by mobsters, racketeers. Not only did they force companies to join up through intimidation and force—cracking heads and kneecaps, setting places of business afire or destroying a garment maker's inventory—they formed what they now called buying directives, bullying their way into the trim and raw material markets, forcing a company to buy exclusively from them and not on the open market.

It was no longer about labor reform—it was just about money. Tons of money. And bloodshed. And extortion. And the politicians had their hands out too.

For a year or two, Abe found a way to push back against what was happening. His union still operated freely, and the only way for a manufacturer to protect themselves was to join a competing union. His. He got threats himself, but went on. But soon the syndicate grew too powerful to fight back against. One by one, they started chipping away at any companies who didn't buy in. The Amalgamated Needle Trade Workers Union started losing membership.

"I can't buy fur unless I go directly through them," a client would complain. "My prices are soaring."

"Abe, you're a good man, I've known you a long time," another would say. "We were always able to do business in the past. But the business has changed. . . ."

"It's only changed if you give in to them," Abe would insist.

One day, he was beaten up in an elevator coming from one of his manufacturers and told if he knew what was good for him to keep his nose out of things.

The Amalgamated Needle Trade Workers Union began to lose its hold.

Then, on the morning of April 24, 1933, things collapsed entirely. The office doors burst open and ten thugs, faces covered, wielding heavy clubs and lead pipes, charged in. They smashed desks and filing cabinets and shattered frosted-glass partitions. Anyone who stood up against them was knocked viciously to the floor. Ezra J. Potash, the union's president, came out of his office. "What's going on?" he demanded. "How dare you barge in here like this?"

One of the attackers struck him on the back with a lead pipe and Potash slumped to the floor. One of the union's longtime employees charged one of the attackers and got clubbed in the head. Blood pooled on the floor. People shouted, "They can't do this. Call the police!"

"We *can* do this," the head of the masked attackers said. "And don't bother with the police. You can be sure, they won't be coming."

It was clear what he meant. The union had paid them off to stay out of it.

"Employees of the Amalgamated Needle Trade Workers Union," the head of the thugs addressed the office. "As of today, there's been a change. You now all work for the International Fur Dressers Protective."

"The Fur Dressers . . ." There was a gasp. Potash pulled himself off the floor. "You have no legal right to—"

"You want us to show you our legal right?" Another club to the back and Potash was on the floor again, blood coming from his scalp. "Any further questions about legalities?" The intruder addressed the crowd. "Anyone feels the need to report anything, you'll get a lot worse than a little bump on the head. You understand? From now on, the Fur Dressers Protective calls the shots here. Anyone objects . . ." he looked around the room, "there's the door."

No one moved.

Until Abe Langer got up on a stool and shouted, "Listen to me. You all submit, you'll be signing away everything you believe in. We'll make sure the press will hear about this. These people are just hoodlums. What they're saying is extortion. They won't get away with it."

Two goons pulled him down and threw him onto the floor. They began to kick and stomp on him. One goon pulled him up and another rammed the blunt end of a lead pipe into his head, a crimson gash opening above Abe's temple.

"I have friends," Langer kept saying. "People will hear about this. You may have the guns and the fists, but I've been around this street longer than you've been alive."

"Friends, huh? In that case, Leon, maybe you oughta show Mr. Langer here to the complaints department." The leader nodded to one of his crew.

"Sure. Follow me, Mr. Langer," the accomplice said. He and one of the others peeled Abe off the floor and dragged him over to the window. The entire office murmured in fear. One of the goons threw open the window. Abe squirmed, trying to wrestle out of their grasp.

The offices were eight stories up over Midtown Manhattan.

"Complaints are on the first floor," one of the two holding him said. "I'm pretty sure this is the quickest way down."

"Please, please," Abe begged. "I have children."

To the shock of everyone watching, they hurled him out. Abe's hands cycled vainly to latch onto a landing that wasn't there. His desperate cry echoed all the way down.

Everyone just stood in silence, a pall of shock and disbelief. No one could believe what they'd just seen.

Abe Langer was one of the most revered people in the labor movement.

"Anyone else have any complaints?" The leader of the intruders looked around.

A few of the women were whimpering.

"Any one of you cares to say something to the wrong people or make a case about anything here, think twice," the leader said, "'cause now you know what's in store for you."

No one moved.

"In that case, welcome to the International Fur Dressers Protective, ladies and gentleman. First order of business is to let your clients know their union has now changed."

Chapter Sixteen

Two years went by. The Crash made things hard for the garment trade.

Still, Raab Brothers grew.

Morris and Sol now made coats for the largest stores across the country. Department stores like Macy's and Bamberger's in New York and New Jersey, Marshall Field's in Chicago, J. L. Hudson's in Detroit, Dayton's in Minnesota, and the Emporium in San Francisco, battling the shift in the nation's fortune, all now came in and worked out buying plans with them. Along with hundreds of smaller shops through the resident buying offices, who, just a few years before, wouldn't even take their call. Their price point gave them the right niche for the country's changing fortune.

After a year, Morris and Sol moved their offices from the cramped, two-room production space on Chrystie Street to larger quarters in a brand-new loft building on West Thirty-sixth Street, in a part of town where many of the clothing companies were setting up. They also purchased an old uniform plant up in Kingston, New York, out of receivership, which came with one hundred workers, where they were able to keep their operations out of sight from the local unions. Morris had developed a tough-guy reputation as one who was uncompromising with their customers. You wanted their line, you had to buy it their way, as it was presented—no concessions, no returns. Unless it was a matter of quality—which, in their case, was rare. Everyone in the industry joked, one guy you didn't want to get into a beef with over how he ran his business was Morris Raab. But he and Sol delivered their product, always as promised, and it generally sold through. And though they were equal partners, the reins of power had shifted; Sol now worked for him. Morris was just thirty-two, but he had fast become a known and respected figure in the trade.

After he and Ruthie married, they moved uptown into a three-bedroom place on West End Avenue with a view of the river. They had a son and named him Samuel, which pleased his mother greatly. Morris couldn't believe that such a perfect little creature had sprung from him, such a rough-and-tumble guy. He and Ruth hired a nanny and she continued her job at a publishing company that printed educational textbooks. He supported his mother, who chose to remain downtown in her familiar neighborhood.

They held lunches at their apartment on Sunday afternoons, where the entire family gathered. Even Harry would drop in, though he continued his infatuation with his old friends and still declined Sol and Morris's invitations to join the firm and begin a real career. He now lived in a small walk-up apartment on Lex and Twenty-third. Morris had a Packard; a boat he and Ruthie kept at a marina in Oyster Bay; more money than he could spend, though most of it he and Sol plowed back into Raab Brothers as it grew. When he held up his infant son, Morris thought back to the hardscrabble kid who had never backed down from fights on the Lower East Side; who had been picked on and beaten in the army; who had dutifully studied the marker maker at Majestic Garment Company and picked up a trade; and who was ashamed to even open his mouth in front of customers or show his obvious lack of education. He couldn't believe the path his life had taken, all the good things that had come to him—most, he felt certain, because he had never just taken no for an answer and settled for what he knew in his heart was wrong: a vibrant woman like Ruthie, who would have been unattainable to a clumsy lug from the Lower East Side who had never read a book; a son, who would now not need a benefactor like Pip had to make his own way in life; a successful business and a comfortable home.

Yet, even in all his good fortune, Morris saw the business had begun to change.

The ILGWU, Amalgamated Needle Trade Workers, and the Fur Dressers Union, were all now squarely in Louis Buchalter's palm. Word was that it was *he* who had gunned down Jacob Orgen on Norfolk Street—he and his crony Jacob "Gurrah" Shapiro. Morris's industry friends who were unionized all complained that the union was squeezing them dry: their workers' dues went up and they had to make good for it, or risk losing them to a more agreeable union shop. And they also had to make onerous payments—protection payments, everyone knew: protection from the union itself, which would make life hell for anyone who balked at them or refused to play along. The union's strong-arm tactics would shut down a company at the slightest resistance, smashing expensive equipment, destroying valuable inventory, even causing physical harm to the owners, who were petrified to stand up to them. These were garment makers, not union crusaders. Who knew where the money they doled out to the unions went? Certainly not to the workers they claimed to represent. More likely, directly into the pockets of the mob. The very people who perpetuated this policy of intimidation. And anyone who stood up to them got hit, and hit hard. Not with picketing or work stoppages, or threats. But with blackjacks and lead pipes; with fire bombings and stink bombs that could render a warehouse full of merchandise not even worth the hangers the clothing was draped on.

What had happened to Abe Langer was talked about in every hushed conversation on the street. The unions were now all wrapped into one large directive, run by Louis Buchalter—who was known as Lepke now, a name that had become synonymous with murder and brutality—and his partner, Gurrah. And it made no difference to them who they crushed, extorted money from, or forced out of business, as they paid off the police or the district attorney's office to look the other way. So far Morris had remained free of their attention. Maybe it was because their main factory was located three hours north in Ulster County, well out of view. Or maybe because Harry was still drinking pals with Mendy Weiss, now one of Buchalter's chief lieutenants.

Or maybe it was simply that Lepke had always held a form of "tough-guy" admiration for Morris, who had stood up to him, even as a kid. But one by one, even the most stubborn holdouts caved in and agreed to let the unions in. It was either that or face the kind of retaliation that no one had the stomach or ability to stand up to and see their warehouses go up in smoke. Whatever the reason, Lepke let Morris alone and never came after him. If he did, he knew he'd be in for a fight.

At least until 1934. When, for Morris, the fight hit closer to home.

When he ran up to Manny Gutman's factory and saw the devastation and viciousness Buchalter and Shapiro had unleashed.

And when staying on the sidelines was no longer possible.

Chapter Seventeen

His heart quickening, Morris stepped inside Rosie's Cigar Shop in Brooklyn, where Buchalter and Shapiro's headquarters was located in the back room. The goon in the check suit who had checked him out outside followed him in, a hand inside his jacket where clearly his gun was located, staying a few feet behind.

There was a tobacco counter, and a clerk behind it; Rosie, no doubt. A couple of legitimate customers buying cigarettes and cigars. Behind the counter, there were boxes and trays of White Owls, Phillies, and Josefinas, and a more expensive array of Cubans in their wooden boxes under lock and key.

There were also two round tables with a couple of men sitting around them in pressed, light-colored suits and fancy shoes. One of them Morris was already acquainted with.

"Mendy." Morris nodded. "Seems you've moved up in the world."

Mendy Weiss sat leaning with his leg crossed, sporting a pair of shiny black-and-white wingtips. Morris had heard he was working for Buchalter now. "Just making a living, Morris," he said, pushing back his Panama hat. "How about you? This your usual cigar joint? You're certainly a long way from Cherry Street yourself."

"I'm here to see Mr. Buchalter." Morris said.

"Mr. Buchalter . . . I'm afraid Mr. Buchalter's not around," Mendy said with a disappointed grunt. "That's too bad, I'm sure he'd be sad to miss your visit. What's your business, if I can ask?"

"My business is with him," Morris said bluntly, "if that's okay with you."

"Sure. It's okay with me." Mendy shrugged. "Just asking."

The heavyset guy sitting next to Mendy with the handkerchief in his breast pocket looked up with the dimmest glint of amusement. "And who the fuck are yous anyway—if it's okay with you, of course?"

"Relax, just an old friend, Arnie." Mendy calmed him. "We all kind of grew up on the same street. So how's Harry, Morris? I don't see him around like I used to. We got him a job at The Green Parrot. Down on Eighth. It seems to take up all of his time these days."

"You'll have to ask him. You probably see him more than me," Morris said.

"I don't know, I don't get around that way so much no more."

Morris looked him up and down, at the loud tie and conspicuous shoes, the uniform shouting the nature of his trade. "Woulda fooled me."

Mendy gave him back a dry, nasal laugh and got up and stretched, like he'd been in the seat all day. He nodded to the goon who had followed Morris in that everything was okay. "Lemme check if Mr. Buchalter has come back in without me knowing. Just to be sure . . ." He went through a door at the rear of the shop.

The heavyset goon with the handkerchief in his pocket said, "Help yourself to a White Owl while you're waiting, buddy. On the house."

"Thanks," Morris said. "But I buy my own."

"Suit yourself, pal." He smiled.

Mendy came back out and held open the back room door. "Your lucky day, Morris. I just managed to catch him as he was on his way out. Come on in."

"Here, Arnie," Morris said to the heavyset gangster, taking a Montecristo out of his breast pocket and leaving it on the table. "Try one of mine."

Before he went through the door, Mendy stopped him and patted him down. "Sorry, Morris, just a formality. You understand."

"I don't even own a gun, Mendy."

"You can never be too sure." He held open the door. "That's what Happy Freidman said to Legs Diamond, and he ended up with seven holes in him. Okay," he said, satisfied. "Go on in."

The back room was smoky and dark, lit only by table lamps that cast shadows everywhere. He saw the big guy, Gurrah, with his large nose that looked like it had been broken at least a dozen times and his sunken eyes, slouching at a table with a deck of cards in front of him, dealing solitaire. He gazed up at Morris as if trying to decide if he was an old friend or an old enemy.

Leaning against a wall was a medium-built man with thick black hair and bushy brows. Morris knew him as Charles Workman. A known stick man. Talk was, he was one of the three who gunned down Little Augie, the others being Gurrah and Buchalter. He was wearing a shoulder holster and no sport jacket.

"Of course, I'm in for Morris Raab!" Louis Buchalter stood up and put out a hand. "Why didn't you let me know you were coming? I'm sorry you had to go through the tenth degree." He was dressed in a dark check suit with a straw hat on the table in front of him, his bow tie precisely tied and a half-smoked cigar in an ashtray. He still had that chummy, affable smile, his cheek puffed out like a wad of tobacco was stuffed inside, though the edges around his face seemed to have hardened in line with the kinds of more serious business he was engaged in now.

Morris hadn't seen him since the night he met Ruthie at the Theatrical Club, six years ago. "Mr. Buchalter." They shook hands. The gangster motioned for Morris to take a seat.

"I'll stand if that's okay."

"Always the renegade, huh, Morris? My sources tell me life's been good to you. That you're a big man now. In your field."

"I'm getting by," Morris said. "Not quite like you though."

"*Me . . . ?*" Buchalter looked around and shrugged. "Forget all the fancy headlines, we scratch out a living any way we can. Jacob . . ." Buchalter leaned back and turned to the hulking Gurrah, who was flipping a card, "you remember our old friend Morris Raab, don't you?"

"I remember I almost turned him upside down and shook the small change out of him," the hulking gangster said. "But that was a long time back." He grinned, showing his gray, uneven teeth. "You look like you're doing well. You got any change on you now, Mr. Raab?"

"Not enough to make it worthwhile," Morris said.

"Anyway, he's gotten too big, even for *you,* Jacob. I think today you'd have to use all your natural charm on him. So what brings you all the way out to our neck of the world?" Buchalter sat up and straightened his tie. "It can't be you've run out of Macanudos."

"I'm here about Manny Gutman," Morris said.

"Gutman . . . ?" Buchalter wiped his mouth, leaned back, and looked to someone at another table. "Am I supposed to know that name?"

"The Isidor Gutman Fur Company," Morris said. "A bunch of your goons here tore his place apart earlier today and doused his face with acid."

"*Acid?* That's surely no fun, I can assure you of that. And what, if I might ask, is your particular interest in this man?"

"My particular interest is that he's a friend."

"A friend, huh . . . ? Well, it wasn't my boys." Buchalter shook his head. "I can assure you of that. Maybe union boys. They can get pretty nasty when they feel they have a point to make. But my boys . . . we're all strictly business now. Right, fellas . . . ? Why don't we send him a nice bouquet of flowers?" He snapped his fingers at the man he'd consulted earlier. "And a bottle of rye. A friend of Morris Raab is a friend of mine. Courtesy of the International Fur Dressers Protective."

"Guess it was the same with Abe Langer too?" Morris stared at Buchalter directly. "Maybe you should send *him* a bouquet."

"Abe Langer? Now I do recall hearing there was someone named Langer who took a tumble from a window somewhere." The lightness drained from Buchalter's face. "He was looking for the complaints department, I was told, and seemed to get on the wrong elevator. Accidents can happen anywhere. You wouldn't want to say it was any more, would you, Morris? Surely not here. Some of my boys might take that the wrong way."

"I know it was your men who did it, Buchalter." Morris glared at him. And then around the room.

Buchalter nodded patiently and then tapped on his cigar. "From what I heard, this Langer was making a lot of threats he couldn't back up, and didn't know how to keep his trap shut. And given what's going on in your particular industry, he seems to have made the wrong bet. At least that's what I've heard." The gangster looked back up at him. "Know what I'm saying?"

"I think you more than heard." Morris looked back at him. "I'm pretty sure it was your men who did it. No one at the International Fur Dressers union would pick their nose without talking to you first."

"I think you overstate my influence, Morris." A plume of cigar smoke wafted between Morris and Buchalter. "You know you've pushed me more than once, and I hope you know, if I didn't like you,

I might take what you're saying in an inamicable way. Which could be bad for you, as people who have made that list tend not to show up for work the next day. Or the day after that."

"I wouldn't be quite that dumb, would I?"

"I don't know, would you, Morris? That remains to be fully seen. But you are pushing your luck about one thing. The union, which some of my men do fieldwork for, is a completely independently run enterprise. It exists only to improve and better represent the cause of the workers to make sure they are fairly compensated for their contribution by their stakeholders. Stakeholders like yourself, Morris. And in proper working conditions. Still, when it comes to day-to-day operations, I have nothing to do with it. Now, do you have another reason for being here, other than to darken my mood, which was high in the sky until you happened in here?"

"I'm here to ask you to call it quits." Morris kept his gaze locked on him. "You've got what you wanted. Control. Money coming in. Money off our backs. Things get any worse, you'll end up in a war. And that's good for no one."

"A war." Buchalter chuckled. "A war with whom, Morris?" He had that chummy grin again, but behind it lurked an icy, determined ire. His eyes fixed on Morris without blinking. "With most people we have pretty good relations. With *you* maybe?"

"Not me, Mr. Buchalter. I don't want no war."

"That's good to hear. Because a war with you, Morris . . ." Buchalter tapped his cigar and sniffed. "That would be a pretty short war. The union is only there to promote goodwill and better conditions for the people who have no means or voice to speak up, say against people like you, Morris. We don't share the fruits of their labor with them. But we don't want a war, as you say, do we, boys?"

Shapiro flipped over a card and shook his head. "Not me. I don't want no war."

"What about you, Murray?" Buchalter asked a heavyset guy with a pockmarked face in the back.

"War? Nope. Not me," he said.

"Or you, Charlie?"

"Me neither, boss. No conflict at all." Charles Workman shrugged and shook his head. "That only puts a strain right here." He tapped his chest. "Right in the ticker."

"See, no one here is looking for any war. Only to make sure everything with our workers runs smoothly. There are a lot of people out there who would characterize that wrongly. But while we're on that subject, Morris," Buchalter looked up and wagged his index finger in the air, "remind me, quick, are you a union shop these days?"

"I'm not," Morris said, "and I'd sooner shut my doors before I would be."

"You'd sooner shut your doors, eh . . . ? Hear that, boys, we're talking to a man of genuine principle here. Someone who takes care of his people paternalistically. We've all heard that before."

Gurrah Shapiro nodded. "Very hard to find these days, indeed."

"You know, you're lucky I somehow like you, Morris. Otherwise . . ." Buchalter flicked an ash into the ashtray and shook his head with amusement. "You'd fucking shut your doors . . . Y'know you and your brother have a way of making me laugh. Speaking of which, how is that boy these days? Haven't seen him around much." He snapped his fingers. "I forget his name?"

"Harry," Gurrah reminded him.

"Yeah, Harry," Buchalter said. "Lot of laughs, Harry. Just like you, he knows how to weave a good story."

"We got him working over at The Green Parrot, Mr. Buchalter," Mendy Weiss, who was still at the door, said.

"The Green Parrot." Buchalter nodded. "Yeah, now I remember, that's where I've seen him. Say, isn't that where Izzy Cohen got shot?"

"And Hy Danzer, I recall as well," Mendy said. "No telling."

"Rough spot, The Green Parrot. Hard to guarantee anyone goes in comes out alive. Tussles break out most every night."

"I'm thinking that sounds like *you're* the one making a threat now," Morris said.

"I don't make threats, Morris." Buchalter tapped his finger on the table and looked up. "You, of all people, should know that. I'm just thinking we ought to find a safer place for your brother. Purely for his own interests, of course. Put that down, Ike. . . ." He leaned back and gestured to the man with the pad. "Now, anything else? If not, me and the boys, we ought to get back to making a living. Ask Rosie about some Cohibas on the way out. I'll see we work out a good price."

"Thanks. But I buy my own, if it's all the same."

"And why not? You're a big shot now. Still, since you came all the way out, we'd just like to show some appreciation."

As Morris passed one of the tables on his way out, he stopped and stared at the heavyset man he'd heard called Leon. "You know, people up at the Amalgamated Needle Workers Union, the day Abe Langer died, said one of the guys who grabbed him was named Leon. . . ."

The heavyset man stared back at him and shrugged. "I wouldn't know about that. Leon's a common name."

"Not that common." Morris headed out.

"I gonna make a rule for you, Morris Raab," Buchalter called after him, "and if I were you, I'd pay attention. Know where the line is, you understand? 'Cause some lines you just can't cross. 'Cause if you do, nothing in the world can save you, Morris. Or your brother. You want to close your doors so badly, I can make that happen, you hear me? 'Cause sooner or later, Morris, everyone's luck runs out."

Mendy took Morris outside, and as the door closed behind them, Mendy said, "I wouldn't be standing up to Mr. Buchalter that way, if I were you, Morris."

"That so? You know, Mendy, I've been standing up to him since I was twelve years old."

"You have, huh?" Mendy chuckled, but not with any levity in it. "Well, I don't have to tell you, do I, Morris . . . you ain't twelve anymore. You *feshtayn*?"

Back in his office, Louis Buchalter called Gurrah over to his table. "You know, Jacob, I'm thinking I've been a nice guy to that man for a long time now."

"Too nice, if you ask me," Shapiro replied. "He'll only go around making problems for us. You'll see."

"We all go back a ways, that's all. So maybe I have cut the guy some slack. And Mendy's always had a hard-on for the guy's brother. But I'm starting to think my goodwill has reached its limit. He's got workers . . . ?"

"Plenty. Plus a shop up in Kingston, I'm told. A hundred more up there."

"A hundred, huh . . . ?" Louis Buchalter pursed his lips. He let out a breath. "So maybe it is time we find out just how tough Mr. Raab really is."

"Just say the word."

Buchalter got up and straightened his jacket around his shoulders. He gave his partner a shrug, as if to say, *All right, go ahead now. It's your call.*

"You want we do it hard or by the book?" Gurrah pulled his large frame up from the chair.

"By the book" was how a union normally organized a company. Start pressing the flesh, promise the world—better wages, more time off, more bathroom breaks. Picket the factory until the owners gave in.

"Hard" was how they'd done it to Manny Gutman.

"You choose, Jacob." Louis Buchalter put on his Panama. "Just get it done. And don't be a pig about it. There's dues to be had here."

Chapter Eighteen

That same day, in a different part of town, Special Prosecutor Thomas E. Dewey stood at the window of his tenth-floor office in Lower Manhattan and looked across the city. It was big, raw, booming—buildings shooting up everywhere in spite of the Depression. But it was also a city in the grip of a menacing contagion.

There was the newly formed crime syndicate: Luciano, with his gambling and prostitution rings. Dutch Schultz, who, with the end of Prohibition, traded in bootlegging for his new racket—the numbers, not only preying on the innocent, who bought their tickets with the hope of an early Christmas, but manipulating the payoffs, pocketing hundreds of thousands a week. Lepke and Anastasia, with their control of the garment and longshoreman unions. And a wave of dead bodies from their vicious new syndicate, known as Murder, Incorporated. The governor had pushed him. Do whatever you have to do. Just clean it up. Take whatever resources you need to do the job. Dewey said to him, only if I have full control. "You have it," Governor Lehman replied. "Just do whatever you have to do."

And early on, Dewey had had some successes. Turning informants on their bosses, tapping phone lines. He'd handed Dutch Schultz to the Feds twice on trials for tax evasion. And they had him dead to rights until the bootlegger's attorneys convinced a judge to move the trial out of Manhattan. Dewey had even gotten a crony of theirs, Leon Weinberg, to turn on Murder, Inc., until the witness ended up in a free fall from the tenth-floor hotel room guarded by three of New York City's finest.

The bastards' money and influence spread everywhere.

But now he had a team of sixty. Handpicked men. Lawyers, cops, tax accountants. People he knew he could trust. Who shared a mission. If these murderers were allowed to show they were stronger than the law, it would be the end of society as we knew it. It was like an ineluctable clash of forces, Dewey called it—two unmovable powers coming together. And there would be but one winner. One winner. And for once it would be the law. He'd had Schultz lined up for conviction twice, and twice he'd wiggled out. Dewey wouldn't miss the chance again.

He went back to his desk and opened the file he'd been paging through a moment before. He stared at photos of the unrepentant killers he would soon see in jail. Schultz was Number One. The bootlegger had left a trail of a hundred bodies to get where he was. Then Lepke. He and his murderous crime partners killed with guns, garottes, ice picks, clubs, even tossing victims out of windows. Then Dewey would move on and throw the full force of the law against Luciano himself. The head of the crime commission. One by one they all would be brought down.

The gangster wouldn't be known as Lucky anymore.

There was a knock on Dewey's office door. "Come on in," he said, closing the file.

One of the young lawyers who had fought to be assigned to his staff, Irving Weschler, stepped in. The kid was raw, chubby, a bit rumpled; he always wore a suit that didn't quite fit. Not a Harvard or Yale guy like so many of his outfit, but rock solid when it came to the statutes. And he was as eager as they come. The young lawyer stepped up to Dewey's desk. Dewey could see the kid was nervous. Who wouldn't be? He'd never even addressed the young man directly before.

"You asked to see me, Mr. Dewey?"

"Sit down, Counselor. Don't be nervous. You may be just the man for one of my assignments."

"I'd be honored, sir." Weschler's eyes came alive.

"You're a local lad, I'm told."

"That's right. From the Lower East Side. Born and bred."

"Pulled yourself up from nothing through your own hard work. Brooklyn Law. Graduated top of your class, I'm told."

"Third." Irv shrugged with a modest smile. "But the only one not currently teaching, I'm told."

"Well, academia's loss is our gain, then. So you know what we're going after on this task force? Organized crime, of course. Both in their traditional venues—gambling, prostitution, murder . . ."

"That's why I asked to be a part of it, sir. It's an honor to be on the team."

"Excellent. But then there's the entirely new activities the mob seems to be involved in today. Extortion, intimidation, labor fraud. Anastasia's got the dockworkers in his back pocket; Schultz, the restaurant trade. And this Buchalter figure—Lepke, as he's now known—he's got the garment unions. We're talking extortion, price fixing. Restraint of trade."

"Yes, sir." Irv waited for him to continue.

"And as you may know, Counselor," the special prosecutor put his palms on the desk, "a racket cannot exist for long without being fueled by three things. It's oxygen to them. The first, of course, is political protection. Someone in power has to be watching out for them. Protecting them. And you can be sure these particular groups have it in spades—people on their payroll in all levels of the government and police.

"Two, they need witnesses who are terrified to speak out. Who are subject to brutal acts of retaliation, to get them to either back down or recant their testimony."

"Yes, sir."

"And three, Mr. Weschler," Dewey said, leaning forward. He knotted his dark brows. "Lackluster and indifferent law enforcement. Even worse, where the motives of such law enforcement, let's just say, may not be the same as yours and mine. You understand what I'm saying, don't you, son?"

"I believe so, sir." Irv nodded, waiting to hear where this was leading.

"So how do we bring down these men? You may well have your own ideas. One, we catch them in the act. In their criminal enterprises. Which is often difficult because of reasons two and three, just mentioned. Either the will to prosecute is not strong, or the witnesses against them recant, through pressure, or, worse, are never heard from again. We can also try to turn their associates further down the lines of authority against them, by lessening their sentences if we have them dead to rights, or through relocation, if necessary. But those situations only present themselves every once in a while, and it's been more than once, of course, that such an accuser doesn't quite make it to trial. Alive, that is."

"Yes, sir."

"Or, there's another way." Dewey opened his file. "We can go after the very source of their enterprise. Hit 'em right where it hurts." He dropped his fist on the table. "In the pocketbook. I'm told you know your antitrust statutes."

Irv nodded. "That was my expertise at the district attorney's office."

"So then you know that to invoke federal antitrust laws, which is where I'm hoping you'll see I'm heading, the racketeering activity must be of such a character as to restrain interstate commerce through the following: the creation of monopolies, through an acquisition or the merging of competing enterprises; the maintenance of monopoly status through the implementation of price fixing, the establishment of retail prices through agreements with jobbers and dealers. And lastly . . ."

"Lastly, the furtherance of the above by agreements between buying and trade associations, including labor unions." Irv finished where the special prosecutor had left off.

Dewey smiled, his mustache widening. "I can see you're a young man who wants to make a difference. Yes, the unions. And that's exactly where we're going to hit them, Counselor. That's where these bastards are the most vulnerable. You're familiar with what's going on with the dockworkers, Teamsters, and the various unions in the garment trade, the Amalgamated Needle Trade Workers Union, the Fur Dressers Protective, and the International Ladies' Garment Workers' Union?"

"Loosely familiar. I know there's been infiltration on the part of certain criminal groups and some physical intimidation along with it."

"Intimidation . . ." Dewey smiled. "If you mean people who resist being hurled out of eighth-story windows and taking over competing unions through brute force, yes, there's been intimidation, Mr. Weschler. There's been that in spades.

"But what you may not know is that these garment associations are then forcing their members to buy raw materials and trims only through union-sponsored suppliers. At prices *they* artificially set. If they don't, they suffer severe consequences: firebombings, stench bombs. Even cracked knees and split heads. Besides assault, battery, malicious vandalism, and extortion, in terms of antitrust laws, it's also clearly price fixing, Mr. Weschler. Restraint of trade."

"But the problem as I see it, sir," the young lawyer spoke up, "is that, to my knowledge, violations of these statutes are ordinarily only punishable by a fine not to exceed five thousand dollars and a year in prison, if convicted. That won't put them out of business."

"That is true. A mere slap on the wrist. But multiple violations, Counselor . . ." The special prosecutor wagged his index finger. "Let's say a dozen, all wrapped into the same prosecution. We can hit them hard and we can hit them right where it hurts—in the bank account. And that's why I've asked you here."

"If you want me to bring myself up to date with the statutes behind these cases I can get started right away," Irv said, eager to prove himself.

"I don't need you to bring yourself up to date, Mr. Wechsler. At least, not yet." Dewey came around the table, opened the file that he'd had in front of him, and dropped two photos on the desk.

"You know these people, Counselor?"

"I know who they are, of course, sir." One was Louis Buchalter. The other—flabby cheeks, dull, mirthless eyes—was his henchman, Jacob "Gurrah" Shapiro.

"I'm going to bring these two sonovabitches down, Counselor. You understand? So what I want from *you*, sir, is not your expertise, but to take advantage of that local knowledge I spoke of earlier, and any associations, shall we say, that you may have." Dewey punctuated his point with an unflinching stare. "The associations of your kind."

"My *kind*, sir . . . ?" Irv looked at him quizzically.

"Find me someone in this garment business who will talk to us. Someone who has faced intimidation by these men, first hand. I want a witness, Counselor. Someone who's either fool enough, or gutworthy enough, to go up against the bastards. And preferably the latter."

Dewey laid the photographs of Lepke and Shapiro out side by side. "Can you find me that person, son?"

Irv looked into the gangsters' somber, empty stares. "I think I can, sir."

Chapter Nineteen

"I'm finished, Morris," Manny Gutman said from his hospital bed. His neck and face were wrapped with gauze, only a slit opening for his eyes. His wife, Helen, sat by his side. "The doctors say I ought to recover. I guess I just won't be putting my face in the sun so much anymore . . . ," he said, coughing a laugh. "No need." Then his eyes welled up with what Morris saw as heartbreak and he looked away. "I'm old enough to understand the writing on the wall when I see it. Look what happened to Abe Langer. In a way, they were kind to me."

"I wish I had been there," Morris said, seething inside.

"And you would have done what?" Manny said. "They had guns and clubs. Got yourself killed is all. Like you almost did with that silly stunt of yours, going out there."

Morris heard the anguish in his friend's voice. "You can rebuild, Manny. You've got more friends in this business than anyone."

"Rebuild?" He laughed and let out a hacking cough, his lungs still raw. "With what? You saw the state of things. Our insurance won't exactly cover half of what we lost. And anyway, what for?

There's no future in it for me anymore. I tried working with these goons. If I buy from them, sooner or later my business dries up and falls apart anyway. And if I don't buy . . . ," he snorted and put a hand to his bandaged face, "then there's more of this.

"Anyway, I'm a garment maker, Morris. I can't stand up to them. Helen and the kids, all they want is for me to do the smart thing and be safe." He turned and put his hand over hers. "Right, darling . . . ? We've had a good run, right? I have some money stashed away. I've always wondered what life would be down South. Everyone's going to Miami. You're a father now. You understand. So don't jeopardize what you have, trying to play the hero."

"I understand by giving in to them, it only makes them stronger," Morris said. "In a way, Abe Langer was right about what he said."

"Abe Langer is dead," Manny said emphatically. "And you'll be too, if you don't smarten up. Even if he was right, now, what does it matter? These are not regular *yiddishers* we're dealing with here. They're cutthroats. They'd just as soon shoot you as shake your hand. Anyway, it's not my fight anymore. It's for people like you to figure out what to do. Though, I advise you, you better watch your step and don't be a hero, Morris. I know you."

"You do, huh?"

"Better than you know yourself. But you want to know my biggest regret? Besides having to close my doors. It's my workers. Many of them have been working for us their whole careers. They trust me like a member of the family. You think these bastards give two shits about where all this leaves them? They claim to be a union—a union of greed and filth, maybe. If I could spit, I would spit on the floor."

"Don't worry, I'll take some on," Morris said. "The rest, I'll ask around. See what I can do."

"Thank you." Manny reached out and patted Morris on the arm.

"No one ever said you weren't a stand-up guy, Morris. My old friend Menushem Kaufman would be proud of you, God rest his soul."

"Though he never once gave me a good word." Morris smiled. "Even at the end, he would call, all the way from Arizona, and insist I was leaving money on the cutting table, and how long can a style possibly be in pleating if you know this job so well? Anyway, I'm not going to let 'em just walk away and get away with it, Manny, whatever you say."

"And you're going to do what, Morris?" Manny tapped his forehead. "This isn't a time for heroes, it's a time to be smart. You've got a good thing now. You know yourself, you can only avoid this for so long. Sooner or later they'll be onto you too, and then . . ." Manny shrugged. "And then you'll have to make up your own mind what to do."

Morris got up. He gave Manny a pat on the shoulder. "Get well fast, old man. I'll look into your staff for you. I'll be back to see you soon."

"Be careful," Manny Gutman called after him. "Helen and I, we don't want to be going to your funeral." He laughed darkly. "At least not before you find the rest of my staff new jobs."

Chapter Twenty

Irv Weschler sat across from Morris in a booth at Lindy's, between Forty-ninth and Fiftieth and Broadway. They sat in the back, the bright lights of Broadway flashing in from outside. Irv had called and reached out to him. He'd moved away from the Lower East Side and out to Brooklyn a couple of years ago. "So how *are* things in the old neighborhood?"

"I don't know." Morris shrugged. He picked at a slice of apple pie and Irv had a plate of their famous cheesecake, and coffee. "Other than to see a manufacturer now and then, or a fabric guy, I really don't get down there much anymore, any more than you."

"Well, we're all proud of you, Morris. My mother says you're doing better than anyone we know."

"Yeah, and how would she know . . . ?"

"From your mother, of course. How else? She said you're the man of the family now."

"I'm just working hard. Doing what I know how to do. But anyway, you're the real big shot, Irv. Fancy law degree. Working for the DA's office. Even your suit fits you now."

Irv laughed. "And you got yourself a great wife. Remember, I was there the night you met. And now a kid too."

"And another on the way." Morris took a sip of coffee. "But you really didn't ask me here to butter me up, did you? If so, here's a roll." Morris pushed across a basket of bread.

Irv put down his fork with an expression of chagrin, as if Morris had seen right through him. "No. I didn't. I have some news too. I'm actually no longer with the DA's office. I'm with Thomas Dewey now. You know him? He's been appointed head of a task force by Governor Lehman. To battle organized crime."

"I read the papers." Morris nodded. Everyone knew Dewey's name. A hard man, but someone who couldn't be bought. Or stopped. Driven. "Congratulations. It sounds important."

"It *is* important," Irv said. He leaned forward and hushed his voice lower. "We're going after some really big fish, Morris. Meyer Lansky. Dutch Schultz. Luciano. All the big boys."

"You'll put more Jews in the clink than I hear this guy Hitler's doing back in Germany." Morris snickered.

Irv smiled, then he looked at Morris and threw out one more name. A name Morris knew well. "Lepke."

"Buchalter . . . ?" Morris's eyes went wide.

"I know you've had your run-ins with him. And I know you know what he's up to these days. I mean, you're in the trade. You'd have to know."

"I know." Morris nodded. He rolled his spoon around in his coffee. "Good luck."

"His syndicate has taken over all the garment unions. He, his sidekick, Jacob Shapiro, and a bunch of violent thugs. So tell me, are you union, Morris?"

Morris looked at his friend and shrugged. "Not yet, anyway. I might as well get out if we do."

"Well, I'm sure you know enough people who are. And who have experienced their shakedowns. We know he's done some violent things, Morris. It's just that . . . It would be good if maybe you knew someone, or even yourself, who might want to help us."

"Help you do what, Irv?"

"Help us put him away. For good."

"Buchalter?" Morris smiled and took a sip of coffee. "Good luck. You wouldn't be the first to try. I hope you got your life insurance up to date." He took a bite of his pie. "Look, anyone I know, ain't so happy with what's going on. But they ain't exactly stupid either. So this is why you asked me here? To get some names? To collect some information. Sure, I'm aware what's going on. You'd have to either be dead or have your head in the sand not to be. Abe Langer was a friend of mine. And Manny Gutman and Monty Rosen, and David Rubin too."

"The reason I asked you here," Irv said, leaning forward and putting down his fork, "was it would be helpful if we could get to talk with someone who might have something to say. Who's faced this kind of intimidation."

"Is that what you lawyers call it, intimidation? Manny Gutman had his whole business destroyed and his face doused with acid. Abe Langer was thrown out of an eighth-story window in front of his whole office. So far, no one's even lifted a finger in any investigation. Not the cops. Not the DA. How's that for intimidation? So, sure, I know people. What is it you want to know? How the cops are all paid off and don't lift a finger against him? How the DA's office has Lepke's own men inside it? How he throws more money around than the Chase National Bank to get tipped off or have cases put in the drawer? It wouldn't surprise me if your own task force, despite the fancy name, is paid off just the same. Buchalter's no dummy. He just sits back and pushes the buttons and collects the checks. Anyone who talks to you, trust me, they know their name will get out and they'll be an empty seat at the Passover table if they open their trap."

"It's not that way here, Morris." Irv looked at him seriously. "You're right, what you say. But now there's new ways to go after them. New laws. Things called antitrust laws. They let you go after people who want to interfere with competition. Who want to impose a monopoly status in their business. Who pressure people into buying a certain way. Through their own cartels. Even unions. We don't have to get them pulling a trigger anymore."

"I've heard Buchalter's got this team of killers that goes around knocking people off for money. Murder, Incorporated, everyone calls it. Why don't you nail him on that, if it's so different now?"

"Because there's no witnesses to those kinds of crimes," Irv said.

"There's plenty of witnesses, Irv. It's just that anyone who would dare speak up usually doesn't make it to the stand. So what makes it different with the garment unions?"

"Because this is the new way, Morris. The way to nail him. And not on a single charge, so he's back on the street in a year. On multiple charges. Dozens, even. He can't intimidate witnesses in them all. All we need is just some people I can talk to."

Morris put down his fork and took a sip of his coffee. "You know I know this joke, Irv. Maybe you heard it? 'Apple pie and coffee, please.' Someone's just off the boat, and those are the only words in English he knows. So every time he goes to eat he orders the very same thing. Apple pie and coffee. Till one day he's so sick of it he can't order it anymore, and he goes to his cousin, who he's staying with, to teach him something else. So the cousin says, 'Pastrami sandwich with mustard and a water.' The guy practices it over and over till he's got it down and then he goes to the restaurant. 'Pastrami sandwich with mustard and a glass of water.' The same waitress he always has comes up to him. 'Pastrami sandwich, please, with mustard, and water,' the guy says. The waitress looks back and goes, 'White or rye?' The guy doesn't have a clue what to say back, so he just shrugs and goes, 'Apple pie and coffee, please.' You know that joke, Irv."

"I think we all know that joke, Morris. Or those people."

"Yeah, I guess we do."

Morris let his thoughts shift to Manny Gutman. His friend was barely out of the hospital. No way he would put him in further danger, even if Manny could be twisted somehow to testify against Louis Lepke. Or any of Manny's friends, for that matter, which Morris knew, they would not. Most of them were just as terrified and had long capitulated with the union to stay in business and remain alive, buying syndicate or not. Morris himself was one of the last holdouts. He looked at Irv, whose eyes were fixed on him, waiting. "Truth is, I don't think I know anybody, Irv."

"No one?" Irv's eyes suggested disbelief.

Morris took another sip of coffee and shook his head. "No."

"What about you . . . ?"

"Me? I haven't had any issues, myself." Morris shrugged and then smiled. "With, how do you call it, intimidation? Nothing direct. Only what I've been told."

Irv nodded, and blew a disappointed blast of air from his nostrils. He placed his fork back on his empty plate. "I just want you to know, it'll be different this time around, Morris. You have my word. These people have broken federal laws. They've stood in the way of open competition. They've created monopolies. These are offenses we can pin them to. Put them away on. All we need is a few people not afraid to talk."

"Well, good luck finding them, Irv." Morris drained the last of his coffee. "If I run into one, I'll be sure and let you know."

They sat in silence for a while. Then Irv said, "So you're not union. How come they've given you a pass so far?"

"I don't know. . . . Buchalter seems to have this crazy respect for me, how I stood up to him a couple of times. You know how a bully always backs down when he's confronted face-to-face. Or maybe it's Harry. He still hangs around with the lot of them. Whatever it is, I think it's coming to an end. We're growing too large. We can't hide under the surface anymore. But I have a feeling that's all changing."

"So what are you going to do?"

Morris dug in his pocket for his wallet. "The truth . . . ? I really don't know." He glanced at his wristwatch. "Look, I hate to break up the party, but I told Ruthie I'd be home half an hour ago. She puts out a nice meal for me. And here I already had dessert."

"I understand." Irv reached into his pocket. "Say hello for me, would you?"

"Sure." Morris went for some money.

"On me." Irv waved him off. He threw a few bills on the table. "On the city, actually. Think of what I said. I promise, it's different this time. And don't be so sure that a bully always backs down. Sometimes when they're backed into a corner, they just come out, swinging harder. And then we've all seen what happens."

Morris said, "I'll keep that in mind. Listen, I've got a car outside." He'd instructed his driver to hold up around the corner. "Can I drop you somewhere?"

"I'm still in Brooklyn," Irv said. "The F train works just fine. But thanks."

They got up, put on their hats, and went outside through the revolving door. At the same time, coming into the restaurant was a large man with deep, sunken eyes in a homburg, followed closely by two other men.

On the street, Irv turned and watched them go inside.

"You know who that is?" Irv asked.

Morris stared back after the man. He shook his head.

"That's Dutch Schultz." Irv turned up his collar. "I guess crooks like cheesecake too."

Chapter Twenty-One

When it began, it began the way Morris had always expected.

A man came up to the office and asked to meet with him and Sol. He was dressed in a wrinkled suit, rumpled hat, and scuffed brown shoes. He had a short gray mustache, and the feel of someone who could relate to the people behind the machines. Morris had seen union front men before.

"Talk about what?" Morris asked, stepping out from the sample room where they put together their design prototypes.

The man looked around, craning his neck here and there, seemingly to get a sense for their operation. He said to Morris, "Your brother's your partner, isn't he?"

"What's he got to do with it?"

"Just that maybe it would be best if he came in and joined us as well."

Morris found Sol down in the receiving department and they went in the glass-enclosed room they used as a showroom and closed the door behind them, though Morris already knew what the scruffily dressed man was there to say.

"Certain parties want to know if you've given any thought to unionizing your operation?" the man said.

"Certain parties . . . ?"

"That's right. They feel like they've given you ample time to establish yourselves and now it's time to talk turkey." He reached into his breast pocket and slid his card across the table. Seymour Haddad. *Field Administrator. Amalgamated Needle Trade and the International Fur Dressers Protective.* "They've asked me to go over the details. Call me Cy."

Morris, pushing across an ashtray for his cigarette, nodded warily. "All right, Cy."

Union organizers were always sniffing around their offices. Most of the firms had caved in by these days, willingly or not, so he and Sol stood out as an opportunity for them, though it was no secret in the trade how opposed Sol and Morris were. As he talked, Cy Haddad kept glancing around, looking through the glass, clearly trying to size up their operation. From his vest, he took a small notepad and jotted something down. "You mind . . . ? My memory isn't what it once was. . . ." He smiled amiably.

"We *have* given thought to it," Morris took a look at Sol and answered. "And I'm afraid my brother and I, we're not interested."

"Not interested . . . ?" the union man said, with a hint of amusement.

"You can see, we're not a big outfit here. Whatever we do, we have to keep a finger on our costs. Otherwise there's no purpose for us to remain in business. You understand? Our only advantage is coming up with what the upper-class women want to wear, and making it at a price. For the rest of the women out there. We lose that, we might as well close the doors. And, unless you can guarantee my workers a better deal than they already get from us, we don't see the point of talking."

"The point of talking...Well, I guess there is no point." Cy Haddad shrugged, giving Morris a sage smile. "Other than, in the view of certain parties, whether you want to remain a going concern or not."

The threat hung in the air and Morris stared back at him. Then he glanced at Sol. He had to hold himself back from telling Cy Haddad to get the fuck out of his place.

Instead he said, "I guess we're prepared to take our chances. As it is, I think you'd find we take care of our workers just fine, and that's what you're concerned about, isn't it, the welfare of our workers? Feel free to ask them. I can't imagine they'd be so eager to change. And now if you don't mind...?" Morris stood up. "I think I'm needed back in the design department."

"And I'm sure you do just that, Mr. Raab," Cy Haddad went on, ignoring him, not moving an inch. "If you wouldn't mind humoring me a moment more and sitting back down. It's funny how everyone feels that way. At the start. 'Our workers are our friends. We take care of them. They've been with us since our first day in business. It's one big happy family here.' Still, what we believe is that it's up to the employees to determine what's in their interest. Not you. So how many people do you have, if you don't mind me asking? Between the warehouse and the sewing department?" The organizer went to the glass and craned his neck. There was the usual chatter of sewing machines in operation, six or seven sewers behind them, the hiss of a steam press, someone draping fabric on a body form, and two cutters working at the tables.

"Around fifteen," Sol said. "It's basically just our sample room here. Most of the production we contract out."

"I see. And in the warehouse? Downstairs?" The union man scribbled something on his pad.

The guy had probably been scoping them out for a week, getting his facts right, before he ventured up.

151

"In the warehouse . . . another eight or so, in shipping and receiving. Maybe we put on a couple more in peak season."

Cy Haddad just nodded, jotting down the figures in his pad with a small, worn-down pencil. Then he looked up and smiled, without betraying the bomb he was about to drop on them next. "And that's not including the operation up in Kingston, I assume?"

Morris stared back bluntly. His eyes went over to Sol's.

"The operation in Kingston," Sol explained, "is not exactly ours. The fact is, it belongs to an outfit called Hudson Manufacturing. They're a jobber we occasionally farm work out to. Right now, I have to admit, that work's pretty steady, so you're liable to see much of our production in there if you pay a visit."

"We already have." Cy Haddad smiled. "And though you may have some predilection against how we operate, Mr. Rabishevsky, let's not pretend we're all idiots, shall we?" The labor organizer tossed his pad on the table. "It's common knowledge Hudson Manufacturing is wholly owned by you and your brother. Alois Ross, the president and general manger on record—do I have the right name?—is, I believe, the husband of one of your floor managers here in New York. Both of *your* names are attached to the lease as guarantors. If you like, I can produce a copy of the check from your account at the Chase National Bank on Thirty-fourth Street just a block or two away, which went for the down payment to buy the assets of the previous business there."

Jesus, just who do they have on their payroll? Morris asked himself.

"We pay them a good wage," Morris said defiantly. There was no point in pushing against what was obvious anymore. "They get the best piece rate in the business, morning and afternoon breaks, and a two-week vacation. Which is more than most in the union can say. We even keep them on in our slow season instead of laying them off, regardless of the work. If we didn't come in there, the place would have shut down two years ago, just like what happened to the previous owners you tried to organize, and then you'd have a hundred more workers on handouts, instead of behind a machine. Besides, I'm not sure the Amalgamated Needle Trade Workers or International Fur Dressers even have a chapter up in Ulster County, so I'm not even sure it's in your jurisdiction."

"As an arm's-length subsidiary of Raab Brothers Manufacturing," the organizer looked back at him, "which is what we, and I'm pretty sure any court in New York would see it as, I'm afraid you're on thin ice on that one, Mr. Raab. It falls under the heading of 'accretion,' which you may want to familiarize yourself with. And unless you're prepared to drag the matter out forever in court, after we do make the effort to organize there, I'm not sure you really want to get into a legal battle over jurisdiction anyway. Not that we let details like that interfere with the lawful rights of workers everywhere to improve their position in life."

"Take a hike." Morris got up and went to the door.

"Gentlemen, I'm giving you notice of our intention to engage your workforce up there to the end of a vote of accepting the Amalgamated Needle Trade workers as their rightful representative. And in your offices here as well. Again, how many did you say you have on payroll?" Haddad consulted his notes.

Neither Morris nor Sol answered.

"Around thirty, I think you said," the organizer scratched at his mustache. "More, in season."

"You can finish your count on the street." Morris glared at him. He held the door open. "Sorry if we don't show you out."

"Now, now . . ." Haddad put up a hand. "I don't need to remind you, gentlemen, that the right of workers to organize into a union and to form such a union has long been decided in the courts and is fully protected by federal law. Any interference, under the recently passed National Labor Relations Act, would not be looked at kindly by us, by the press, or by the courts."

"I think what my brother meant," Sol tried to smooth it out, "is that we'd be happy to explore the conversation, though not right at this point in time."

"What I meant," Morris said, glaring at the man, "was to continue your count out in the street and go fuck yourself, Mr. Haddad. Buchalter sent you, didn't he?"

Cy Haddad blinked. "Sorry?"

"Lepke? Gurrah? This came from them, right? They gave you the word to come up here and harass us, right?"

"I work for the Amalgamated Needle Trade Workers and Fur Dressers Union, Mr. Raab, and I'm not aware of anyone in our offices by either of those names. Besides, I thought I made it clear, lawful organization is not harassment in any form. It's protected by federal law."

"And so is me not throwing you out the window like you did to Abe Langer . . . Protected by the law. But let me ask you, just for argument's sake, what's your base labor rate?" Morris pressed.

"Eighty cents an hour is standard. With two percent raises annually."

"And how much do we have to pay?"

"How much do you have to pay?" Haddad stared at him blankly. "I don't understand."

"You said let's not pretend we're idiots," Morris said. "So let's don't. Everyone knows the union demands protection money as part of the deal. You know, what you refer to as the Workers' Benefit Plan."

"You wouldn't stand in the way of your workers' welfare, would you?" the organizer said with a practiced smile.

"If it went to the workers, no. Maybe we wouldn't. But the world knows it goes to you. Anyway our workers already make ninety cents an hour. And with piece rate, they can earn another forty to fifty in peak season. Or more."

"Then why be so foolish as to resist," the organizer said. "Take our deal. You're already ahead of the game."

Morris felt his temper rise and held back from throwing the union man out. "As I said, Mr. Haddad, go back and tell whoever you have to we're just not interested."

"Cy," the union man said again with a smile.

"I don't care if you were Bella, my own mother, sitting in front of me," Morris said. "Our answer's the same."

"All right, all right . . ." The organizer folded his pad and put it in his inside pocket. "Nevertheless, I'm advising you of our intent to speak with your work staff, as is our right. And if you know what's good for you, and you both seem like savvy businessmen, unless you want the Feds breathing down your back, not to mention a bit of persuasion from other loyal union folk, I wouldn't interfere. You can save yourself a whole lot of trouble by just agreeing to come on board. It's always easier that way. If they trust you the way you say they do, I'm sure your people will go for whatever you propose. They're generally easily led that way."

He folded his pad.

"What you don't want, to be sure, are any work disruptions. Things like that can get very messy. Very messy, indeed. I'm sure you've had experience with what I'm talking about." The union man stood up. "Maybe someone you know."

"My brother and I will give it some thought," Sol said, knowing he was referring specifically to what happened to Manny. He got up as well and held the office door open for him. "But I think you heard what he said."

"Noted." The union man got up. "That's what everyone says. . . . Then, once the benefits are pointed out to them—sometimes graphically, I'm afraid—eventually they see what's best." He took his

155

hat, smoothed it out along the brim. "*If,* as you say, you intend to remain a going concern. I'll convey what you say to my bosses. They won't be happy, of course. But it's how things sometimes have to go. I'm sure you'll be seeing us again, Mr. Raab. Quite soon. And don't bother, I can find my own way out."

"We weren't offering," Morris said. He let the man go out, watching him peek once or twice around the cutting room, and the receiving area, to see what was going on. "So, Cy . . ."

The organizer turned around, maybe hopeful there would be some reconsideration.

"Long as you're up here, you want us to press that suit for you before you leave?"

Chapter Twenty-Two

A week later, the union sent in the troops to accost his workers on the street.

Old guys. Jews. Italians. Tradesmen. Loyal, union folk.

People like Morris's staff. Even a few women. They intercepted them on the street outside as they left at the end of the day. "You work for Raab Brothers?" they would ask. "Are you happy? Can we talk?" Wearing union signs. "Just a minute is all we need."

They looked like people who were being forced to give them the spiel. Who knew they were pressuring workers into a raw deal, but were forced into it. "You'd all like to make more money, wouldn't you?"

After Cy Haddad's visit, Morris and Sol had rounded up the staff in the cutting room. "Some people may want to talk with you," Morris told them. "It's their right to do so, so Sol and I can't interfere. If you think things sound better with them, it's your right to take a vote and have them represent you. Before you do, you ought to talk with your friends in other companies who have made a deal with them. See how life is for them, which I think you'll find isn't always as promised. Ask how things are, and how business is—are they busy or slow? Are they growing? I'm not saying it's bad for everybody, but we've always tried to treat you fair and do right by you. Just remember, if you choose to accept them, my brother and I, we can no longer stand up for you directly anymore. Only the union can. That has to be clear."

"So what should we do?" asked Felix Kupperman, one of their tailors, who was about sixty, and looking kind of helpless. "We all like it here, Mr. Raab. You treat us good. And with respect. We don't want to upset things as they are."

Morris looked at Sol. Sol said, "All you can do is what you think is right for you. It's a new world. We can't advise you. Just remember, you've always gotten a fair shake from Morris and me. And since you've been with us, business has always been good, right?"

"That's right," many of them murmured.

"The only thing is," Morris said, "you ought to know, you decide you want to keep things the same, things are liable to be different around here."

Now, Morris and Sol looked out the window at six P.M. as the sewers, pattern makers, and warehouse men left and were met on the street by union workers set to talk with them. They put out their hands and greeted them like they were meeting long-lost friends. Like their welfare was even a speck on their minds. They only wanted a deal.

Buck, the Negro vagrant who camped out near their entrance, and who Morris rarely left without handing a dollar to, was edged further down the street.

"You know we're not going to beat this, Morris," Sol said, looking on. The union had women too, who spoke Yiddish to them. And gray-haired grandmas from Little Italy, telling them how easy life was for them now. You never have to ask for a raise. It's all in the agreement. Any grievances, the union handles it for you.

"Felix Kupperman told me they're making it pretty tough on them," Sol said. "They say if they don't agree, they'll close the place down and then they'll *all* be out of work. They say even if business is good now, it's only a matter of time before it turns down, and then who else but the union will have their backs? Some of the people say they're even coming around to where they live, and threatening them on the street, on their way to work, if they don't vote to sign up. He said some of the people are scared."

"They're selling them all down the river," Morris said. "They gotta show they're adding something, so they take what we pay them and add thirty cents an hour to it. In six months, we'll have to raise our prices."

"Still . . ." Sol looked at him with kind of a helpless expression and took off his glasses. "It's not really in their hands anymore, Morris, it's in ours. All this, it's for us, not them. You know what's going to happen if we keep saying no."

"We have to say no, Sol. What other choice is there? You know what happens if we cave in. It's not just our sewers and warehouse staff. . . . It's who we'd be forced to buy from too. It's how much we pay for our furs and fabric. Not to mention how much we'll have to pay them to keep them off our backs. You know very well they don't care who stays in business and who doesn't. They're just bleeding the whole industry dry. It's just a shakedown, Sol, to them. Another racket. We're not talking about a real union here. . . . We're talking about a bunch of thugs and killers who found a new scam."

"Maybe I'm just not as strong as you, Morris," Sol said. Morris could detect a weariness in his voice. "I'm good with numbers, following a plan, not standing up to hoodlums. Those people, whether it's Lepke or Gurrah or whomever, they respect you. They respect that you're tough. That you're a bit like them. But, sure as day, one day they're going to come after us. You know that as well as I do. And what then . . . ?" He indicated their workers outside. "Maybe this time we should try to strike a deal."

"You want a deal so bad, Sol, go see what you can strike. And see how we can stay in business." Morris shut the window. "My fifty percent says no."

"Well, my fifty percent would like to remain fucking alive," Sol said.

Morris had never heard his brother swear.

Sol looked at Morris and nodded with an air of futility. "All right. Well, I have one idea how we can hold 'em off. At least for a while. We do have *one* ally over there."

Morris looked back, what his brother meant settling in on him. "You mean Harry."

"We always talked about bringing him in. Maybe it's time."

Chapter Twenty-Three

Sunday afternoons, Morris and Ruthie had the family up for lunch at their apartment on the Upper West Side.

Sol and his wife Louise and their sons David and Paul took the Lexington Avenue train down from where they lived on the Grand Concourse and then the crosstown bus. Morris's sister Anna and her husband Leo rode in from Brooklyn. Bess's too. Their mother, Bella, usually took the subway from the Lower East Side, always declining Morris's requests that she take a cab, which he'd be "happy to pay for," as far too lavish. (Though, against her objections, they always put her in one for the trip back home.) Even Harry came most weekends. It was nice to have him a part of the family again. He had taken like a dream to Morris's son, Samuel, and the boy to him as well. It took everyone back years and years. Harry like a kid again, laughing, rolling around on the floor, chasing around Samuel, who could barely walk he was laughing so hard. Other than Morris and Sol, the family members had gone their own way for several years, living in different parts of the same city. And it made Morris feel good to see them all, the Rabishevskys back together. Like back on Cherry Street. And it made him feel especially good that it was his wife, Ruthie, who had made it all happen.

One Sunday in May, Morris and Sol asked Harry to come with them out onto the terrace overlooking the Hudson River. "There's something we want to talk to you about," Sol said.

Harry handed Samuel over to Ruthie. "Sure."

Gin fizz in hand, Harry threw himself into the wicker chair on the balcony, while Sol and Morris sat on the love seat facing him. "It sure is nice out here," he said, admiring the clear, blue day and the view of the cliffs of New Jersey unobstructed across the river. "So, what gives?"

"We've been talking," Sol started in. "We want to ask you again to come into the business."

A decade of managing pool halls and speakeasies where gambling went on had put a little money in Harry's pocket. He rented a small apartment on Twenty-eighth and Lex. Over the years, he'd paired up with the occasional girlfriend, the casual type you'd meet in such places, but never anything serious. But it wasn't hard to see in the way he tumbled around with little Sam that inside he longed to have a family of his own one day, though with his life how was it ever possible?

Harry shrugged and took a sip of his gin. "We've talked this over before. You both know I'm not cut out for the nine-to-five thing. Sitting behind a desk. Besides, what would I even do? Stamp purchase orders?"

"You leave that to us. We'll teach you," Sol tried to assure him. "Things have grown, Harry. We can no longer do it just ourselves. And just so you know, it ain't nine to five at all. More like seven to seven. Six days a week. But the sign on the door says Raab Brothers. And we want to finally make it official. Otherwise, we'll have to bring someone in from the outside."

Harry looked over at Morris. "You okay with this, too?"

"'Course I'm okay with it. Things are changing, Harry. Not just for *our* business. We're talking about you. You're not hanging around with a bunch of street toughs anymore who take tourists for a ride or bang a few knees. They're killers now. You know what they do these days, as well as me. Mendy. Maxie. Buchalter. It's called Murder, Incorporated. They kill. For hire. And you know what they did to Manny Gutman in the union. It's time to say good-bye to them, Harry. So, yeah, we're both okay with it. We want you to come in."

"What would my job even be?" Harry hunched his shoulders and shrugged. "I don't know anything about making clothes."

"You don't have to know about making clothes. We'd find you a role. You could manage the warehouse. Or the receiving department. You get along with people. That's important."

"Receiving?" Harry took a sip of his drink and looked at Sol with a smile. "Receiving what?"

"Piece goods, Harry. Fabric. If you could log in bottles of booze, you can take an inventory of bolts of fabric."

Harry grinned, as if this was confirmation that it was all a bad idea. "See, it just goes to show you."

"And I promise you'd be making a helluva lot more money than what these guys throw at you now," Morris said. "That's tip money, Harry."

Harry put his head back and looked out over the river. "Well, it would be nice to finally be able to put something away. I look at you guys and I see how well you're doing. But . . ."

"But what, Harry?" Morris leaned forward. "These guys you're tied up with are bad. I know you think of them as your friends. But you're a patsy to them. They use you for a laugh or to do odd jobs. Then they'll toss you aside, and where will you be? You'll see, one by one, they're all going to go down. Prison, Harry. Or the morgue. You don't want them to drag you down too."

Harry sat back in the high-backed wicker chair. "I read the

headlines. I'm not exactly stupid, y'know. I see what's going on. I ask myself all the time, why did I make the wrong choices? All these years I've watched you and Sol, seen what you've put together, how you've built this thing, something important, from scratch, our name on it, and I think sometimes, yeah, it would be nice. Why do *I* have to be on the outside? That maybe I deserve a little respect too."

"You've wanted that, Harry," Morris said. "You know why . . ."

Harry nodded and let a long exhale out his nostrils. "Yeah, I know. I know."

"Harry, you've been beating yourself up a long time. Time to let it go."

He was silent for a while, his thoughts taking him somewhere, then he smiled and nodded again. "I really like being with your kid, Morris."

"And you'd have a chance to finally meet the right girl," Sol said. "Start your own family. Anyone can see how you are with Sammy."

"So what do you say?" Morris said. "Like we said, the sign on the door says Raab Brothers. We've waited a long time."

Harry nodded and peered past them out at the water. A barge went by. On its side, *McKenzie Maritime.* A tug sounded its horn. "Look at that. It would be nice to have my name on something," Harry said. "It would be like, you meant something in life. You mattered."

Sol said, "That's what we're offering you, Harry."

Harry turned back around. "You say you'll teach me, huh? I'm not starting with very much, I'm afraid."

"Mr. Menushem Kaufman once said to me, 'You watch, you learn. Only way to pick up this business.'"

Sol said, "Like Morris said to me, it ain't exactly rocket science. Otherwise, we wouldn't be doing it. None of us exactly went to Harvard."

"Listen," Morris said, grinning, "for what it's worth, Harry, you stayed in school three years longer than me."

"Not that it got me very much," Harry acknowledged ruefully. "Or I paid much attention."

Morris got up and went over and stood by Sol. "So what do you say?"

Harry seemed to run it through his head. Then he finished the rest of his drink and put the glass down. "I say, I think we should finally give 'em what the sign on the door says."

Elated, Morris went over and put out his hand. "Just one more thing... Whatever happened in the past, Sol and me, *we're* first now. You say good-bye to your cronies. You can't have both. We're your family. This business, it means everything to us. And it will to you too. From now on, you sit at our table, not theirs. You understand what I'm saying?"

"I won't make you ever doubt that, Morris. I'd never put them first."

"In that case . . ." Morris glanced at Sol, who gave him a final nod. "Welcome to the business, big brother." Morris and Harry shook, a little tentatively at first, then as the grin widened on Harry's face, heartily, and Morris pulled his older brother close.

It was the first time he had embraced his brother in almost thirty years.

Sol came up and gave him a hug of congratulations too.

"Want to make it official?" Morris motioned to the family inside. "There's someone waiting in there who I think would give the world to hear this news."

Harry looked through the glass at his mother in a chair. "I guess." Then with a wide grin, he said, "Why the hell not?"

The three of them went back inside. Everyone stopped talking and just looked at them. "We just had a board of directors meeting,"

Sol announced. "Harry's agreed. We're going to make an honest man out of him. He's going to come into the business."

"Raab Brothers," Harry said, grinning widely, "will finally live up to its name."

"Harry, that's wonderful!" Ruthie said, and went over and gave him a hug. Morris and she had discussed this many times.

"Mazel tov!" Sol's wife, Louise, beamed happily.

"We need to have a toast," Ruthie said. "I know just the thing." She ran into the kitchen to find the bottle of champagne and the fancy flutes they'd been given at their wedding that they'd been keeping for such an occasion.

"So what about you, Ma?" Harry looked at her. "You happy too?" He stood there, his drink in hand, waiting.

It took a moment for her to say anything, seemingly thrown back to a moment in time she had long shut out. Maybe back on that street, a brother's guilty tears soaking her skirt. *I'm sorry. I'm sorry* still echoing in her ears. Then she looked at her grown, aching son with a nod that after thirty years seemed to put that moment finally behind her. Eyes glistening, she nodded and said in her broken English, "Nothing could make me happier in the world."

She got out of her chair and opened her arms to him. And he melted in her long-sought embrace, tears smearing his face, home again, for the first time in years.

Chapter Twenty-Four

Lepke and I ran into each other not long afterward.

It was at Aqueduct Racetrack. It was a beautiful autumn day and I'd taken a box there and brought Ruthie, along with one of my largest customers, Reg Leavis, who was merchandise manager of Strawbridge and Clothier in Philadelphia in those days. He was up for the weekend with his wife. I think her name was Alice.

It was a warm autumn day, and the ladies wore blue-and-white dresses, Ruthie's with blue nautical trim and a wide hat, and the men, we still dressed in sport jackets and Panamas.

I bet the ponies every once in a while. And occasionally on baseball with Lief O'Malley, who sat in the booth of his tavern across the street from my office. My wife disapproved, of course, but when I won, sometimes big, I'd always buy her something: a fancy brooch, a necklace. Once, I even got her this new Buick convertible. I guess she always knew where the money came from. And when I lost, well, we didn't talk about that so much.

That day with Reg Leavis, we never bet more than twenty or thirty dollars on a race. And mostly, we let the women pick the bets. We were just having fun. I knew as much about picking ponies as I did about the stock market, which was no more than the last person who came up and gave me a tip.

Come the seventh race, we were talking about leaving and heading back to the city when Ruthie pointed at the racing form and said, "Look, there's a horse in the next race named Sammy! Sammy's Siren. Our son is Samuel," she said to Alice Leavis. "And he has this police car he plays with. He's always making a siren noise. We should stay and bet on him, Morris."

"He's twenty to one," Reg Leavis said, looking at the racing form. "It says he's won only once, and on a wet track. It seems he prefers the mud."

"Well, I've got a hundred that says he's a winner today," I said loudly, and peeled off a hundred-dollar bill.

"Morris!" Ruthie looked at me reprovingly. "My husband's always trying to be such a show-off," she said to Alice with a flustered smile.

"I'm not trying to be a show-off," I said back to her. "I mean, if a guy can't even bet on his own boy, who can he bet on? We should just pack up and leave now." I glanced at Reg for support. "You agree?"

"I'm in for twenty myself," Leavis said as well, "though I think this colt Fire Island is the one to bet on in this race. His odds are down to three to one."

"All right, all bets are in," I declared. "Let me get the runner." Back then, in the private boxes, bet runners placed the wagers for the bigger patrons, so they didn't have to go up and fight the crowds at the windows. "If we win, we're all going to Delmonico's for dinner. On me!"

I was looking around for the runner when I heard someone call out my name. "Morris Raab!"

Louis Buchalter came up to me, wearing a white sport coat and straw hat. He and two others were passing by our box. His union was all over me these days, harassing our workers, snooping around our *facilities. He was about the last person I wanted to see. Especially in front of the ladies.*

"Mr. Buchalter." I acknowledged him grudgingly.

"This must be your wife. We've had the pleasure once, if you recall," he said. He put out his hand and he and Ruthie shook.

"Of course I remember, Mr. Buchalter," Ruthie said. I'd talked to her about him from time to time, about what was going on. "How are you?"

"As well as could be. Meet my friend Arthur," Buchalter said. I'd seen the face somewhere: pale complexion, drooped, melancholy eyes. A thin, crooked mouth that didn't seem so eager to smile. "But his friends just call him Dutch."

I remembered I'd seen him once before—with Irv at Lindy's. Dutch Schultz was one of the most feared crime bosses in the city. I realized I was shaking hands that had probably pulled the trigger on dozens of murders. "Mr. Schultz."

He had just come off of two well-documented tax evasion trials, the last where it was said he literally bought off an entire upstate New York town, where the trial had been moved. The papers said it had made Thomas Dewey so mad, he said he wouldn't have a restful night of sleep until he put him in a cell in Sing Sing for good and turned the key himself.

His shake was kind of limp and sweaty. "Mr. Raab."

"And this is his friend, Otto Berman." Buchalter motioned to the slight, balding man with the high forehead, trailing them. "Otto's not so social, but he's a mathematical genius," Buchalter said. "Give him your birthday and he'll tell you how many days you've been alive, just like that." He snapped his fingers. "Care to test it out, Mrs. Raab?"

"I'm not sure a lady cares to reveal that sort of information, Mr. Buchalter, but why not? April 10, 1904, Mr. Berman. Be my guest."

The dark little man barely scratched his nose, and came back quickly. "Nine thousand, four hundred and ninety-four," he announced.

"How's that, Mrs. Raab?" Dutch Schultz chuckled. "Make you feel old?"

"And how do we know he's right," Ruthie questioned.

"He's always right," the Dutchman said. "Trust me, you can take it to the bank."

"Three hundred sixty-five times twenty-six. Plus four leap years," Berman explained. "You can do the math later if you like. You'll see it's quite correct."

"That's quite an accomplishment. And do you put this talent of yours to any good use, Mr. Berman?" Ruthie asked, as the bugle blew for the next race and the horses came out on the track.

"After the eighth race, given the crowd size, he's known to be able to calculate just how much the gate will be at the end of the day," Buchalter said. "Down to the dollar. In fact, he can tell my friend Arthur, here, just how much we have to bet to achieve a desired number."

"How impressive," Ruthie said to Alice Leavis with an edge of sarcasm. "And why is that such an important skill?"

I knew that Dutch Schultz was known to be big into the numbers racket now. And that the last three digits, which were what the payoffs were set to, were pegged to the gross that day at the track. So if someone could correctly estimate the gross, it could be worth a ton of money to him. Millions. "It just is, honey," I said to her.

"Say, I'm glad I ran into you, Morris," Louis Buchalter said. "Morris has a sizable garment company," he explained to his friends. "And the two of us are looking to see if we have anything in common, business-wise. You mind if I stay and chat a moment, Morris?"

"It's a free world," I said. "My friends and I were just about to place a bet."

Schultz and his man Berman said they'd catch up to him back in their box and moved along with quick good-byes.

Buchalter said to me, "I understand some people from the Amalgamated Needle Trade and the Fur Dressers Union have been in touch."

I said, "Funny, they've been making this big point of saying how you didn't have anything to do with the union."

"I'm merely an interested party, that's all. I just like to keep the peace, however I can make that happen. Anyway, I hope you'll become more receptive to what they have to say. Your husband's a stubborn man, Mrs. Raab," he said. "But you must know that."

"He's stubborn, but I usually find that he's right." Ruthie backed me up.

"Funny, my wife always says the same thing." Buchalter chuckled. "So how's your brother anyway? Harry, right? I hear you're doing your best to make an honest man out of him."

"He's doing just fine," I said without giving much away. "He's learning the trade."

"Well, good for him. You know I always kept an eye on that young man. I guess he doesn't need me to look after him anymore."

His thin smile came to rest on me, and I couldn't decide if the bastard was making a threat or not. But keeping my cool in front of the women, I said, "My brother Sol and I thank you for that. But from now on, that's our job."

"Well, I'm glad to hear that. Anyway, who can guarantee anything these days?" He shrugged. The kind of shrug that meant there was something behind it. Which if we weren't in front of a couple of thousand people, I might have asked him if he had something he really wanted to say. "Look, I'll let you all get back to your afternoon." He checked his watch. "Very nice to spend some time with you all. You said you were placing some bets?"

"We were about to," Ruthie said.

"Then maybe I can offer some advice. One of our horses is running in this race. Number Four. Fire Island. Me, I don't like to bet so much—I don't like to risk anything on something out of my control—but the Dutchman . . . he takes it all very seriously. I see the horse is on the board at three to one. You may have a good result if you take a chance on him."

"Thanks, but we're placing our money on Sammy's Siren," I said. "Our son is named Sammy."

"Is he, now? Isn't that nice. . . ." Buchalter checked the board. "Twenty to one, I see. I didn't take you for such a chaser, Morris. If I were you, I'd give some thought to what I mentioned. Number Four. He's been training very well, the Dutchman tells me. And he would know."

I put my hand up to signal for the bet runner. The Leavises and Ruthie told them what they wanted to do and I peeled off some bills.

"Ten thousand dollars on Sammy's Siren to win," I said.

Ruthie, who'd been doing her best to ignore things, turned around, completely pale. "Morris, what are you doing?" she gasped.

"And another two thousand to place," I said. With trembling hands, the shocked runner made out the marker. I signed it and stuffed it back into his hands. "All on Number Six. Sammy's Siren."

Buchalter shook his head and gave me a crooked smile. "You got balls, Raab, if nothing else. Mind if I hang around a bit longer and watch the race?"

"It's a free country," I said. "If you got nothing better to do."

"Oh I got lots better to do. But seeing your face after might be more entertaining than the race."

A small buzz went up from the people around us as word got out I had made such a sizable bet, and people were pointing toward me.

"Morris, have you gone crazy?" Ruthie said to me under her breath. The Leavises looked on, not really understanding what was happening. A few people around us who heard placed bets on him as well and held up their tickets to show their support. The air bristled with excitement.

"Just watch the race," I said to Ruthie. "Sammy's Siren is going to win."

The horses pulled into the starting gate.

"So you don't bet?" I asked Buchalter.

"Not on the races." He pulled up a set of binoculars.

We looked on as the horses loaded, then after a pause, the gates opened with a clang. "And they're off!" the track announcer shouted.

Then Buchalter added with a shrug, "But others I'm close to do."

The race was seven furlongs. A little less than a mile. A tangle of colorful silks and pumping legs burst out of the gate. They ran close to us on the rail and I could hear the pounding of their hooves as they galloped by. Bolting to the front I saw the tall brown horse. Number Six. Sammy's Siren, taking the lead. "You see, Ruthie."

"He'll run himself out like that," Buchalter commented. "That colt's only setting the pace."

"We'll see about that," I said. I'd never felt so sure of anything in my life. I started cheering. "C'mon, Sammy! C'mon!"

Buchalter watched through his glasses, not saying a word. Fire Island, the Number Four horse, was trapped in the pack, in eighth place out of ten. "I'm told he's a closer." Buchalter looked at me.

"He'll have to be," I said. Inside my heart was racing.

On the back stretch Sammy's Siren maintained his lead.

In front of me I heard Ruthie, who generally could care less about things like this, screaming loudly, "Come on, Sammy's Siren! Come on!"

The horses rumbled around the far turn. I couldn't see across the field, but the board still had Six maintaining his lead. But I could see a horse starting to weave its way through the crowded pack.

"Watch," Buchalter said.

I'd rolled up my Racing Form and slapped the seat in front of me. "Come on, Sammy! Come on!" We were all up on our feet. Six was now in front by a full length. He wasn't tiring. In fact, he was looking like this was his day. Stronger and stronger. He didn't need the mud.

His lead widened to two lengths.

By that time we were all cheering him on. Even Reg Leavis. Everyone knew there was a lot more on the line than just a race. Not to mention a small fortune. "C'mon, Sammy!" I kept urging him on, whispering it under my breath. "Come on!"

As they rounded the last turn, Sammy's Siren still held the lead. Buchalter, still peering through his glasses, said, "Your horse seems to be tiring."

"Don't worry, he'll hold it," I said.

Only a quarter mile to go.

"I'm afraid not. He's done. These things aren't left to chance, Morris."

As the horses hit the home stretch, the stands let out a roar. My blood was like a locomotive through my veins. A long shot was in the lead and looked like he had the distance to win. Everyone was feeling it, shouting, "Go, Sammy!"

Suddenly a horse came out of the pack, the jockey whipping him.

It was Number Four. Fire Island. He set his sights on Sammy's Siren's tail, still a couple of lengths ahead.

He started gaining.

"I told you, he's a closer," Louis Buchalter said matter-of-factly, looking through his glasses.

A furlong to go, it was just the two of them now, separated from the pack. Sammy's Siren still clinging to the lead. Which was only a length now, but with every stride Fire Island was making up ground. As they came along the last pole, they were stride for stride. The crowd was on their feet, roaring.

"C'mon, Sammy!" I kept saying. Ruthie and Alice Leavis were on their feet screaming too. "C'mon!"

Only another twenty yards or so . . .

Then, with only a few strides remaining, Sammy's Siren seemed to run out of gas. His stride faltered, and Number Four, Fire Island, surged past him. In fact, at the wire, a couple of more horses had caught up to him and galloped by, the crowd emitting a collective groan.

"Too bad." Buchalter put down his glasses and said to me, "I thought for sure I said to bet on Fire Island. I told you, the horse can close."

Though I was completely empty inside, I did my best not to show the slightest trace of disappointment.

"Me, I never bet though. I think I mentioned that, Morris. If there's one rule I live by, it's never bet against the house. Especially when you can be the house. Know what I mean?

"So I'll be sending someone by again. I'd be pleased if you could give him a bit more of your time than the last time and we can amicably work something out. Mrs. Raab, Mr. and Mrs. Leavis . . ." Buchalter tipped his cap to them. "Nice to be with you."

He cast me kind of a sage smile and left.

"Morris, how could you?" Ruthie said to me, as furious as I've ever seen her. "What were you trying to prove?"

I merely sat there and unfurled my racing form and turned the page. "All right, who's up in the next race?" I said.

Chapter Twenty-Five

The next day two men dropped off a case at Raab Brothers, addressed to Morris's attention.

He closed his office door and opened the briefcase.

It was full of cash, bundled inside. It came to $12,000. Just what he'd lost the day before. Along with a note wrapped around the bills: "My apologies, I must have somehow distracted you yesterday. I was sure I said Number Four."

It was signed, "Your friends at the Amalgamated Needle Trade Workers and Fur Dressers Protective."

Morris stared at the packs of bills. All hundreds and fifties. There wasn't a second where he actually gave a thought to keeping it. Instead, he packed the case back up and called in one of his warehouse men who occasionally ran errands for him. "Take the car. I want you to make sure this case gets back to its owner," Morris said.

"Where to, Mr. Raab?" the man inquired.

"A tobacco shop. In Brooklyn. The corner of Livonia and Saratoga. I want you to ask for Mr. Buchalter."

"Buchalter?" The man's eyes opened wide, as Buchalter was a name everyone in the industry knew. "Okay." He nodded warily.

"You'll be fine. Make sure you put it in his hands."

When the briefcase came back, clearly full, Louis Buchalter closed his office door and stared at it for a full minute, his mind fixed on what to do. Because of its weight he didn't even have to check what was inside.

Finally, he undid the lid and took out the uncounted wads of bills. He felt something snap inside. The guy had balls, that was all he could say. And to some extent, Louis had enjoyed the game of cat and mouse, and seeing how far he would go. But that was over now. It had gone on too long, and now it had to end. He had put the ball in Morris's hands and had made it clear how he wanted it to proceed. Pack by pack, he stacked the bills on the table.

He called in Gurrah.

"Morris Raab . . . ," Louis Buchalter said, nodding to the stacks of bills. "I know I asked you to go slow."

"Did you really expect him to keep it?" his partner said.

"I don't know what I expected. But all bets are off now."

Gurrah waited. "You say the word, boss."

Louis flared his nostrils and then he stuffed the cash into a drawer. "The word is, the game is over, that's all. Just do what you have to do."

Chapter Twenty-Six

The following day, at the 500 Club atop 500 Seventh Avenue, as Morris's lunch partner, Larry Zices, got up and went to the men's room, another friend from the business, Morty Zimmer, came up to his table.

"Mind if I join you a moment, Morris?"

"Sure. Sit down."

Morty was known as a quiet, easygoing guy, but today he seemed nervous and agitated. He owned a competing coat company, but, far from being a fighter, he had long ago struck a deal with the fur dressers union to get them off his back. At one time his firm was one of the largest in the industry, but word was, business hadn't been nearly as good since. He sat down in Larry's empty chair.

"You know, I'm kinda friendly with my union guy, Morris . . ." Morty looked around to see if anyone at the next table was eavesdropping and lowered his voice. "Cy Haddad."

"I've met Cy." Morris nodded.

"He mentioned something to me today. I thought you ought to know. He said you had better watch out. Usually I take that kind of thing with a grain of salt—everyone's pissing off everybody these days. But he didn't seem to mean it in a general way. He meant, like, imminently, Morris. Everyone knows you're not doing business with them. I think you're going to get hit. Today. Tomorrow. Soon."

"Did he say where?"

"No. If he even knew. He's just the rep, of course. Maybe the warehouse. Maybe the next time you make a delivery. Ike Goldman told 'em to take a hike and they set one of his trucks on fire. Just that you got to watch out, Morris. You know how these guys operate. You can't just thumb your nose at these people. It ain't good."

"It ain't good for who, Morty?"

"Ain't good for anybody, Morris. The union. The rest of us. It ain't good for business. It just agitates everything. Things need to quiet down."

"I'll watch out for myself, Morty, thanks," Morris said. "So tell me, Cy Haddad put you up to tell me this?"

The coat man blinked and the guilty hunch of his shoulders implied that he had. "Look, I'm just being a good citizen, Morris, that's all. No one would want to see anything bad happen to you."

"Thanks for that, Morty." Morris moved his fork to the side of his plate. "So tell me, how're things going for you? Since you became such a good citizen?"

"You know well as I do things ain't what they used to be. I try to be a good soldier. You know me, you cut your deal and then you make the best of it, right? Those companies the union controls, they're making a go of it. The rest . . . Margins are thin. How's it going with you, Morris?"

"It's going fine, Morty," Morris looked at him more closely and saw how uncomfortable he was. "Just fine."

Morty spotted Larry coming back across the room. On his way, he stopped at another table to shake hands with someone. Morty got up. "Cy said, if you want, you could give him a call. He might be able to work something out."

"He did, huh?"

"All I'm saying, Morris, is, if I were you, I'd give it a bit of thought. You know you can't beat them. You may make this big show of standing up to them. Maybe you're just a tougher guy than the rest of us. . . . But you won't win."

Morris looked at Morty and nodded.

"Maybe think about that call. I'm pretty sure Cy could help smooth things over for you. Here, here's his number." He passed Morris a card. Morris looked at it. *Amalgamated Needle Trade Workers and Fur Dressers Union.*

"I already got his card, Morty, but thanks."

"We all like you, Morris. No one wants to see anyone get hurt. We're all in this together, right?"

"I appreciate hearing that. Pass on a message for me?"

"Sure, Morris." A ray of hopefulness lit up Morty's eyes, maybe thinking his intercession had done some good.

"Tell him not to wait by the phone. Know what I mean?"

"Oh." Morty flattened his mouth in disappointment. "He ain't gonna like hearing that, Morris. My guess is, no one will."

"You're right; let me see if I can say it differently then. . . ." Morris pushed back his chair. "Tell him to go fuck himself. Will he like that better?"

"Take care of yourself, Morris," Morty said, in the way you might say it to a dying friend in the final phases of a disease and who you might never see again. "I was only trying to be a good friend."

Morris said, "You take care too, Morty," but for the first time, he knew things had changed. And he should take it seriously.

The following night he knew why.

Chapter Twenty-Seven

That night, we had a big delivery scheduled. To B. Altman in the city and Bamberger's in Newark, New Jersey.

1,250 coats. Thirty grand tied up in it. The truck backed into our loading bay, but before we brought any inventory out, I stood in the cold in my black bowler and long vicuña coat, an eye peeled to both ends of the street, because if Morty was right, I figured this was where it would happen.

The street was dark, almost empty. The sewers, salesmen, and warehouse men rolling their racks, who during the day made the place buzz with activity, had long gone home for the night. Across the street, a lone push-boy guided a trolley of fabric, the wheels clattering on the pavement. It all looked calm. When my lookout on the corner of Seventh and Thirty-sixth gave me the all clear, I flung open the truck's cargo door and waved my warehouse team into action.

"Let's get her loaded up fast. We have a delivery to make."

Six workers in beige smocks and flat wool caps hurried out, wheeling the metal racks crammed thick with garments. Inside the truck, a double row of steel bars lined each side. They loaded the coats, each of them squeezing ten at a time right below the collars and transferring them onto the bars. I kept my eyes on the street, expecting at any second the sudden rumble of a sedan accelerating from around the corner or the sight of men in dark coats slinking out of the alley across the street. I knew the people we'd pissed off weren't exactly the types to let such a warning go by without acting on it. But in minutes we got the truck loaded up. Nothing out of the ordinary, so far. Like any delivery, on any other night.

Not what might well be the last night of my life, a voice inside me said.

"That's all there is, Mr. Raab," Leo, my warehouse foreman, said, as the last of the racks was loaded on. Two of his guys tightened a cord around the garments to secure them on the ride. Then they took the empty racks and wheeled them back up the loading ramp into the building.

I got set to hop up into the truck.

From inside the dock, Sol stepped out. He had on a vest and tie, like he usually did, a banker's cuff around his sleeves. He wiped his hands clean. "That's the lot of them, Morris."

"All right, let's start her up," I called. "Vito, Louis, you're in front. First stop is Altman's. Let's go." Their receiving dock was on Thirty-fifth between Fifth and Sixth, only a few blocks away.

The two hopped into the cab, Vito behind the wheel. He started the ignition.

"You know you don't have to do this," Sol said. "There are other ways."

"We've got thirty grand tied up in this shipment. That's a month's payroll, Sol. What other ways."

"Other ways that say losing thirty grand makes a whole lot more sense to me than losing your life," Sol answered. "You've got a family now, Morris. A kid. Another on the way. There's no harm in just hearing them out."

"We've already heard 'em out, Sol. And we've seen what happens next. Don't be so worried. We've been warned before."

"We have." He looked at me warningly. "But one of these times, they're going to be right."

I beckoned him with my fingers. "C'mon, give it here."

"I got an uneasy feeling on this one, Morris."

"C'mon, Sol, give it here."

He blew out his cheeks acquiescently and went back inside for a moment, and came back with the Remington double-barreled shotgun, which would take out anything within ten feet wide of the blast. He handed it over with a dubious shake of his head. "You know you're a fool, don't you? I ever tell you that?"

"Only since I was about fifteen." I rested the gun on the floor of the truck's cargo bay and hoisted myself into the back.

"Yeah, well, it still applies."

I wrapped my hand around the handle of the truck's cargo door and gave him a final nod. "All goes well, I should be back about eleven."

"And if it doesn't?" Sol looked up at me with a kind of finality in his eyes. "Go so well . . ."

I gave him a grin. "Then you better find yourself another partner, big brother. Unless you've finally found the knack of how to sell these things."

With a rattle, I flung the metal cargo door down, but Sol put out his hand, stopping it from shutting.

We gave each other a long look. In it was Cherry Street and the rugged road out we had traveled. Harry and Shemuel. Sol's dreams, where he thought life would take him, all collapsed into mine. We were as different as two people could be and still come out of the same womb.

He merely glanced down to the truck's floor. "Your coat," he said, bringing my attention there. "You paid an arm and a leg for it. Who knows what's been in there. Watch out it doesn't drag on the floor."

I gave him a quick smile back. "Thanks." Then I brought the cargo door down the rest of the way.

I stood there, a wall of darkness and silence separating us. I thought about throwing the door back open, like there was something between us that was left unsaid. That needed to be said.

Instead, I heard him close the latch and give the truck a hard slap. "C'mon, what are we waiting for, paint to dry? Let's get this thing going."

Up front, Vito threw the truck in gear and I felt it lurch out of the loading bay onto Thirty-sixth Street.

I bent down, picked up the wooden stool there. Put it underneath me and sat down. Then I noticed my coat. It was dragging, just like Sol had said. I lifted the hem and brushed off the dust. Who knows what's been in here.

Then the truck lurched forward and I rested the shotgun across my knees.

The first stop took only minutes. The truck's doors opened at Altman's and we dropped off a hundred and twenty-three fur-trimmed coats. The rest we had to get to Bamberger's across the river in Newark, which meant heading downtown on Twelfth Avenue all the way to Canal and the Holland Tunnel, which now cut a good three hours off the trip there and back.

So far so good. I relaxed, taking a seat back on the stool.

On the ride down, thoughts flooded through me over whether what I was doing was right. Since I was a kid I was always standing up to people stronger than me. And it had always gotten me by. But Sol was right, thirty grand wasn't enough to get a bullet in the head. But he could be right a hundred times, I thought, and still not quite see. It wasn't about the money any longer. They'd never be happy until they bled us dry. Half my friends had already closed shop and were out of business. Or had landed in the hospital with cracked heads or broken ribs, or like Manny, a lot worse. It may be called a "union," but all it was was just another racket. Once you paid, you paid again and again. You didn't stop paying. Sometimes you simply had to hold your ground, I resolved, otherwise they'd be moving you an inch at a time and taking another piece of you that was rightfully yours. I looked at my hands. The hands of a pugilist past. They'd never been the hands of someone who'd given up that inch.

Not ever.

Surely not now.

The truck rumbled onto Canal, only blocks from the tunnel. The end-of-the-day traffic was all backed up as honking cars and trucks funneled into the entrance.

"So far so good, huh, Mr. Raab?" Vito called back. There was a narrow window to the front, for the driver to look in the rear, which I could see through.

"So far, so good." I had to agree.

We stopped at a light only a few car-lengths from the tunnel, and I began to think, maybe Morty was only blowing smoke after all. We'd had threats before; and up to now they'd left us be. Maybe it was easier to put the screws to some other small operator. Who didn't have the spine to stand up to them. Someone who buckled when the heat was turned up. Who—

The light turned, but the car in front of us stayed put. Vito hit the horn. "This idiot in front of us don't know how to drive, Mr. Raab. He's just sitting there. What's with you, buddy, you asleep . . . ?" He honked one more time. Someone behind us did too. "This crazy bastard doesn't want to move."

I got off the stool and reached in my coat pocket. I pulled out two double-ought rounds and inserted them into the twin barrels of the gun. "Just do whatever they tell you, Vito."

Through the small window I could see the car doors open and two men leap out of the car in front of us and rush the truck's cab from each side. One pulled open the driver's door and put a gun to Vito's face. "Get out of the truck, buddy. Open the cargo door!" The other dragged Louis roughly from the cab.

"Listen—" Vito stammered back. "We don't have the keys for back there. They're—"

The man put the barrel of his revolver between Vito's eyes. "You got a family, fella?"

"Yeah, I got a family," Vito said. "A wife and two kids."

"So if you want to go home to them tonight, you'll get out from behind that wheel and open the fucking door."

The man dragged him out of the cab and pushed him around back, following him.

My heart started to beat, hard. I heard the sound of the outside lock being opened. I shut the gun's barrels and pulled back the hammers with a firm double-click. You don't have to do this, a voice inside me intoned. These are killers. Just put down the gun. You can make everything just go away, just like Sol said.

A second voice insisted that this was the one thing I had to do.

The cargo door flung open.

Three men in fedoras and dark coats looked up at me with surprise.

"I'm sorry, Mr. Raab," Vito said as they threw him to the pavement.

"That's all right, Vito," I said, leveling the shotgun at them. "These men were about to take a step back."

The thugs on each end had handguns; the one in the middle held a satchel with a stream of smoke coming out of it, which he had been about to lob into the truck. But as he spotted the shotgun aimed at his chest, the man's eyes widened and he lowered the satchel to his side.

I knew what was inside.

Not explosives, but something called ammonium sulfide. Once it made contact with the atmosphere, in seconds everything inside the truck would take on the stench of rotten eggs. It could ruin a warehouse full of merchandise just as effectively as if it were a real bomb that blew the entire place apart.

The men on each side of him brought up their guns.

"I said take a step back," I said again.

I kept the shotgun barrels aimed directly at the man with the stink bomb, who had dark eyes, thick, bushy brows, and the kind of steely coolness that barely even acknowledged I had a weapon pointed at him.

"I know you," I said, recalling him from my visit to Buchalter's office. "You're Workman."

He was a part of what the papers called Murder, Incorporated, and was reputed to be with Buchalter and Gurrah the night Jacob Orgen was gunned down. A true killer.

"Well, if you know me," he said, "you'll do what's smart and step down from there. Before things start to get messy."

"Seems to me they are already a bit messy," I replied. "At least, in my book."

"Not that messy." Charles Workman curled a smile. "At least, not yet."

The truth was, I'd never even pointed a weapon at anyone before, much less pulled the trigger. And now here I was aiming at three button men who I knew wouldn't spend a whole lot of time thinking on it if they had the chance to do the same to me. My mouth was as dry as cotton and I could feel my heart bouncing rat-tat-tat against my ribs. "Your call, Mr. Workman." I kept my gun steady. "But I did ask you to step back."

"We got two guns, you only got one." One of the thugs smirked, steadying his revolver at me.

"And your aim's likely better than mine as well," I acknowledged, "being professionals. Still, I figure you never know how these things go." Even the spray from this close in could take a head off without much fuss. Maybe all three.

Grudgingly, they looked at each other and complied as one, taking a step back.

"You know you ain't gonna stop this." Workman glared up at me. "What's ordered is ordered. And you know by whom." He glanced at the satchel in his hand. "If I have to take this back with me, I can promise no one'll be very happy. It'll take a lot of explaining."

"In that case, feel free to put it down right over there," I said, dipping the Remington toward the sidewalk and giving him a slight smile. "But I'm pretty certain if your men there decide to take things into their own hands, you won't be the one making that argument."

Workman inched into a thin smile himself and nodded back. "Yes, on that I would have to agree."

Suddenly car horns sounded. A couple of nearby drivers rolled down their windows, not aware of what was happening. "C'mon, what the hell's going on? Move! We don't have all night." My impression was that the two with the pistols were likely giving thought to which was the better choice: to be blown halfway back to Houston Street, a foot-wide hole in their chests, or to go back and tell Louis Buchalter they were unable to carry out his orders.

Seconds ticked by. A thought wormed through me that depending on what their answer was, that was how much longer I had to live.

Finally Workman seemed to think the better of it and lowered the satchel. He shook his head disgustedly. "You don't have any idea what you've just done."

"My lucky day, I guess?" I said, taking in a breath.

"Lucky day, huh . . . ?" Workman chuckled. He sniffed back with the disbelieving look of a hunter who was sure he had shot something dead, but yet still the thing continued to hop around as if nothing had happened. "More like you just signed your own death warrant, Morris. Over a bunch of fucking coats."

Suddenly the sound of a siren could be heard, a few blocks behind us.

Someone in the car in front jumped out and said to them, "Charlie, Otto, c'mon, we gotta get out of here."

Workman just continued to stare at me, the siren growing louder.

"Charlie!" One of the goons on the end grabbed the killer's arm. "We gotta go. Now."

With irritation, Workman wrestled his arm away and tossed the smoking satchel harmlessly onto the street. An odor like rancid eggs began to emerge.

"Lucky day?" He flashed me a baleful glare. "A mentsh on glik is a toyter mentsh," he said. "Feshtayst?"

"Ich feshtayn." I nodded, looking down at him.

He gave me a final shake of his head and then the three jumped back into the sedan in front of us. It started up and bounced onto the pavement through the light, screeched at the corner, and disappeared.

Only then did I let out a deep breath and felt just how fast my heart was racing. My shirt was damp with sweat.

I lowered the gun.

"Mary Mother of God, Mr. Raab." Vito jumped up and dusted himself off. "That was the bravest thing I ever saw." He stood there in awe. "I was sure they were gonna . . . What was it he just said to you?"

"Said to me?"

"Yeah. In that language you guys speak."

"He just said he'd be seeing me is all, Vito. In shul."

"Shul?"

The siren grew closer. The lights of a police car could be seen now weaving through traffic, maybe two blocks behind. Vito looked toward it. "Should we wait, Mr. Raab?"

I glanced at the stink bomb on the pavement. The last thing I wanted to do was to lodge a complaint. "What say we just close it back up now and get the hell out of here? I think we've lost enough time."

"My thoughts exactly, Mr. Raab."

I climbed back onto the truck and he shut the outside door and affixed the lock again. Then he jumped back in the cab and started the engine. This time, the truck went forward, feeding in with the traffic heading into the tunnel, as the cop car finally pulled up to where the commotion had been and two policemen hopped out.

The only sign that something had happened was the stink bomb lying on the sidewalk.

"But I think you're ribbing me, Mr. Raab?" Vito called back when we were safely in the tunnel. "What that guy said back there. I don't think he mentioned shul at all?"

"I guess he didn't," I agreed.

A mentsh on glik is a toyter mentsh, *was what Workman had said.*

An unlucky man is a dead man.

This isn't over, he was saying.

And I knew exactly what he meant.

Chapter Twenty-Eight

Ruthie was furious at Morris when she heard what he'd done that night.

"Are you just trying to get yourself killed?" She looked at him accusingly, preparing herself for bed. "I know how you are, Morris, but if you don't value your own life, at least give some thought to ours. Sam and the one inside here." She put a hand on her belly. "And me. We don't work for you. We're your family."

"I am thinking about you." Morris sat down on the bed and pulled his tie off. "I'm thinking about protecting what we've worked for for the next twenty years."

"No. You're thinking about this tough-guy image you feel you have to live up to. You're the same as your friend Buchalter, Morris. You just don't shoot anyone. You easily could have been killed tonight. If either of those guys had started shooting . . ."

"But they didn't."

"Not this time." She turned at the makeup mirror. "But for how long."

"So what do you want us to do, Ruthie? Tell me. I'll do it. You

191

want us to just give in? I give in, I basically work for them. We have to raise our rates, I have to buy from who they tell me I have to. I have to pay them protection. We do that, Ruthie, we might as well close the doors. You know better than anyone, it's not who I am."

She turned around and sat on her stool. "Tell me, are Sammy and I at risk?"

"No." Morris shook his head. "It don't work that way."

"So how does it work? You keep acting like a cowboy until one day I get a call that you're dead?"

Morris unbuttoned his shirt and sat there on the bed. His voice almost cracked. "This isn't just what I do, Ruthie, this is my business. Sol's and my business. We're not just going to give it up. I don't see what else there is I can do."

Ruthie came over and sat next to him on the bed. "You go to the police then."

"The police. That's a joke, right? The police are in their hip pocket. The police will only laugh and tell me to work out a deal with them."

"What about your friend then? Irv. You mentioned he was working for that special prosecutor now. Dewey?"

"And tell him what, Ruthie? Someone named Workman tried to hijack my truck. We bring in the Feds, that's when we do get ourselves in trouble."

"Then make a deal with them, Morris. What else is there?"

"I told you, we work out a deal with them, we might as well close our doors."

"But you'll be alive. And your kids will have a father, Morris. Not some martyr, who never found a fight he would back down from. What are you afraid of, not living up to this image we all have of you? You're smart, Morris, but you're too damn stubborn to see what's right in front of you. I married you because I felt I could trust where you would take me. You said it yourself. And I have trusted you." She put her head on his shoulder and squeezed his arm. "I love you. I don't want to go down that road alone."

Morris put his arm around her, his eyes slung straight ahead, Ruthie leaning on him. "You won't have to. I won't let that happen."

"I know you won't. But please. You could have been killed tonight. For the first time, I'm starting to get scared."

Morris thought about what Charles Workman had said at the end. *An unlucky man is a dead man.* He was lucky tonight. But Workman wasn't a good enemy to make. Any more than Buchalter was.

"We're not the same, you know. Buchalter and me."

Ruthie nodded on his shoulder. "I know. I'm sorry."

"And trust me, he's not my friend."

Chapter Twenty-Nine

After talking to Sol the next day, Morris placed a call he'd never thought he would ever make.

To Cy Haddad.

As much as it left a taste of guilt and shame in his mouth, maybe Ruthie was right on this one. There was no choice anymore. It was just he and Sol and Harry in a battle they couldn't win. If it continued, the next time might leave her without a husband and Sammy without a father. Even Sol said this was the first time Morris had made any real sense since he first came back with those orders from Muriel Mossman.

"I'm happy you've come around," the union organizer, who appeared not at all surprised to hear from them, said. "I'll pay you a visit, tomorrow. Say around five thirty. Does that work for you? Or six. It's best if the people up there don't see me around. And I may bring another person with me."

"Tell Buchalter I only negotiate with him," Morris said. "Otherwise, no deal."

"I'm afraid that's not how it works, Mr. Raab. Mr. Buchalter doesn't have anything to do with the day-to-day activities of the union. How about I come up and give you the rough edges of how it works. I assure you, your new willingness to come to an understanding will definitely be communicated to him."

The next day, Haddad and a short, pasty-faced guy in a suit, named Goldman, an attorney on the union's payroll, came up at six thirty, after Morris's staff had left. They sat in the glass-lined showroom where the conversation had gone so poorly only weeks before, the cutting room and the piece goods department just outside.

After the predictable song and dance about how great this would be for their workforce, Morris said, "I give you my workers here; the factory up in Kingston is off-limits."

"I'm afraid that's not going to happen, Mr. Raab," Cy Haddad said.

"Why not?" questioned Sol. "It's out of anyone's view. No one will even know whether they're in or out."

"It's in *our* view," Cy Haddad said. "And it falls under the heading of accretion. It's part of your company. Unless you'd like to challenge that in court."

"It's not part of our company," Morris said. "Any more than it's in your jurisdiction."

"Then stop putting your work up there," the union man said. "And take yourself off the lease as guarantor. And see how long the place stays open. Anyway, soon we'll be opening a charter in Ulster County," said the lawyer. "So we have every right to organize up there."

Morris asked himself how such a person had traded away his soul. How they could do the bidding of an outright crime syndicate.

"Fuck accretion." He scoffed at Sol. "They only want it because that's where the real dues are." He shrugged. "So how about, you give us two years up there, as is, and then we'll agree?"

"We can probably do one year," Cy Haddad said.

"Two."

"Sorry. That's all the leverage I've been given. One is all we can do," the union man restated. "We can't be seen to be weak."

Morris looked at Sol. If they signed, they were helpless. He knew he was just trading away his business.

"But you buy through the union's preferred vendor list," Haddad added.

"We can't buy through the vendor list. They just give kickbacks back to you. The whole reason we're even in business is because of our price."

"Everyone buys through the preferred vendor list. No exceptions," the union man said. "Especially to you."

It was Buchalter squeezing him. That was plain and clear. Morris felt an ache in his gut. An ache of helplessness and the evaporation of control. "Tell me, how much do you get from your vendors?"

"I don't know what you're talking about," Goldman, the union lawyer, responded.

"Two percent. Three? How about we buy where we want to buy and we cut you back the difference?"

"Everyone buys from the list," Cy Haddad insisted. "That's not negotiable. Just ask your friend Manny Gutman. I think he'd vouch for that."

Morris gave Haddad a spiteful glare. Somewhere the union man had had his hand in what had happened to Manny. It was likely he who had informed on Manny, that he was buying pelts from outside their agreement. Morris suppressed the urge to leap across the table and take Haddad by the throat.

"Our people in the production room and the warehouse. They've been with us from the start. How much do they have to contribute?"

"Four percent dues. Deducted straight out of their paychecks.

Our accounting office will be in touch with you. You know we get to monitor the payroll."

Sol said, "So explain to my brother and me just how they're better off?"

"You're so concerned about them being better off, pay them the four percent yourself. We're offering you peace, and that's gotta be worth something to them too. And once they sign they have no way to appeal on wages other than through the collective bargaining agreement, so you're removed from it, is the way *I* would look at it."

"And what about protection?"

"Protection?" The lawyer raised his brow. "I thought we established there was no such thing."

"You know very well what I'm talking about. Protection money. From Sol and me. It's no big secret. Everyone pays it."

"There is a three percent company fee payable monthly on all union payroll, that goes to the workers' fund for unforeseen contingencies."

"Unforeseen contingencies . . . ?" Sol asked.

Haddad shrugged. "Such as making sure your work doesn't get interrupted in an unforeseen stoppage. Or in the case of an unforeseen emergency in your warehouse, say a flood you didn't expect, or a fire, there'll be money to compensate your workers in the time they're down. . . ."

"Protection money." Morris stared at them. "From yourselves."

"Call it what you will." Cy Haddad sighed. "Just make your peace with it. And because of your long-standing relations with parties close to the Amalgamated Needle Trade Workers and Fur Dressers Protective, that fee has been graciously cut back to two percent. For the next two years. To give you an easy adjustment."

Morris gave him a derisive smile. "Tell Mr. Buchalter thanks."

Cy Haddad and the union lawyer closed their files. "These are the broad terms. The rest, for your protection, it would be good to discuss it with your own attorney. Do we have an agreement?"

Sol said, "The four percent we're forced to ante up between our current workforce's dues and the two or three percent you're looking for from us is about the margin we make at the end of the day."

"These are the terms, I'm afraid," Cy Haddad said. "Others seem to manage. Should you not want in, however, I'm afraid I can't vouch for how things might go."

Morris said, "My brother and me, if we agree to your terms, we'll essentially be staying in business to pay you. The union."

"It's not so bad," the union organizer said, with the calculated indifference of a man who knew he had all the cards at the table. "You charge a little more. You cut back here and there. People manage to get through. And on the plus side, you take the worry of your own labor negotiations off your shoulders. And look at it that we don't hassle you anymore. From now on, we're all just friends. Working for the same cause."

Morris looked at Sol and then at the lawyer. "Draft a letter. We'll see."

"Of course, you understand that the failure to pay at any time would be looked at very discouragingly," Haddad folded his fingers, "and we'd have to encourage your work staff to respond accordingly."

"You mean, strike."

"Nasty word, but just so you know. Or not abiding by the terms of the agreement . . . That would be very bad as well. I like to say this up front. That's a situation you do not want, trust me." He closed his notebook and looked at the lawyer. "Are we set?"

Morris felt like a gristmill was grinding his intestines. They were trading in their workforce for the security of remaining in business. And for how long was anyone's guess. They were being squeezed, bled of whatever profit they were making. They couldn't work any thinner. What was the point of even being in business?

"If so, I should have the paperwork for you to sign in the next day." The lawyer stood up.

Morris thought of Ruthie. And Sam. He was doing this for them. He glanced at Sol. His brother had a similar look.

They were trading away their business.

"It's been a true pleasure reaching an understanding with you, gentlemen." Cy Haddad nodded firmly. "And welcome to the Amalgamated Needle Trade Workers and Fur Dressers Protective." He put out his hand.

"Just send us up the paperwork, Mr. Haddad," Sol said.

The union man stood up and smiled. "Cy."

Morris looked at him. "You speak Yiddish, Cy?"

"Of course. I'm from Ocean Avenue in Brooklyn," he said.

"Gey tren zich," he said. Go fuck yourself. "Have a good day."

They waited for the union man to leave, then Morris said to Sol, who was still sitting across the table, "Charles Workman was right."

"About what?"

"We just signed our own death warrant."

Morris walked and walked before he went home that night. The traffic was heavy on Broadway as he made his way through the bright lights and crowds all the way up to Fifty-ninth Street and the park.

If there was any one rule he lived by, he had always been truthful to himself. He had never been afraid to stand up. Since he was fifteen and in the army, he had never backed down.

He paid a visit to Manny Gutman. He was at home now, a large, three-bedroom apartment with a balcony on Park Avenue. The Isidor Gutman Fur Company had been closed since the incident. Helen took him in to Manny, who was in the den, reading.

His hair was white and distinguished-looking, but his face still bore the bright red blotches of the union's acid attack.

"What's the occasion, Morris?"

"Whatsamatter, can't I just come up and see an old friend?"

"I know you a long time, Morris," Manny said, "and your face doesn't seem to be saying this is a personal call."

Morris told him about their talks with Haddad.

"I'm sorry to hear it," Manny said, "but I always knew it would come to this. Ruthie is right, you know. You have to make a choice."

Morris said, "I sign that piece of paper, I might as well close up shop."

"And you might as well close up shop if you don't. Look at me." He pointed to his face. "You want this for yourself, Morris? You want this to be your life?"

Helen brought them coffee and they watched the fish in his aquarium for a while.

"I spent the summer on the Jersey Shore in Deal. This winter, we're planning a trip to Havana. Life ain't all bad."

"I'm thirty-one years old, Manny. Not seventy-two."

"You're smart. You could do a million things. You've got some money put away, right?"

Morris shrugged. "Some."

"You're up here, right? You want my advice? Sign the contract. Milk it for as long as you can, then walk away. Walk away in one piece. One day, the Feds will come down hard on these people. This business is part of your blood, you can always come back then. In the meantime, go out West. Maybe make pictures. Isn't that Goldwyn guy a friend of yours?"

"This is all I know how to do, Manny."

"You think that, Morris. But you better decide just how much it means to you. You want to be riding around in that truck with a gun in your lap for the rest of your life? You got a gal who loves you, and a beautiful son. You may think you can outlast them, Morris, but look at me. One time, someone's gonna pull that trigger. You won't be so lucky.

"You see that big red scaly one there, swimming around." He pointed to a fish. "Scorpionfish, they call it. Rare as can be. From the Caribbean. Pretty as they come, right? But in there he's the boss. Watch him. It's dinnertime now. You don't want to get in his way when it comes time for a meal."

"You trying to tell me something, Manny?"

"Me? Nah, I got no good wisdom anymore." He put the fish food down. "Just be sure what you want, Morris. Because you're gonna have to live it. What you do next, it's gonna be the most important step of your life. And I don't want to have to come all the way back from fucking Cuba for your funeral."

"Trust me, I don't want you to either, Manny."

Chapter Thirty

The next morning, a messenger dropped off the letter mapping out the terms of their agreement. It was longer than Morris had expected, with pages and pages of legal warranties and representations that they'd have to show to their lawyer. But legalese aside, Sol confirmed it was what they had said.

Both knew if they signed it, they were pretty much signing away their lives.

They slept on it one last night. Morris went home and while Ruthie prepared some dinner, he played with little Sammy on the couch. The boy was wearing his New York Yankee pajamas, number three on the back, belonging to the Babe. Nothing made Morris feel happier than to hear his son giggle happily, than to feel that this red-cheeked innocent thing had sprung from his rough seed. "Shake the hand of the man who shook the hand of the man who shook the hand of the Big Bambino," Morris rang out merrily, tossing his boy in the air. And every time Sammy would put his hand out, Morris would playfully pull it away.

"Shake the hand of the man who shook the hand of the man who shook the hand of the Babe," he said again.

Sammy laughed.

Tomorrow, they'd have to make their decision. Morris reflected on his life. He could've been on the street selling papers if Mr. and Mrs. Kaufman hadn't taken him in and seen something in him, and given him a chance. He'd always heard people talk about how much luck was a part of where you ended up in life, or how much was due to character. How much you actually brought to your own fate yourself. Morris was generally never much interested in such conversations, but right now, it seemed important to him, as it became clear, holding his son, how whatever he had achieved in life, whatever mattered, had come to him because *he* had taken the decisive step. He had studied Mr. Beck for two years, and at fifteen years old told Mr. and Mrs. Kaufman he was ready to handle his job. When they finally had to sell their company, at twenty-three years old Morris had opened his own business and convinced Sol to come along. When he took his samples to see Muriel Mossman, as inexperienced as someone could be on their first sales call, it was he who had tossed them over her partition while others just waited in line. No one else would ever have dared. And he had pursued Ruthie when he was nothing but an uneducated lug full of plans but with nothing to show for them, when a woman like that was but an unattainable dream for someone like him.

Raab Brothers—it was the one constant in his life. The one thing he knew, like he knew there were five fingers on each hand. The one thing they could count on. If he signed that contract, the company wouldn't be his anymore. Oh, his name might still be on the articles of incorporation, and he and Sol might still sign the checks; he might even decide who they would sell to and who they wouldn't.

But they would own it. Lepke, Gurrah. Even Cy Haddad. The union. They'd be calling the shots. And if he continued to fight them . . . He tickled Sammy on the ribs and made him laugh. If he fought them he might not be around to see his boy ever go to school. They were squeezing him because he had stood up to them so publicly. If they squashed them, they'd squash everyone. He and Sol, they would be working as hard as they were now, but for free. What choice was left for them? To go to the Dewey commission? To Irv? What could he really tell him? That three of Buchalter's henchmen had tried to damage his inventory? That wouldn't be enough to put Workman away for a week, let alone put the pressure on Buchalter. And it would bring the mob down on him with a force he could never fight back against.

Anyway, Morris wasn't the kind of man who ran to the cops or anyone else to solve his problems for him. Manny Gutman had said, *Whatever you do next, it's gonna be the most important step of your life.* "I only know how to do this one thing," Morris had told him. This one thing. And he knew that well. He might not be book smart, but he'd still amassed a lot of learning in life, and this business, this was what he knew. He tossed Sammy up in his arms and caught him. "Shake the hand of the man who shook the hand of the man who shook the hand of . . ." He caught himself. Emotion rushed into his eyes. His son laughed. He threw him up in the air again.

What truly mattered—that was what he had only begun to understand.

"Everything all right in there?" Ruthie called from the kitchen.

"Everything's fine," Morris called back.

All fine.

What he had to do, he understood, was somehow trust that the things that had taken him this far in life were the same things he could trust now. In Sammy's playful eyes, he saw a glimmer of what would be one day. What Morris would pass on to him. One day his son would want to know, what kind of man was his father? What did he stand for? What did he believe in? What would his legacy be?

That he was a man who had stood apart? Or put his principles aside, and played the game like everyone else?

Morris had never been one who was able to say things very clearly. What came out of his mouth was still sometimes rough, garbled. But he still felt them. Deep in his heart, in his soul, he felt things just as fiercely as if he could say the words as elegantly as Ruthie or Irv.

Raab Brothers was his life.

"Up with the Babe!" he said to Sammy, tossing him high. In his baseball pajamas and tiny Yankee cap, the number three sewn on his back. "I saw him play a few times. Did you know that? I took your mother once. It was our third date. I remember it clear as if it happened yesterday." He flicked the bill down over Sammy's eyes. "He hit two that day."

"What are you two doing?" Ruthie said, coming out with a tray of chicken and a salad.

"Can't a guy just horse around with his son?" Morris said, faking umbrage. He put Sammy on his lap. She put the tray down on the coffee table and sat next to him. He put his arm around her.

"Something's wrong?" She kept at him. "I can tell, Morris."

He smiled. "What could be wrong?"

That was a beautiful day, was all he was thinking. The two of them. At Yankee Stadium. A row behind the dugout. The sky as blue as her eyes. He remembered the polka-dot dress she wore with a wide straw hat.

That day, he'd felt like the most important man in the whole world, next to the prettiest girl in the park. He knew he would marry her from the moment he'd gone up and asked her to dance.

The Babe hit two.

The next morning, he met Sol for coffee before work.

Morris tried to gauge from his brother where they stood. "So . . . ?"

His older brother stared back at him. "You're looking at me like I got a hairpiece off-kilter or something. . . ."

"I'm asking if you're still up for signing that document?"

Morris waited while Sol put two sugars in his coffee and stirred in some milk.

"We both know, we sign that letter, we can take six, eight percent right out of our bottom line. That's all we make now. We raise our prices, maybe we can hide it for a while. Till our customers catch on."

"And maybe we *can't* raise our prices. Maybe the market says no," Morris said.

"Maybe it does. But the fact remains, we're no longer working for us, Morris. We have partners now. Partners who don't give a shit whether we do well in business or not, so long as we pay them. . . ."

"So what are you proposing?" Morris looked at him with a sparkle of surprise lighting his eyes.

Sol stirred his coffee. Then he looked at his brother with kind of a sage smile. "You remember when I came and got you and drove you back home that day, from Fort Slocum, after you enlisted. When your army unit was about to ship out?"

"I remember."

"You probably thought I felt some kind of anger toward you at taking you back, 'cause I was always like the parent telling you what was right and what was wrong."

Morris smiled. "You didn't say a word till we were back across the Brooklyn Bridge."

"Maybe so. But when I heard what you'd done, taking on those *petselehs* in your unit, and never once even telling us about it, it wasn't anger I felt toward you. I just couldn't say it then. It was pride. God-honest pride, that I had the toughest little brother in the whole world, a whole lot tougher than me. And you know why? Because he wasn't afraid to stand up when things got tough. For himself. For all of us. And I remember thinking then, driving, when am I gonna be able to stand up for him?"

"That so," Morris said, with a surprised grin. "I always thought you felt I was the dumbest SOB on the Lower East Side."

"Maybe you were. But I learned something from you nonetheless. That some things are worth fighting for and not giving up on so easy. Some lines you just have to cross, even when everything says that you can't. So if we have to close up shop because of this, we close. . . ." Sol put down his coffee. "But my fifty percent says, and I must be crazy to even think this, I'm damn well not gonna let those goons make that decision for me." He smiled. "I don't need to be spending my whole day and half the night stuck with you if I can't at least make a little money out of it."

Morris stared at his brother and curled back a smile. "You'll see, Sol, we'll make a little money out of it yet."

"It may be on our deathbeds, but . . ." Sol smiled too. Then he grew serious. "You know what's going to happen, don't you?"

Morris nodded. It wouldn't be easy, and yes, it would bring all hellfire down on them.

Sol said, "I'm not a fighter, Morris. You know that."

"That's okay. I can do that enough for two."

"You'd better, then. *L'chaim.*" He raised his coffee cup.

"*L'chaim.*" Morris clinked it back. He smiled. "Say a *bracha* for us." A prayer. "And Sollie . . ."

"What?" his brother said. He stirred his coffee, brooding.

Morris winked. "I like spending time with you too."

Chapter Thirty-One

After a long lunch at Sardi's, at which he celebrated one of the truly sweet victories of his career, Cy Haddad was back at his desk, feet up, hands behind his head, having decided he wasn't going to do much for the rest of the day.

The two gin and tonics he'd had at lunch didn't exactly put a lid on that feeling.

If there was one thing he enjoyed about his job, beyond the day-to-day complaints and worker grievances he was always dragged into, and the tedious labor regulations he had to enforce, it was bringing some puffed-up *potz* who thought he was bigger than the union to his knees. Someone who thought Haddad had sold out in life, and made no secret about telling him that to his face. Sure, he once had dreams, like anyone did. About helping people who were without rights. Who were disadvantaged and without a voice. He had watched his old man toil in a livery factory on Wooster Street, never making enough to buy his kids real coats for the winter. The embers of the Triangle Shirtwaist fire had made dreamers out of many of them back then.

But over twenty years things had changed. It was no longer like that now. And he just didn't have the balls or the caring to fight it anymore. So maybe he had sold out, Cy thought. Maybe that voice inside him did jab at him before sleep every night. But why should he have to live like his father had? Never as much as a ten-dollar bill under his mattress. What did a labor organizer make? Not even enough to buy a nice car. Cy had a fucking boat in a marina! Why should these owners have all the rights, or their workers?

He deserved his share too.

But watching someone like Morris Raab brought down to size— someone who had mocked him, who had wanted to toss Haddad out of his shop—that's what made his own capitulation in life all the more tolerable. Enjoyable, in fact.

All that other stuff, well, that was long ago. . . .

"Mr. Haddad." The receptionist brought back the envelope he'd been expecting, delivered by messenger.

Cy looked it over. It pleased him to see the Raab Brothers' return address. He knew exactly what was inside.

Not just a contract, but their complete capitulation to the deal.

Cy had even squeezed them by the balls a little harder than he'd had to. Buchalter had told him a year and a half on the Kingston plant. He'd gotten them down to one.

No, now they were about to be like partners.

That *pisher* Raab would never throw him out of his place again.

"Get Mr. Goldman on the phone for me, Suzanne," he called to his secretary. He'd affix his name on it, representing the union, then send it along to his boss. Once it was countersigned and made official, Morris Raab and his brother would as much as be working for him!

He took out the letter and wet his index finger. He picked up the fancy fountain pen one of his clients had given him, the one he used for just such pleasurable occasions.

He flipped straight to the signing page.

A lump knotted in his chest. His stomach turned. The lines for the two signatures he was expecting to see were just a blank.

Not exactly a blank. There *was* something written there, which Haddad let his eyes roll over, feeling the saliva in his mouth turn to acid, partially in rage, and, if he had to admit it—in a place deep inside he thought he had lost touch with—partially in admiration too. And a wave of sadness. Sadness because maybe secretly he still admired men like that. Men like he wished he was. Who he might have been once. But now that was all moot anyway. They weren't going to be around that much longer. They were as good as dead.

Written on the last page, in big bold print where their signatures should have been, were three words, in Yiddish, which Haddad still knew enough of to understand: *Kack zich oys.*

Go shit on yourselves.

Chapter Thirty-Two

For the next several nights, Morris, Sol, and Leo, their warehouse manager, slept at the office on mattresses, guns by their sides. The cage doors to the warehouse were locked shut. They let the workers in each morning at seven thirty and back out at six at night. It was October and the warehouse racks were crammed with newly received inventory. Two-thirds of their year's revenue would be shipped in the next two weeks.

Once or twice each night, a clattering noise would be heard that woke them all with a start and made them spring for their guns. Either a rumble from the hallway outside or the elevator arriving suddenly would send them scrambling to their feet, sweat trickling down their faces, waiting for the doors to open, guns and lead pipes raised.

But it always turned out to be nothing more than the boiler rumbling unexpectedly or Silvio, the building's night caretaker, making his rounds. Then Sol would laugh, the kind of nervous chuckle that comes from a disaster averted, blowing a relieved blast of air from his cheeks, or Leo would pat his heart as it regained its normal rhythm.

"I'm not exactly cut out for this kind of work," Sol would say, holding the Smith &Wesson Morris had shown him how to use.

"Don't worry, when the time comes, you will be," Morris said, "when there's something to protect. I'm just sorry to drag you into this."

Sol, who had never stopped going to shul regularly and who read the Torah every day, would simply smile at Morris. "You know, the Pirkei Avot tells us it is not our responsibility to finish the work of perfecting the world, but we are not free to desist from it either. You'd know that, if you ever went back to shul."

"Yeah, well, thanks for not desisting," Morris would say back, laying his gun down and climbing back on the mattress. "When they come."

But they didn't come. Not just yet. The attack against them they were all preparing for never materialized. There was no reply from Cy Haddad. Or Buchalter. According to all the newspapers, Buchalter had far deeper problems to worry about. The special commission under Thomas Dewey was coming down hard on him and his crony, Dutch Schultz. The gangsters' various headquarters were being raided by Federal agents and bins of records seized. The Feds were now able to tap into phone lines, and no one knew who was listening. Mob foot soldiers were being slapped with subpoenas and charges, trying to squeeze them to turn on their bosses. Everyone was looking at their own organization and trying to lie low. Maybe the worst had passed.

At some point, Sol went home for a night, then, when nothing happened, Morris did as well. Harry, who was slowly taking over the role of warehouse manager, took Leo's place. They knew they couldn't keep protecting themselves in this way forever. The outer doors to the warehouse floor were secure—they were iron, heavily reinforced, bolted from the inside. It would take a cannon to get through them. They even hired an off-duty policeman to stand guard at night outside the building. Morris or Sol never failed to take responsibility for locking up for the night, to make sure the gates were secure and the alarm, a loud clanging bell which could be heard a block away, was set.

One night Sol's son was ill and he had to rush home. Morris had promised to go to a trade association dinner; he'd committed to making a short speech about a colleague who was being honored. Harry said he'd lock up the place himself. It was the height of their season and their warehouse was filled to the rafters with new stock to be delivered over the coming weeks. More than half their year's revenue was hanging on those racks. And a good part of that went to pay back their factors, who had extended them operating funds against their orders.

"Go ahead, Morris, don't worry," Harry assured him. "I'll be fine."

"You've got to make sure the outer door is secure." Morris finally relented. "See . . . ?" He rattled the latticed metal window and shook the door to show how it didn't budge. "And double-check the alarm is set."

"Stop worrying." Harry patted Morris on the shoulder. "I've locked up my places a thousand times over the years. I know what has to be done. So go to your meeting. Leo'll be here with me. We're going to get a head start on pulling the L. S. Ayres and Carson's order. We'll be fine."

"Okay. I'll check back after dinner."

Harry said, "You worry too much, Morris. We'll be fine here. Do what you have to do. Go on."

"All right, then," Morris said, putting on his coat and hat. He was unable to feel just right. At the door he looked back and smiled with a wistful shake of his head. "Ayres and Carson's, huh . . . ? There's two names I never thought I'd hear come out of your mouth." He and Sol loved how Harry had taken to his new responsibilities. "I'm at the Lambs Club, if there's any problems. Just pick up the phone and call."

"Enjoy your evening, Morris." Harry waved him out.

For the next two hours, Harry, Leo, and a couple of warehouse workers who had stayed on pulled the two large orders for shipment and transferred them to the front racks, where they would be packed up in boxes in the morning. Anyone could see Harry had taken to the work and taken even stronger to the connection of working side by side with his brothers. He knew he might not have been blessed with the sharpest mind in the world or the most ambition. But what he did have now was a place in life. For the first time he felt he was actually building something, not just dallying around without purpose, without a plan. He knew he had a long way to go before he was ready to be trusted to actually run something, but the trust they had showed in him thus far, even letting him stay that night with all that was going on, was worth the thousand drinks he'd been bought at Mendy's establishments or the hundred-dollar bills stuffed in his breast pocket by his old cronies.

When they were finished, Leo said, "That's it, Mr. Raab. Okay, for me and Tommy to leave?"

"Sure. Go ahead. Take off," Harry said. "I'm just gonna count it and make double sure it matches up to the picking tickets one more time."

"You're sure? Mr. Morris would be okay?"

"Don't you worry, boys. Enjoy your night." Harry waved them off.

"See you tomorrow then, Mr. H."

Harry liked it when they called him that. The warehouse men left and Harry took the picking tickets and started double-checking the shipment at the front rack. L. S. Ayres. Indianapolis, Indiana. Store 1. Style 2510. In navy. The sizes ranged from small to extra-large: 1-1-2-1.

It all matched up perfectly.

He went on to style 2521. Size range, the same. He counted one by one. It checked as well.

He proceeded to Store 2. . . .

Suddenly he heard the freight elevator clatter to a stop on his floor. Harry jumped. Everyone in the firm was on pins and needles these days. He had thought about going to see some of his old friends just to ask them to lay off. Just for old times. But things had gone too far with the men upstairs who actually called the shots for him to have any sway. Still, his time with them all had to count for something, right?

But he stood with his brothers now.

He looked out, and to his relief, it was only Silvio, who shuffled out of the elevator in his khaki uniform. He peered through the grating in the gate and saw Harry, the warehouse lights still on, and gave him a wave. "Just checking who's around. I saw the lights outside."

"I'll be staying." Harry waved back at him. "Thanks."

"Okay, then, have a good night. And let me know if you need some coffee. I got some brewing down there."

"I will."

Silvio went back in the elevator and pulled the metal cage door down. It clattered loudly as the doors came together, heading back down to the basement.

Quarter to eight now. Harry went back to checking the count for tomorrow's shipment. It took another twenty minutes. Six hundred and twenty units between the two stores.

When he was satisfied, he shut the cage door to the warehouse and made sure the padlock was locked. Then he went down to the second floor, where the offices and factory floor were located. He thought he'd just run out and grab a quick dinner from the automat on Thirty-fourth Street and take it back up. He'd only

215

be gone a few minutes and there was that off-duty cop they'd hired on guard at the door. They had a roast turkey and mashed potatoes special, Tuesdays, and a honey cake that reminded Harry of the *lekach* his mother made back on Cherry Street.

He was salivating.

He looked at his watch—eight fifteen now—and threw on his coat and hat. Everything was calm and secure. He wished he *could* sneak out tonight, just for a couple of hours. The Furillo-Rosen fight was at the Garden. Lennie Rosen was the middleweight making every Jew proud—18 and 0. Maybe two fights now from the title. Not that he had a ticket or anything, and it would definitely be a packed house. In the old days he would have surely been handed one, likely in the first couple of rows—"Here, Harry, enjoy the fight"—just for picking up the tab of one of the big shots at The Green Parrot.

But not now.

He took his key and went up front to make sure the alarm was set and to double-check the outside door, just like Morris had told him.

He'd only be gone a minute.

As he flicked off the lights, the phone rang. One ring, then two. For a second Harry thought about not picking up. Then he thought it was probably Morris, or Sol, checking in on him. He had to show them he could handle things without them peering over his shoulder. But if he didn't answer they'd only be nervous. Hell, knowing them, they'd probably still be nervous after he'd been there twenty years.

He went to the phone at the front desk and picked up. He was actually glad they would hear his voice here, taking care of things. "Raab Brothers . . . ," he answered, expecting to hear one of them.

But it wasn't.

"Hey, Harry, glad I caught you," the familiar voice said. "It's been a while."

It made his heart come to a stop, a torrent cascading back over him, a torrent of the past, a dark part of him he thought he'd put aside.

"Hey, Mendy . . ."

Chapter Thirty-Three

I knew from the start I should've gone back and checked on him.

At eight thirty, the dinner over, I toyed with the thought of going back. Making sure Harry had done what I'd told him.

But at some point, another voice said I had to learn to trust him. Give him some room; he was doing a good job. That's what Sol told me I had to do. Harry was working hard, handling the warehouse and the receiving department just fine. Like he'd been there from the start. Even Leo seemed to have taken to him. And it seemed he had broken off with his old friends. At least he hadn't mentioned them in months.

He was a Raab brother now. Which made me happy. So let him act like one, I reasoned. Besides, we'd stationed a guard at the front entrance. An off-duty cop who'd been vouched for by Irv. He seemed like a stand-up guy. And I hadn't seen Sammy for days now. Besides, Ruthie would love that I'd snuck home unexpectedly. We hadn't had an hour for each other in a week.

She'd love it even more that it was Harry who was holding down the fort.

So instead I hailed a cab. "Ninety-third and West End," I said to the driver.

Chapter Thirty-Four

Officer John McGuire braced himself against the chill. It was one of those raw October nights that felt more like the dead of winter, the wind whipping off the Hudson. He'd been in the department for three years now, married to his sweetheart for the past two, with a little one on the way. And had a record that was clean as a whistle. He'd never had as much as a dollar bill put in his hand to look the other way. So when the sarge said some people were looking for after-hours help and pretty much just to stand around, McGuire was quick to raise his hand. Three nights a week. Ten bucks a shift. And it was only for a week or two, he told his wife, Sarah. Who couldn't use a little extra cash?

The homeless guy who shared the stoop was huddled in a threadbare coat, muttering to himself. It was after eight, and everyone had gone home. He'd waved good-bye to the last of the Raab Brothers employees about an hour ago. He'd told John he'd be back to check on things in a couple of hours.

But standing there, virtually alone on the darkened street, the wind knifing through his bones and only the occasional cab going by, McGuire decided it wasn't worth it, no matter how much it paid. Spending eight hours in the cold. Away from his wife. After a long shift of his own. Catching a couple of hours' sleep before his next one. He'd fill out the week, what he said he'd cover. Then he was done. He put his hands in his pockets and bobbed up and down on his toes. Must be forty tonight. He checked his watch—six hours to go—then watched as a dark sedan slowly inched its way down the street.

You hear that, Sarah. Don't be mad at me. Come Friday, done.

McGuire kept an eye on the car, figuring it would head on to the light on Sixth, but it stopped, virtually in front of his building, and he stood there, watching it for a minute, wondering if the driver was lost or something. The windows were dark; it was hard to see inside. What did they want here? There were no businesses open other than the Irish bar across the street, where McGuire wished he could be right now, with a hot Irish coffee. Then—

The front passenger's door opened. A man in a gray coat and hat pulled down over his eyes stepped out.

He had his hands in his pockets and came up to him slowly, as if he was about to ask him directions. He seemed to check both ways down the street, then, satisfied, looked up at McGuire. What he said sent a tremor down his spine.

"You're an off-duty cop, right?"

McGuire wasn't sure how to answer. He put a hand inside his peacoat, searching for the handle of his gun. "Who the hell are you?"

"Doesn't matter. I'm just someone passing the time of day. What's your name, son?"

"Why don't you be smart and just move on?"

"No matter. I already know your name. It's McGuire, right? Officer John McGuire."

McGuire's eye roamed to the car's rear passenger window, rolling down.

He took a firm grip on his gun.

The man in the coat and hat stepped closer. McGuire had been told what he might expect, but he also knew that the last thing Lepke or anyone in that kind of business wanted was to take down a cop.

"So here's how it's gonna go, Johnnie." The man took his hand out of his coat. "I can hand you this envelope, which contains two thousand dollars, and you can go take a leak in that bar across the street. A nice, long one. Say twenty minutes. Or I can nod to my friend in the car back there and he can put about a dozen holes in your chest in the next ten seconds."

The dark muzzle of a gun appeared in the window, a machine gun.

McGuire sucked in a breath.

"So that's the choice, Johnnie-boy. What do you think? Seems like an easy one to me. Take a twenty-minute leak with two grand in your pocket that no one will ever know about. That's what, at your level on the force, Johnnie, close to six months' pay? Or, make your little lady a widow. But you gotta make it now, son." The man took another step and held the envelope out to him. "You choose."

Even in the brisk night air, a stream of cold sweat poured down McGuire's neck. His dad was a cop and his dad before him had been one. He'd never taken as much as a dime, swore he never would. And he didn't want to start now.

"Time's a-ticking, Johnnie." The man glanced behind and McGuire saw the dark barrel protrude from the rear window and heard the bolt of the machine gun click. "We can't stand out here in the cold all night."

"Gimme the cash." McGuire nodded anxiously.

"Wise choice, Johnnie-boy." The man grinned, and put the envelope into the young cop's sweaty hand. "Relax, Officer, your job's done for the night. Now take a hike. And remember, you have any sudden regrets about this—and you never know when that sort of information comes our way—you and that pretty wife of yours will be lying beside each other at Coleman's Funeral Hall on Dicker Avenue, instead of having that baby. Understand?"

McGuire swallowed and nodded. "I understand."

"Now go take that leak like I said and come back in say, twenty minutes, okay . . . ?"

The young cop stuffed the envelope in his coat pocket. Without even glancing at the car or its license plates, he hurried across the street.

Chapter Thirty-Five

The phone was ringing.

Morris clawed out of sleep and reached across to the night table to pick it up. At twenty past twelve in the morning, whatever it was couldn't be good news.

"Morris, it's me," his brother Sol said. Sol's home number was listed as the first to call in the case of an emergency at the office.

Morris was alert in seconds. "What's happened?"

"Bad news. They torched the warehouse, Morris. The fire department is there now. I called Harry. He's blithering like an idiot, going over and over that he locked up properly; that when he left everything was fine."

"Left . . . ?"

"Morris, listen, everything there, it's all up in flames. I don't know how much is salvageable. The fire department's putting it out now."

"Sol, we have over half a year's inventory in that warehouse," Morris said. The racks were jammed to the rafters.

He heard Sol blow out a sobering breath. "Yeah."

"I'll be there in twenty minutes." Morris hung up, staring blankly, Ruthie sitting up now. The consequences, what this all meant, came crystal clear to him. September and October, everything they had was in that warehouse. Every bit of cash. Every note to their factors. Every IOU. Tied up in finished stock.

Harry left?

Ruthie looked over, seeing Morris's expression. "Morris, tell me."

"It's our warehouse." He swallowed, the taste bitter and warm. "Someone torched it. Everything's up in flames."

"Oh, Morris." She grasped his arm.

He jumped out of bed and grabbed his slacks, which were hanging over a chair. "I've got to get over there, Ruthie."

It took him a little over twenty minutes, having a little trouble hailing a cab at that time of night. The sight of flames leaping out of their fourth-floor window made his stomach turn, and he felt as helpless and empty as he'd ever felt in his life.

Sol was in front of the building, looking up, his hands in his pockets. "We're ruined, Morris."

At 2:30 A.M., when the fire department had finally extinguished the blaze, they walked around the smoking third-floor warehouse area, inspecting the damage.

He didn't need some fancy accountant to tell him how things stood. This was their biggest season in business to date, and most of what they'd hoped to ship in the next forty-five days was hanging on those racks, now either charred or drenched, but in either result, not worth the hangers they were hanging on. Whatever wasn't up in flames, the soot and heavy smoke had ruined them just the same.

"We've got insurance," Morris said to Sol.

"It might cover the property damage," Sol nodded, "and rebuild the offices. But all the inventory, where all our cash was, and all our orders to be filled—it'll only cover a fraction of what that was worth."

Even with their success, they were a small company and everything was still run hand to mouth. The kinds of handwritten ledgers they kept gave no idea of the true cost of each garment, exactly how much fabric they had in inventory, all the money sunk into fur collars and trim.

But it was even deeper than that. Morris saw it in the sobering resignation stamped on his brother's face as he scanned what remained of their business. The real loss was all the orders that would not be filled. Orders they had borrowed against with their lenders. Inventory they couldn't properly account for. The work staff, who they wouldn't be able to pay. Debts that would surely be called in.

"Is there any way we're not finished?" Morris said.

For the first time he could ever remember, he didn't see lightbulbs of reason trying to make sense of things in his brother's eyes. Instead they were dim, smoldering, barely flickering. Beaten. And Morris thought he saw something else in them.

They were tired. Tired of the constant climb. Tired of fighting.

"There's no way," Sol said, rubbing his face. "You know how it works better than me. Our factors have advanced our working capital against our orders. Now we can't fill them. They're going to be calling in that money, Morris."

"I can call in favors too. If we can get the goods, we can turn around production pretty quick."

"A fraction, maybe. And even if we *were* able to remanufacture a share of it, we'd miss our shipping windows. You know as well as I do, the stores will go out and fill them from someone else. You think we're the only company making fur-trimmed coats? But it's worse than that, Morris. Our whole payroll was wrapped up in that stock." He looked over the rows and rows of singed, dripping coats. "You have any money in the bank?"

Morris nodded. "Some."

"Me too. I guess we could put that up against what we owe. The factors might take it and settle. That might keep us in business. We'd be broke. We'd be a shadow of what we were. And who's going to keep the plant in Kingston going? They rely on us. It might be best to go into receivership. Our factors may advance us something, against our reputation, to recoup their debt."

"Receivership?"

"It's the coat business, Morris. You miss your shipping window, your stock's worth sixty cents on the dollar the next day. A month from now, half. That stock was our company's blood, Morris. Raab Brothers was just the name on the door. Everything we had was wrapped up in it."

Their whole dream was crashing down on them in those smoldering embers; it might as well have been their building that had collapsed. Or one of them harmed. "It's my fault," Morris said. He drew in a deep breath and gravely shook his head. "I pushed them too far."

"Maybe we did." Morris's older brother looked at him and put a hand on his shoulder. "There'll be time for all that later. Truth is . . ." he forced a thin smile, "we're likely no worse off than if we had signed that union contract in the first place. Only we got here quicker. And we can't take a dime out."

Morris looked over at Harry, sitting at his desk with his head in his hands, ashen. "We were fools to trust him, Sollie."

"Go easy on him, Morris. The guy's a mess."

"Go easy on him? He was supposed to stay here."

"He's our brother, Morris. He realizes he screwed up."

The fire lieutenant whose team had fought the blaze came over, and a police captain, named Burns. "I'm Lieutenant Cade," the fireman, in a dark blue uniform and a white cap, said. He put out his hand.

"Thanks for what you could do," Morris said.

"A real shame . . ." The captain took off his cap and ran a hand through his white hair. "My sympathies. I've seen this kind of thing before."

"Seen what?" Morris looked at him, detecting a tone of falseness in the man's sympathy.

"You see that boiler over there. . . ." Each floor had a steam boiler of its own that produced forced heat in the winter. "You can see how it just blew. Look at that valve. The fire, you can see how it just swallowed up those bolts of fabric over there and made a beeline for the warehouse."

"That fabric wasn't there earlier," Morris said. Cotton, wool—anything that would go up fast. He pointed to a material storage area. "We keep it over there."

"That I can't contest," the fireman said. "I can only account for what I see. You can see the damage it did for yourself."

"You're saying this was an accident?" Morris looked at him angrily. "I can smell the gasoline they poured on them. Those clothes were doused in it."

"Gasoline, you're saying?" The lieutenant sniffed in twice. "I'm not as sure. You smell it, Captain?" He turned to the police investigator. Burns shrugged. "No, I'm afraid it's a boiler explosion in my book. That's how I have to put it down. You think people came in here to do harm? I don't see any sign of forced entry. Anyway, the door to the warehouse area wasn't even ajar. The lieutenant here talked to the guard you had stationed outside."

"Fine boy, McGuire," the police captain said. "I knew his father on the force. We also spoke to the building's caretaker. Both of them claim they saw no one going in or out. Unless it was someone on the inside, if that's what you're alleging? You might want to take a look at your own staff. Most times, that's what it breaks down to be. No, I have to agree with Lieutenant Cade here. A boiler mishap, that's my read. Common today. We're lucky the whole building didn't go up."

The two men looked at Morris, flatly, as if Morris wasn't seeing something that they saw clearly. They were probably both in Buchalter's palm. Morris saw it in the fireman's phony sympathetic and fixed blue eyes. Sure, he'd seen this many times before. He'd likely been paid off on each one to write it up as an accident of some kind.

Cade shrugged. "You can appeal any findings, of course. Feel free to bring in your own experts. Anything we do here is merely preliminary. But what will it get you? A lot of red tape is all, I'm afraid."

"You realize that what you're alleging may well put us out of business?" Sol said accusingly.

"Well, it'll just drag it on at a big cost. But it's something you must decide. Do you agree, Captain Burns?"

"I'm afraid so." The police captain shrugged. "That's the way it is with city hall."

The fire lieutenant walked away, instructing his crew to wrap things up.

Morris said to Sol, "You spoke to that guard we hired?"

"He says he went across the street to the bar just to take a leak and when he came back he spotted smoke upstairs. It was him who called it in."

"And he didn't see anyone go in or out?"

"You're free to talk with him if you like."

"He's lying, Sol. Or they got to him too. Just like these guys. And what about Silvio?" The night caretaker.

"In his office in the basement, the whole time."

Morris looked at him, anger coursing through his veins. "You know this is a fucking setup, don't you?"

"I know it is, Morris. But it is what it is."

Their gazes drifted over to Harry.

Morris said, "It was his responsibility to make sure the place was secure. I went over it with him, step by step. No one heard the alarm, the doors were not broken through, so whoever did this, they either had a key or they were let in. Take your pick. Either way, you know he's involved, Sol."

Their brother was leaning on his elbows at his desk, his face damp with sweat, his head in his hands.

He stood up nervously when they came over to him. "It was locked, Morris, when I left. I swear. And I only was going to run out and get a bite. I double-checked the doors myself, just like you said. On my life. You said to set the alarm and I did. I don't know how this happened."

"Sol said he called you later and you weren't here."

Harry grew pale, fidgeting. "All right, I left at eight fifteen after picking the Ayres order. You know I wouldn't let you down."

"You left for where?"

Harry pressed his lips together and ran a hand through his slicked black hair. "I don't know, Morris. Just out."

"Out, Harry . . . ?" Morris continued to press. "Out, where?" You didn't have to be a police detective to see that he was keeping something to himself.

"I locked the doors. I put on the alarm. There was a guard outside. The place was buttoned up."

"*Where,* Harry? You were supposed to be here. Sol said he tried to reach you earlier. Where were you?"

Harry swallowed and finally let out a breath. "All right, I went to the fights. At the Garden."

"*The fights?* I left you at six o'clock. You never mentioned going to the fights. You were going to pull the L. S. Ayres order, that's all. Where'd you suddenly get tickets?"

"What does it really matter how I got tickets? Someone called."

"*Who*, Harry? Who called? Who were you at the fights with?"

"Look, I know I screwed up, Morris. I realize that. But I didn't let anyone in. I swear. And I locked the door, like you said. I give you my word."

"Your word. Look around the place, Harry—your word isn't carrying a lot of weight with me right now. I want to know who called you. Who were you at the fights with?"

"All right. But it's not what it seems," Harry said, starting to perspire. "I was with Mendy. He called, just as I was getting ready to run out and grab something to eat. He asked if I wanted to join him at the Garden. He had ringside tickets, Morris, and it was that fighter we like, Lennie Cohen. Everything seemed safe. I just couldn't pass it up."

"What time did you try to reach him, Sol?" Morris looked at Harry accusingly.

"All right, all right . . . Afterwards, we might have had a beer or two. Just to hash around old times. Nothing more, I swear. I haven't even seen him since I came to work here, honest to God. But you have to believe me, I didn't let him in, Morris. I locked up like you said. I swear it on little Sammy, Morris, you know I love that kid and wouldn't—"

"Don't you use my son to try and get out of what you did." Morris grabbed him by the collar.

Sol pulled them apart, cautioning, "Morris . . ."

Harry was stammering now, his nerves taking over, his eyes flitting between Harry and Sol. "I only meant it's 'cause I love him, Morris. Tell him, Sol. So you know I would never wish him harm."

"I know you love him, Harry." Sol shrugged. "But I'm sorry, I can't help you here."

"I told you you had to make a choice," Morris said, his voice carrying across the floor. A few of the firefighters, mopping up, turned around. "This was our business, Harry. Our business. That we built up from nothing with the dirt under our fingers. While you danced around with a bunch of bootleggers and killers . . ."

"I know it's your business, Morris. And I wouldn't do anything to hurt it." Tears flashed in his eyes.

Morris jabbed a finger in his chest. "Someone let them in, Harry. They didn't break in, they walked in. Who? Someone opened the door and said, *Here, make yourself at home. Here's the boiler. Burn the fucking place down. While you're at it, move those bolts of fabric over there to accelerate the flames.* And you just happened to be with Mendy Weiss when it was all going down."

Sol put a hand on Morris's shoulder. "Morris."

"You're a snake, Harry." Morris let him fall back against the desk. "You've got no backbone. I'm sorry about what happened to you as a boy. With Shemuel. I know it's haunted you your whole life. But you're your own person now. And this is on you. You're empty to me now. You're not part of us here anymore, whatever's left. Pick up your things and get out. And that goes for our home too. I don't want you there on Sundays. I don't want to see you with my son."

"Morris," Harry said, pleading. "I love that kid. And he loves me."

"I don't want to even hear your fucking name again if I can help it. You're dead to me from now on, Harry. You understand?"

Tears welled up in Harry's eyes. He tried to stammer back some kind of response, but in the end all he could do was nod, accepting it like he always knew it would come to this in the end, and shrug his shoulders with resignation. "Yeah, I got it, Morris. I do."

"Give me your key."

Harry let out a breath and looked to Sol.

"Harry, give me the fucking key," Morris said, "or so help me God, I'll put my fist down your throat and tear it out of you."

Harry nodded and dug into his pocket and pulled out a key ring, unscrewed the one he was looking for, and pulled off the key that went to the Raab Brothers back door.

He put it on the desk.

"I'm telling you, Morris, whether you want to believe me or not, I don't know how they got in. Okay, maybe they did sucker me out. But when I left, the place was locked up, tight as a drum. You can hold it against me all you want, for the rest of my life if you have to, but it wasn't me that let them in."

"Sure, Harry." Morris turned away as Harry grabbed his jacket and went through the iron gate. He stood there, took one look back with a resigned exhalation, and went down the stairs.

Sol picked up the key and put it in his pocket. "He's our brother, Morris."

"Not anymore."

Sol sucked in a breath and looked at his brother with sad, beaten eyes. "You're going to need to make a police statement," he said. "Harry might have to testify as well."

It took a second for what Sol had said to sink in. "What do you mean, *me* . . . ?"

"*You,* Morris." Sol looked at him rsignedly and shook his head. "I'm done too."

"What do you mean you're done?"

"Just what I said. Whatever happens now, I think I've been done for some time."

"Sol, come on . . . ," Morris said. He felt his insides sink like a weight. "We can rebuild. I'm not going to let this totally sink us."

"I'm just not a fighter, Morris. Not like you. You rebuild. Me, we both know I was never really cut out for this work from the start." He put a hand on Morris's shoulder. "I'm done, Morris. I'll help you through whatever settlements there are. Then I'm out."

Sol shuffled away, and Morris stood there gazing at the smoking, soaked warehouse, their dreams gone up with it. Sol had been with him since the very first order they'd received.

Morris peered out the iron-gated door after Harry.

He was gone and the door closed.

Morris heard the rattle as the door shut tightly and Sol headed down the stairs. Raab Brothers, which a day ago contained dreams enough for all of them, had lost two partners that night.

Chapter Thirty-Six

So I started out all over again, this time on my own. Our inventory wasn't worth a dime. Our unshipped orders were canceled. Our factors called in all our debt. I had nothing to offer them, nothing but my word.

Which in the end did turn out to be worth something.

We had to shut down Raab Brothers, of course, and the plant up in Kingston. We let a hundred workers go, including the handful of Manny Gutman's sewers we had taken on. All of which broke my heart. In a night we had gone from a company on its way up to one in shambles. With as many people with claims against us as we had customers. But I struck a deal with my factors. I promised them I'd pay them back a hundred cents on the dollar for every dollar we owed if they staked me in a new venture going forward. I didn't want to be in the coat business any longer. It was primarily one season and it was always a challenge to keep the manufacturing operation busy and the cash flow steady over a full year. For a while, I'd been thinking about maybe getting into the dress business. The '20s had ushered in new styles of shorter, more stylish dresses, and that's what women seemed to want these days. And the dress business had three seasons—spring, summer, fall—not just one, and therefore a constant flow of orders I could borrow against. So after Sol and I disposed of what was left, he went on to something else and I started from scratch again. I used the same philosophy as we had with Raab Brothers, knocking off the fancy styles I saw in all the department store windows and manufacturing them at a more affordable price. Many of my friends gave me a shot. Instead of taking pleasure at our misfortune, they all pitched in to help me back up. I guess they secretly liked the way I'd stood up to Lepke and the union, even though it had left me close to broke. The factors loaned me. The fabric people advanced me piece goods. Even the stores came through for me, an order at a time.

Those first signs of support meant as much to me as when Muriel Mossman gave me my first orders all those years ago.

It was a tough time for the family though. Sol and I remained close. He helped me close up Raab Brothers, but there was almost nothing to parcel out, as the factors came in and gobbled up everything worth anything that they could put their hands on. After a while Sol took a new job—a safe and steady one, like he always said he wanted—as the manager of a printing company. He joked, "Can't exactly be over the hill at thirty-eight, can I?" He even got some catalog work in the garment trade.

Harry, I wasn't sure how or what he was doing then. Truth was, I didn't care. He made his choice: He had sold us out. Once, I thought I saw him across West End Avenue as I was on my way to work. Our eyes met for a second, and I was sure he was about to cross the street and come over to me. But he only took a step and stopped. And I just got into my car and drove off. I looked at him in the rearview mirror as I drove away. He looked like a man trying to cross a wide stream who didn't know what his next step should be. There was no room in my heart to forgive him. Sunday afternoons at the apartment were different in those days. Sol and his family came up less. Our son missed his uncle Harry and we told him that sometimes families just got into fights, though I know Ruthie took him out to meet Harry more than once when I wasn't around. I didn't care how Harry got by. My mother was angry at me for dividing the family. "It's always your pride," she said. "You always need to prove you're the big man, so be one, Morris." "I can't," I said. I told her he'd made his choice. "I'm not talking about his choice." She looked me in the eyes. "I'm talking about you, Morris. And this Buchalter person. You brought it on." I heard Harry and Mom saw each other once in a while as well, when I wasn't around.

Starting over, money was tight again for us. All of the flashy cars and fancy nights out were now a thing of the past. I had to pay the rent out of what money I'd been able to put away, and while I had some, it wouldn't last forever.

1935. That year, we had another child. A girl. We named her Lucy. Lucy Frieda Raab, after Ruthie's favorite aunt, so I named the new dress firm after her: Lucy Fredericks.

It had a bit of a ring to it, no?

Those days, the union left me alone. Why not? They'd already broken me. I was small potatoes now. Who cared if I was starting over on my own at a tenth the size? And anyway, they had their own issues to deal with. Dewey's task force, which was finally gaining steam, was all over them like glue to paper.

The task force was all over Dutch Schultz too, closing down his restaurant-protection racket, threatening his lucrative numbers business, trying him on charges of tax evasion, not once, but twice. After his second trial, it was like Dewey had a personal vendetta against the man. Every paper in the country carried the headline. NOTORIOUS MOBSTER DUTCH SHULTZ, ACQUITTED. And a picture of him, surrounded by the poor, local fools he had bought off who had eagerly set him free.

Still, his luck couldn't last much longer. The government had it in for him. He couldn't make a call without fear of it being wiretapped. People in his organization began to face their own indictments and turned on him. And Lepke . . . He was next on Dewey's list. They were nabbing lower-level henchmen and trying to turn them against their bosses. But unlike with Schultz, every time they got close to Buchalter, he always seemed to be one step ahead. He always knew how to reach a turncoat informant before he made it to testify at trial. Like he knew what was coming. Mobsters were scared then, trying to stay out of the headlines. And I was only a tiny pisher now. Not worth their time. I took a small space in a building on Thirty-sixth Street. All I started with was a sample room with a pattern maker and three sewers from my old firm. What we sold, we shipped right out of the back room. It was a whole different game now. There were three seasons a year so everything moved quickly. I began to pull myself off the ground. We contracted out all of our production. I didn't take out a dime, until I finally paid every factor back a hundred cents on the dollar on what I owed them.

But for every person in the coat business, there were a hundred in the rag trade. A lot more competition. I didn't know if I could make a go of it or not. For a while, it was order to order.

Then one day I got a call from Abe Zincas, the buyer at Interstate stores. "Style 8102. Color navy, Morris. Got any around?"

"8102?" I didn't even know the style by number. It wasn't one of our better sellers. I had to look at the sketch. It was a little nautical number, with a navy-and-white-trim bib in front. I said, "Let me look at the stock sheet. Why?"

"Because it's sold twelve out of twelve in the first week. You got a clicker, baby!" A clicker was something you couldn't keep in stock. "I'd take a hundred if you had 'em in stock."

Three weeks later I had his hundred. And a thousand more ready to ship. The manufacturers had to hold them. I didn't even have a warehouse to put them in.

8102.
After that, I was a dress man forever.
It brought me back to life.
But it also brought the hammer of the union back down on me.

Chapter Thirty-Seven

"I wish you had called me, Morris." Irv sat next to Morris at the bar at 21 Club, eight months after he'd been in his new business. It had been a long time since they'd spoken. "I heard you had some trouble. I tried to reach out to you. Maybe I could have helped. But you never returned my calls."

"They were troubles of my own making," Morris said. "Things I thought I could handle myself. I just got in over my head. I didn't want to put you in the middle."

Truth was, Morris knew, the last thing Buchalter needed to hear was that Morris had run to the Feds. He would have put him out for good.

Irv stirred his rye and soda. "A suspicious warehouse fire. A bogus fire department report. A cop standing outside who didn't see anyone going in. I'm not sure I'd say those were entirely of *your* own making, Morris." Irv looked back at him. "And I get why you didn't want to get me involved."

Morris's old friend had kept much of the baby fat he'd had as a kid. Now, he had dark, wavy hair and wire-rimmed glasses, and eyes that reflected some of the gravity and rough edges that came with taking on the kind of people he was trying to put away.

Morris asked, "How'd you know about all that, anyway?"

"It's my job to know about all that. And I might have been able to help you, if you were serious about going after the people who did it."

"If I were serious . . ." Morris sniffed amusedly. "I'll call that a joke. Anyway, I know who did it, Irv."

"I mean serious about finally putting them away, Morris. For good. We're not the New York City Fire Department. We don't have our hand in someone's pocket. You read the papers. You see we're making progress now. Dutch Schultz—I know we've been close to shutting him down twice, but the next time he steps across the river into New York, he's ours. We're shutting his lucrative numbers racket down. And your friend Buchalter . . . he's up next on the dance card. One or two people in your business have even begun talking to us."

"They have, huh? And what's happened to them?"

One of them had taken an unexplained fall out of a hotel window in the place they were being protected in. "A canary can sing," Lepke was said to have remarked, "but they sure can't fly." The other, part of the fur dressers union, recanted everything before trial when the front windows of his home on Long Island were riddled with bullets.

"Look, I've just started up again, Irv." Morris sipped his scotch. "I promised Ruthie, I'm gonna do things differently this time. We've got two kids now. . . ."

"And I heard they're beautiful." Irv grinned. "I guess they must take after Ruthie." Morris smiled too. "Still, that doesn't sound like the Morris Raab I knew."

"Is that why you asked me here, Irv? You want me to show you a picture of the kids?"

"No." Irv finished his drink. "That's not why at all. You want to know why?" He stood up and tossed a few bills on the bar. "C'mon, walk with me."

"Where are we going?"

"Just walk." He nudged his way through the bar crowd to the back of the restaurant. Morris took a last sip of his drink and went after him.

Near the rear, where carvings of jockeys and paintings of racehorses adorned the wood-paneled walls, they came to a spot near the kitchen, red-vested waiters and busboys hurrying by. A brass door handle protruded from the wall. Otherwise, Morris wouldn't have even known there was a door there. Irv twisted it open and motioned Morris inside.

The room was small and dimly lit, hidden from the public. It was clearly a holdover from the restaurant's speakeasy days. The only furniture was a table that could seat around eight.

But there was only one man sitting at it. Legs crossed, jet-black hair slicked back, mustached, in a gray pinstripe suit.

"Mr. Raab . . ." The man stood up, extending his hand. "I'm Thomas Dewey."

The special prosecutor's face was one of the best known in the city in those days. The sharp cheekbones; the dark mustache; dark eyebrows; the obsidian, narrow slits for eyes. He was the one public figure with the integrity and backbone to stand up against the mob, and along with Eliot Ness in Chicago, one of the most admired lawmen in the land.

Morris had met a lot of famous people in his time—politicians, athletes, gangsters—but he was proud to shake this one's hand.

Dewey motioned to the table. "Please have a seat."

Irv pulled out a chair in between them, leaving Dewey and Morris face-to-face.

"What's your drink, Mr. Raab?" the special prosecutor inquired. He raised a finger and a red-vested waiter came in.

"Scotch."

"Mine as well. Macallan Twelve, all right with you? I keep a bottle here." When Morris said that it was, Dewey looked at Irv to see if he would have the same and then the waiter ran off to fulfill their orders.

"Sorry for all the secrecy, Mr. Raab," the special prosecutor said. "These days, if we met in public, there'd be a team of photographers flashing their bulbs before you even took a sip, and both our faces would be on the morning edition of every paper in the city. I can't imagine that association would work to your benefit either."

"No, it wouldn't," Morris said. He looked around. "Your private room?"

"The city's. I just use it for occasions."

Their drinks arrived and Dewey lifted his glass. "To the public order. And to whatever it takes to get it restored."

"L'chaim," Morris said, lifting his glass, unsure if he should feel honored at the invitation or angry at Irv for setting him up.

"To life, yes," Dewey said. "To life well lived."

The three of them took a sip. "The reason we asked you here, Mr. Raab, with all this subterfuge, is to try and interest you in a bit of a bargain. Counselor Wechsler here says you're a man who's not afraid to consider one. You're well aware of what we're doing . . . ?"

Morris nodded that he was. "You'd have to have your head in the sand not to be."

"We're going to systematically rid this city of the criminal vultures who have drawn their sustenance from it for the past twenty years. As you may know, we've got Arthur Flegenheimer, known to most as Dutch Schultz, under our thumb right now. He may have gotten off that trial, but he can't even venture back into the city where all of his business is located without being picked up. The mayor's got an open warrant against him if he as much as sets his foot back here."

"Word is, he bribed a whole town to get out of it the last time," Morris said.

"That may well be true," Dewey conceded. He took a sip of scotch. "But I've got sixty prosecutors, tax experts, and forensic investigators who promise me it won't happen again if we do nab him. Are you a betting man, Mr. Raab?"

"I've been known."

"Well, I'd bet on my side the next time around. And after Schultz, we're on to the rest of them. Luciano. Anastasia. And then Lepke and his pal Shapiro, in the garment trade. Which Assistant Prosecutor Weschler here tells me you have some firsthand familiarity with, and which is what brings you here."

Morris said, "I came here to have a drink with an old pal, that's all. Irv may have told you I don't snitch on people and I can handle my own matters in life."

"He did. He did say that. He said you were a very stubborn fish to reel in. But I wonder, Mr. Raab," the prosecutor looked at him, "just how is all that stubbornness and independence going for you these days?"

"I'm not sure I understand what you mean?"

Dewey put down his drink. "I heard you had built up a big business, Mr. Raab, until a handful of months ago, and that you were one of the very few garment company entrepreneurs who stood up to Mr. Lepke and Mr. Shapiro and refused to buckle under to the unions."

"I suppose that's true."

"And for all your steadfastness and moral compass, you were threatened in a variety of ways, including the attempted hijacking

243

of one of your delivery trucks, where you were forced to defend your property yourself, and, in further retaliation, your warehouse filled with goods was set afire, which resulted in your business shutting down. Do I have that right? I commend you for that stubbornness, Mr. Raab, and determination, but I'm afraid such steadfastness will not be victorious on its own. What I'm offering is the power of the strongest law enforcement team ever assembled in this state to help you rid us of these vermin for good."

"I'm just a garment, guy, Mr. Dewey." Morris shrugged and took another sip of his drink. "But in my estimation, what I would tell you is, it won't work."

"What won't work, sir?" Dewey inquired.

"Your big-shot team. Any more than the last one did. Or the one before that."

"It will work, Mr. Raab. This is no charade this time, I assure you."

"It won't, respectfully, as long as your own house is the first one you need to clean up," Morris said firmly. "How do you think Schultz and Lepke have been able to beat your legal team thus far? Twice now."

Dewey stared at Morris. "You didn't strike me as a cynic, sir, but as a man of action."

"The New York City Fire Department signed off on some completely bogus explanation to write our warehouse fire off as a boiler accident. My little son with an Erector Set could have looked at the place and told you the inspector was full of shit. But what isn't full of shit is that Buchalter's got his men there squarely in his palm. Time after time, when people stood up against them, people with some guts, your vaunted New York City Police Department declined to even look into it. I personally know one who lost his life when he was flung out of an eighth-story window and another who had acid thrown in his face, who both tried to stand up to them. You turn state's evidence against Murder, Inc., you know better than any, you usually don't make it to trial."

Dewey nodded. "I'm aware of all these things. Including the tragic circumstances behind the death of your friend Abe Langer. Were I the district attorney, I assure you those crimes would not have gone uninvestigated.

"But I want to assure you, it's not only the Schultzes and the Lepkes we're going after this time around, Mr. Raab. But the corruption and collusion that has ingrained itself in and infected our city agencies as well. From the police to the fire department to the DA's office. We're going to wipe out the contagion, Mr. Raab, from the heart out, as well as those in the carcass who have enabled them. Wherever it falls. I've got a hundred thousand call logs my investigators are painstakingly making their way through, conversation by conversation. These people will have to worry every time they pick up a phone, whether in some candy store in Brooklyn, or in city hall."

Morris sipped his scotch. He looked at his watch. "You said you wanted to talk to me about some kind of bargain."

"We need people who aren't afraid, Morris," Irv stepped into the conversation, "who can testify against the extortionists. Firsthand. We feel, once people stand up, there'll be many others who won't be afraid to follow."

"We're not just going after murders, Mr. Raab. We'll get them where it hurts them most. In the bank account. On restraint of trade. Extortion."

"You know as well as me, Irv," Morris shrugged, "what happens to those who go state's evidence against Murder Incorporated."

"We know," Dewey took over for his aide, "and while we can't offer you anything as an inducement to come forward, other than to do the right thing and help us finally rid this city of them for good, we do know you're trying to rebuild a business for yourself, and there are always various things that come up that may be helpful in that—city contracts, say, uniforms for the mass transit department or the police, big contracts, and enterprise loans. . . ."

"The man who can't be bribed is trying to bribe the rest of us when he needs some help." Morris shot a smile to Dewey.

"Not bribe. We don't look at it that way. We just know you'd be taking a risk, and risks should be rewarded, if they are successful, just like in business, don't you agree?"

"We need your help, Morris," Irv said. "You've faced them down firsthand. People respect you. They'd come on board if you led the way. Right now, everyone's scared. Just give it some thought."

Morris glanced at his watch and said, "We'll see."

"We know you've known Louis Buchalter a long time," the special prosecutor said. "Since before he took the name Lepke. Assistant Prosecutor Weschler says, at times, he's even shown a liking for you."

"He didn't seem to show much of a liking when he burned my business down." Morris smiled cynically.

"Still, maybe he'd trust you enough to in some way implicate himself. If we fed you a kind of narrative. Of entrapment. It's not easy to get close to him, Mr. Raab. Maybe for the good of the city, you'd be willing to wear a wire."

"A wire?" Morris put down his drink and the tightening of his jowl said there was no way he'd agree.

"Dutch Schultz is as good as gone, Mr. Raab," the special prosecutor said. "But this Lepke-Buchalter character . . . He's far more protected. Maybe even from the inside. He's consistently been able to stay a step ahead of us. We need someone who's close."

"I figure you don't speak Yiddish, Mr. Dewey?"

"No, I can't say I do." Dewey smiled.

"Then I'll let Irv translate. *Gey fiefen ahfen yam.*"

Irv looked at Morris and shrugged. Dewey waited. "If I translate it loosely, sir," Irv said, "it means, go peddle your fish somewhere else."

"You've got the wrong man, Mr. Dewey. Irv could have told you that." Morris drained the last of his scotch and got up. "I wish you luck, though. Now, I'm afraid I have two little ones at home, so I'm going to have to say goodnight."

Irv stood up too, but the special prosecutor remained seated. "I appreciate your time, Mr. Raab. But I don't want you to underestimate my determination to get this job done. I know you have two young children and a charming wife. And as you've noted, with reason, it hasn't always fared well for those seen to have cooperated with the government when it comes to these types. . . ." Dewey looked at him. "Not at all . . ."

"I'm not sure I understand just what you're saying, Mr. Dewey?" Morris stared back. He looked the special prosecutor in the eye.

"I'm saying, as clearly as I can, sir, you can work for us, in secret, and help us rid the city of these vermin. Or, we can let the word out in other ways that you're working with us, if you get my drift. And see where the chips fall."

"A man with my lack of experience in the law might take that as just your own Ivy League form of extortion," Morris replied. "What would you say, Irv?"

His friend was silent.

"We just want your cooperation, Mr. Raab," Dewey said. "Any way we can. Now let me tell you what a pleasure it was to have this chance to meet you."

Chapter Thirty-Eight

That fall, no one was feeling the heat of Thomas Dewey's reach more than Dutch Schultz.

By the slimmest of margins, the mobster had successfully escaped conviction on two federal tax evasion charges. Most people, including Schultz himself, knew if he was brought to trial a third time, he would be going away for a long time. New York City Mayor Fiorello La Guardia issued standing orders that if Schultz as much as stepped across the river into the city, where the vast majority of his business was located, he should be arrested on sight and taken into custody.

That October, the crime syndicate commission that had been formed by Albert Anastasia, Joe Bonanno, Lepke associate Jacob Shapiro, and Charlie "Lucky" Luciano met in secret at a restaurant in the Bronx, to figure a way to carve up Schultz's lucrative numbers racket once the gangster was inevitably put away.

Banished to New Jersey, Schultz set up his headquarters at the Hotel St. Francis in downtown Newark, worried that on the other side of the river a power grab had arisen within his own ranks, centered on his once-trusted lieutenant, Bo Weinberg, who was now peddling himself to the commission as someone who could run Schultz's operation. Incensed, the Dutchman called for an emergency meeting and braved the price on his head to attend the secret gathering in Brooklyn.

Schultz cockily assured them he wasn't going anywhere. That in fact, he had already dealt with his rebellious lieutenant who just weeks before had tried to make the case before them that going forward they should deal with him. "He won't be coming around here no more," he chuckled. And indeed Weinberg was never heard from again. Schultz claimed he had a plan that would get the heat permanently off his back. And theirs.

He asked the commission to approve the murder of Thomas Dewey.

Though the Dutchman was known as a man who harbored no reservations about spilling blood, with over 130 murders attributed to him, even the commission members, the most hardened crime bosses in the city, were taken back.

"It'll solve all our problems," Schultz argued. "You don't think when this country hick is done with me, he's not gonna turn his attention to all of you? How are your union rackets going to hold up?" he asked Shapiro. "Or you, Albert . . . ?" He turned to Anastasia. "When he's turning your pimps and hookers into government informers. Every weekend he goes up to his farm in Putnam County. A baby could do it with no problem."

At first, Shapiro and Anastasia, who shared no qualms themselves about killing anyone, voiced their approval. They said the Dutchman was right on one thing: they had to show this ambitious lawman where to draw the line. "In the past, they always knew: they stay on their side of the street, we stay on ours," Shapiro said.

But the rest felt such a plan was far too reckless, and could bring the wrath of the entire legal world upon them. It would turn the deceased federal prosecutor into a martyr. Right now, people liked their gambling and their whores and even their drugs, and the quieter the better.

"This isn't like icing some stupid cop who doesn't get the message," Luciano said. "Dewey is the most visible lawman in the state. In the country. There's talk he may even be next in line for governor. We kill him, the government'll come down on us with a vengeance like we've never seen before."

"If you don't, when he's governor, this guy'll be in your guts like a bad piece of fish," Schultz said. "Best get it done now."

The members told Schultz they'd mull it over and get back to him in a few days. But everyone at the meeting knew the Dutchman would likely go through with it no matter what they said. They figured he was probably already plotting it in secret.

The world was shifting, Luciano, Bonanno, and others, like Meyer Lansky, knew. Once-flamboyant figures like Dillinger and Capone, Baby Face Nelson, and Bonnie and Clyde were all riddled with bullets or living out their days in prison. It was becoming more of a business. Giving the people what they wanted. Gambling. Prostitution. Even drugs if that's what it was. Reckless killers like Schultz were becoming a thing of the past. They just didn't understand how the game was played now.

Not to mention, they all knew the Dutchman had the richest crime racket in the business to carve up if something happened to him.

A day later, Albert Anastasia met with Louis Buchalter again. He told his friend he had another favor to request of him, this one straight from the commission.

They owed Schultz an answer, Anastasia said, and he asked Lepke to deliver it.

It just didn't come back exactly how the Dutchman was expecting.

Chapter Thirty-Nine

Harry was working in one of Mendy's pool halls on Forty-sixth Street off Times Square, a block from the giant flashing Hydrox Ice Cream sign.

It was the only steady work he could get these days. Opening and closing the place, handling the front-of-the-house receipts—the real money came from one of Buchalter's bookies who operated out of the back room. Since his separation from Morris, Harry could barely afford the apartment on East Twenty-eighth Street. He even had to take little "gifts" of twenty to thirty dollars from his mother, just to cover the rent. The mother who for years had barely looked his way and called him a pudding-head and Mr. Upside Down. "Ma, please . . . ," he would beg her, "don't," fighting back shame. But still she would fold a bill she'd saved up and stuff it into his jacket and go, "Just take it. What am I to do with it? It came from your brother anyway." It made Harry feel like a child all over again, but he had no other choice. He put it in his pocket.

He wanted so badly to tell Morris that he hadn't betrayed him. He'd screwed up, sure. Royally. He knew he should never have left that night, even though he'd locked up before he left, just like Morris had instructed him. But both Sol and his mother said that just wasn't going to happen anytime soon. She said, one day the family would heal and come back together. *"Nor Got veyst,"* she would say with a wistful wave about when that time would be. Only God knows.

At four P.M. Harry was polishing the tables for that night's crowd, mostly down-and-outers who lived on the street in the neighborhood and gambled to afford a drink, when Mendy came in.

Harry balled up his cleaning rag, surprised to see him. "Mendy."

"Listen, I have a job if you want it, ace." Mendy invited him over to a corner of the floor where no one was around. "A way to put a little cash in your pockets. I bet you could use that, huh?"

"The last time you said that you and Maxie Dannenberg robbed Sheffler's jewelry store and left me hanging there," Harry said. He knew who Mendy worked for now—he was no longer a petty hoodlum who never hurt anyone. Now he was a known lieutenant for Lepke, the most notorious killer in town. And while Mendy had clearly suckered him out that night, the night of the fire, he always claimed he had nothing to do with what had happened up at Raab Brothers; he'd seemed genuinely sorry to hear about it. Besides, he had given Harry this job.

"Yeah, and how'd that work out for you in the end?" Mendy grinned. "Anyway, you decide. But I'm talking some real cash in your pocket. And all we need is a ride. A real breeze, out in the country to New Jersey. Our regular driver's under the weather. You know how to drive, don't you, chief?"

"I can drive," Harry said. "I used to chauffeur my brother around."

"Well, that's all we're looking for," Mendy said. "And it pays pretty well."

"How well?" Harry asked. He could use a little holdover, of

course. Rent was due and there was this suit at Raleigh's he'd had his eye on.

Mendy shrugged. "I dunno. Say a grand."

It was like a lightning bolt rippled down his vertebrae. A thousand dollars would pay his rent for the next three years. He wouldn't have to keep taking handouts in secret from his mother, which filled him with such shame. But it also meant *something* had to be up for them to pay that much for just a ride.

"What's going on, Mendy? A thousand dollars doesn't just fall in my hands every day."

"Don't you worry about it, ace. You just be here. Around seven. Tonight. We'll be in touch. And if you like, what do you say I give you a down payment, just to whet the appetite, so to speak." He dug into his pocket and came out with a wad of bills, and peeled off three one-hundred-dollar bills and folded them into Harry's palm. He'd never held such an amount at one time—at least, that he could keep.

"Just a ride in the country, you say, that's all?"

"That's all we're talking, chief. It's Jersey. What's even there? And don't you worry, we'll even supply the car."

For that kind of money Harry was well aware something big had to be going on. He was no fool. But working for his brother, doing the nine to five, getting a steady paycheck every week, well, that hadn't worked out so well either. So the hell with it, he thought. He knew he was crossing a line somewhere, one he might not so easily climb back from. *But for a grand!* He looked at the three Ben Franklins. "Okay, Mendy." Harry stuffed the cash in his pocket. "I'll be here."

A little past seven, Harry's nerves were getting the best of him, and he was almost wishing whatever it was he had agreed to would turn out to be a false alarm, when he got the call.

Hop a cab, Mendy said, and meet him up at 178th and Fort

Washington Avenue, right near the George Washington Bridge. He'd see them outside a liquor store on the corner.

"Who else is coming?" Harry asked. Sometimes you could tell just from who the players were what was going on.

"Ah, don't spend your time on that one now, sport. Just wear your driving shoes."

"I don't have driving shoes, Mendy." Harry looked down at his brown leather oxfords.

"Just get up here on the double."

Harry threw on his jacket and straightened his tie. He wanted to look presentable, as he might be driving someone important. He told Bert he might be gone for the night, that Mendy said he was in charge, and he'd try to be back to lock up around midnight. He hailed a cab outside. The whole ride uptown, he had the edgy feeling in his gut something wasn't on the up-and-up. *Just a ride in the country, huh? It's in Jersey, what else is there?* He knew what his friends did. Maybe they were going to bury a body out there. Or maybe threaten someone, outside the city. He could always drop out, he surmised. It wasn't too late. He could just give Mendy back the cash and say sorry, it wasn't for him after all. They could find someone else. It was like the cash was burning a hole in his trousers.

But when the cab pulled up to where Mendy said to come and he saw Mendy leaning on a black Plymouth, Harry paid the fare, leaving the driver a respectable tip, and got out, saying only, "Hey, Mendy, I'm here."

The Plymouth was about as inconspicuous as a car could be, with Connecticut plates. Which seemed strange to Harry. Whose car was it? It had a large backseat, set back from the driver. Someone was already in the back. Almost a shadow. He tried to see who it was.

"Ready?" Mendy slapped him amicably on the back. "Right?"

"Right as Eversharp," Harry said, parodying the advertisement, though in fact he was nervous as hell.

"That's good, chief," Mendy said. "Climb in."

Harry opened the driver's door and climbed in behind the wheel. The keys dangled in the ignition. He glanced behind him to see who was there, and that's when his heart bounced against his rib cage. Charles Workman was sitting there in a long coat. He gave Harry a perfunctory nod. Harry knew something bad was up tonight if Charles Workman was part of it.

Workman was a known button man for Mendy's boss, Lepke. Mendy climbed in next to Workman and shut the door.

"So what's going on tonight, fellas?" Harry asked.

"Don't you worry about that part, Harry. All you have to do is drive."

"Okay. Where, then?" he asked.

"Start with across the bridge."

The George Washington Bridge was just a block north of them. Harry took a glance behind him, trying to make out what they might be carrying. There was a black satchel on the seat between them. He felt a bead of sweat wind down his neck. It was too late to back out now, no matter what was going on. "Okay, gentlemen." Harry turned the ignition. The engine rumbled. "Over the bridge it is."

He did a U-turn back down Fort Washington to 179th Street and onto the bridge.

"Take Route 2." Mendy leaned forward. "South."

"All right. How far we talking, Mendy?"

"Just take it. We'll tell you when."

It was eight thirty P.M. Traffic was light. Harry cracked the window a bit to cool himself off because he was sweating through his shirt. It was October; there was a chill in the air. Mendy and Workman were talking, low enough that Harry couldn't quite make out what they were saying. He kept watching them in the rearview mirror. They were stoic, looking out the window. "Want to clue me in where we're heading?" he called back.

"Just watch the road, Harry." Even for Mendy, he seemed unusually tight-lipped.

Harry knew he had gotten himself in something that even a grand wasn't enough to cover.

They drove another thirty minutes. *A ride in the country,* Mendy had called it.

"Get off at the Newark Turnpike," Mendy instructed. "Then continue straight. Onto Kearney Avenue."

"Newark Turnpike. Okay." Harry nodded. What was going on in Newark?

"You said go straight?" Harry called back.

"Yeah. Onto Kearney and then Fourth Street." Downtown Newark. Harry had been there once or twice before. It no longer sounded like a ride in the country. And that was worrying him.

He followed Fourth to Broad as they approached downtown. Warehouses and office buildings jutting into the dark sky. Banks. Hotels. The occasional lights flickering.

"Turn left on Park Place," Mendy directed him. "Then a right onto East Park."

"East Park, you say?" Where the hell were they heading? Harry also understood enough about the business to know this was well out of their territory, if something was really happening.

By now, it was nine thirty. They found themselves in a quiet corner of downtown Newark. There wasn't a whole lot of traffic around. Not like in New York. Harry saw the façade of the Hotel St. Francis up ahead, the name lit up, maybe twenty stories tall. That's when his heart started to pound. He knew from reading the papers just who was holed up there these days.

What did they have to do with someone like the Dutchman?

"Slow down," Mendy leaned forward and directed him. "You see that restaurant straight ahead?" A sign outside said *The Palace Chop House. Steaks. Seafood.* It was a small, two-story, stand-alone building. The sign was lit up in lights. Just down the block from the St. Francis.

"I see it."

"Pull up across the street in front of that truck." Mendy pointed. "And you can ditch the engine."

"Okay." His heart pumping, Harry did as he was told. There was a vacant lot to his left. A few people lingered on the sidewalk, maybe heading to or from the restaurant. He stopped, took a deep breath, and switched off the ignition.

They sat there for a while, across from the restaurant.

Then Mendy leaned forward. "So the thing is, we're going to be going inside there for a couple of minutes, Harry. As soon as we're out of the car, I want you to pull around and wait for us right in front. Keep the engine running. We shouldn't be too long, only a few minutes. Just wait for us to come out."

"What's gonna go on, Mendy?" Harry asked, his voice cracking. Every instinct inside him told him he already knew.

"Don't you worry yourself about it, chief." Mendy patted him on the shoulder. "We're just gonna have a little talk inside, that's all. Nothing to get all worked up about. Right, Charlie? We'll be back out before you know it. Everything'll be fine."

"Okay." Harry cleared his throat and caught Mendy's eyes in the mirror. "This ain't no drive in the park, is it, Mendy?"

Mendy smiled. "All you have to think about is to come around and wait for us outside with the engine on. You got it, Harry?"

"Engine on." Harry's hands were now covered in sweat. "I got it."

He felt Mendy squeeze his shoulder. "That's my man."

It was quarter to ten now. A few people were emerging from the chophouse, couples walking back toward the hotel. Some businessmen, who maybe had one too many gins and tonics, loudly saying good-bye. One or two searched down the block for vacant cabs.

At ten sharp, Charles Workman glanced at his watch and said

to Mendy, "Time to go." He grabbed the door latch, just as a cab pulled in front of the restaurant, so they just sat back and waited for it to leave. The cab looked like it was waiting for a particular fare. They all sat there in the darkened car, Mendy and Workman waiting. Harry perspiring. "Fuck it's doing there?" Mendy grumbled.

"Relax," Charles Workman said to him. "He gets to make a living too."

Finally a man and a woman came out, waved their good-byes to someone still inside the place, and climbed in. The cab turned the corner a block down.

Harry heard Charles Workman sigh and utter, "All right, then?" In the rearview mirror he could see the two men stuff their guns into their belts and close their jackets and coats over them.

They opened the rear doors.

Harry sat there, his hands fixed to the wheel, his body rigid as stone. Outside, Mendy rapped his knuckles against Harry's window. Harry rolled it down. "Remember, pull in front," Mendy said again. "And whatever you might hear, just stay calm and wait until we come out."

"I'll be here, Mendy."

"Knew I could count on you, ace." Mendy winked. "Oh, and one more thing, just so you know . . ." The gangster's grin disappeared. "You drive off with us in there, you're a dead man, Harry. You understand that, don't you?"

Harry nodded. This was no ride in the country. That was clear.

Chapter Forty

Once inside, Mendy and Workman nodded hello to the maître d'. Workman said, "We'll just take a drink at the bar."

The bar was long and ornately carved, with a large glass mirror on the other side, behind the booze. They sat down. "Two scotches," Workman said. They glanced in the mirror. In the dining area, there were about five tables still occupied, diners chatting, laughing, some with napkins in their collars, cracking into lobsters or cutting steaks.

They could see the Dutchman. He was sitting at a round table near the back with three others. One, Mendy could see, was that accountant guy, Berman. Everyone called him Abbadabba, who the fuck knew why? He had a white napkin stuffed in his collar and he was happily cutting through a large hunk of meat. The other two were Abe Landau and Lulu Rosenkrantz, Schultz's longtime bodyguards. He was sad to see Lulu there. They went back a ways.

"Gentlemen, we stop serving at ten thirty, will you be dining with us tonight?" the bartender asked, sliding across their scotches.

"Give us a minute," Workman said. "We'll see."

"Take your time. Just to let you know, that's all. To your health, gentlemen. . . ."

"L'chaim." Workman tipped his glass to him and took a gulp. Mendy too.

They listened to the din coming from the tables, waiting for the right moment. Then they watched in the mirror as Schultz, in a gray suit and flowery tie, got up, glanced their way a second—Mendy's heart jumped almost as if the killer recognized the two of them sitting there—and then headed to the rear of the restaurant and down a small corridor leading to the men's room. Workman elbowed Mendy. "I'll take the Dutchman," he said. "You take the table."

"All right." Mendy nodded.

"We won't be needing a table after all," Charles Workman said to the bartender, getting up. "And by the way, if I were you, I'd get down."

It took a second for the man to comprehend just what Workman meant, then the bartender's eyes stretched as wide as if he'd just received a fifty-dollar tip, and with a glance at the maître d' up front, he dipped below the bar.

Workman ducked his face beneath his hat and headed toward the back after Schultz. At the table, something must have been funny, because Berman and Landau burst out in laughter, and, distracted, didn't notice Workman as he went by. Mendy, following, put his hand inside his jacket and grabbed hold of the Smith & Wesson.

He and Workman shared a last glance and then Charlie went inside the men's room after Schultz as Mendy walked up to Schultz's table and took out his gun.

"Hey, Abe," Mendy said cheerily, as the corpulent bodyguard chugged down a swallow of water. Landau's wide-eyed gulp indicated he knew what was going on, and there was nothing he could do. He coughed out the water, just as Mendy put a bullet into the bodyguard's throat and another into his chest. Blood spurted all over the steak he was eating, a spray of water coming out of his mouth.

At the same moment, three loud pops came from inside the bathroom.

Lulu Rosenkrantz, a giant of a man, leaped up, fumbling inside his jacket for his gun. Mendy squeezed off two into him as well. He fell back against the wall, blood smearing the restaurant's faded wallpaper. Otto Berman was the least threat. He likely wasn't even carrying. With the other two down, Mendy put two through the startled accountant's white napkin. His eyes went wide and his face pitched forward onto his steak.

Workman came back out, nodding quickly to Mendy that the job was done. Abe Landau had managed to get up and find his gun. He thrust out his arm, squeezing shots off wildly. Diners dove for the floor with horrified screams, ducking under their tables.

Mendy threw his gun down and dug out his backup. He and Workman just stood there, arms extended, firing.

Outside, Harry's heart was rat-tat-tatting like a jazz drummer playing an endless solo. He sat glued to the wheel, focused on the steak house's front door. Mendy and Workman had been inside an awfully long time. He started to think maybe they *were* just in there to talk. Maybe that's all this was—a sit-down of some kind. Like Mendy had said. Sure, he was full of shit about it all being just a ride in the country. He guessed he knew that going in. For a grand.

But that still didn't mean they were actually here to kill someone.

Especially the one person he knew who happened to be residing next door these days at the Hotel St. Francis—the most feared mobster in the country.

Any moment he didn't hear gunfire was a good one, Harry assured himself, swallowing.

In the rearview mirror, he suddenly saw headlights advancing in his direction. *Shit.* As the lights came closer, Harry's eyes grew wide as he realized what it was. A fucking Newark police car. Coming down the street. *What was it doing here?* His heart began to inch up his throat.

Following it, a bead of sweat wormed down Harry's neck and inside his collar. *What should he do? Just sit here? Pray it just went by?* He'd done nothing wrong to attract attention. Sitting here, with his engine running, he could just be waiting for someone inside. And as long as it was quiet in there, they'd be none the wiser. They couldn't exactly tell what he was here for just from looking at him.

Or could they?

Harry's tongue felt dry as sandpaper. *Why a cop car now? Of all the times. Why . . . ?*

It advanced down the street at a snail's pace, maybe checking out the cars. The Palace was a known hangout. They probably even knew Schultz was inside. By this point, Harry was so scared he could barely breathe. He sat there, his foot bobbing, ready to hit the gas with everything he had. He couldn't let go of the wheel. He just watched in the side mirror, sweat inching down his cheek, as the car drew closer and closer. He felt like just gunning the gas and taking a powder. But if he did, he knew he was as good as dead when Mendy and Workman came out. No, he had to just sit tight where he was and pray they went by. He had to summon the nerve. His throat was coarse as sand. He swallowed.

Then he thought, what if the policeman stopped and asked what he was doing here? *Just waiting for my friends inside, Officer,* he would say. They couldn't be suspicious of that.

But what if the shooting started just as the cops approached him? What then?

Oh God . . .

It was only seconds, though it felt closer to an hour. Finally the police car pulled up parallel with him, Harry not even acknowledging it, keeping his eyes straight ahead. For a second he was sure it was going to stop and the cop inside would roll down his window and ask why he was sitting there with his motor running, and no matter what Harry said, he'd put it all together. His heart came to a stop. Either that or Mendy and Workman would start shooting at that very moment, and Harry wouldn't know what to do.

But to his great relief, the police car continued slowly on, passing him. It made its way deliberately to the corner, stopping there for another moment, staying so long, Harry was screaming inside: *Can't you just go on? Go on! Please, turn. Go.* Finally the car did turn. He continued to sit there, dry-mouthed, counting slowly to ten. Out loud. Taking breaths between each number. Then he paused silently for a full five seconds until he continued. Until he was sure the car had gone.

He blew out his cheeks with an audible sigh of relief.

His shirt was fully soaked.

It had now been a full five minutes that Mendy and Workman had been inside, and he'd heard nothing. Yes, maybe they were just here to talk. Maybe Mendy hadn't been kidding. He was always such a kidder, Harry knew. Maybe they were all just sitting around a table right now, while Harry was sweating. With a drink. Workman, Mendy, and that other person—Harry didn't even want to utter his name—shooting the breeze, laughing, and—

Suddenly he heard a barrage of gunshots coming from inside.

So many shots, he couldn't count them. They wouldn't stop coming.

He started to breathe heavily and his shirt was encased in sweat. He pumped the gas, over and over, ready for them to dart out. *C'mon, Mendy, come on.* More shots. *Come out now. Please.*

Two people on the street started running.

He sat there like Mendy had ordered, but then he prayed that the first people out that door would be Mendy and Workman, and not someone who worked for Dutch Schultz.

To Mendy, Otto Berman looked dead at the table. Lulu Rosenkrantz had collapsed against the wall, clutching his chest. Mendy had put rounds into Abe Landau several times, but the guy was somehow still moving, fumbling for his gun.

Workman just stood there, continuing to fire: *Bam, bam, bam, bam, bam.*

"Let's go," Mendy yelled. He was now out of bullets in his backup. The job was done and they'd both better get the hell out of there.

In a crouch, he darted toward the entrance.

Most of the patrons had either taken cover beneath their tables or dashed behind the bar. The few women in the place were screaming holy hell.

Workman stepped closer to Rosenkrantz and kept unloading. Somehow the big man still hadn't fully gone down, and his body was just taking hits. Mendy sprinted out the door. Outside, he ducked into the backseat of the Plymouth, which was running, Harry at the wheel. "Let's get the hell out of here!"

"Where's Charlie?" Harry shouted.

"He's coming now."

Harry gunned the gas, expecting to see him any second. No one came out. "He's coming, *when . . .* ?" Harry screamed. Every second stretched out like an eternity and he could hear more shots inside. *What was going on in there?*

He feared the cops who had just passed by would hear all the ruckus and come back around. There were passersby on the street who, startled by all the shooting, had ducked behind a vehicle across from him. A part of Harry was kind of thrilled that they might think him involved. "We've got to get out of here, Mendy!"

"He was right behind me."

Still more firing.

Then silence. They waited a beat. "C'mon, Charlie . . . ," Mendy said under his breath.

Nothing.

"Fuck!" Mendy shouted, shaking his head.

Harry turned around. "There's a cop car not far away, Mendy. He passed by a minute or two ago while you were inside. They might hear. Where the hell is he?"

Mendy was growing rattled too. "I don't know!"

They waited, a count of five. Still, no sign of him. But every second they remained it grew more and more dangerous for them to stay. What if Charlie had been killed? And one of Schultz's henchmen burst out the door, firing? They couldn't just stay there. He had no gun, and Mendy was likely empty. They'd be sitting ducks. Mendy remained fixed on the door. "Give it five more seconds." Five seconds that to Harry felt like twenty. *Where the hell was he?* Sooner or later, the cops were going to come. They had to get out of there.

Workman had to have been shot. He wasn't coming.

"Okay, drive!" Mendy finally shouted, slamming the door.

"We can't just leave him, Mendy."

"I said, *drive*!" Mendy shouted again. "Get moving. Something must have happened. Now!"

Harry wasn't sure what to do, and waited one last beat to five, fixed on the door. *Come on, Charlie. . . .* He put the car in gear.

"I said fucking drive, Harry!" Mendy pointed his gun at Harry's head. "Or so help me I'll pull you out of that seat and drive the fucking thing myself."

Harry hit the gas. The Plymouth lurched forward. As he pulled away, he kept his eyes peeled on the canopy in the rearview mirror. He slowed one final second before he turned the corner.

Nothing.

He swerved and drove away.

"Something must have fucking happened." Mendy shook his head. "I told him we had to leave. He just kept firing."

They turned two streets down and headed back to Broad Street in the direction of the turnpike.

"Who was it?" Harry asked, glancing back nervously.

"Don't go too fast. I don't want a fucking cop to pull us over."

"Who was it, Mendy? Who did you guys just kill?" He drove down Broad, and thought about looping back one more time to see if Workman had come out. But it was too late now. And Mendy would have shot him.

"It was Dutch Schultz, right, wasn't it?"

Mendy said, "Just drive."

"It was Schultz, wasn't it, Mendy. Tell me! You just killed Dutch Schultz." Harry headed toward the highway, keeping a steadying foot on the gas.

"Yeah, it was Schultz," Mendy finally said. A smile crept onto his puffy face. "You're gonna be famous, kid. It'll be in all the papers."

Harry's heart was beating so fast he thought it would burst through his chest. By morning, every paper in the country would have the headline: *Dutch Schultz Gunned Down in Newark*. And he'd been the getaway driver. On a hit on the most feared mobster in all New York.

"What the hell did you get me into, Mendy?"

"Relax, kid, you just earned yourself a grand."

"You can keep it. I don't want your grand!"

He drove, retracing their steps back to the tunnel. But his mind strayed, to back in front of that restaurant. To that passerby, the one ducked behind a car across from him, crouched down. Their eyes had met and the guy must have thought, *That driver there, in the car, behind the wheel, he's a real button man. He was one of the crew that took out the Dutchman.*

And for the first time that night, Harry smiled.

Chapter Forty-One

Inside the Palace Chop House, Abe Landau had somehow kept returning fire at Charles Workman. No matter how many bullets Workman had put into the fat SOB, he wouldn't die. And that moose, Rosenkrantz, he wouldn't stay the fuck down either. They were writhing and trying to reload, blood leaking all over them. They both must have been hit five or six times.

Workman knew he had to make a run for it. Mendy could only wait so long. But he was pinned down behind a table which he had turned upright to avoid being hit, dishes and tableware crashing to the floor. And now even his backup gun was empty. Abe Landau was struggling to pull himself up to his feet. The police could be here any second.

"That you, Charlie?" Landau called out. He extended his arm and fired twice in Workman's direction.

Workman crouched, making himself as small as he could. The bullets went right over his head. Then he thought, the hell with it, and made a dash for the front entrance. Landau pulled himself up, his legs wobbly, barely supporting him, clutching his side, and continued shooting. Somehow the shots missed.

Workman burst through the front door and onto East Park Street, set to dive into the car.

It wasn't there.

Not in front of the joint. Or across the street. Where someone was crouching behind a car. Or down the block. He looked around helplessly.

Those fuckers . . . They'd left him there.

"Fuck you, Mendy!" he shouted, looking helplessly down the empty street.

He knew he couldn't stay there. There had been dozens of shots. The cops would be there any time. He turned and headed down East Park. He was in Newark. In hostile territory. The Dutchman's territory. Who knows, even the cops might be on Schultz's payroll here.

Behind him, the front door of the restaurant burst open. To Workman's disbelief, Abe Landau, staggering like a wounded bull, came out. He spotted Workman down the street and, bright red blotches dotting his chest, he turned and pointed his gun at him. He grinned.

Standing there, Workman was a sitting duck.

One shot fired wildly into the air. Landau almost lost his balance. He kept pulling on the trigger, once, twice, three times, until Workman could hear only useless clicks. He was out too. He threw the empty gun on the street and took a step toward Workman. The guy must have seven bullets in him, Workman thought in disbelief. *Go down.* Then Landau wobbled sideways, losing his footing, and fell into the trash cans with a deafening crash.

This time he stayed down.

Workman gave out a laugh. How fucking lucky could he be? They'd done it—they'd iced Dutch Schultz. Iced his whole gang. But now he had to make it back to Brooklyn. Before the rest of Schultz's men or any cops who were on his payroll got on his trail.

He turned and took off at the corner. He couldn't believe Mendy and that weasel Harry had just left him there. What a bunch of cowards.

Well, they'd have one helluva surprise waiting for them back in Brooklyn.

Chapter Forty-Two

At 2:00 A.M. at his headquarters in the back of the cigar store in Brooklyn, Louis Buchalter wasn't a happy man.

Somehow, Dutch Schultz had survived.

At least, so far, that's what the press was claiming. They said he had two bullets in his chest and abdomen and was at Newark General, talking up a bloody storm. Babbling.

Somehow that crazy fuck was going to make it, Buchalter lamented. And he would know who had done this to him.

Buchalter would have to report to the commission later that day.

Still, that wasn't the only reason he wanted to kill someone that moment.

Mendy Weiss had made it back to the shop around midnight. At first he was giddy. They'd done it. They'd iced Dutch Schultz.

"Not according to the news," Gurrah informed him. "He's still alive."

"Alive?" Mendy chortled, disbelieving. "That's impossible."

"Giraffes tap-dancing at Carnegie Hall are impossible. Schultz is still alive."

"So where's Charlie?" Buchalter asked.

"Charlie didn't make it." Mendy shook his head.

"What do you mean Charlie didn't make it?" Buchalter got up out of his chair.

It didn't take a fucking police chief to know Workman was a part of Buchalter's organization. If his body was found at the scene, you wouldn't have to be Rembrandt to put that picture together.

"We were waiting in the car. There were a ton of shots in there," Mendy said. "He never came out, Louis. At some point, we had to go."

"You had to go . . . ?" Buchalter looked at him, ire coming into his face. "You're saying you left him in there?"

"He never came out, boss. We waited. We had to get out of there. We heard all kinds of shots. Something must've happened."

"You're damned right something fucking happened," Buchalter said, his eyes aflame. This was an even bigger problem than the Dutchman alive. Now he had to answer to Luciano. Schultz still had friends. Powerful ones. If he lived, he could point the finger at whoever had done this. And if Charlie was found in there, that was proof enough. This could start a war.

"Who was the driver?" Louis asked Mendy.

"Some guy I picked up. He did fine."

"I asked you who the fucking driver was, you tell me," Buchalter glared at Mendy and asked again.

"Harry." Mendy shrugged, clearing his throat.

"Harry?" Buchalter squinted in disbelief. "Harry Rabishevsky?"

"You wanted it done quick, Louis. My usual guy was in Detroit. He did just fine."

"He did fine. . . . You come back with Charlie, he did just fine. You just better hope that bastard fucking dies, Mendy." He jabbed his finger at him. "You just better hope."

Mendy sat down, suddenly a sheen of sweat all over his face.

"Here." Gurrah handed him a handkerchief and placed a bottle of rye in front of him. "Pour yourself a drink. And go through how it happened."

Mendy took them through it step by step. How they went in and sat at the bar. How Workman went into the bathroom after Schultz, and Mendy had taken the table. Berman, Landau, and Lulu Rosenkrantz eating steaks.

"Lulu Rosenkrantz was there?" Gurrah interrupted with a shake of his head. "Too bad. I always liked the guy."

How Mendy had heard two or three shots coming from the men's room and how he'd then shot Berman, Landau, and Rosenkrantz, dead on, multiple times. "Charlie came back out and we both continued firing."

If Workman was dead, Buchalter wasn't sure how he wanted things to play out. If the Dutchman died, the Feds would be looking Louis's way for the murder. If he remained alive, it would start a war. Either way, he had a bad report to bring to the commission who had ordered the hit. This kind of screw-up was bad for business. Up to now, he'd always handled things cleanly. That was why when they needed something done, they said, "Go to Lepke." Someone would definitely have to pay.

No, Schultz just had to die, he decided. That was paramount. He looked at Gurrah. He'd already begun thinking. Maybe they had to make another move against him while he was in the hospital.

"So what do we do?" Mendy asked, his tie loosened, his collar wide, a film of sweat on his brow.

"I make a rule for you, Mendy." Buchalter pointed at him. "You don't have to be thinking about that part. You just keep praying Charlie turns up. That's all."

An hour passed. Then two. It wound into four. They kept the radio on. Schultz and his crew were still at Newark General, all in critical condition.

Suddenly they heard commotion coming from the shop outside. The door to their offices opened.

Charles Workman stepped inside.

Mendy bolted up as if he was looking at a ghost.

"You filthy coward," Workman said, and went over and grabbed Mendy by the collar. "You fucking left me."

"You never came out, Charlie," Mendy said, putting up his arms. "There were shots. We didn't know what happened. We waited as long as we could."

"As long as you could? I coulda been fucking killed in there. Abe Landau came out after me and I was out of ammo. He had six shots in him but he was able to do it. You, you just took off."

"We didn't take off, Charlie. You never came out! Anyway, I'm just happy to see you alive."

"No help from you." Workman put him down and glared at him.

"So how the hell did you get back here?" Buchalter asked.

"I walked. Crossed half of fucking New Jersey. That area all belongs to the Dutchman. Anyone found me, without ammo, I was as good as dead. I hopped a ferry across the river, a tram over the bridge, and walked half of Brooklyn here. This ain't right, Louis." He jabbed a finger at Mendy. "You took a powder. You don't leave a man on a job. I've been doing this too long. You gotta pay."

"I tried to tell him to stay," Mendy said, looking at Buchalter, seeing he was in a real bind. "But Harry, he got scared and hit the pedal. By the time I knew what was happening we were three blocks away. We couldn't go back."

"I thought just a moment ago you said he did fine?" Gurrah looked at him.

"He *did* fine. Up until then. It just got a little crazy. We heard bullets left and right." He turned to Workman. "And you never came out. How're we supposed to know if you were shot or what . . . ?"

Workman said to Buchalter, "I don't care. It's a rule. You don't drive off. Someone's gotta pay."

"We'll get into that later," Buchalter said. "Right now, we have bigger problems."

Workman poured himself a drink from the bottle of rye. "What problems?"

"You didn't hear?"

"How could I hear anything? I been lugging my ass all over Jersey and Brooklyn the past four hours."

"Schultz ain't dead."

"What do you mean, he ain't dead? I hit him three times. Dead on."

"Well, you shoulda hit him five times," Buchalter said. "He's at the hospital. And according to the reports, very much alive. If he lives, you know what's the story then? We got a war on our hands."

"If I hit him five times I'd have nothing left to walk back in that restaurant with. Anyway, relax. He'll be dead by tonight. Trust me."

"How can you be so sure?" Buchalter asked. "You a doctor in your spare time too, Charlie?"

"I don't need to be no doctor. I shot him with rusted bullets. Just in case I couldn't get a clean shot. Trust me, if the bullets didn't do the job, the infection he's gonna get from them will. Landau and Lulu too."

"Infection . . ." Buchalter looked at Gurrah with a widening grin. "You wasted your talents, Charlie. You should be teaching at Harvard."

Workman said, "I promise he won't last the day. But that still doesn't satisfy my wrong." He scowled at Mendy balefully.

"One thing at a time," Buchalter said. "The Dutchman first."

Charles Workman turned out to be right about Schultz. He died later that day of complications from gunshot wounds.

As did Landau, Rosenkrantz, and Berman, shortly after.

Then it was on to the matter of Charles Workman's restitution.

Chapter Forty-Three

Three days later, at a restaurant in Brooklyn, Albert Anastasia, Jacob "Gurrah" Shapiro, and Louis Buchalter listened to Workman and Mendy hash out what had happened.

"It ain't kosher," Workman said. "You don't take a powder on your partner in the middle of a hit. I was left alone. Without no gun. In very hostile territory. If any of the Dutchman's men had run into me, I'd be on a slab at the morgue next to them instead of in front of you. And that would be very bad for the whole organization," he looked up at the three members of the committee, "if I was traced back to any of you."

"You didn't come out," Mendy said in defense. "We did wait. As long as we could."

"How long?" Gurrah questioned.

"I don't know, a minute maybe. Maybe more. There was tons of shooting inside. When you didn't follow me out, we thought you were dead."

"You still don't leave," Albert Anastasia said, "unless you know for sure."

"I don't leave, there could be cops down our backs. Then where would we be? You tell me, Louis, Jacob. This ain't my first job. How long do you stay?" Mendy was clearly nervous. It was he who had hired the driver. It was up to him to play it by the book. His eyes appealed to his three bosses, but their faces didn't give him much reason for relief. He knew that the penalty for leaving his partner there to get shot was death too.

"I told him to wait," Mendy said, suddenly changing his stripes.

Albert Anastasia questioned, "Who?"

"The driver. Harry. The guy just took off. I did my best to get him to stop. What should I have done," Mendy appealed to Buchalter and Gurrah, "shoot him too?"

"You left me there to rot," Workman said. "No way I'd have done the same for you."

"So who was this driver?" Albert Anastasia looked around.

"Someone named Harry Rabishevsky."

"And who found him?"

"I found him," Mendy said, swallowing guiltily. "He works for me."

"He works for you. . . ." Anastasia glanced over at Buchalter. "He ever do a job like this before . . . ?

"Look." Mendy stood up, a quiver of desperation cracking his voice. "Maybe I made a mistake with him. You wanted the job done quick and my usual people weren't around. He's not used to a lot of shooting. He just got spooked and hit the gas. I told him to stop, Charlie's still in there." Mendy turned to Workman. "I know I have to own up for bringing him on."

"All I'll say is he seemed fine to me when we went in," Workman said with a skeptical glare.

"First, you said he did good," Gurrah said to Mendy, "now, it's he got spooked and hit the gas. Which is it, Mendy?"

"I was just trying to cover up for him." Mendy looked across at his jurors. "He's a good guy. You all know Harry."

"Yeah, we know Harry," Buchalter said. "That's the problem. He should never have been on the job."

"Well, someone has to pay, that's for certain." Anastasia tapped his beefy index finger on the table. "Otherwise, we become a laughingstock. We gotta show, we do this kind of work, we mean business."

Mendy nodded. He had sweat stains on the back of his jacket. He saw this could go very badly for him. Badly indeed. "Look, you know me too, Louis," he appealed. "And I've done a lot to deserve your confidence."

Mendy and Charlie were asked to step out. They sat, uncomfortably, at opposite ends of the bar while the three bosses met among themselves and deliberated Mendy's fate. In half an hour, which seemed an eternity to Mendy, Gurrah stepped out and asked them back in.

Mendy took in a deep breath.

"So here's the thing," Albert Anastasia said, "we all agree, someone's gotta pay. Mendy, none of us believe you're being entirely truthful with us. It's entirely possible you told him to drive. This Harry guy . . . Charlie said he wouldn't make a move without you telling him to."

"That's what I saw." Workman turned to Mendy and shrugged.

Mendy's eyes were dark and hollow. He knew he was in trouble.

"But it's your crew, Louis." The Italian turned to Buchalter. "So you choose. Just make it quick, whoever it is. So people know we back up our business."

Buchalter nodded and looked at Mendy.

"Louis, please . . . ," Mendy begged. "We did the job. I've proved myself to you over a lot of years."

"Yes, you have, Mendy. But you know what I think? I think you fucked up." Buchalter pointed accusingly. "I can't say what I would have done, I wasn't there. Still, between the two of you, I have to say, you're far more valuable to me than Harry."

Mendy let out a breath, feeling the sweat on his back start to cool.

"Just as long as it's someone," Anastasia said.

"You okay with this, Charlie?"

Workman thought it over a second, then shrugged. "Long as someone pays. Just don't count on me to do any more jobs with you so quick." He glared at Mendy.

"Okay, then." Anastasia crushed out his cigar and stood up. "You guys make up as friends. I got a babe waiting for me."

"You're closest to him," Buchalter said to Mendy.

Mendy nodded with flattened lips and blew out a deep breath through his nostrils. "I've known him since we were kids back on Cherry Street."

"You're right, he's a nice guy. Everybody likes Harry." Buchalter got up. "I remember that night at the Theatrical Club. He knows how to make you laugh." He shook hands with Anastasia and put on his hat. "It's your mess, Mendy, you clean it up."

"Yes, boss." Seeing the meeting was over, Mendy went to the door with relief.

"And Mendy . . ." He turned. "You're a lucky sonovabitch, you know that, right? Anyone else, we'd be talking about you here."

Chapter Forty-Four

"So Harry, a few of the guys want to show their appreciation," Mendy said over the phone. "About the other night."

"What about Charlie?" Harry asked. He was happy to hear Workman was okay, but nervous about how it might've made him look, since he'd been the one behind the wheel. "I heard he was mighty ticked off."

"Charlie? Water under the bridge. Things like that happen in the big leagues. But, big picture, the Dutchman's dead. That's all that matters. So whaddya say you come on out to Dov's tonight?" Dov's was a bar in Bensonhurst where Lepke's crew hung out from time to time. "Say, around eight. Come on around the back. We got a little celebration planned in the back room. A bunch of the guys'll be there."

"I got work, Mendy."

"Hell with work, you know how big this is for us? I'll get Bert to cover."

"I guess," Harry said after a pause. "As long as you're sure there's no hard feelings? You did tell him it was you who pushed me to leave?"

"Look, if there's anyone Charlie should be mad at, it's me, right? Trust me, no hard feelings at all. Right as rain."

So Harry put Bert in charge of the pool hall and took the tram across the Brooklyn Bridge. He walked the eight blocks in the rain to Ocean Avenue, where Dov's was situated, in a two-story brick building on a quiet corner.

On the way, he thought about how he had tried to make a go of it straight, but it just hadn't worked out for him. It always seemed like the deck was stacked against him. Maybe this was his place. He felt like an outcast to the family. He knew he had disappointed them, his brothers. He'd always felt different. Going all the way back to Essex Street, and the thing they never talked about. Which he played over and over a thousand times in his head.

But these guys, they'd never judged him. They'd never looked at him with shame or accusation. He never felt like an outcast here. So maybe it was right that this was where he'd ended up. He had helped knock off Dutch Schultz. People would be telling the story for years. He might as well join the celebration.

Maybe this was his family now.

Outside Dov's he tipped his hat to a young couple passing by. *Dutch Schultz, huh?*

Maybe his star was on the rise after all.

He tried the door, but it was locked. Odd, and the lights were dimmed inside. But Mendy had said it was a private celebration. In the back room. Maybe they closed the place. He had said to come around the back.

So Harry went through the alley to the back entrance. A couple of cars were parked there.

To his surprise, Mendy was there. With Oscar Hammerschmitt. He always liked Oscar. They called him "Heels" because he knew how to tap dance.

"Hey, whaddya know," Mendy came up with a wide grin, "the man of the hour."

"Hey, Mendy. Oscar." Harry was surprised that they were waiting for him outside.

"Harry." Oscar gave him a wave of hello in return. "How's it cookin'?"

"So what do you say we go in?" Mendy went to the back door. "A bunch of the guys were asking where you were. This new situation promises to be a very good one for the organization."

"What situation?"

"What situation?" Mendy slapped him on the shoulder. "With the Dutchman gone."

"I didn't see any lights on," Harry said, looking through the window.

"We closed the place, champ. They're all in the back room, waiting. C'mon." Mendy opened the door. "After you, sport."

Harry went in ahead of them. He'd been in the back room several times. He'd drunk a lot of whiskey there during Prohibition, and sometimes there were even girls, though almost everyone in the group, save him, was married. Of course, that never stopped anyone from enjoying themselves.

He expected to hear the usual wave of noise and raucous laughter when he opened the door. When these guys got together you could always count on it being a loud time. But in fact, it was eerily quiet. And as Harry stepped inside, it still looked like the lights weren't even on.

To his surprise, the room was completely empty.

"What's going on, Mendy?" He stood there for a moment trying to figure out if this was a joke, until he realized what was happening.

"Sorry, Harry. Nothing personal," was all he heard behind him.

"Tell Morris I didn't do it," was all Harry said. "He'll understand."

"I will, sport. I sure will."

He closed his eyes.

Oscar put a gun to the back of Harry's head and pulled the trigger.

Harry dropped where he stood.

He never felt more than a wave of darkness washing over the light. Lying in his own blood, he looked up and a face somehow came to him.

He looked quite the same and even had on the same shabby clothes he was wearing the last time Harry saw him. In the street, turning back, with that same wide grin, relishing his moment of triumph, before the rumble of hooves swept over him.

"Hi, Shemuel."

"Hi, Harry. Where you been?"

His brother held out his hand, but this time didn't impishly pull it away as Harry reached for it. Instead he wrapped it around Harry's shoulders, with a smile both welcoming and forgiving—forgiveness, how badly Harry had always wanted to feel that all these years—as he led him toward the light, elbowing him amiably. "By the way, you owe me five zuzim."

Chapter Forty-Five

Morris grabbed the early edition of *The Daily Mirror* on his way home from work.

The newsstand hawker shouted, "Gangland killing! Gangland killing! Read it here!" as the crowd on Thirty-eighth and Broadway rushed by.

Morris plunked down a dollar, which included ninety-five cents for the newsboy, folded the paper under his arm, and walked in the October chill the twenty blocks up to Central Park. His mind was stuck on a work matter he'd faced earlier, a bolt of fabric he had rejected on a style he needed out the door in two weeks. On Fifty-ninth Street and the park he put out his hand for a cab and unfurled the paper. As his eyes hit the front page, Morris felt a weight in his stomach drop in freefall and his legs almost collapse.

In an oversized photo under the bold headline, IT'S BEEN NICE TO KNOW YA, HARRY, was his brother—eyes shut, a trickle of blood oozing from his mouth, crumpled against a waste bin.

Morris's heart came to a stop. "Oh my God, Harry!"

Focusing in on the blank, expressionless face, unable to pull himself away, Morris pushed back the elevator falling in his chest, trying to make sure.

But he knew. As soon as his eyes fixed on it. There was no mistake. Propped up, an arm twisted beneath his side, like a drunk who'd slept it off on the street.

Feeling like his heart was sliced in half like a slab of meat, Morris turned from the bustling street to read the article:

The body of Harry Rabishevsky, manager of a Manhattan pool hall and a bit player in the Lepke-Shapiro crime ring, was found earlier, left on a Brooklyn pier, a popular dumping ground for mob victims, dead from a single gunshot wound to the back of the head.

"Oh Jesus, Harry," Morris uttered, stretching the paper wide. A few passersby turned to look at him as they went by.

The victim, who was said to be a friend and hanger-on to several well-known crime associates, such as Louis Lepke and Mendy Weiss, had no known criminal history of his own. Speculation arose that his death was either a warning to the Lepke crime syndicate, sometimes known as Murder, Incorporated, or the notorious crime clan cleaning up an internal matter of its own.

Lepke's syndicate was suspected of involvement in Tuesday's brazen, bullet-riddled executions of the infamous mobster Dutch Schultz and three of his lieutenants at a popular restaurant in Newark, New Jersey, though it is not known if Rabishevsky played a role in those killings or what else might have prompted his execution. But sources close to the paper say the victim was suspected of having played a part in the Dutchman's bloody murder, possibly as the getaway driver.

"Getaway driver?" Morris uttered out loud. He found a bench along the side of the park and sat down. *Harry?* Harry had no criminal involvement of his own. He was merely attracted to the easy life of these people, that's all. The glamour and the approval they gave him. How they made him feel important. *But getaway driver . . . ? For Dutch Schultz's rubout.* That was impossible.

Harry wouldn't even know what to do around a gun but duck.

Morris kept his eyes fastened on the lurid photo, unable to accept that the face his eyes were boring into was his own brother's. A cold sweat spread down his back. Morris had pushed him. Pushed Harry away. Sure as day, Morris'd sent him scurrying back to them. But Harry had made his own choice when he let Mendy Weiss back in his life. When he chose his old friends over his family. And Raab Brothers was in ruins because of what he'd done. He, Sol, Ruthie, Sammy—Harry'd taken them all down with him.

Morris thought back to the last time he had seen him. Across the street from their apartment building, maybe a year ago now. Surely hoping to mend things, his arm tentatively raised in a greeting, as Morris, barely acknowledging him, looked past him and ducked into a cab.

Morris closed his eyes and folded the paper under his arm. He had never given Harry the chance to explain.

He hailed a cab and sped uptown to his apartment. As soon as he opened the door, Ruthie threw her arms around him, tears filling her eyes. "You heard what happened?"

Morris showed her the newspaper.

"Sol just called. They're saying he was part of the gang that executed that awful mobster, Dutch Schultz?"

"I know what they're saying," Morris said. On the ride uptown, he had read the article three times, each time finding it impossible to believe what he was reading, that he was seeing his brother's face.

"He would have done anything for them, Ruthie. If Mendy Weiss said jump, he'd have jumped, right through that window. I know how you probably feel about this, but look at what he did to us."

"By that point, he would have done anything for someone's approval, Morris."

"It's not about approval, Ruthie. People don't just get killed. There's a reason."

"He was your brother, Morris."

"I know he was my brother." Morris went over to the settee in the foyer and sat down.

"All he wanted was to prove himself to you. To be a man in your eyes. We pushed him to them, Morris, as surely as if we pulled that trigger ourselves. And look what they did. We're as responsible for what happened as they are."

"No." Morris pulled her to him. "That's not true. He's the one who made his choice." He put his head against her. "Mom has to know. She'll take it hard."

She had already buried one twin.

"I have to call Sol." He stood and folded the paper. "And whatever you do, don't let Sammy see this."

After stopping off at their mom's and leaving Ruthie and Sol's wife Louise there with her, Morris and Sol went down to the morgue at Belleview to identify the body. A doctor met them and led them to a wall of refrigerated lockers. The room had the cold, antiseptic smell of disinfectant, making Morris wince.

They wheeled Harry out on a gurney. He looked fairly tranquil and composed, a sheet covering his torso. If he had a bad bone in his body, you couldn't tell it from his placid complexion. To Morris, for all the guilt and conflict he knew his brother had felt, and for the violent end the papers said he had met, Harry looked as at peace as he had ever seen him. Sol gave a glance to Morris and nodded to the doctor. "That's our brother."

"I'm sorry," he said, and made a motion to an aide to take the gurney away. Sol put out an arm to stop him. "Can you give us a second, Doc?"

"Sure. You'll have time at the funeral home." The doctor shrugged. "But I don't see why not."

He and the orderly left the stark examining room. Morris and Sol just stood there, looking down at their brother.

"He looks pretty peaceful," Morris said. "Considering."

"That he does. How are you doing in there, Harry?" Sol leaned over and said. "Can you hear me somehow? We're so sorry for you. I hope you didn't feel a lot of pain. How'd you ever get involved in this thing, Harry? Is everything okay?" Harry's eyes were closed and there was a soft, dull sheen on his face. The back of his head was shaved. They'd cleaned up the blood.

"Whatever you want to say, he didn't have it easy, Morris. He spent his whole life torturing himself for what happened to Shemuel. Or feeling Mom blamed him. And she did. He was her favorite, you know?"

"Who?"

"Shemuel. We never discussed it, but it was true. You were too young to remember."

"Shemuel's been dead for thirty years, Sol. At some point you have to let it go. He made his choices. We worked hard to build that business up from the ground and he tore it down, like that, in one day. Maybe you can, but I can't get past that."

"Cut him a break, Morris. He's dead. Whatever you want to say, he was ashamed even to be around us. For what he did. That's the only reason he got involved with those guys. They didn't judge him like he felt we judged him. Some things you just can't let go."

"I didn't judge him," Morris said. "He just never wanted to face up to being a man and moving past it."

"You're hard. He was still our brother, Morris."

"You think he did this? What the papers are saying?"

Sol leaned over Harry and put a hand to his cheek. "It feels weird. Cold. I don't know. It just doesn't seem like him. If I was gonna kill someone, I wouldn't exactly have used Harry. No offense, Harry. . . ." He smiled.

Morris smiled too. "Yeah, he wasn't exactly Charles Lindbergh behind the wheel."

The doctor cracked open the door again. "I'm afraid I need the room."

Sol looked across to him and nodded. Then he took one last look at Harry. "I'm sorry, Harry. I'm sorry for how you had to live your life with all that shame. I'm sorry if you felt we all thought less of you. We loved you all the same. Even with . . . Even with what you did to us. I forgive you, Harry. You're still my brother, and you didn't deserve this."

The doctor came over and took the sheet to drape across Harry's face.

"Hold it a second." Sol stopped the doctor from covering him. "Can you say that, Morris?"

"Can I say what?"

"That you forgive him. Can you forgive your own brother? Look at him."

A lump formed in Morris's throat. He looked down at Harry. The dull, grayish cast on his face. He remembered him years before at the Theatrical Club. All jokes and laughs. Mendy, Maxie. Buchalter. Surrounded by all the people he trusted, but who in the end, set him up and killed him. Morris was certain. Even back then Harry couldn't get up and come over to them. Even then. Morris wiped a tear away.

"No," he said. "I can't. I can't forgive him, Sol." Morris glanced up at the doctor and nodded. He draped the sheet back over Harry's eyes and wheeled him toward the wall. "I'm sorry, Harry, but I can't forgive you. But I can't forgive them either. He trusted these bastards, Sol. And they just set him up and made him a patsy for something. They have an empty hole in their chests where their hearts should be. I can't forgive him, not like you want, anyway. Not yet. But I can't forgive them either. That's the best you'll get out of me now."

Chapter Forty-Six

After the funeral, Mendy Weiss, Maxie Dannenberg, and Ike Lipschultz stopped in for a shivah call at Morris's apartment. Buchalter and a bunch of the boys had sent flowers. Morris told Ruthie to dump them down the chute. Special Prosecutor Dewey's office had sent a nice arrangement too.

"Meyn simpatye," Mendy and the two others muttered to Bella with a kiss to each cheek. *"Zeyer antshuldigt far deyn onver."* Very sorry for your loss. Mendy looked over at Morris, who was nursing a glass of scotch. "Excuse me," he said to Morris's mother, and came over.

"You got a lotta fucking nerve coming up here," Morris said.

"Harry was our friend too," Mendy said. "Trust me, we find out who did this . . ."

"Shouldn't be so hard. You shouldn't have to look too far."

"Morris, listen, you think this was our work, you'd be dead wrong," he said. "We want to find out same as you."

"You burnt our business down."

"That was business, Morris. You knew the risk. If I recall, it was me who told you not to piss off the boss. But this isn't the time."

"No, it's not. But tell me, Mendy, did Harry play a part in that killing? Like the papers say?"

Mendy didn't blink. "Don't ask me stuff like that, Morris."

"I've known you a long time, Mendy, and you'd lie to your own mother if it would save you a buck. Did Harry drive the car that night, like they're saying, with what happened to Dutch Schultz?"

"You know I can't talk about business, Morris," Mendy said.

"Go fuck yourself," Morris said, "and you can tell your boss too."

"I'm gonna put that down to the situation," Mendy said, grabbing his hat. He eyed his cronies. "I think it's time we go."

People were looking over. Ruthie came up. She took Morris by the arm. "Morris, come over here, my aunt Iris would like to meet you. . . ."

Morris turned to Mendy. "I find out that's the case, that you did suck him in, you and I are gonna have some things to discuss, Mendy. And it won't matter how far back we go. You understand? He was your friend. But he wasn't like you. He had something. In here . . . ," Morris tapped his chest, "something you hadn't covered over yet. He was your friend? You fucking used him for a laugh and then you put a bullet in the back of his head. Guys like you, you don't have friends, Mendy."

"I'm very sorry, Mrs. Raab, if we caused any unrest," Mendy said. "You have our respects."

"Thank you," Ruthie said. "But maybe it's best that . . ."

"We're leaving." Mendy nudged Maxie and Ike who muttered again, "We're very sorry, missus. . . ."

Morris gave Mendy a look. They both knew what was in it.

They'd crossed a line. Both of them. Buchalter too.

And there was no turning back from it.

Chapter Forty-Seven

At the funeral, the rabbi who had presided asked, *What does it mean to be a good man?*

After, Morris sat at the bar at the Hotel Chesterfield, nursing a scotch.

Did it simply mean love of God? If so, Harry didn't measure up on that one, the rabbi joked.

Or to do good deeds? Performing *mitzvos,* or observing the commandments? Or to live with *tzedaka,* righteousness. Perform acts of charity. Or any of a hundred ways the Torah would describe it.

Seen this way, Morris fell short too.

Harry was about as far away from *tzedaka* as a man could be.

He was weak. He couldn't be counted on. He built nothing of his life. When he was needed most, he wasn't there. He was no *mensch*—a decent, honest person who could be trusted. He spent his days around bad types.

But he was gentle. He wouldn't hurt a flea. Morris only had to watch him playing with Samuel to see that. It was as if he saw his twin reborn in that boy. And he had a good heart.

And Sol was right, he had shouldered the burden of his brother's death his entire life, along with his mother's sorrow at the loss.

Morris could not see how he would knowingly take part in a rubout, especially of Dutch Schultz. He wouldn't kill anyone.

These people had used him. Used him for something. They chewed him up and spit him out on the sidewalk like a wad of spent tobacco.

What does it mean to be a good man?

Morris felt a hand on his shoulder and he looked around. "Irv." His old friend took a seat next to him. "Listen, thanks for coming the other night."

"Of course. I'm really sorry you have to go through all this."

"How about a rye?" Morris asked. The bartender came up to them.

"Wish I could, but I have to get back to the office." Irv waved him off. "We've got a lot of big doings going on."

"So, you find out anything for me? On Harry."

"Look . . ." Irv leaned closer and said in a low voice, "I know you don't want to hear this, but some of our sources on the street confirm that it was Harry who drove the getaway car, just like the papers are alleging."

"Harry?" Morris leaned back and shook his head. "My brother may have sold us out, Irv, but he didn't have the balls or the lack of conscience to get involved in something like that."

"Maybe he needed the money."

Morris thought about it. He knew Bella was helping him out. Maybe Sol was too. How much could he have made, polishing the wood in a pool hall? Still . . . "So why would they have killed him?"

"The word on the street is, Harry was given up. By one of their own. The guy's rumored to have been one of the shooters. Maybe it was to keep the peace. Either way, you know where it comes from."

"Buchalter," Morris said.

"The fish stinks from the head." Irv nodded. "So have you had a chance to think it over? What we asked? Can we count on you, Morris?"

Morris took a sip of his drink. "The rabbi the other day, at the funeral, he told this story. 'A famous rabbi said to a student, "You must repent one day before your death." "How do you possibly know what day you will die?" one of his followers asked. "You don't," the rabbi answered. "So better to start today, since you may die tomorrow."'"

"What do you have to repent for?" Irv looked at Morris and asked.

"Me? I don't know. But I'm thinking maybe Harry felt he did." Morris looked at Irv. His own face said he was wrestling with it too. "So tell your boss, I'm in. All the way. For whatever he needs of me."

Irv smiled widely. "That's great, Morris. Welcome to the good guys."

"Good guys, huh?" He finished his drink. "We'll see. Just let me know what you need me to do."

PART FOUR

UNDER MANHATTAN BRIDGE

Chapter Forty-Eight

Morris would start off the conversation with something like, "Meet me for coffee. I need to talk to you about something."

It got deeper from there.

He went to see three people in the industry whom he knew had faced strong-armed repercussions from the union. Two were clothing manufacturers and one was a fur trimmer who had been pressured to join the directive. Sid Berlin had a budget coat firm; his rabbit fur collars were initially dressed at a nickel apiece. Soon it was raised to eight cents, then ten. When he refused to continue, the union thugs came up to his place with lead pipes and smashed his cutting tables and sewing machines. When he succumbed and raised his prices, his business fell by a third.

Hy Dresher made couture dresses. He was known as the "dresser to the stars." Theater and movie stars wore them; his clothes were only in the toniest stores like Bergdorf Goodman, Bonwit Teller, and Saks. He told Morris a similar tale. He received intimidating phone calls and was told that his offices would be stink-bombed if he didn't comply. His workers were threatened and his deliveries hijacked, right off the street. Two of his fabric suppliers were met by armed thugs. Everyone knew Lepke and Gurrah supplied the muscle.

David Mittleman was a furrier who stopped using the directive when he was notified that his prices would increase, effective immediately. When he went back to his existing suppliers, he began to receive threatening phone calls. First at the office, then at home. Two of his delivery trucks were stopped and stench bombs were hurled inside, his inventory ruined. When he still wouldn't agree, he was clubbed in the stairway to his offices and sent to the hospital with a fractured knee and three broken ribs.

"I want you to listen to me," Morris said to them. "We have to end this. It will just take a few of us to stand up, and I'll be at the front of the line. I just want you to talk to Dewey's operation. You can make up your own minds."

"I want to rid the business of these bastards same as you," was the usual reply. "But all they're gonna do is toss a few slammers in jail and then run for public office. And we'll still be here. And the bigwigs, they'll still run the union. And who's gonna stand up for us then?"

"It's different now," Morris would answer. "There are things called 'restraint of trade' laws. I can't fully explain it, but they can nail them on running a monopoly and price fixing. And not just the muscle—the guys in charge. Lepke. Gurrah. Just talk to them. It'll all be done in secret. No one will ever know."

"If word gets out, Morris, we'll be dead."

"Then I'll be dead with you," Morris said. "But if we don't fix this, in terms of our businesses, we already have one foot in the grave."

He asked each who their union rep was, who would know if they weren't complying. They all had the same answer.

Cy Haddad.

So they talked.

One by one, over weeks. At first in back rooms of restaurants and watering holes. Eventually at Dewey's offices on Center Street, rushed out of unmarked cars, accompanied by their lawyers. It took about three visits each; over months. Each time convincing them a little further of the task force's seriousness of purpose and the depth of the cases they had assembled to put those who ran the unions away.

They were assured their identities would remain secret, even through the grand jury hearings, until a trial. Accusation by accusation, the special prosecutor began to map out the case against Lepke and Gurrah. Price fixing and extortion. Pressuring clients through force into buying only through the union's directive. Violations of the Sherman Antitrust Act. Gradually, more small operators came on board, each with their own stories. For the first time they had actual witnesses, not just whispers and innuendos. The evidence against Lepke and Gurrah was clear cut.

"We just need one more case," Irv said. "A witness who could sway a jury in a way that's beyond the numbers."

In the end, Morris went back to the most convincing witness he knew. The one who had suffered most.

"Manny," he said one afternoon, when he'd gone up and visited his friend at his apartment, "it's time to tell your story."

This time Morris's friend didn't say a word.

"Just talk to them," Morris said. "You'd be one of seven people pointing fingers. They can't fight us all. You'll be fully protected. Dewey promises it. And I've seen, he keeps his word. Only the prosecutors will know your name. Anyway, just talk to them. Let them convince you, not me."

"I'm sorry about your brother," Manny said, "and I know you have a grudge to bear against these people. But these things always have a way of leaking out."

"I know that better than anyone," Morris said. "And we both have a grudge to bear. But it's different now. They're going after all of them this time. And it's not the local police. These men haven't been infiltrated. Manny, I know you've already paid a huge price. But your testimony would put it over the top. Just think about it, okay?"

Manny knitted his fingers together and finally let a blast of air out his nose. "Okay."

"That's all I'm asking, my friend." Morris patted him on the shoulder and got up to leave.

"Morris, sit down. Don't go yet."

"All right." Morris sat back down.

"You see *The Times* yesterday?"

"I might've. What about?"

"Albert Schoenberg died."

"Albert Schoenberg . . . ?"

Schoenberg was an Orthodox rabbi who was well known for his efforts to organize a Jewish state in Palestine. Both by raising money through the Jewish community here and putting pressure on international governments. Morris had given money to the cause himself at industry fund-raisers.

Manny shrugged. "The *mishnah* states that the world will be sustained no matter what tragedy as long as there are thirty-six *tzaddikim* left in the world. You know *tzaddik*, Morris?"

"Saints, I think," Morris said. "Right?"

"Kind of. You would know if you went to temple more. Anyway, it's more like a truly righteous person. People devoted to doing good deeds. Rabbi Schoenberg was surely one of them. It's said that, as long as at any time there are still thirty-six such men left in the world, the world will not perish. No matter what evil is let loose in it."

"What does any of this have to do with the union, Manny?"

He got up. "I may live to regret this," he said, "but if you're gonna go the distance on this, which it seems that you are, I may have something that can be of help to all of you." He went across to a dresser and dug to the back of a drawer. He came back out with something wrapped in a white handkerchief.

He handed the bundle to Morris. "Here . . . It's not doing anything in here, except collecting dust. Might as well put it to some use."

Morris unwrapped the cloth and removed whatever was inside.

It was a cigarette lighter. A nice one. Silver. On the front, there were two initials engraved.

O.H.

"Whose is it?" Morris looked at him.

"It belonged to the little prick who led the raid on my company. The one who did this to me." Manny put a hand to his cheek. "He was about to set fire to our pattern library. The bastard wasn't just content with destroying our skins and machinery, he wanted to drive the nail in the coffin and put us out of business for good. I must have pried it loose when I grabbed on to him and tried to stop him."

Morris looked at it. The lighter could connect someone there that day. It could convict someone.

O.H.

"This is good, Manny." Morris held it in his hand like a weight on a scale. "You've had it for over a year." He started to wrap it back up. "Why now?"

"You came to me."

"I came to you before, Manny."

"So you did." Manny nodded. He took a breath. "Thirty-six *tzaddikim*, Morris. Thirty-six good men. That's all the world needs. With Rabbi Schoenberg gone, I guess I figured maybe they'd need one more."

Chapter Forty-Nine

Oscar Hammerschmitt was five foot nine, with fists like meat hammers, thick lips, and dull, droopy eyes. He had boxed a bit as a youth at the Jewish clubs, but was far too short to really go anywhere, so he took a job as a butcher. He started doing odd jobs for the mob when they needed something done that involved his special skills. First, with Little Augie. Then as a full-fledged member of Lepke's gang. Not that he was ever a threat to rise too high in the organization. Brains weren't Oscar's specialty. But if you needed something done that required his form of persuasion and not too many questions asked, Oscar was the one you called.

He sat in the small interrogation room staring at the mirror at the 19th Precinct station in Bensonhurst.

He'd been picked up outside the hotel where he boarded, the Hopkins, in downtown Brooklyn. Two detectives had taken him in after breakfast, pulled him right off the street into their car.

"What's the charge?" Oscar asked. They could have gotten him on a hundred counts, but not these guys. These guys were errand boys. Bunko and fraud. Plus, his boss had them all in his palm any-way. Whatever they wanted with him, by lunchtime he'd be back on the street.

"You got a license for that gun?"

"Yeah, I got a license," Oscar said.

"You drive a car?" the other detective asked.

"Sure. I drive a car."

"Then double parking."

These rubes had no idea what they had walked into with him. All he'd have to do was make one call.

But they didn't offer him a call. They took his possessions and booked him on the traffic charge and let him sit in the station room for nearly an hour. Finally, two men came in. One was short and pudgy, in a gray suit, lawyer written all over him.

The other, which made Oscar sit up and do a double-take, was none other than Thomas Dewey.

"Guess by now you've figured out," the famous prosecutor smiled thinly, "this isn't really about double parking, Mr. Hammerschmitt."

"If it is, you guys must really be hard up for a conviction." Oscar grinned.

"I'm Special Prosecutor Dewey," Dewey said, taking a seat across from Oscar.

"I read the papers. My mom's a big fan."

"Tell her hello then. This is Assistant Special Prosecutor Irving Weschler from my staff." Pudgy opened a file and took out a pad and pencil. "We'd like to ask you a few questions, if that's okay?"

"Maybe I want my lawyer," Oscar said.

"You'll have every opportunity to call for one." Dewey opened a file as well. "But in the meantime just hear us out. I predict in a matter of minutes your life is about to change. And decidedly for the better."

"For the better, huh?" Oscar sat back and lit up a cigarette. He might as well hear what they had to say. They'd made a point in getting him here. "It's a free country." He shrugged. "At least that's what they say. Fire away."

"Good, Mr. Hammerschmitt. I agree, it is." He nodded to his chubby associate.

"You work for the Lepke and Gurrah crime organization," the lawyer started in.

"Uh, that's not how I would say it exactly."

"Let's not play around with each other, shall we? You do jobs for them. And for the Amalgamated Needle Trade Workers and the Fur Dressers Union. You're what's known in the trade as a slammer."

"I work for the fur dressers union." Oscar nodded. "But you got it wrong. I'm a field organizer."

"A field organizer . . . ?" Dewey squinted, as if just to be sure he heard him correctly. "You specialize in labor relations."

"Yeah, labor relations." Oscar laughed. "When they have an organizing problem they call me in. I do my best to get it solved."

"Like we said, you mean you're muscle?" Dewey clarified. "You strong-arm people when force is needed?"

"I would say I can be very persuasive." Oscar grinned. "When it comes to solving problems."

"All right, let me ask you." Thomas Dewey turned the page. "Have you ever heard of something called ammonium sulfite?"

"Don't think I have, Mr. Dewey. I didn't do so well in science class back in school." The gangster smirked.

"Me either, actually." Dewey nodded amiably. "My worst subject. But to speed things up, it's a compound that when exposed to the air emits a strong sulfur-like odor. It's commonly used in stench bombs, Mr. Hammerschmitt. You must know of these, in your work?"

"I know what they are." The gangster shrugged and glanced at his watch. "This going anywhere?"

"It will, Mr. Hammerschmitt. Count that it will. So have you ever been asked to deliver a stench bomb?" the prosecutor asked. "Say, as a warning. To a stubborn client, who wouldn't come around? From the union perhaps. Or maybe as a message from Mr. Lepke and Mr. Shapiro themselves? In your capacity of solving organizing problems so persuasively?"

"No, I don't think I have," the gangster said. "But can we cut to the chase, Counselor? I have appointments. You said this was gonna change my life."

"And we're getting to that, Mr. Hammerschmitt. I promise we will. Just hear us out. So, changing subjects ever so slightly, what about sulfuric acid? Have you ever heard of that?"

The gangster lit up another cigarette and took in a drag. He shook his head.

"Very potent, I understand. It has a hundred chemical uses, I'm told, but one of them, a bit out of the ordinary, and pertinent in the particular field you're in, is to have a harmful effect, say, on fabric or even fur or skins. Have you ever come across that, Mr. Hammerschmitt?" Dewey stared. "In your line of work?"

"What did you call it?"

"Sulfuric acid."

The gangster rubbed his mouth with his hand and shook his head.

"I didn't quite hear that, Mr. Hammerschmitt?" Dewey said.

"No, I don't think I have, Mr. Dewey. Sorry."

"It would surely be dangerous work if you had, so I'm sure you'd remember. You can only imagine what might happen if such a substance came in contact with your skin? The result would be very bad. Or, say, a client's skin. In your union activities. That might be looked at as a form of assault, not just persuasion. Assault with intent to injure. And with a deadly weapon. If some came in contact with you, say by someone throwing it on you, liberally," Dewey thrust his hands forward like he was tossing a basketball, "I bet you'd look at that as an assault, wouldn't you?"

Oscar wasn't the swiftest boat in the marina, but he began to see where this was going.

"I didn't hear your answer, Mr. Hammerschmitt. Can you say it again for me? I bet you'd be downright incensed. If someone threw it on you. Wouldn't you look at that as an assault?"

Oscar shifted in his seat. He flicked off an ash. "I might." He nodded slowly.

"Fortunately it doesn't specifically matter what you think, because as far as the New York State penal code is concerned, intent to injure with an object capable of doing bodily harm is regarded as a Class A felony and I don't think anyone would have much difficulty thinking sulfuric acid, especially if they saw photos of the harmful result of such an attack, was such a weapon."

"You know you told me my life was about to change for the better." Oscar looked back at them. "So far, I only have the feeling it's getting worse."

"Ah, and we're about to get to just that, Mr. Hammerschmitt," the special prosecutor said. He nodded to his partner.

"On May fifth, two years ago, at approximately ten fifteen A.M., the offices of the Isidor Gutman Fur Company were broken into by a gang of club-wielding thugs with concealed faces," the pudgy lawyer started in. "When asked why they were there, the leader of this group claimed it was in response to the company, after repeated warnings, not adhering to an agreed-upon directive to buy raw materials only from union-approved sources. In other words, not on the open market, by their own choice, but from a supplier chosen by the union who maintained a higher price. Did you happen to be among that group of intruders that day, Mr. Hammerschmitt?"

"Never heard of the company." Oscar shook his head. "Now if we can—"

"After the company's president, one Emmanuel David Gutman," the lawyer pressed on, "tried repeatedly to convince the group to leave, he was struck, thrown to the floor, savagely beaten in front of his staff, and the company's inventory of finished goods and raw materials, as well as expensive machinery, destroyed. They're in the fur business, Mr. Hammerschmitt, so pelts and hides which were quite valuable were mutilated into worthless strips. And expensive sewing machinery was destroyed by lead pipes. You still claim no knowledge of this event?" the lawyer asked.

"Yes, I do." A stream of sweat wound its way underneath Oscar's collar. "And I'm getting ready to leave now," he went to stand up, "unless you're intending to charge me with something. . . ."

"I'm saying we'll be happy to give you that choice in just a minute," the lawyer said. "So, please sit down."

Oscar remained standing.

"Sit down." Special Prosecutor Dewey narrowed his eyes at him.

Oscar lowered himself back down.

"After the skins and pelts were rendered useless," Pudgy continued, "the leader of this band of thugs took a container of sulfuric acid and doused the finished coats and uncut hides, damaging them beyond repair. As Mr. Gutman was on the floor begging them to stop, the leader of the group took what remained of the sulfuric acid and threw it at Mr. Gutman, causing severe burns over his face and neck, permanent skin discoloration, and extreme pain. You can imagine how being doused with such a highly corrosive form of acid would feel?"

"Not so good, I would think," Oscar said, clearing his throat.

"That's right. Not so good, I think too, Mr. Hammerschmitt. By definition, an act of physical assault with intent to cause bodily harm. Maybe even death, it might be construed. Which would make it attempted murder. But this is all just hypothetical, anyway, of course, since you were not there."

"Yeah, hypothetical, of course," the gangster chuckled. "So if I can—"

"One more thing," the special prosecutor said. "In the tussle before he was assaulted, as Mr. Gutman tried to stop the man he identified as the leader of the group from lighting an assortment of his clothing patterns on fire, something fell out of the intruder's hand. Mr. Gutman picked it up. Which is why we asked you here." The lawyer went into his case and came out with something wrapped in a white handkerchief. As he slowly unwrapped it, Oscar's heart started to thump loudly. The second Oscar's eyes fell upon it, he looked away and stared glumly at the floor. He had known for months it might resurface one day and come back to haunt him—but he'd not wanted to ever go back and look for it, as it would make him appear like a dumb lug.

Dewey placed it on the table between them.

It was a silver cigarette lighter. With a monogram engraved on it.

The initials *O.H.*

"There's a lot of people with those initials," Oscar said. "Doesn't prove shit."

"Yes," Special Prosecutor Dewey nodded, "I admit, left to itself it doesn't prove 'shit,' as you say. A hundred people could have the same initials. *O.H.* Even in your specific line of work.

"But of course you already know what was among your personal items taken off you today, when the detectives took you in?"

This time it was Dewey who dug into *his* jacket pocket. He took out a lighter, almost identical to the one on the table, with the same filigree scroll and engraved initials. *O.H.*

Oscar's throat went dry.

"I guess you must have sincerely missed it," the prosecutor smiled, "after it fell out up there. I commend you on your taste."

"Still don't mean fuck-shit." The gangster stared at Dewey, a baleful glare in his eyes. "Only way you can convict me on that is if that guy wants to own up to it at trial. And that's never a sure thing. Otherwise, it's just a lighter. But on reconsideration, I think I will take that lawyer now."

"That's your option," Dewey said. "But I would beg to differ on a point. I think it does mean 'fuck-shit,' Mr. Hammerschmitt. In fact, what I think it means, just to lay it out for you, is extortion, assault with a deadly weapon, criminal vandalism. Manslaughter in the first degree, at the very least. Maybe attempted murder. I wouldn't think there's a jury in the country that would have trouble placing you directly at the scene where these incidents took place based on what we have on that table, and more, as the chief perpetrator of these charges. A conservative estimate at trial, if we were to convict, would say thirty to forty years. And the indictments of this committee are under federal time. You're how old, sir?"

Oscar rubbed his meaty face. "Thirty-two."

"Thirty-two. You may indeed get out, at sixty or seventy. But I did promise that if you stayed here to hear what we had to say, your life could dramatically change for the better."

Oscar sniffed in his nose loudly. He massaged his face. He reached for another cigarette. He lit it and tossed the match in the ashtray. "I'm listening."

They did bring in a lawyer. Not Oscar's, of course. He couldn't trust that his own lawyer wouldn't be on the horn to his bosses the moment Oscar hung up from him. A court-appointed lawyer. A fancy one, to work out the details of their plea agreement.

The real interrogation began the next day.

"How many of these special assignments did you personally participate in, Mr. Hammerschmitt?" Thomas Dewey asked him.

"Maybe ten, fifteen." The gangster shrugged. "We didn't exactly keep records on that sort of thing. Hard to keep track."

"And how much were you paid for your work?"

"Paid? Fifty to sixty thousand a year," Oscar said. "Plus money for outside labor, if we needed it."

"Outside labor?"

"Additional personnel. Slammers. Sometimes the situation required it."

"Kind of funny," Dewey said, smiling, "the union enforcers having to use outside labor."

"Yeah, hilarious," Oscar chuffed. His dress shirt was sweated through and opened to the chest, over a sleeveless undershirt. A two-day growth was on his face. At least seven Old Gold butts lay crushed in the ashtray.

"Anyway, it was highly profitable work, it seems. And who would alert you that such an action was necessary?"

"We'd get a call. It could be from a couple of people. The orders always came from above."

"Names, Mr. Hammerschmitt." Dewey tapped his index finger on the table.

"Gurrah. Jacob Shapiro." Oscar flicked his cigarette.

"Lepke?"

"If it came from Gurrah you could assume it came from Lepke too. Those two are like butter and bread."

"And what about from the union?"

"What about the union?" Oscar asked.

"Who would alert you from the union that your kind of work was needed for a recalcitrant client?"

"Re-*calcitrant* . . . ?" The gangster screwed up his eyes.

"Someone who didn't want to play the game, Mr. Hammer-schmitt."

"Oh. There were a couple of them." Oscar shrugged again. "There *was* one I worked with mostly."

"And who was that?" Dewey pressed.

"This guy, Cy Haddad."

"Haddad. Write that down if you please, Mr. Hammer-schmitt."

He described how the situation would generally proceed. A company would refuse to comply with some aspect of the agreement. Often it took just a phone call to convince them to fall in line. Other times, a visit. To wave the flag, as it was called. Usually the guy got back in line quick. Once in a rare while someone was just stubborn enough that they needed to do some real work. "Those were the calls we liked best." Oscar grinned. "We got to show off our skills."

"Your skills?" Dewey asked for clarification.

"Yeah," Oscar said, lighting up a new smoke, "at persuasion."

"And you're certain your superiors were aware of these actions?" Dewey asked. "Mr. Shapiro? And Mr. Lepke?"

"'Course they were aware," the gangster chortled. "They're the bosses. We talked about it many times. They paid us bonuses based on how good we'd done."

"How good you'd done . . . ?"

"Whether or not the company got back in line."

"And how good were you at what you did?"

Oscar nodded and grinned crookedly. "They always got back in line."

Irv and Dewey pressed him in detail about specific conversations. What was Mr. Gurrah's reaction? What did Mr. Buchalter say?

313

"What did they say?" Oscar bunched his thick lips and shrugged. "Once he may have said, 'Good job'? Another time, 'Here's two tickets to the Yankee game.' Or 'Go take a week in the Bahamas.'"

They went over it and over it again until they had enough. Enough to confirm Lepke's and Shapiro's day-to-day control of the fur dressers union. And the use of intimidation and violence to enact their illegal schemes. Extortion. Restraint of trade. Price fixing. Not just one count. Several. If Hammerschmitt talked on the stand, it was enough to put them away for years.

After three days of spilling his guts, he was done. Oscar stamped out maybe his hundredth cigarette in the ashtray. "So I don't have to spend no jail time? This is all good, right? You got enough."

"It's all good," Dewey said. "But still not quite enough for that, I'm afraid."

"What are you talking about? I got him lined up on a silver platter for you."

"On union violations. Maybe some antitrust charges, yes. Each carries a maximum prison term of only five years. The actual physical assaults will be harder to prove."

"Wait a minute! You said if I told you what I know, you'd set me up somewhere. After the trial. I got it in writing."

"What I said, Mr. Hammerschmitt," Dewey elaborated, "was that that depended on what you know."

"I told you what I know."

"That's up to you, Mr. Hammerschmitt. If you want to find yourself on some beach somewhere, instead of upstate, I'm hoping there's more."

Oscar sat, rubbing his face. Dewey waited. The gangster got up. He went to the wall and leaned on it with his palms outstretched. Finally he turned around. "I know stuff."

"Then let's hear it, Mr. Hammerschmitt," Dewey said. "We're all ears."

Oscar came back to the table. He let out a breath and sat back down and laughed. "How you guys gonna keep me alive?"

"You let us worry about that."

"*You* worry about it, huh?" He snorted. He took a long sip of water and looked at them like he was signing away his life with what he was about to say. "I was once a driver," he said. "Back in '28. I drove them out. Both of them."

"Drove who?" Dewey pressed. "Where?"

"Lepke. Gurrah. They did this job. I'm not sure who it was for. I heard Albert Anastasia. It was this candy store owner. Maybe you heard of him. Blinky Cohen."

"I know of Blinky Cohen." Dewey nodded and looked at Irv. Pictures of Cohen's bloodied body had made the front pages of all the local papers. The crime was still unsolved.

Oscar grinned. "Then maybe you also heard he ain't around no more."

Dewey looked at Oscar sternly. "You're sure it was them? Lepke, Shapiro. They did the killing?"

"'Course I'm sure. I was the driver. They even came back out with a box of Cracker Jacks and laughed about it."

"Cracker Jacks. I like that." Dewey smiled, got up, and plopped down a pad of paper in front of Oscar. "Start writing."

An hour later, they had eyewitness testimony to first-degree murder, a crime that could put Lepke and Gurrah away for good, not just a few years. Maybe even get them the chair. Oscar Hammerschmitt finished and pushed the tablet back across the table, ashen, empty. He looked at Dewey. "There."

"All right, one last question, Mr. Hammerschmitt. And then you have your deal."

"You guys don't give up, do you?" He took a drag on his cigarette. "What's that?"

Dewey leaned in close. His eyes were fixed and alive. "Who killed Abe Langer?"

Chapter Fifty

Louis Buchalter was worried sick.

In the back room of Rose's Steak House, a Kosher restaurant off Ocean Avenue in Brooklyn, he sat, finishing up a bowl of borscht. A plate of herring and a bowl of *kreplach,* potato dumplings, sat nearby.

There was one other place set at the table.

Buchalter knew the special prosecutor was preparing indictments against him. Charges related to his union activities. Buchalter had the finest lawyers; informants wherever he could spread a buck. He had people who could intimidate anyone who even thought about raising their right hand. But this time he had a troubled feeling. It was funny, he thought, with all the shit he'd done, that what he could end up going to prison for was union fraud. Extortion. Price fixing! He knew he couldn't be like Schultz and propose to kill Dewey. It would be like killing the president now. He'd end up just like the Dutchman, and that's not the way he wanted to go. When these kinds of situations arose, his instincts told him to go on the offensive. If they were going to nail him for something, he laughed, let them get him for something big. Not for cracking a few kneecaps. Or throwing a stink bomb in a few warehouses. But with the union, there were too many people involved. People left evidence, witnesses who would talk. The days when you could just solve a problem by bashing a few heads were over. Phones were tapped. Underlings were promised deals if they'd roll over. The tide was shifting. Government spies were everywhere.

That's what tonight's meeting was about. He had to find a way to change that tide.

There was a knock, and Moe Stein, one of his men, stuck his head in. "Our guest is here."

Louis wiped his mouth with the napkin and stood up. "Show him in." He buttoned his double-breasted jacket.

Albert Anastasia came into the room, while his bulky body-guard remained outside. "Louis." He put out his arms, and they gave each other a warm hug.

"It's taken you long enough to come to *my* neighborhood." Louis shook his hand warmly and motioned for the Italian to sit down. "So you here for that circumcision?" Louis grinned.

"No more than you came to my neck of the woods for a shave." Anastasia laughed. "But I am looking at what you've got laid out here." He turned his flattened nose up at the soup. "What is that? It looks like pink paint."

"It's borscht. It's made from beets, Albert. It's Russian."

"Russian, huh? What about those?"

"Herring. They're little fish. Kinda like anchovies. You like anchovies, don't you, Albert?"

"What is it, you Jews don't know how to eat any more than you know how to shave? Why don't you just bring me a steak? Medium rare. It said they had steak here on the front door."

"The best steak." Louis snapped his fingers and a waiter hopped out, and back to the kitchen.

"And you got a glass of wine here? You Jews drink wine, don't you?"

"We'll have to get you to a Seder next." Louis chuckled. "Yeah, we got wine. Kosher."

They drank and talked about business until the Italian's steak arrived. About the Dutchman's murder, and if there were any problems for him from it. Nothing yet. And how they were carving up Schultz's numbers rackets in Harlem. Everyone, including Louis, would receive a share. It would be a nice piece of change. Then the Italian looked at him. "This is all good news. But you don't look so happy, my friend. Is that why you asked me here?"

Louis put down his wineglass. "I got word the special prosecutor has built up some evidence against me. He may be preparing some indictments."

"And how do you know this, Louis?" They'd all been trying to buy someone inside Dewey's department.

"I know a lot of things, Albert. That's my job."

"All right. What kinds of indictments?"

"Things related to the garment union. New kinds of charges. Things called restraint of trade. Violations of the Sherman Act. Labor racketeering. Intimidation and extortion. It says we forced people to buy from our own vendors instead of on the open market."

"And you do this, Louis? Right?"

"Of course we do it, Albert. Anyway, each carries a five-year prison term, if convicted."

"Five years . . . We've all done time, Louis. It ain't so bad in there. You can still run things."

"Five years per indictment. There could be ten of them. That's fifty years."

"Ah, I see . . . ," the Italian said, cutting into his steak, which had arrived. "Of course, the key word I heard you say was, *if* convicted.

This is actually pretty good," the Italian said, nodding with approval. "Who woulda guessed. So these complainants against you, Louis, they're just who . . . ? Regular people?"

Louis nodded. "Industry people. Furriers, garment makers, a few fabric mills we pushed out."

"And just to be clear . . ." The Italian put down his fork. "You put Dutch Schultz in the grave and you're being taken down by a bunch of furriers and garment makers? That's a laugh." He snorted. "Just fucking take care of them, Louis. One falls, they all have a way of developing a faulty memory."

"There's too many of them, Albert. Someone's gotten them together."

"So, you're saying, what, your union's been out-*organized*?" Anastasia laughed again. "Kind of funny. Don't take this the wrong way, but that directive thing you got going, you *have* been kind of a pig about things. Maybe you did bring this on yourself."

"You'll be next, Albert."

"You know this for a fact, Louis?"

Louis cast him a sobering stare, indicating that he did.

Anastasia let a long breath out his nostrils. He cut off another piece of meat. "My sense is in these kinds of things, there's always one person who's out in front on it, who the rest look up to. Y'know . . . ? You make that person go away, the rest, they all kind of look in the mirror and lose their nerve. I know in the past you've had some success at that kind of thing."

"There is someone . . . ," Buchalter said. "Maybe a couple of them. He and this guy we burned up. Who are leading the others."

"So then take care of them." Anastasia cut into a *kreplach*. "You know these things ain't half bad either," he said. "Dough?"

"Potato."

"Hmmph. Like gnocchi, huh? So back to what you were saying . . . This guy . . . ?"

"You remember the driver we had to take care of after the Dutchman? Who took the rap for Mendy . . ."

"I remember." Anastasia reached for another dumpling.

"It's his brother."

"*His brother?* You think it's a personal thing?"

"No." Louis shook his head. "We go back a long ways. This has been coming for quite some time."

"*So?* Take care of it, then. You don't look so happy about it though."

"This guy's pushed me a hundred times. We go all the way back to when I ran card games on Delancey Street. He was pushing me even back there. He's kind of like me, in a way. He's a tough sonovabitch, and he doesn't back down from much. Not scared. He'd make a great one of us," Louis grinned, "except he's not. He's legit. You know, *good.*"

"Good . . . ?" Anastasia stared at him blankly. "So what's your fuckin' problem then?"

Buchalter took in a breath. "I know what I'm gonna tell you is gonna sound a little strange. *Feygeleh,* as we call it."

"*Feygeleh?*"

"I don't know. . . ." Louis wiggled his hand. "Like a woman or something. You know, queer. But I was always thinking, if I wasn't me, you know, what I do, but you know, in some other life, something legit . . . I could be him."

"You could *be* him . . . ?" Anastasia stared solidly at Louis, his jaw wide. An incredulous smile crossed his lips. "Someone *good,* you're saying?"

"Yeah, good. I know it sounds a little crazy. But, Albert, but yeah, the thought's crossed my mind."

"And that's why you let this guy push you around so long? 'Cause he reminds you of you?" Anastasia's lips curled into a smile. "Listen, you're not smoking that shit we sell to the niggers, are you, Louis?"

Buchalter laughed and waved it off. "No. I told you, it's a little crazy, Albert. You never thought about anything like that?"

"If I did, I wouldn't tell nobody," the Italian said. "So you know what I think? I don't think you do '*good*' so well, Louis. I think you oughta stick to what you know. Lemme ask, you looking for some kind of dispensation here? You know, just 'cause I'm Italian, doesn't mean I'm the Pope."

"No, I was just talking." Louis Buchalter shrugged with kind of a vague dimness in his eyes. "Forget I said it. You're right on what you say."

"You know you once did me a favor." The Italian leaned forward. "With that Yid with the candy store. So maybe you want us to handle this thing for you? If it's so tough. I'm happy to pay back the debt."

"No." Buchalter finished up, wiped his mouth, and pushed away his plate. "You know me, Albert. I handle my own business."

"Then take care of your business, Louis. This ain't like you. Make him disappear. Both of them. And without a trace, so the task force and the papers don't get all over you. You gotta nip this thing before all these people feel they're the ones who have the power. And you end up in the can. 'Cause once you're in there, all kinds of shit will come out. How did you call it, this idea of yours . . . ?"

"*Fegeleh*," Louis Buchalter said.

"Yeah, *fegeleh*. What's *fegeleh* is letting this guy shit all over you, Louis. Make him disappear. And anyone else who thinks they're a big shot. And not so noisy. The people don't like noisy these days. Something out of the public eye."

Buchalter nodded thoughtfully. "I'll take care of it, Albert." But there was something else bothering him. Something potentially worse.

Something he didn't dare mention till he knew for sure.

One of his men, Oscar Hammerschmitt. Word was he'd been picked up by the cops.

And no one had heard from him in three days.

Chapter Fifty-One

Manny Gutman went twice a week to his club, the Young Men's Philanthropic League, in a Victorian town house off the park on Seventy-ninth Street.

He bundled himself up, put on his hat (which hid the scars on his face), and walked the three blocks up Madison, where he would grab the afternoon *Mirror* and maybe a packet of gum. He always chatted with Vinnie, the newsstand owner, about the weather, the state of the country, even about how the Jews were having such a rough time of it back in Germany.

Then he would make his way to the club, read the headlines over a coffee, the Sports section too, how City College, where Manny had gone to school, was the basketball class of the city these days. Maybe he'd play a few games of rummy, if some of the other old-timers were around.

Manny had felt old this past year, with his company closed. These days, his biggest decision was whether to wear a green or red scarf.

Often he thought about the way in which he'd been forced out.

Sure, he could go over what it was like then with the other old-timers over cards. "Back in my day . . . ," they would say. But his day had come too soon. He stewed and stewed until he felt ashamed he had not done all he could. That was why he had finally given the lighter to Morris. The one that had come off of his attacker. Not so much out of goodness as he claimed; the desire to see that person caught. To get back a piece of what they'd stolen from him.

But because it gave him life. It made him feel connected again.

After a year trying to pretend he still had a purpose in life, it made him feel alive.

That afternoon, as he left, it was particularly raw out for early November. Another month and he and Helen would go to Miami. He waved to the doorman on his way out. "Gabe."

"Afternoon, Mr. Gutman."

"Need anything while I'm out?" He always asked, though Gabe had never once requested a thing.

"Maybe about ten more degrees, all I could ask for," the doorman said, his hands in gloves.

"I'll see if I can work that out," he said, and headed up to the corner.

As he turned, behind him, he thought he saw a set of car lights go on.

He crossed over Park on Seventy-fifth Street and then walked to Madison, past all the fancy town houses. There was one, he was told Theodore Roosevelt once lived in it. He glanced behind him. He thought he noticed the same car following, a big sedan, a Pontiac or something, creeping at a snail's pace behind him. But he could be wrong. He'd been lost in his own thoughts. He'd told Helen this morning that he'd decided he finally had to stand up. He wasn't going to be afraid anymore, and he felt good about it. He'd show these bastards in court, in the end.

Maybe this would even give the Isidor Gutman name back its pride.

Hands in his pockets, Manny waited for the light to change. The newspaper stand was just ahead. Maybe Freddie or Phil would be at the club today. Loudmouths, living in the past. The lot of them.

But Manny Gutman was about to reclaim his future.

Crossing the street, he heard the rumble of an engine picking up.

He turned, shielding his eyes from the glare of the oncoming lights.

Chapter Fifty-Two

Morris was still at the office after seven when Ruthie called.

"Morris, I have terrible news," she said. "Helen Gutman called me. Manny was hit by a car on his way to his club tonight. He's dead."

Dead? Morris felt the weight in his chest and sat down. Manny was his oldest friend in the business. "Did the driver stop?"

"No, that's the worst of it. Apparently he just kept on going. Oh, Morris, this is just terrible, isn't it?"

"Yes." The sweats came over him and his stomach dove into a freefall. His mind raced to the only possible conclusion:

It had to be connected. It had to be a response to what Manny had given him. The lighter he had taken from the thug who ransacked his business, which Morris had passed on to Irv. But how could they possibly know? Irv promised this would remain strictly confidential until they'd decided how to handle it. Who else knew? There had to be an informant up there. Morris's head spun wildly. Which made him think about all the others he had lured in. *Poor Manny.* He'd suffered so much already. Only a week ago, Morris had convinced him to step out from his silence, to become a witness against these murderous thugs. If it was true, what Morris suspected, then this wasn't some random act, but a retaliation, a way to keep him silent. Morris was as much a part of his death as them. He had as good as driven that car himself.

"Where's Helen?"

"She's home. Some of her family are there. She's a complete mess, of course."

"I have to go up there." He had to find out more.

"Do you want me to come too?"

"No. I want you to stay at home, Ruthie." If they knew about Manny Gutman, then they likely knew about him too, and the people he'd been organizing to testify against them. And their families. "Stay with the kids. It's important. I'll call you."

"What do you mean, it's important, Morris? What do you know about this? There's something you're not telling me."

"Nothing, Ruthie. Just wait to hear from me. That's all."

In a daze, he closed the style book he'd been going through, planning out next season's line, threw on his jacket and coat, and locked up the steel outer door. It was raining outside. Cold for November. He grabbed an umbrella at the gate and pushed the button for the elevator.

His mind flashed through how they possibly could have known.

Dewey had sworn to Morris that it wasn't like before. Back then, the police and even the city government had been infiltrated by the mob, giving them a heads-up when investigations were under way, selling the name of who was testifying against them. This time it was tight as a ship. But Morris knew, these people could always buy their way in. Money could buy anything. Or put a gun to someone's head. Or threaten their family. *Poor Manny . . .* All he had wanted was to live out his life in peace. Go to Miami, Havana. Do a little gambling. See the Carmen Miranda shows. He'd already suffered enough. But

Morris had lured him back in with the promise that they could actually do something this time. A promise he could not keep.

And now . . . Standing in the hall, he felt his stomach churn. Now Manny was dead too. Helen was a widow. Morris jammed his finger against the button for the elevator. Where the hell was it? What was taking so long? He felt a rage sweep over him and he slammed his hand against the wall in anger and complicity. *Goddammit, Manny. I'm sorry.*

The elevator door finally opened. He went in, pushed the button for the lobby. It was the service elevator, large enough for several trolleys of fabric to fit in. He felt sweats take hold of him. Guilt. Shame. It could have been anyone, he knew. Anyone. It could have been some hurrying cab, or some drunk behind the wheel, coming from a bar. He had to find out. It didn't have to be Buchalter. But he knew the handwriting. Abe. Now Manny. They didn't stop. If you stood up to them. *They just kept on going.* Hearing the floors pass by, he felt certain it had to be them.

At the lobby, the elevator rattled to a stop, the door opened, and Morris rushed out.

Directly into the path of two men. They seemed to be waiting for him. In overcoats, fedoras drawn down, their hands stuffed in their pockets. One had a thick nose and a mole on his cheek. The other . . .

The other, he knew.

And he knew he was in for trouble.

It was Charles Workman.

"Hello, Morris." Workman's eyes were dark and smiling. "I think I owe you one, don't I? And I'm a man who always tries to pay his debts."

"I guess they let any scum in here." Morris looked at him, bracing.

The two rushed forward and took hold of him. Morris swung

his umbrella, catching the one with the mole near his eye with the umbrella's tip. He howled, putting a hand up to his face.

Workman forced Morris back into the elevator. By that time his partner had recovered, a trail of blood streaming down his face. "You're a fucking dead man," he said.

Morris tried to rip free, but Workman's hand was out of his pocket and there was something shiny and flashing in it. Morris held his breath.

"Gurrah said he wished he could be here himself," Workman said. "But this'll have to do." He thrust out his hand and Morris felt a searing pain slice through his abdomen. The air went out of his lungs. His legs gave way. He tried to push his attackers off, even with the knife inside him, but then it was out again, a gleam of silver, blood on the blade.

His blood.

Workman thrust it into him again.

Morris sagged against the elevator wall. He tried to grab onto Workman's arm.

"No one seems to want you around anymore, Morris. Your nine lives seem to have run out."

He drew the blade back again.

Morris knew another stab would send him to the floor, and he'd be done then, unable to fend them off. He summoned whatever strength he still had left before Workman pushed the knife in again, bull-like, and threw him to the side and tried to run out of the elevator, a flower of sticky blood spreading on his shirt. The guy with the mole struck him in the abdomen near the stab wounds, sending a lightning bolt of pain up Morris's spine. He gasped and fell to the floor. He knew he had to get to his feet. If he could somehow get to the door and outside he had a chance, was all he was thinking. Fighting the pain, Morris tried to force himself out of the elevator. The guy with the mole grabbed onto his waist and threw him down.

Morris kicked at him, pain lancing through him. The man was struggling to bring out his gun. Morris tried to scramble to his feet, just as Workman squared his knee into the center of Morris's back, pinning him back onto the floor. He sucked in a breath that made him shudder with pain. But he had to fight through it. He pushed up. Workman kneed him back to the floor. *Just get to your feet,* Morris willed himself. *To your feet.*

He couldn't.

"So how you feeling now, Morris," Workman chided him, "still your lucky day?" He jabbed Morris in the side again through his heavy coat, the pain shooting all the way down to his toes. Morris's heavy wool coat and sport jacket had probably kept the knife from going in all the way, but the next one, Workman would likely twist it all the way up to his gut. Morris spun around and wrapped his hands around the killer's wrist, slowly inching the blade away from him. Fending off the other assailant's gun hand with his legs.

He could only hold out so long.

He heard the gun go off. He cringed and smelled the acrid scent of either burned fabric or flesh and held his breath. The guy with the mole was tangled up with him, the muzzle against Morris's coat, but somehow the shot had gone wild. A searing burn sliced through his side, no more than a glancing blow, but the next one, he knew, would be deadly. He kicked the man off of him and tried to wrestle the gun away in a desperate clinch. Workman came back with the knife. If the killer freed his fingers and pulled the trigger again, that would be all there was.

Suddenly, behind them, the front doors opened. "What's going on in there?" someone yelled. "Sweet Lord, is that you, Mr. Raab?"

It was Buck, the vagrant who lived on the street outside. Whose hand Morris had put a dollar in most days as he left for the night.

"Get the fuck out of here!" Workman shouted.

"I'm gonna call the police," he said. "There's a car up the block."

The two assailants distracted, Morris kicked himself free. The attackers couldn't exactly murder someone with someone else looking on. They didn't know who Buck was. He could be the night manager for all they knew. Someone they'd have to take care of afterward if they went on.

Morris forced himself up and stumbled toward the door. Almost in reach of it, he heard the crack of a gun, two of them, and a searing pain ran through his thigh. He lunged for the front door, sure he was about to feel another one in his back and that would be it.

"Buck, get out of here," he said, and pushed the vagrant back outside. "Run." Morris put a hand to his abdomen. Blood spilled all over his palm. He could feel it damp and sticking against his shirt. There were drops of it on the floor. And his leg was deadened.

The two men had gotten up and were coming after him.

Doubled over, he staggered out onto Thirty-sixth Street. What was packed during the day with workers and salesmen was pretty much a graveyard now. Morris knew, if the two caught up to him on the street, alone, they'd shoot him right there on the pavement.

Down the block, Morris spotted a blue-and-white police car, just like Buck had said. It was parked about thirty yards down the street toward Broadway. He hobbled toward it—crouched over, sucking back the pain, his hand pressing the hole in his gut, blood leaking out of him. A cold rain slanted into his face.

Behind him, Workman and his partner came out of the lobby and headed after him.

He didn't know if he could make it to the car. He looked back again. The two were catching up to him, walking briskly, concealing the guns in their coats, maybe ten yards behind.

Morris's fear was that the police car would drive off before he reached it. He tried to scream, but nothing came out. He could barely suck in a breath. What he should have done, he knew, was head across the street into O'Malley's pub. They couldn't follow him in there.

He put up his hand to signal to the cops. Another ten yards. He glanced behind again. Workman and his partner had stopped. *Thank God,* they were afraid to go any farther. Morris ran the last six or eight steps and slammed his hand against the passenger's side window. "I need help! I'm stabbed," he shouted. "These two men are trying to kill me." He stood, his knees buckling, against the side of the car, gasping both in pain and alarm as the gangsters just stood there watching him, rain pelting him, the flow of blood matting on his side.

Behind him, instead of beating it out of there, Workman merely seemed to smile.

The passenger's window of the police car rolled down. Morris shouted again, "I need help. I've been stabbed."

"That so?"

To his shock, instead of a cop appearing, a gun came out the window.

"You look like you could use a ride, Morris. Why don't you come on in?"

Holding the gun to his face was Mendy Weiss.

Chapter Fifty-Three

Morris turned and sank back against the car. His body was numb and empty. There was no point in running.

Mendy hopped out and opened the rear door. The cop behind the wheel spun around. Morris recognized him instantly. It was the prick captain who had been there at the warehouse fire. Burns. It was no big surprise, just a confirmation he didn't need. Morris had known the moment he heard him back up the lieutenant that he was Lepke's man.

In a second, Morris was flung face-first onto the cop car's backseat. His abdomen was on fire. Charles Workman squeezed in after him, digging his gun into Morris's ribs. "Make a wrong move, Morris, and it ends right here. Hop in, Mendy." Mendy climbed back in the front.

"Start her up," Charles Workman instructed the driver.

"I don't like this, Charlie. I don't like this at all," the captain said.

"Just drive, Jack. You know where. You're not paid to like it or not. It's a little late for any pangs of conscience."

Grimacing, the police captain started up the engine.

Mendy turned back. "I told you to back off, Morris. We gave you every chance."

"Go fuck yourself, Mendy." Morris spun his head around.

Workman dug his gun deep into Morris's gut. Morris gasped. "You got the urge to fight it out, Morris, we can always end it right here."

"You do that, you can clean up the car," Burns looked around and said.

"You know where to send your complaints, Jackie-boy. You just drive."

Every time Morris took in a breath, he winced in pain. As he lay there, the gun in his side, the blocks going by as the police car sped downtown, his thoughts flashed to Ruthie, Sam, and Lucy. He wondered if they would ever know what had happened to him. If he would disappear. Or if they'd find him, like Harry, behind some garbage dump, tomorrow's headline in the *Mirror*. That was the hardest part. That he would never see them again. That Lucy would never even know him. "Where are you taking me?" he asked. The rain continued and he heard the windshield wiper squeak on the glass.

"Don't give too much thought to that, Morris," Workman sniffed. "You must've pissed enough people off that no one wants there to be any sign of you from now on."

The car turned right, heading south, and soon, a couple of quick turns more, it picked up speed. Eventually they were on bumpy cobblestones, which meant to Morris they were on East Street, heading south. At some point, Morris lifted his head and saw the dark, hulking shape of the Williamsburg Bridge go by.

"I said, get down." Workman pressed the gun in deeper.

Morris realized there was no way out now. He was bleeding inside his shirt from the knife. The bullet in his thigh was just a glancing blow. But the next one surely wouldn't be.

"How do we get over there?" Burns asked.

"Get off under the Manhattan Bridge. Stay along the river."

It was clear what they were going to do with him now. Morris saw it. What did Workman say? *No one wants there to be any sign of you.* The river was just a stone's throw away. They pulled off and wrapped around along the piers. Dark wharfs lined the shore. Warehouses interspersed with tenements. The bridge rose high above them, a massive dark shadow, like the hull of an enormous black ship. They were going to dump him there. In the East River. Where he swam as a kid.

That was going to be his resting place.

"Over there. You see Pier 36. Easton-Marley Freight," Mendy said, pointing.

"I don't like this," Burns said. "There's a guard."

"Of course there's a guard. Don't worry, it's been arranged. You're a cop, aren't you? Just tell 'em you're here about a possible theft. They're expecting us."

The policeman pulled up to the gate. He glanced back at Workman nervously and rolled down his window. "Someone called about a theft here."

"Yeah, theft . . ." The man at the gate sniffed. "All the way to the end. Go on in."

"Call the police! They're gonna kill me," Morris shouted.

"Yell all you want," Workman said. "No one gives a shit about you here. Anyway, good one, Morris," he chortled, considering the vehicle they were riding in. "Call the police."

"How 'bout you go and catch a smoke, " Mendy leaned over to the guard and said. "Twenty minutes should be enough."

"Will do."

The gate opened and they drove down the dark pier, passing stacked towers of containers and trestles. Morris could smell the river, oily and dark. Near the end of the pier, Burns pulled the car up and stopped. "This is as far as I go. I'm not comfortable anymore."

"All right," Workman said, "let us off here. Why don't you wait outside the gate, Jack, in case anyone gets ideas? You remember what it was like to be a cop, don't you? C'mon, Morris." He jabbed him with the gun. "End of the ride."

Mendy came around and opened the door. He took Morris by the collar and dragged him out of the backseat, onto the pier. Morris sucked in a breath against the pain.

"Come on, get up now." Charles Workman prodded him with his shoe. "This woulda been a whole lot easier on all of us if you'd just let me do the job back there."

"C'mon, Morris," Mendy said. "Up and at 'em." He yanked him to his feet.

The policeman swung the car around and cracked his window. "I'll see you boys outside then. Have a good night, Mr. Raab. I'm sorry it's worked out for you like this. Me, I would've just taken the message back in your warehouse and not rocked the boat."

Morris wiped the blood off his lip. "Go to hell."

"Don't you be judging me now, lad. If I were you, I'd use the time to prepare to meet your maker. Get on with your work now, boys. You can be sure you won't be disturbed." The police car drove off, leaving Morris, Mendy, and Workman on the dark pier.

Workman dug the gun into Morris's back. "Start walking."

"Where?"

"Where do you think, Morris? The Bronx? Ebbets Field? Straight ahead, smart guy." He waved his gun toward the far end of the pier.

There were crates and trellises everywhere, the lights of the Lower Manhattan skyline looming behind them. He could shout all he wanted, Morris knew, scream bloody hell; out here, no one would hear a thing. He walked. Across the river a Rheingold beer sign blinked in neon yellow script. The span of the dark bridge loomed above them. The occasional lights of cars heading to and from Brooklyn twinkled in the heavy night.

"We used to swim off these docks, remember?" Morris said to Mendy as he walked to the edge of the pier.

"That we did, Morris."

Morris looked north to the next pier, maybe a quarter mile away. It was once the Fourth Street pier, he recalled, where as kids they would play. The pier was dark now, a trawler moored, barely a light on it. Morris said, "I used to make it all the way over to that pier over there without even coming up for air. We called it Little Dublin back then. All Irish and Italian."

"Probably still is," Mendy laughed, nudging him with his gun, "'cept they're in the dockworkers union now."

Workman pointed. "You see those crates. Stop over there." He pushed Morris toward them. A slick, slanting rain began to beat into Morris's face.

"Coulda picked a prettier night to do this," Mendy chuffed.

Morris shrugged. "All the same to me."

Workman stopped behind a stack of containers near the tip of the pier. "Here."

Out on the river, a horn sounded. A barge coasted by, dark and silent. Morris contemplated screaming for help, but the breeze was coming in against him. No one would hear. No one would hear ten feet away, let alone hundreds out on the water.

There was a heavy chain rolled up on the dock.

Workman began to uncurl it. "Boss wants no trace of you. You know, we ordered up a wheelbarrow full of cement, you being such a big shot and all, but this was quicker. You won't take no offense, I hope?" Workman brought the chain over to Morris and wrapped a loop around his shoulders. "Mendy, boss said it's your fuckup, so it's yours to do."

Morris turned to Mendy, who was still holding his gun on him. "Your fuckup? What did he mean by that?"

"Nothing," Mendy said. "Just business. Let's get on with it."

"Oh, go ahead and tell him, Mendy," Workman said. "Who's he gonna tell? The fish? He deserves to know. I think Mendy's got a message for you."

"What message?" Morris looked at him. Anger rose up in him. Rain pelted him in the face. "You're talking about Harry?"

"Harry? Nah. Charlie's just being a prick, that's all."

"What happened to him, Mendy? You can tell me. What's the difference, anyway?"

"I told you at the shivah, Morris, I don't know what happened to him."

"Oh come on," Workman said. "You're a big guy, Mendy. The guy's about to go in the drink. You can own up to it." He'd picked up about six feet of heavy chain and, kneeling, started to wrap it loosely around Morris's ankles.

Morris kept his legs as wide as he could. He looked at Mendy. "You were there, weren't you?"

"*There?*" Workman chortled amusedly. "I'd say he was there."

"Shut the fuck up, Charlie," Mendy said.

"I knew it was you, Mendy." Morris glared, his anger surging through him. "You piece of shit, I knew Harry didn't have it in him, however you suckered him into doing what he did. And you killed him, right?"

Mendy didn't answer.

"You killed him."

"Well, I didn't exactly have fun doing it," he finally snapped. "I always liked Harry. But it was either him or me, so what choice was there."

"Him or you? What do you mean?"

"Go on, Mendy, tell him." Workman fed the end of a length of chain around Morris's waist. "Who's he gonna blab it to, anyway, the fucking carp?"

"Fuck you, Charlie." Mendy glared, rain pouring off the brim of his hat. "I screwed up, that's all. Charlie here thinks I ran out on him on the job. So someone had to pay."

"The Schultz job . . . ?"

"You know damn well what we're talking about, Morris. It was in every headline in the country."

"So you let him take the hit for you?" Morris stared Mendy in the face. "Your pal. The guy you grew up with. The guy who would have done anything for you. What'd you do, tell him you were gonna take him out for a beer, and put a bullet in the back of his head?"

"Something like that." Workman grinned. "Now . . ."

Mendy wiped the rain off his face. "Well, I guess you were right about something, Morris. People like me, we don't have any friends. Anyway, he said something, for what it's worth. At the end. To you. You might as well hear it."

"What?"

"He said, 'Tell Morris, I didn't do it.' I didn't do it. Those were the last words he uttered." He laughed bitterly. "Whaddya think he might be talking about, Morris?"

Anger lit through Morris's veins. In seconds Mendy was going to pull the trigger and Morris would be pushed in to sink to the bottom of the East River. No one would ever know his fate. He no longer felt pain anywhere. Just rage. And a helplessness that he could do nothing about it. "You pulled the fucking trigger, didn't you?" He kept his eyes fixed on Mendy.

Mendy was silent.

"You pulled the trigger, you piece of shit?"

"Yeah, I pulled the fucking trigger. Or one of my men did. But *you* sent him back to us, Morris. You pushed him out. So where the hell could he go? He came to us. 'Tell Morris, I didn't do it.' Right as we dropped him, Morris. That's all he had to say. Trust me, he was a lot more ashamed in front of you than he was angry at me for doing it. He knew what it was about. So how does that make you feel? Not such a big shot now, right?"

Workman looped the chain loosely around Morris one more time. Then the gangster brought it back up to wrap around Morris's shoulder.

"So, tell me, Mendy, *did* he do it?" Morris asked. "Did he let your boys in that night? When you torched the warehouse. I know you called him. I know he went out with you."

"Did he *do* it?" Mendy chuckled in his face. "You poor sap, you don't even know, do you? You had the fucking warehouse manager who was being pushed out of his job. Leo, or something. He let us in."

"Leo?"

"We just needed Harry out of the way, that's all. So I took him to the fights. He was always a sucker for the fights."

Morris looked at him. For the first time, tears fell down his face, mixing with the rain. Harry didn't do it. That's what he'd said at the end. When his friend had put a gun to the back of his head and he must've known what was happening. The person he trusted most, taking him down. *Tell Morris, I didn't do it.* Maybe he should die. Morris swallowed, a weight in his own chest pulling him, even stronger than the chains.

"Anyway, enough talk now," Workman said. "Let's get on with it, Mendy. I'll fix the rest after."

Mendy brought his gun up to Morris's chest. Morris looked him in the eye.

"Whatsamatter, Mendy." Morris smiled. "You can do it to my brother, but not to me?"

"Get it done, sweetheart," Workman said. "If you're too much of a woman to pull the trigger, I'll be happy to oblige."

"I can pull it." Mendy waved the gun at Workman. "Sorry, Morris."

He hesitated one more second, then brought the gun back, steadying it at Morris's chest.

That was when Morris lunged forward, crashing into Mendy like a bull busting through a fence. The force sent them both toppling off the edge of the pier, and they fell, an eight-foot drop into the cold, black water. The gun went off. Morris felt a hot jolt sear into his side.

They went under.

In his heavy coat and with the chain draped around him, Morris gulped a lungful of air into his lungs as he was pulled down. He still held on to Mendy, who tried to break free of his grip and pull the trigger. But Morris latched onto the gun and elbowed Mendy in the face, trying to wrench it free. The chain was looped around his shoulders and ankles, but there was a gap from Morris having kept his legs apart, and he was able to kick his ankles free. Still, it continued to drag them both to the bottom.

Air bubbles leaked from Mendy's mouth, rising rapidly. They were about eight feet under now, the water dark and murky. Mendy squeezed off another shot, but it missed Morris narrowly, Morris forcing Mendy's hand back and mashing his arm against one of the wood pylons securing the pier. Mendy's other arm thrashed wildly as he tried to kick free and get himself back to the surface.

Morris continued to hold on to him.

Twenty seconds elapsed. Morris kept hammering Mendy's gun against the pier. Somehow Mendy managed to twist his hand free, and wrestled the gun in front of Morris's face with an expression that read, *it's over now,* and squeezed on the trigger. But the gun harmlessly clicked and clicked.

Jammed.

Mendy's lungs began to give out. The gun fell out of his hand. Morris continued to hold onto him, shrugging the chain off his shoulder. *Thirty seconds.* Mendy kicked frantically, trying to wrench himself free, but Morris's coat and the chain wrapped around him continued to weigh them both down. Morris held on.

Forty seconds now.

Mendy's eyes grew wide with panic. Morris just kept him there, staring into the face of the man who had killed his brother. It didn't matter whether they both died. *You know what he said, before I dropped him?* All sense of time disappeared. Close to a minute had now elapsed. Mendy's cheeks were puffed out now, trying to hold on to every breath, and his eyes showed fear and alarm.

Above them, Workman tried to maneuver himself around the side of the dock and get off a shot—at either of them, at this point he didn't care—but they were under far too deep.

Slowly Mendy's lungs began to empty. He thrashed his legs, desperately trying to kick Morris off with the last of his strength, but his efforts only used up more oxygen and he began to weaken. His eyes were almost begging now, no longer fierce and explosive. Just afraid. With one hand, Morris pinned him against the pylon, and with the other, unlooped a length of chain from around his own shoulders and, a mask of panic emerging on Mendy's face, Morris looped the chain around the gangster's neck and then around the crossbeam supporting the pier. Eyes wide, Mendy violently shook his head, letting in more water. Kicking desperately.

Morris felt his own oxygen start to deplete.

With his free hand he unwrapped the rest of the chain from around his own neck. Morris had been under a long time as well, over a minute now. His own lungs began to burn.

Mendy's grip suddenly went limp, his eyes wide. Suddenly there was no longer struggle or panic in them, just a kind of helplessness, then surrender, and an acceptance of his fate. Then just calm.

His mouth parted and his eyes were fixed. He stared into Morris's face.

His own lungs bursting now, Morris wriggled out of his coat and

342

sent himself upward. He maneuvered along the side of the pier to the far end and broke the surface, gasping and heaving, sucking needed air into his lungs. His side felt like it was on fire. He put a hand to it and there was blood on it, diluted by the water. He felt his own strength fading. Somehow he had to get out of here.

On the dock, Workman heard him break the surface and rushed around the side, craning over the edge, trying to get an angle. "Is that you, Mendy?" When there was no reply, he pointed his gun and squeezed the trigger, two, three times, aiming at Morris's coat floating on the surface. Bullets disappeared in the black, lapping tide.

Morris dove back under. He heard two more shots as bullets streaked through his coat. Without surfacing, he pushed away from the dock and swam. He kicked until his lungs ached again and his side and right thigh throbbed with pain. This time he came up out of Workman's range. He saw him still on the pier, searching the black water, unsure where Morris was. He went back under, swimming toward the Fourth Street pier, just as he had done as a kid. He moved further and further away. When his strength was on the verge of giving out, he ducked his head up from under the tide, sucked in a deep breath, and saw the new pier, now just yards in front of him. He ducked back under and swam for it, virtually out of breath, bleeding, almost unable to move his arms another stroke, and with a final, exhausted grasp, latched his fingers onto the pier. If they hadn't make contact he might have gone under for good. He gasped. On the far side of the pier, he located a wooden ladder affixed to it and, straining, using every fiber of strength he had left, pulled himself up. He was completely spent, his lower body deadened. Nothing hurt anymore—he was numb all over. He collapsed as soon as he was on top, gasping loudly, gulping heavy breaths into his lungs, only the feeling of blood leaking out of him convincing him he was still alive. He had no thought of getting away.

Even if Workman found him. He didn't have the strength to stand. He'd lost a lot of blood. It occurred to him he might still die here.

And if he did, Morris thought, if that happened, that was okay. In the end, maybe he didn't deserve to survive. Harry hadn't. Or Manny. He realized now what he had done, and tears fell down his cheeks mixed with rain. He had cast his brother away, wrongly, and it had cost Harry his life. Morris felt the blood ebb out of him. Mixed with grief, shame.

Dying, it wasn't that hard. They had managed it.

Ruthie . . . He saw a pretty face take shape in front of him. *You were the best thing ever to happen to me.*

"You okay, sir?"

Morris opened his eyes. A black man, likely a night watchman, knelt over him. Looking almost amazed that this hulk who had crawled out of the water was somehow alive.

"Call the police," Morris said, gasping. "I've been shot."

"Okay, okay. You just wait there, all right," the man said, putting out his palms to Morris to reassure him. "I'll be back in a jiffy, you hear. You just wait there." He ran off.

"Wait!" Morris called after him. Using every bit of strength he had left, he rolled onto his side and pulled out his wallet from his sodden pants. "Not the police." He searched around in his wallet and took out a card. It was soaked, like everything on him, but the name and number were still visible. "Call *him*." Morris handed the watchman the card. He breathed heavily. "Tell him you have Morris Raab."

"Who?"

"Morris Raab."

The guy ran off. Morris lay his head back on the pier. He felt the irrepressible urge to sleep. He used to play here. The only way they could get cool in the summer. The rain had lightened on his face. He looked up. From behind a passing cloud, the bright orb of the moon was trying to push its way through. He drew in a breath that told him he was going to live.

The card belonged to Special Prosecutor Thomas Dewey.

Chapter Fifty-Four

Morris heard a whoosh and a groan. Another whoosh and a groan.

He opened his eyes.

An oxygen tube and an IV line were affixed to him. As he'd felt himself passing out on the pier before help came and the medics reached him, he hadn't known if he would ever wake up again.

"Hey there," a familiar voice said happily. A scent he knew was close by—apricot—and a sweet image came into focus next to him.

He smiled. "I was sure I would never see you again," he said, his mouth coarse as sandpaper.

Ruthie smiled too. She squeezed his hand. Her eyes glistened with gratefulness and happiness. "For a while, me either."

"How long have I been out?" He glanced around, getting a sense of where he was. A large, single room. Flowers against the wall. Lots of flowers.

"Two days." Her eyes glistened with tears. "The doctors weren't sure you would even make it. Oh, Morris . . ." She rested her head on his chest and squeezed him. He knew without her saying a word what she wanted to say.

"You know I love you more than anything and I knew what I was getting when I married you," she shook her head, "but this has got to end, Morris Raab. I need you. We all need you."

He rubbed his hand softly against her face and smiled. "You know, when I saw you in that club, I thought you were the most beautiful thing in the world. I don't know how you even let me into your life."

"You were light on your feet. Remember?"

"That's all it was, huh?" He gazed at her. "But now I feel it even more."

She took his hand and smiled too, her eyes flooding. She brushed a tear off her cheek. "For a while I didn't know if you were going to pull through."

"Takes more than a bullet and a couple of stab wounds to put me away." He tried to laugh. The pain hit him. He winced.

"Are you all right, Morris?"

He smiled, letting his eyes wash over her. "Now I am."

"Anyway, it was two. Two bullets. One went through your side and the other they had to take out of your thigh. Not to mention the ruptured spleen. From the stab wounds."

He nodded.

"And two fractured ribs."

"Like I said." Then he shut his eyes a second and nodded solemnly. He tried to recall what had happened.

"You just can't keep fighting all by yourself, Morris. . . ." She wrapped his hand in hers and squeezed. "You just can't. I can't believe I almost lost you."

He thought about telling her how close it had actually been. How they had jumped him in the lobby and he wouldn't have even made it out to the street if old Buck hadn't stuck in his head. Morris would put a whole lot more than a dollar in his palm next time.

And then the fight underwater with Mendy as he tried to free himself from the chains. In the end he thought it best to just not say anything. Ruthie was strong and independent, but right now, even he knew that was a story for another day.

"I still feel terrible about Manny," he said.

"I do too."

"Have they found out anything more?"

She shook her head. "Whoever hit him has never been found."

"I got him killed, Ruthie. I was the one who pushed him to testify."

"He was a grown man, Morris. He made his own decisions."

Tsaddikim, Morris recalled. Thirty-six good men. Those were his reasons.

For a while, they didn't say anything. She took his hand and rested her head on his stomach. "Anyway, you just take it easy now. There'll be enough time to talk about that later."

Sol came in. He smiled. Morris gave him a sheepish wave. Sol said, "Anna and Bessie are outside. We took Mom home. She hadn't slept in two days."

Morris nodded.

"I'll go see to them," Ruthie said. "I'll see you in a while, okay?"

"Ruthie," Morris called after her as she was at the door. "Thanks."

"Thanks?" She looked at him quizzically. "For what?"

"For forgiving me," Morris said.

She smiled.

Sol came up to the bed. He put a hand on Morris's shoulder and sniffed a laugh. *"Ich zol azoy vissen fun tsoris. . . ."* he muttered. I should only have half the trouble you cause for me. "You know that, don't you?"

"So you keep saying, Sol. But don't make me cry."

Sol waited for the door to fully close so that they were alone. "Anything you want to talk about?"

"It was Mendy, Sol. I put a chain around his neck and left him there, under the pier. It was him who killed Harry."

"Mendy?"

"They suckered him into driving the getaway car on the Dutch Schultz thing, and when they drove off with Charlie Workman still inside, I guess someone had to pay. He didn't do it, Sol."

"He didn't do what?"

"The fire. It wasn't him who let them into our place. It was Leo."

"Leo . . . ?"

"Mendy told me. I guess he didn't like that Harry was taking his job. He let them in." Morris closed his eyes. "I threw him out of our lives and it wasn't even him."

Sol took in a deep breath through his nostrils. "He still shouldn't have left though."

"No, he should never have left. Gimme some water?" Morris glanced toward a pitcher on his night table.

Sol poured some into a glass and tilted it toward Morris's lips. Morris's throat was parched. He put his head back down. "Mendy said to me, before we went into the drink, that Harry said, 'You tell Morris, I didn't do it.' Those were his last words. I sent him back to them, Sol. This never would have happened if I hadn't been such a stubborn fool."

"You are a stubborn fool. But it's not the time for that now. You're safe. Your wife wants her husband back. Your kids deserve a father." He squeezed Morris's arm and grinned. "So you can still swim it, huh? They found you all the way over on the Fourth Street pier."

"Yeah, but I had to come up twice. For air."

"Still . . . Not bad. Though it seems a waste of a pretty nice wool coat to me."

He gave Morris another sip of water, then put the glass back. "The rest of the family would like to see you."

349

"Sure. Send them in."

"Just so you know, they've stationed a guard outside. Oh, and there's a couple of people from the city with badges on who'd like to talk with you too."

He took them all through it. Workman and the guy with the mole in the lobby. Mendy. The corrupt police captain, Burns. He said that they'd find a body still wrapped in a chain underneath Pier Six. He had said he would only speak with a detective that Special Prosecutor Dewey sent. The special prosecutor actually came up to see him that first day. After the two detectives took down his story, he asked Dewey if he would remain behind. "I've been doing some thinking," Morris said to him. "There's something I need to talk to you about."

The next afternoon, Irv came by to visit.

He seemed unsettled, and shaken. "When I asked you to get involved, Morris, I didn't mean quite like this," he said, forcing a weak smile. He put his hat on the chair.

Morris smiled back.

"You'll be happy to know, we've picked up Charles Workman and we got him dead to rights. Oh, and your police buddy, Burns. He denies everything, of course. But he's got a history that goes back twenty years."

"Can you get him a message from me?"

"A message? Maybe. I have some friends on the force."

"Tell him I said it's time to think about meeting his maker, Jackie-boy?"

Irv looked back quizzically.

"He'll know what I mean. So what about Buchalter?"

"There are things brewing on that. Big things. I can't talk about them now."

"Good." Buchalter had ordered the hit, of course. And likely the hit on Manny too.

Irv stepped up to him. "You really had me worried, Morris. I couldn't have lived if we had lost you. You need anything in here?"

"Long as that guard stays on duty out there, they're taking pretty good care of me."

"Trust me, Dewey wouldn't let him leave if an earthquake hit the building. He handpicked the men himself. You can't even get down the wing unless you're a doctor or family."

Irv squeezed his shoulder. "You've done good work, Morris. The whole thing's going to bust right open. You rest up though. I'll stop back in a couple of days. You know, I couldn't have slept with myself if you didn't make it." Irv picked his hat up off the chair and went to the door.

"Irv."

His friend turned. "Yes."

"You know you have a leak in the department, right?"

"A leak? What makes you say that?"

Morris shrugged. "Me, there coulda been a dozen people who knew I was trying to round people up. But Manny . . . that lighter . . . there were only a handful who knew about that."

Irv looked back, his mind ratcheting through what Morris might be saying to him. "I'm truly sorry about your friend Manny. I met him a couple of times. We're looking into it, and if it's connected in any way, heads will roll."

"You know, I've been thinking about a couple of things. . . ." Morris leaned himself up.

"You shouldn't be pushing yourself, Morris. What?"

"On the pier. As I was passing out. You'd think my mind would've been on maybe never seeing Ruthie again. Or my kids. But it was on something else. You remember how we used to swim off those piers?"

"You mostly." Irv grinned. "I just jumped in and tried not to get pushed around."

"Well, I recalled something, lying there. You remember when you started going to that new school in Irving Place but you needed someone to get you through the Irish and Italian neighborhoods?"

"Of course. You took your life in your hands back then. Not like now. Why . . . ?"

"And then you found someone. A *yiddisher,* remember? You remember what you said about him?"

"I barely remember anything back then, Morris. That was twenty years ago. Look, I'll stop back up and—"

"I know it was twenty years ago, Irv. But what you said was—I recall it like yesterday—this guy we found, he's even tougher than the Italians or the micks. He'd come back from some reform school upstate and had formed his own outfit. Who was that guy, Irv? You must remember his name?"

"Jeez, Morris. Abe or something. I think he got pinched and ended up in jail. I mean, who can go back that far? We were kids."

"I know we were kids, Irv. But you had to pay him for over four years, so I thought you might recall. Abe, huh? And then I recalled something else. Which has bugged me to this day."

"What's that, Morris?" Irv's expression changed. He glanced at his watch. "I'm meeting my mother in Brooklyn in an hour. She sends her best, by the way."

"That's nice. Tell her thanks. But I was thinking about that night at the Theatrical Club in Harlem. The night I met Ruthie . . ."

"I wore that evening suit that was two sizes too big for me. She was part of those girls. From Columbia and Skidmore."

"Later on, you remember who came up to the table?"

"Not sure I do." Irv's tone grew taut, no longer patient.

"Louis Buchalter," Morris said.

Irv nodded. He tapped his index finger against his hat.

"He was being his usual prick self. Ruthie and I turned down an invitation to go to his table. But as he was leaving he said something I always wanted to ask you about. I could never figure it out. At least, till now . . ."

"At least till now . . ." Irv's look had hardened. "I'm not sure I like where this is leading, Morris."

"It's leading everywhere, Irv. It all keeps coming back to there. You know what I mean? With Manny dead, I just started thinking. He acted like he knew you, Irv. Buchalter. You remember what he said?"

"No. I don't remember, Morris. What did he say?"

Morris looked at him. "He called you, Counselor, Irv. Counselor. As he said good-bye."

"Counselor . . . ?" Irv looked back at him, uneasily, the gears of his brain churning to stay ahead of where this was going. "I'm not sure I like what you're—"

"Just how would he know that, Irv?" Morris continued to stare at him. "That you were studying law. He wouldn't, of course. Unless you *did* know him. I got to thinking . . . unless he was the one who gave you protection all those years. Just tell me if I'm off base, here, and I'll stop. Was he?"

"Was he what?" Irv stared. His voice had gotten thin.

"Was he the one who gave you protection, Irv? Back then. I think I deserve an answer."

Irv stood there, air leaking through his nostrils, his cheeks sagging, the steady whoosh of the mechanical pump the only sound.

Then he let a breath out that had been inside him twenty years.

"I'm only going to tell you this once, Morris, and if it ever comes up again I'll throw a libel suit on you so large it'll take down your new business as well. I've done a lot of good in this job. I've put people who deserved it in jail. As an ADA, I stood up for people who had no one else to defend them. I'm not going to let myself feel ashamed. Whatever I do.

"But you have no idea what it was like for me back then. Always being the weak one. Afraid. The pudgy little bookworm who always had his head in his studies. Not like you, Morris. You were always able. And strong. You didn't even have to think twice when it came to standing up for yourself, no matter how tough someone was."

"Your bookworm habits got you where you are in life, Irv. Look at you."

"The only sliver of respect I had in life, Morris, was being your friend. And that's what made it even worse. You remember that big scholarship to Brooklyn Law I received? We had that big celebration?"

"Yes."

"Without that, I would have been working behind the counter in some bakery on Delancey Street. Or selling shoes somewhere, saying my whole life, 'I came within an inch of going to law school.' You want to know where that money came from? There *was* no scholarship. You understand?"

Morris stared at him.

"So yes, Louis was that person. He's always been that person to me. You always said you'd do whatever you had to do to get out, and me—I did what I had to do too.

"But here's the thing . . . I put a lot of bad people away. In the balance, I've done a lot more good than bad. And I never, ever meant to put you in any harm, Morris. On that, I swear. That was a part of it between him and me, from early on."

"What do you mean, that was a part of it, Irv?"

"Why do you think he let you get by with so much, Morris? Because of your brother? *Harry?* Your brother shined their shoes. Or because you're such a tough guy? Anyone else, you would have been in some garbage can ten years ago. I'm sorry, Morris, but I've been your friend a lot more than you'll ever know."

Morris just looked at him.

"So yes, maybe I have given him a nod from time to time when the heat got too close. Does that make me a bad guy? Can you ever not do more good, even when you do something bad? I admit, there are times I look at myself in the mirror and the whole thing makes me retch. Other times, I think, it's just part of the job. He's given me names too. But I've never thrown a case, and I never meant to put you in any danger, Morris. God's honest truth. And no one's happier than me to see you here, okay, and we're still gonna get Lepke. So what damage has it really done, in the end?"

"Damage?" Morris looked at him. "Manny. There's the damage, Irv."

Irv squeezed his hat and went to the door. "You were always my friend, Morris. You protected me when we were young. And I've protected you. You just never knew."

He left, holding open the door for Ruthie to go back in. "He's looking swell," he said, and gave her a hug.

"What was that about?" she said.

Morris was left with the whooshing of the breathing pump. "Nothing."

It was nine P.M. and visiting hours were over. Ruthie finally went home. Morris was resting. He heard a knock on the door. "It's open."

Thomas Dewey stepped in. In a gray double-breasted suit, collar pin, and striped blue tie.

"Mr. Dewey."

"How're you doing, Mr. Raab? I hear you're making excellent progress." The special prosecutor came over to his bed. "Not many people get to go through what you did and live to tell about it."

"I'm a lucky man."

"You diminish yourself, son. With what you've accomplished."

"No, trust me, I was lucky."

The special prosecutor looked around the room. "I was going to bring you some flowers. But I didn't think you were the flower kind of guy. Though as I look around, I see you've already received your share."

"You get shot . . ." Morris grinned, "all of a sudden you have friends you didn't know you had."

"And 'a man is who his friends are,' isn't that right? Where did I hear that before? Twain, perhaps."

"Dickens, I think," Morris corrected him. "*A Christmas Carol.*"

"*Dickens?*" The special prosecutor screwed up his eyes and smiled. "At all times you continue to surprise me, Mr. Raab. In any case, instead of flowers I brought you something else. Something I believe you'll like much more."

"What's that?"

"Indictments. Charles Workman. Louis Buchalter. Jacob Shapiro. Seymour 'Cy' Haddad. Not only on their illegal union activities; there's now a murder rap we can nail them on too. I promise, they're all going to be off the streets for a very long time, if not for good."

A feeling of vindication pulsed through Morris warmly. "That's great."

"Oh, and two others you may not know, but who I think you'll be happy to hear about. Leon Burmeister and Leopold 'Fuzzy' Cantor? Have you heard of them?"

Morris shook his head.

"They were the two who tossed Abraham Langer out the Amalgamated Needle Trade Union building."

Morris closed his eyes. A wave of emotion built up inside.

He smiled.

"Oh, and you'll be happy to know that police captain, Jack Burns, has been chirping like a parakeet to save his own skin. See, you're looking better already, Mr. Raab. Though you certainly do have your share of wires attached to you."

Morris pulled up his bedsheet. He removed a small black box with a wire coming from it that was hidden there. "I think this one actually belongs to you. The doctors couldn't figure out just what the hell it was doing anyway." He handed it to Dewey.

"It was doing the public good. I'm sorry, Morris. I know that was a hard thing for you to do."

"I think you'll be pleased with what's on there. So what's going to happen to him?"

"He'll likely be arrested. Depending on what's here. Who knows, he might be able to cop a plea himself. He might well know something worth trading. *If* . . ." Dewey's mustache edged into a smile, "he can find himself a good lawyer."

"He's my oldest friend in the world. I've known him since we were kids."

"If what's on this is what I think is on it, he also kept a cold-hearted killer one step ahead of the law for many years. A lot more people ended up dead because of that, Mr. Raab. Very nearly *you* as well. That's the way I'd look at it."

Dewey wrapped the microphone wire around the recorder and placed it in his coat pocket. He went to the door. "There's nothing easy about this kind of work, Mr. Raab. I know how hard this was for you to do. A friend is a friend."

"Yes, he was a friend." Morris nodded. He tried to smile but his side ached and all there was was the whoosh of the automatic lung. "But Manny Gutman, he was my friend too."

Epilogue

1992

The day was bright and clear, the crowd large on the square of the campus on Seventh Avenue and Twenty-fifth Street.

Morris looked with pride at the gleaming six-story glass-and-stone building that bore his family's name.

His son, Sam, was there. A grandfather himself now. With his kids. And his daughter, Lucy, with her family too. Two of Morris's grandchildren were lawyers; another, on the M&A team at Merrill Lynch. With their own children. Sol's family was there as well. But Anna's and Bess's, those just seemed to have drifted away with time. Even though most of them still lived in Brooklyn.

They were waiting on the mayor to arrive.

"So I guess this brings us to the end," Morris said to the pretty black woman in the yellow suit, an associate professor at FIT, who put together the taped archives of the founding fathers of the industry for the event. For weeks, Morris had been going back through his life with her.

"Yes, Mr. Raab." She smiled. "I think that it does."

He was no longer large in frame. A heart attack and a bout with

stomach cancer had taken care of that. And his hair had thinned. Still,
his rough, calloused knuckles bore resemblance to the fighter he'd once
been. And from the day he'd pulled himself out from that river, two
bullets in him, he had walked with the trace of a limp.

He'd begun to repeat himself a bit, his family said.

"I forget, I ever tell you how I made it big?" he asked her.

"I think you've told me just about everything," the professor said.

"It was during the war," he went on, either ignoring her or not fully
hearing how she'd responded. "World War Two, I mean. This time I
was too old to sign up. Up to that point, I was just getting by in my new
business. There was still a Depression going on. But after Pearl Har-
bor I got this contract from the army to make women's uniforms. They
needed anyone who had a sewing plant back then. The first order was
for fifty thousand units. Then another fifty. It was enough to get me by.
They gave me this big chart of measurements to figure out the size
scales. You know, average heights, weights. They had all that infor-
mation. And you know what I saw?"

The professor smiled politely, having heard it all several times be-
fore. "Why don't you tell me, Mr. Raab?"

"I saw that over half the women were five foot four and under. The
stores, all they wanted was stuff that was made for a model. But that's
not how the average American woman was. So after the war we made
dresses based on the army's measurements. A little short-waisted.
Slightly shorter in length. Petites, that's what they're called today. But
back then, we just called it 'the All-American fit.' And after the war it
just stuck. All of a sudden we were rolling.

"In 1964, we went public. I can't remember, did I tell you that?
On the American Stock Exchange. We were the biggest dress firm in
the country. In every store. You ask any woman, they knew the name
Lucy Fredericks. Still do . . . But things were changing. Things are
always changing in this business. I learned that from Menushem
Kaufman, my first day on the job, God rest his soul. Women no longer

wanted to dress that way. So a few years later, my son, Sam—he runs the business now; he has for twenty years—he got us into sportswear. And that's when we got really big. A few years later we switched over to the New York Stock Exchange. LFR is the symbol. It still is. . . ."

"You've had a wonderful career," the professor acknowledged.

"Oh, and I almost forgot, given all we talked about, did I tell you that in 1955 we went completely union. There were good people running it now, not like before. So we built this big production facility in Wilkes-Barre, Pennsylvania. Now, of course, everything's made in Asia. Now it takes three months to turn around a number; I used to do it in three weeks. These young guys, they all have fancy degrees—my son, he went to Wharton—but sometimes they don't have, you know . . ." He snapped his fingers. "This. Zip. My first employer, Mr. Kaufman, told me that." He shook his head. "Over seventy-five years ago . . ."

"Look, there's the mayor." The professor pointed to the familiar face surrounded by three aides, shaking hands and heading toward the dais. "You sure you don't want to be up there, Mr. Raab, with your family? Let me take you."

"They'll wait. So I told you what happened to Buchalter and Gurrah, right?"

"Well, I know they spent the rest of their lives in jail, or in Buchalter's case . . ."

"Like Dewey said, not long after they tried to take me out, they were all arrested. Along with that Workman guy and the two mugs who tossed Abe Langer out that window. They got the chair. That police captain, Burns, he decided it was easier to put a bullet in his head than face the music. Irv, they got him too. He ended up spending two years in prison, then moved out West to get away, and I think bought this window franchise—he could never practice law again, of course. Anyway, his mother said he did well. But I never talked to him ever again. Got a letter from him once, but . . .

"Buchalter went on the lam for a while, but they got him eventually.

By that time they had booted the whole lot of them out of the union. But I did see him once again though."

"You saw him?" The professor looked at him, this time with surprise. "That you never told me. Where?"

"In prison. In the death house; 1944, I think. It was the day before he died.

"I got this message. From Dewey, actually. By that time he was governor. He said Buchalter wanted to see me. He was scheduled for execution the next day. I said, 'Why me . . . ?' He said, 'I don't know why. He's refused all visitors, except his wife. But he asked for you.'

"I thought about it a bit. I mean, I had nothing to say to him. Except good riddance for what he did to everyone, especially Manny. It had been nine years. But the next day I had a driver take me up to Sing Sing. It's in Ossining. Forty miles up the Hudson. The death house is separated from the regular prison. It's right over the river. They took me into this room outside the cells. Just a table and two chairs. When he came out, he looked different than I'd ever seen him. About twenty years older. Heavier. Tired. He no longer had that cockiness in his eyes. His hands were shackled. He even said thank you to the guard who held the chair out for him. If I didn't know it was Louis Buchalter, I would never have guessed in a million years.

"He smiled when he saw me. Like I was an old friend. A man like that, I doubt he ever had any real friends. He sat down. He asked about my family. 'That cute wife of yours,' he says. He remembered being there the night we met. 'The Theatrical Club,' he says, 'right?' I go, 'Yeah.' 'Nice place,' he remembered.

"I ask him if they're treating him okay and he shrugged and smiled at me and said 'It ain't the Ritz. But tomorrow, I get the white curtain treatment,' he said with a laugh. White curtains is what they drape over the other cells when someone goes by on their way to the chair, so they don't have to see him. I said, 'I'll remember that if my wife ever wants to redecorate.'

"He laughed. Then he changed and got all serious. I figured this was why he asked me there. He asks me if I ever wondered why he let me get away with so much? I told him Irv had said it was because of him. That he was protecting me. I said, 'But I always thought it was because of Harry.'

"He listened, then shook his head. 'No.'

"Then he says something that almost knocked me over. He said it was because he always kind of admired me. This is Louis Lepke talking. How everyone else always bowed down to him, 'cause they were afraid. Even the people who worked for him. But I always stood up to him. I never did bow down. And in a way, he always respected that. He said that if he was ever straight in life, he figured he would want to be someone like me. Brave. Who didn't take no guff from people. Who didn't back down. Like all the rest. It showed I had pride.

"I said it wasn't really about pride. 'When you're scared,' I said, 'you're nothing but a prisoner. You go to sleep scared, you wake up scared. Like you're in this prison. But the moment you decide to stand up, become brave, you're free. Free of everything that holds you back. You can do anything. You don't have to think about it anymore.'"

"And what did he say to that?" The professor looked at Morris.

"He just smiled and said, 'Gee, I never really thought about it that way.'

"So I said maybe I should let him have the time to himself now, if that was all, and he nodded yes. But before he got up, he went, 'You know why I really asked you here, Morris?' And I shrugged and said, 'No. Why . . . ?' And he went, 'Y'know, I ain't sorry about much. About what I've done. It is what it is. But the one thing I am sorry about is what happened to your brother. Harry. It should've never happened that way.' He shook his head. 'It should have been Mendy.' Then he looked at me and kind of smiled. 'But I guess Mendy got what was coming to him in the end.'

"I said, 'Yes, I kind of look at it that way.'

"As they were taking him away, he turned back, his hands in chains. 'I got a rule for you, Morris Raab. . . .' He winked and pointed at me."

"What was it?" the professor asked.

"He never told me. They just took him away. Twenty-four hours later, he was dead."

Ruthie and Sam came up to him from the crowd. Morris said to them, "Here's that professor I was always telling you about. You know, I've been telling her about my life. For the school. They're going to put it in a tape."

"Sorry to have to pull you away, Dad," Sam said. "I know how he loves talking about old times. But we have a building to dedicate. And the mayor's here now."

"Trust me," she said to Sam and Ruthie, "the pleasure's been all mine."

"All right . . . all right." Morris started to head away. "You can see, I don't walk so good now," he said to the professor. "Not like before. Heel-toe, heel-toe. I learned that in the army."

Then he stopped. "Hold it a minute!" he said, and pulled away. "There was something else I wanted to tell you. It's very important."

"Morris, please . . . ," Ruthie pleaded. "She's probably busy. And we have to get started now."

"That's okay," the professor said, noticing Morris's face, which had a sudden pallor on it. "What, Mr. Raab?"

"I wanted to tell you, Sol and I, we went back to Essex Street once. Where we first lived. In 1965. He's dead now, of course. He had a stroke in '86. He dropped right at his club in Tenafly, New Jersey. That's where he moved to. On the second tee. His family's over there." He pointed.

"Anyway, it had all changed. Our old building—it was just a tenement back then—it was gone. There was a fancy new apartment building there. Lots of younger people around. The butcher, who had a shop below us, and the stable, of course, on the corner, they were long gone. We just stood in the street outside. Where it had happened. Over sixty years before." Morris looked at her. Suddenly, tears pooled in his eyes. "You know what I'm talking about, don't you?"

"I know what you're talking about, Mr. Raab." The professor nodded.

"Shemuel and Harry."

"Dad, we've got to go," Sam interrupted, "there are—"

"Wait a minute." Ruthie stopped him. "I've never heard this, Morris."

"That's because I was never so good at saying things, Ruthie. But I still feel them. In here." He tapped his chest. "Like anyone else. And I felt this weight come over me that day. Like nothing I'd ever felt before. Sol put his arm around me and said, 'You can say it now, Morris.' I remember, I put my hand in front of my face so he wouldn't see me cry. But I was crying. He could hear me. You know what I'm saying, don't you, Ruthie . . . ?"

She looked at him and nodded, tears welling in her own eyes. "I know what you're saying, Morris." She took his hand. "I know."

"I'd never felt so weak-kneed. I tell you I thought I was having a heart attack. Right there. All that time. And I had judged him wrong. I had pushed him back to them. I might as well have killed him myself. So 'Say it, Morris,' Sol says to me again.

"And I did say it at last. I wiped the tears back and said, 'I'm sorry, Harry. I forgive you.' Right there in that street. 'I forgive you,' I said again. 'And I hope to God you forgive me too.'

"You hear what I'm trying to tell you, don't you?" He looked at the professor, an aching in his old, gray eyes.

"Yes. I hear you, Mr. Raab." She put her hand on his arm. "I do."

"I want that on the tape. Because it's part of it. You understand?"

"I understand. I'll make sure it is."

"It's part of who I am."

"Come on, darling," Ruthie said. "They need to get this on the road.

364

And you're the guest of honor. You were wrong, but look what you've done for him, Morris, in your own way, to help make it right. If he were here, he'd be so proud."

"All right then. Just so it's in there," Morris said one last time.

Ruthie led him toward the rows of seats. A few people clapped. Morris looked back at the professor one last time. He took his seat, in the front row. The mayor came up and shook his hand.

It was all there, right in front of him. Something that would stand for his life; a life of some breadth, some might say. That would be here for years and years. Forever, maybe. Or at least, Morris laughed to himself, till someone new came along and gave them more.

He looked at the name on the building, letters reflecting the sharp rays of the sun.

THE HAROLD RAAB CENTER FOR THE ARTS

He always said how he wanted his name on something.

Acknowledgments

Twenty million immigrants came to this country between 1880 and 1920, and in many ways, this is the story of one of them. The only one in his family born here actually, in 1902, who went from the mean streets of Brownsville, Brooklyn, and a sixth-grade education to run the garment factory he apprenticed in at the age of twelve by the time he was twenty-one; battled the unions controlled by the Jewish mob (and was proud to show the knife wounds, courtesy of Jacob Gurrah, Louis Lepke's henchman, to prove it); and grew the dress firm he named after his daughter, Leslie Fay, into an iconic national brand.

That man was my grandfather.

It's a first-generational story that could be told by many American families, whether the protagonists grew up to be teachers, doctors, dry goods retailers, Wall Street icons, or garment men. Freddie Pomerantz was the "hero" of our family tale, and while he felt embarrassment over his lack of formal education his entire life, to us he was not only the toughest, but the wisest man we knew. Fittingly, his legacy today is that his name sits prominently over the entrances of buildings on several college campuses. Growing up, he was the most powerful influence in my life, and I'm proud to tell his story, with only a few embellishments.

When I first planned out this book I went to the library of the Fashion Institute of Technology in New York and met with Karen Trivette, Head of Special Collections and College Archivist there. I was looking for background on the early years of the garment business, and she turned me on to microfilm of issues of *Women's Wear Daily* back from the 1920s and '30s and a couple of tattered, first-person accounts that looked like they hadn't been checked out in years. She also gave me a gift I will never forget: "Many of the founding fathers of the industry have recorded their own stories," she informed me, "as part of the permanent archives here. Your grandfather was among them. Would you like to hear it?"

And that is how thirty years after his death, I heard my grandfather's voice all over again. Uttering the phrases that were always part of the rough, street-honed way he talked: "You hear what I'm saying to you, don't you . . . ?" And, "So help me God, it's as if it happened just the other day." And, "So to make a long story short . . ." As real and familiar as if he was sitting in front of me, in his den or at the club, and I was a kid again, no older than the age he started out himself in business, and he would look me in the eye and tell me with such clear-eyed conviction that I grew to believe it myself and still do to this day: "You can do anything you want in life, anything— if you want to do it badly enough."

For men like that, it was just that simple.

Listening, I have to admit I wept a bit. It was as if he had never died, just gone away for a while, and now he was back. As animated and alive as the last time I saw him. (More so, in fact, as that was in the cardiac ward of Good Samaritan Hospital in West Palm Beach in 1986 and he died that day.) In so many ways *The Last Brother* is his story, his rags-to-riches tale. His *Great Expectations*. But it's also the story of an era, a Jewish generation's boy-to-manhood tale: of hope and success; of tragedy and violent crime. And an industry's tale as well. One I grew up in myself before I ever even thought of writing a page. Not the glamorous fashion industry that it has evolved into today, but a rough, go-for-broke, all-or-nothing way out of the grim, overcrowded streets to which half of American Jewry can trace its roots.

Growing up, and as someone who spent fifteen years in the clothing trade before I turned to writing, I got to know many of the "founding fathers" Karen Trivette spoke of. They were all tough, uncompromising men. *Animals*, they were called, by their employees and competitors. Feared, but respected. Even loved. But what they all shared in common was this single-minded drive. They had *this,* as my grandfather would say, snapping his fingers. "And you can't learn it in Harvard." (Another thing they shared was generosity, as many of them, including my grandfather, gave away more than they left behind when they died.) None of these men went to college, but they founded companies like Jonathan Logan, Russ Togs, Bobbie Brooks, and Leslie Fay, and they came to dominate the women's dress and sportswear business from the 1940s to the '70s. Each took their own path to success, and some eclipsed my grandfather in wealth, but any of them would tell you, around a gin game or after a round of golf, that Freddie Pomerantz was the toughest of any of them. As a generation, their lack of formal education coupled with their success will likely never be seen again. These were true Button Men. And I miss them.

People commonly ask, how does a book begin? In this case, I was literally having a beer with fellow thriller writers David Morrell and Daniel Palmer and for whatever reason I was talking about some family stories, especially the one of my grandfather in his delivery truck guarding his shipment of coats with a loaded shotgun, which I'd thought of including in a book. When I finished, David looked at me with a gleam in his eye and said, "What a great scene! You have to write it." And for the first time it got me thinking of my grandfather's life as something other than the subject of family lore. So thanks for the push, man. Without it, I'm not sure I ever would have made the move to do this.

In the writing of this book, several books were instrumental to getting the full flavor of life on the Lower East Side, the early garment center years, the Jewish Mob, and the plight of the Jews in America in the early 1900s:

The Rest of Us, Steven Birmingham. Syracuse University Press, 1984.

How the Other Half Lives, Jacob Riis. Dover Press, New York, 1971. (Originally published by Charles Scribner and Sons.)

Triangle: The Fire That Changed America, David Von Drehle. Grove, New York, 2003.

Tough Jews: Father, Sons and Gangster Dreams, Rich Cohen. Vintage, New York, 1999.

The Family, A Journey into the Heart of the Twentieth Century, David Laskin. Penguin, New York, 2013.

Fourth Street East, Jerome Weidman. Pinnacle Books, New York, 1971.

Satan's Circus, Mike Dash. Broadway Books, New York, 2008.

Ready-Made Miracle: The Story of American-Made Fashion for the Million, Jessica Daves. Putnam, New York, 1967.

Jewish Literacy, Rabbi Joseph Telushkin. William Morrow, New York, 1991.

Billy Bathgate, E. L. Doctorow. Random House, New York, 1989.

Legs, William Kennedy. Penguin, New York, 1983.

I'd also like to thank my team at Minotaur/St. Martin's. My editor, Kelley Ragland, for rounding a lot of rough edges that I dropped in her lap into shape; Andrew Martin (for his title epiphany), Hector DeJean, Jen Enderlin, and Maggie Callan. And Simon Lipskar and Celia Taylor Mobley from Writers House. Your enduring support makes my task far easier and occasionally lets me even shine.

—AG